The Forgotten

Echoes from the Past Book 2

by Irina Shapiro

Copyright

© 2017 by Irina Shapiro

All rights reserved. No part of this book may be reproduced in any form, except for quotations in printed reviews, without permission in writing from the author.

All characters are fictional. Any resemblances to actual people (except those who are actual historical figures) are purely coincidental.

Contents

Prologue 6
Chapter 1 7
Chapter 2 13
Chapter 3 20
Chapter 4 24
Chapter 5 31
Chapter 6 38
Chapter 7 43
Chapter 8 45
Chapter 9 52
Chapter 10 56
Chapter 11 63
Chapter 12 70
Chapter 13 74
Chapter 14 83
Chapter 15 94
Chapter 16 99
Chapter 17 101
Chapter 18 107
Chapter 19 115
Chapter 20 119
Chapter 21 127
Chapter 22 130
Chapter 23 138

Chapter 24 140

Chapter 25 143

Chapter 26 147

Chapter 27 151

Chapter 28 153

Chapter 29 159

Chapter 30 167

Chapter 31 175

Chapter 32 180

Chapter 33 187

Chapter 34 193

Chapter 35 199

Chapter 36 205

Chapter 37 211

Chapter 38 215

Chapter 39 220

Chapter 40 225

Chapter 41 241

Chapter 42 253

Chapter 43 261

Chapter 44 269

Chapter 45 276

Chapter 46 280

Chapter 47 285

Chapter 48 290

Chapter 49 299

Chapter 50 306

Chapter 51 316

Chapter 52 322

Chapter 53 326

Chapter 54 338

Chapter 55 344

Chapter 56 355

Epilogue 364

Notes.. 370

Prologue

She never felt the fatal blow. After the terror and pain of the past half hour, it almost felt like a caress, a cool hand on the brow, comforting her and telling her that it's all right to close her eyes and let go. She stared up at the stormy sky as she fell, its low, threatening clouds heavy with rain and the air thick with the cries of seagulls. There were shouts of angry men and calls for justice as well, but she never heard those. They were nothing more than a roar in her ears, blending in with the crashing of the waves on the shore as the storm intensified.

She lifted her hand, reaching for something unseen, and let it fall as her gaze fixated on a brief glimmer of sunlight peeking through the gloom. A single bird wheeled just above, its wings spread wide as it glided toward the sea. It was the most beautiful thing she'd ever seen, and she smiled, wishing she could watch it forever.

At last, she allowed herself to close her eyes. She had no more reason to fight. She knew with unwavering certainty that her boy was gone, and now she was free to go too. She slipped away, quietly and without a fuss, as undemanding in death as she had been in life.

Chapter 1

New Year's Day 2014

Dunwich, Suffolk

Dr. Quinn Allenby huddled deeper into her coat in an effort to keep out the bitter wind as she walked toward the ancient graveyard of what had once been the Leper Hospital of St. James. Several locals milled about, hoping for a glimpse of the grave, but for the most part, the cemetery was deserted on this Wednesday morning. The day was cold and damp, with a thick mist blurring the edges of the crumbling ruins and making the landscape appear almost gothic. Bare tree limbs formed an intricate lacework pattern against the leaden sky, but their trunks melted into the gauzy mist that swirled between the weathered crosses and left a slick coating of moisture on every surface.

"Here, take my gloves," Gabe said, handing Quinn a pair of leather gloves that he pulled out of his coat pocket.

Quinn accepted the gloves gratefully and pulled them on after taking one last look at the beautiful diamond ring on her finger. They'd been engaged for less than twenty-four hours, but instead of celebrating and sharing the news with their families, they were in Dunwich, of all places, summoned by Rhys Morgan of the BBC to come and examine the remains that had been unearthed by a curious terrier on his morning walk. Rhys was pacing just outside the tent, a mobile phone pressed to his ear as he talked animatedly to someone on the other end. A young man with a video camera stood idly by, exchanging looks of bitter resentment with a middle-aged woman who was in the process of adjusting the lighting to better illuminate the scene. Rhys likely dragged his employees away from New Year's Eve celebrations and brought them to this bleak village for something that might be nothing more than the mortal remains of a medieval leper.

To Quinn, Dunwich was probably one of the saddest places in England. Some referred to it as the 'Atlantis of Britain', but in Quinn's opinion, that was too romantic a name for a bustling port city that slid into the sea and was reduced from a population of several thousand to less than one hundred. Dunwich had once been the capital of East Anglia, with a port to match that of fourteenth-century London, but a series of terrible storms coupled with a powerful coastal drift eroded the coastline, permanently covering about a square mile of the town with seawater.

Of the original structures, the ruins of the Leper Hospital and Greyfriars Franciscan Priory were the last remnants of the medieval town. The Franciscans had wisely moved their priory further inland in 1290, and the Leper Hospital had been built far from the main population for fear of contagion. The port and the rest of the town, including twelve churches, were fifty feet underwater, with the last proud structure, that of All Saints' Church, succumbing to its fate and vanishing into the North Sea in 1922. Now, the village of Dunwich numbered a handful of houses, a museum, and a pub, and was a melancholy spot on the face of the Suffolk coast.

"Quinn, glad you could make it." Rhys's tone was brusque as he rang off and strode toward Quinn and Gabe. "And Gabriel Russell. Even better. Two archeologists are better than one, I always say," he chuckled without mirth. "You two seem to be attached at the hip these days," he remarked caustically.

Gabe threw Quinn an expectant look, but Quinn ignored it. She saw no reason to share their news with Rhys. Quinn had to work with Rhys Morgan, but they didn't have to be friends, especially not after what she'd learned from her mother. Rhys was not her biological father, but he could have been, being one of the three men who assaulted her mother when she was a teenager. He'd contacted Sylvia and tried to make amends, but Quinn could never truly forgive him or give him her trust ever again.

"So, what have we got?" Quinn asked, pulling aside the white tarpaulin and stepping into the tent that had been erected above the grave. Rhys was right on her heels, his excitement palpable. He'd been searching for a suitable subject for the next installment of 'Echoes from the Past,' a program about archeological mysteries, hosted by the renowned Dr. Quinn Allenby. What the viewers didn't know was that Quinn was possessed of a rare gift, which Rhys exploited shamelessly to flesh out the characters and learn their secrets. Quinn was able to see into the past when holding an object belonging to the deceased in her bare hands, an ability that often left her feeling heartbroken and frustrated. Rhys clearly hoped that this new find would be another mind-blowing mystery, one to rival the first episode of the program, entitled 'The Lovers.'

"What we have here is a shallow grave on the fringes of the cemetery," Rhys replied. "There's no headstone, no coffin, and the deceased, who appears to have been a child, is buried face-down. I've already cleared it with the local constabulary, and they're sure that the burial is not a recent one, so they have no professional interest in it."

Quinn squatted down next to the grave with Gabe peering over her shoulder. She'd seen many graves and many human remains, but something about this particular one made her swallow back tears. Unless the deceased had been a very short adult, it had to be a child, a child who'd been dumped face down into a hole and left to rot — a child who was unloved, unmourned, and unwanted. Or was he? Rhys was right; there was a story here, and probably a very interesting one.

"Well?" Rhys prompted, impatient as ever. "What do you think?"

"I won't know anything for certain until the bones are excavated, cleaned, and tested. But here is what I do know. The skeleton appears to be that of a child. It was buried face down as a sign of disrespect, possibly even as a punishment. Prone burials were used throughout history to humiliate the dead and their families. I have no way of knowing if the child died of natural causes until a bone expert examines the remains. I would like to dig several trenches in the immediate vicinity to see if there are any more such burials. I can't imagine that it was just the one. We might need to get permission from the diocese, given that we'd be disturbing a patch of land bordering hallowed ground. Rhys, I'll leave that up to you. Let me get my tools and protective clothing. I don't want any contamination of the site. Gabe, perhaps some of your students might like to volunteer. This is an excellent learning opportunity, and I need someone to do the grunt work," Quinn added with a smile.

"I'll call the Institute. In the meantime, I'm at your disposal."

"When was the last time you held a trowel in your hands, Dr. Russell?" Quinn teased. Gabe had given up digging in the dirt to become head of department at the UCL Institute of Archeology in London, having had his fill of practical experience. Despite his complaints to the contrary, he enjoyed the role of administrator and liked being around young people, who were enthusiastic and eager to get their hands dirty. Gabe patted his pockets, a look of consternation on his face.

"I can't find my mobile. I must have left it at yours," he said. They'd left in such a hurry that morning that it was entirely possible that Gabe left his phone behind. He had a habit of leaving it wherever he used it last, and that would have been in bed last night when he texted his mum to tell her that Quinn had said yes.

"Here, use mine. The Institute is in the contacts," Quinn said, holding out her mobile to Gabe.

"Thank you."

Gabe stepped off to the side to call his assistant, Sherry Lee. She wouldn't be in the office today, but would get his message as soon as she came to work tomorrow and put out a call for volunteers. Gabe handed Quinn back the phone and blew on his hands, which were turning red with cold.

"I think we've done all we can for the moment," he said, giving Quinn a hand up.

"I'd like you to get started as soon as possible," Rhys protested. "Dave, here, will film the excavation and the removal of the bones. I thought it'd be a nice touch for the opening scenes of the episode. People like to see what the remains looked like *in situ*. Drinks on me at six," he added in an effort to pacify his disgruntled employees.

"Right. Let's go get our kit," Gabe said as he escorted Quinn out of the tent. "Are you all right?" he asked as they walked back toward his car where all their equipment was stowed in the boot.

Quinn shrugged. "I wish I could just walk away from this one."

Gabe turned Quinn to face him and placed his hands on her shoulders. "Why? What's bothering you? Did you see something?"

"No," Quinn shook her head. "But there's something about this case that disturbs me. Probably because someone saw fit to purposely disrespect a child, even in death. It's unsettling."

"Yes, it is. Do you want to speak to Rhys about opting out?" he asked, already knowing the answer. Quinn was under contract to finish out the series, and Rhys, being the consummate showman, would never pass up a dramatic, disturbing case because of the tender sensibilities of his star. Quinn was a professional and would behave like one. But there was one way in which she might be spared the gruesome details of the child's life and death: if there were no personal objects found with the remains. That way she would be flying blind, using only scientific data, her heart not engaged.

"No, I have to do this, but perhaps I'll get lucky."

"Fingers crossed," Gabe said with a warm smile, knowing exactly what Quinn was referring to.

Quinn crossed her fingers and returned his smile. It helped to know that he understood her so well and was there to support her.

Chapter 2

They'd taken a room at The Ship, the only inn in town, which was surprisingly modern and comfortable. The rest of the rooms went to Rhys and his assistants, and the student volunteers, who had to share. Dunwich wasn't exactly a hub of tourist activity, so the inn had a limited number of rooms. Quinn claimed the chair closest to the fire and cautiously moved her feet toward the flames. The warmth began to spread from the soles of her feet upward, making her sigh with pleasure. After a week of digging in the mud, the damp and chill had seeped into her bones, leaving her feeling cold even after a scalding hot bath, but part of the chill wasn't entirely physical.

That first day, Quinn and Gabe walked over to the beach, drawn by the screaming of the seagulls and the strange history of the place. The beach was eerie and deserted, the sky low and threatening. The foaming waves rolled onto the beach with frightening frequency, the sea indifferent to the damage it'd done. Quinn looked out over the roiling sea, her eyes scanning the area where the old town would have been. She tried to picture Dunwich as it might have appeared in the early fourteenth century. Quinn imagined the bustle of activity as the townspeople went about their business, and the forest of ship masts visible from every part of town. She glanced toward where All Saints' Church had once stood. There were still people alive today who could recall seeing it perched on the cliff before the tower finally collapsed into the sea in 1922, the cliff eroded by the pounding waves.

"Let's go," Quinn said to Gabe as she turned her back on the hungry sea. It frightened her, and she wanted to get as far away as possible from its fearsome power. They never went back to the beach, concentrating instead on the ancient grave and spending quiet evenings at the inn.

Quinn and Gabe worked on their own for two days, carefully unearthing the child's remains until reinforcements arrived in the form of four upperclassmen. By that time, Rhys had received permission from the diocese to search the grounds, but was expressly forbidden from disturbing any existing graves or excavating hallowed ground, which was absolutely fine, since the burials Quinn was looking for would not lie within the perimeter of the cemetery.

Quinn continued working on the original grave while Gabe helped the students mark two new trenches, which would extend horizontally on either side of the open grave. If anyone was buried within ten feet of the child on either side, the volunteers would find them. They came upon the second skeleton on the third day, a whoop of excitement coming from the trench on the right. The other two students looked sour, having nothing to report but a broken beer bottle, several modern-day chunks of metal, and a plastic lighter.

"Quinn, you'll want to see this," Gabe called out as they carefully removed the top layer of earth, mindful of disturbing the remains. Quinn climbed out of the grave and went to take a look. Most of the skeleton was still lodged in the ground, but there was no mistaking the position. It'd been buried face down, with no sign of a coffin or any remnant of a shroud.

"This one is definitely an adult," Gabe said as he took in the size of the skull and length of the spinal column. The legs were yet to be uncovered. Quinn nodded in agreement.

"Can we excavate this one ourselves, Dr. Allenby?" Tara Moore asked, eager to work independently. Of the four students, she was the most driven, and the most meticulous in her methods.

Quinn liked her immensely, and was eager to encourage her in any way she could.

"Since you were the one to find it, you get to be in charge, Tara. Dr. Russell will observe and guide."

"What about us?" John Myers demanded from the other trench.

"Give it one more day. If you don't come up with anything by end of day tomorrow, you may join in. There's enough work for everyone."

John and his partner looked sour, but nodded in acquiescence before returning to work. Quinn hoped they wouldn't find another grave; two prone burials were more than enough, but they had to be thorough, as did she. She labeled and bagged the bones then went back to carefully sifting through the disturbed earth in search of anything they might have missed. After nearly a whole day on her knees, trowel in hand, she found nothing. The body hadn't been buried with any personal objects; there was nothing in the grave, not a scrap of leather or a piece of metal. Quinn breathed a sigh of relief, thankful not to have to delve into the life of the buried child. She declared the grave finished with and was about to move on to the second grave when there was a cry of triumph from John Myers.

"Dr. Allenby, I found something."

"Let's have a look," Quinn replied and walked over to John, who was cupping something in his hand. His partner craned his neck to get a better view of the find, his mouth drooping with envy.

John opened his hand to show Quinn what he'd found. In his palm lay a dirt-encrusted chain. It had a pendant of some sort, but it was so blackened by earth and time that it was impossible to tell what was depicted on it.

"Show me exactly where you found it," Quinn requested, annoyed that John had removed it from its resting place. Where something was found was just as important as what was found. John pointed to a spot between the two graves. He was still clutching his find, reluctant to surrender it to Quinn, who had a plastic baggie at the ready.

"How deep was it?" Quinn asked, studying the disturbed earth.

"It was just here," John replied, showing Quinn the little hollow where he'd found the necklace. "Do you think it belonged to one of them?"

Quinn shook her head. The necklace was discovered between the two graves and had been situated much higher than the skeletons, so chances were that it was buried at a later date. Or perhaps it hadn't been buried at all. Someone might have simply dropped it years ago, and over time, layers of earth covered the trinket. It wasn't a modern object, given its location, but it likely wasn't as old as the graves.

Quinn held out the bag, and John reluctantly dropped the necklace into it. "Will I get credit for finding it?" he asked, making sure to face the camera as he uttered the words.

"Of course," Quinn replied. "Although, I doubt it has anything to do with our skeletons. However, I will send it to the lab along with anything else we find at the site." John looked pleased and gave a thumbs-up to the camera before returning to work. Quinn slipped the bag into her pocket and walked to the second grave, where Tara and Jade were hard at work. Rhys appeared at Quinn's shoulder, eager to find out more about John's find.

"What do you reckon? Is that necklace significant? Did you hold it in your hands?" he asked in a quieter voice.

"No, I didn't. I don't think it's relevant, but I can't be sure until it's been analyzed. Have patience, Rhys."

Rhys rewarded her with a guilty smile. "You can't fault me for being curious. Knowing what I know…" He let the sentence trail, giving Quinn a meaningful look to remind her that he was in on her secret.

"I'll be sure to let you know if there's anything to tell," Quinn replied. She had no desire to have this conversation in front of other people. Rhys took the hint and changed the subject.

"Could this have been a plague pit?" he asked as he handed Quinn a cup of tea. She accepted gratefully and stopped to consider while she took a sip of the scalding liquid that instantly warmed her. It was hard to tell how old the remains were just by looking, but they didn't strike her as plague victims. The first wave of the plague swept through England in 1348, brought on trade ships from Europe by afflicted sailors and rats that contaminated the grain. The effect of the plague had been devastating, and townspeople all over England went from burying their dead properly to just dumping their bodies into mass graves and covering them with lye, but these graves did not fit that pattern. Quinn had never seen bodies buried face down. The plague victims, although not properly laid out or buried in coffins, were always buried face up and laid out side by side or atop the other bodies if there were too many. These two burials seemed deliberate and malicious.

"No, Rhys, I really don't think these two were plague victims," she said, confirming Rhys's suspicions and making him a happy man. He didn't want plague victims; he wanted foul play and a story he could dramatize to his heart's content.

The second grave was much like the first. There was nothing. Whatever fabric might have gone into the earth with the body had completely rotted away, and there were no metal objects that had survived. Quinn dismissed the students, who were more than happy to be done with the gruesome task, and took one last look before giving the okay to fill in the grave. She was about to climb out when she noticed a tiny sliver of black peeking out of the soil. Quinn reached for a brush and swept aside bits of earth, not using the trowel for fear of damaging whatever was underneath. The object proved to be a cracked bit of leather. Quinn carefully dug around it until she unearthed a disintegrating thong decorated with an iron cross. The metal was brown and flaky with rust, but surprisingly still intact. It must have stayed protected from the moisture in the ground somehow, perhaps having gotten trapped in the folds of the shroud, if there had been one. Quinn carefully bagged the cross. This was her only link to the past, and she would study it carefully once she was on her own.

The remains were labeled and sent off to Dr. Colin Scott, pathologist and bone expert, who would hopefully have some preliminary results for them in a few days' time. The students went about filling in the graves, setting the cemetery to rights, and writing up notes about the excavation. Rhys returned to London with his people, deeply satisfied with the footage and ready to start planning the next phase of the project. He even had Quinn conduct an in-depth interview with the elderly lady whose dog found a femur. She'd been terribly flustered at first, but then, having been seduced by the camera and the bright lights, went on and on, eager to tell her story.

Quinn tore her gaze away from the leaping flames in the hearth and reached for the plastic bag containing the cross. She'd meant to study it earlier, but something inside her protested loudly at the thought of gazing into the past of its owner. Gabe bent over Quinn, kissed the top of her head, and gently removed the bag from her hand. "Not now, love," he said, sensing her apprehension. "Not now."

Quinn had to admit that she was only too happy to set the trinket aside. She wasn't ready. Not yet. The last case had left her feeling horrified and depressed. The brutal death of Elise, Lady Asher, and her lover James Coleman, which Quinn had witnessed firsthand, had been worse than anything she'd ever experienced, and she fervently wished, as she had many times in the past, that she wasn't possessed of her strange gift of seeing into the past.

Gabe threw another log on the fire and took a seat, beckoning for Quinn to come and sit on his lap. He wrapped his arms around her, making her feel a little less anxious, and moved his lips along the column of her neck. A pleasant shiver ran down Quinn's spine, helping her to put the remains and the artifact from her mind. They would return home tomorrow morning, and her research would begin in earnest, but for tonight, she wanted nothing more than to spend a few peaceful hours with her gorgeous fiancé, and to forget all about the past.

Quinn leaned against Gabe as he slid his hands beneath her jersey, cupping her breasts. She eagerly surrendered to his touch, enjoying the sensations that began to course through her body as he pulled off her top and began to kiss her breasts. She felt Gabe's arousal against her thigh and her body instantly responded to his desire.

"Come to bed," Quinn murmured as she slid off Gabe's lap and pulled him toward the antique four-poster.

Chapter 3

Quinn wrapped a scarf about her neck, grabbed her purse, and followed Gabe out the door into the frigid January morning. At least the sun was out, which was something, given the weather they'd had over the past few days. It had been dreary and cold, the damp seeping into the bones, and the chill radiating from the inside out. Gabe would drop her off at the mortuary on his way to the office, and they would meet up later at Gabe's flat.

"Did you take your mobile?" Quinn asked, amused by Gabe's absent-mindedness. A week without his phone nearly undid him, despite the fact that she had hers and there was a telephone in their room at the inn.

"Got it," Gabe replied, patting his pocket. "I've had a dozen missed calls from Scotland and a message from an attorney in Edinburgh. He said it's urgent that I return his call."

"Do you know anyone in Edinburgh?" Quinn asked as she settled into the Jag and turned up the heat.

Gabe shrugged. "I know a few other academics, but no one who'd call me on my mobile. They would contact me through the Institute or via email. I can't imagine what this is about. I'll ring him when I get to the office. Perhaps he has the wrong Gabriel Russell."

"Well, I've had a message from Sylvia," Quinn confessed, noting Gabe's askance look. "She said that Jude is just about finished with his tour and should be back in London in a few weeks. She'd like to have me round for dinner so that I can finally meet the boys."

"You don't seem pleased," Gabe remarked as he swung the car out of the drive.

"I've dreamed of having siblings since I was a little girl, but siblings have things in common, having grown up in the same household. Even if they are as different as night and day, they still share childhood experiences and memories. Logan and Jude never even heard of me until about a month ago. They're strangers to me, as I am to them. I'm a little nervous about meeting them. They might resent my intrusion into their lives."

"I'm sure they'll love you," Gabe said, giving her hand a squeeze.

"But what if I don't love them? What if we have nothing in common and sit there in awkward silence? That's worse than having no siblings at all."

"Quinn, no family is perfect, and few siblings have the close, uncomplicated relationship that you envision. There's always resentment, rivalry, long-festering hurts, and ongoing arguments."

"How would you know? You're an only child," Quinn chuckled.

"But my mum is one of five. Not a single family gathering goes by without someone exhuming the past and rehashing their grievances ad nauseam. I think my mum and Aunt Janice enjoy bickering. It's the bedrock of their relationship."

"Do her brothers join in?" Quinn asked, curious about the family dynamic.

"They have their own established pattern, but they goad each other just as much as their sisters."

"Will you come with me to meet my brothers?" Quinn asked, feeling slightly more optimistic.

"Of course. I'm curious to meet them myself. Will you be inviting the Wyatts to our wedding?"

"Oh Lord, I haven't thought of that. I can't imagine that Mum and Dad would feel comfortable knowing that Sylvia would be there."

"So, you've finally told them?" Gabe asked. Quinn had picked up the phone a dozen times to call her parents to tell them about finding her birth mother, but every time she set the phone back down, unprepared for the conversation that was to follow. She knew it would hurt her parents, and she wished to spare them the pain, despite knowing that at some point she'd finally have to tell them the truth, especially since they would be coming for the wedding. It was easy to hold off, since her parents had retired to Spain a few years ago and were happily living in Marbella, but Quinn couldn't stall forever.

"Yes, I called them just before we left for Dunwich. It wasn't a very long conversation."

"What did they say?" Gabe asked as he eased off the gas. Traffic was building up as they got closer to London proper.

"Not much, which is exactly how I know they are upset. Normally, they would ask a million questions and savor every detail, but they both got quiet and then said they had to go; they were meeting someone for lunch. Mum said she was happy for me, which, in essence, means that she's not happy for herself."

"They are just feeling a bit insecure. They've had you all to themselves for thirty years, and now your biological mother is a part of your life, and they can't help wondering if your feelings toward them might change."

Quinn threw Gabe a look of pure incredulity. "You seriously think that I will love my parents less because I finally met Sylvia?"

"I don't think that, but they might. They feel threatened, especially since she's an unknown quantity. Give them time. They'll come round."

"I hope so," Quinn mumbled as she tried to picture a meeting between her mother and Sylvia Wyatt. The two women were so different. Quinn hadn't thought of it before, but now that she imagined both her mothers in the same room, an unbidden thought popped into her head: *Sylvia is not the type of woman you trust with your husband.*

Chapter 4

Quinn's heels clicked on the linoleum floor as she walked down the corridor toward the mortuary. The strong smell of disinfectant was still there, but this time it didn't hit Quinn as hard, possibly because she was prepared for it. A young Asian woman caught up with her, smiling in recognition. Quinn had met her last time, when she worked on the case of Elise de Lesseps. Sarita Dhawan was Dr. Scott's assistant, and a very competent pathologist in her own right.

"Dr. Allenby, nice to see you again. Dr. Scott is expecting you," Sarita said. "He performed most of the tests himself this time, since these remains are older and more fragile, but he allowed me to assist," she added, clearly displeased at not being allowed to perform the tests on her own.

"I can't wait to hear what you two have discovered," Quinn replied, hoping to mollify Dr. Dhawan's professional pride.

Dr. Scott rose from his seat behind a computer and came to greet Quinn. "Quinn, lovely to see you. We really must stop meeting over decaying bones and have a cup of coffee one day."

"I'd love that," Quinn said, and meant it. She genuinely liked Dr. Scott and would enjoy chatting with him about something other than death. Colin Scott looked trendy as ever with his sandy hair pulled into an artistic bun. Not many men could pull off a man-bun, but Dr. Scott was one of them, his chiseled bone structure accentuated by the lack of hair around his face to distract from its perfect symmetry. His blue eyes sparkled with excitement as he offered Quinn a pair of latex gloves and invited her to walk over to the twin slabs where the skeletons were laid out, illuminated by harsh, fluorescent lights. Sarita Dhawan hung back, waiting to be included, but Dr. Scott took no notice of her. Quinn tried to suppress a smile as she suddenly realized that Sarita Dhawan had a bit of a crush on her boss and was desperate for his attention, which, at this moment, was completely focused on the remains.

"Dr. Dhawan and I have performed a series of tests, including carbon-14 dating, a CT scan, and DNA sequencing. The results of the DNA sequencing take some time, but here's what I can share with you right now. What we have here are the skeletal remains of a prepubescent boy, aged somewhere between ten and thirteen, who died approximately seven hundred and fifty years ago, which would bring his date of death to somewhere in the late thirteenth or early fourteenth century."

"I thought he'd be younger," Quinn interjected, surprised that the boy might have been as old as thirteen.

"He was small for his age," Dr. Scott explained. "And people of that time were generally shorter and slighter due to lack of proper nutrition and less-than-varied diet."

"Please, go on," Quinn invited, eager to hear what the doctor had discovered.

"I performed the CT scan before cleaning the bones in the hope that we might find something which is not obvious to the naked eye and might have been washed off during the cleaning, but nothing save a few stray fibers were revealed. If you take a look here," Dr. Scott said, pointing to a jagged crack in the frontal bone, "you'll see a crack. This is the cause of death — blunt force trauma, which probably resulted in a subdural hematoma. The child had several broken bones, but they appear to have been old injuries that had healed or were in the process of healing. Either our lad was accident-prone, or someone hurt him intentionally and on a regular basis. Given the time period, I'd go with the latter."

Dr. Scott patted Quinn on the shoulder as she blanched at the thought of the child being regularly beaten. "I'm sorry if this is upsetting," he said, his look of amusement alerting Quinn to the fact that the remains on the slab were nothing more than a puzzle to him, not what was left of a human being.

"And the fibers?" Quinn asked, eager to move away from the subject of child abuse.

"I believe that the fibers come from a burial shroud. The fabric had been coarse and undyed, consistent with the type of cloth that might be used in a burial. I think that the child was buried naked, which would explain a complete lack of any other fibers or objects."

"Is that all you can tell me?" Quinn asked, surprised by the lack of information.

Dr. Scott smiled apologetically. "Unfortunately, we were unable to find any hair follicles or bits of nail which might have yielded his DNA. Sarita extracted two teeth, which she ground to a powder and will use for a DNA reconstruction, but that takes months, I'm afraid."

"I see. And what can you tell me about the second set of remains?" Quinn asked as she moved toward the adjoining slab where the adult skeleton was laid out.

"This skelly belongs to a woman who was in her mid-twenties to early thirties. She was in reasonably good health when she died, and had given birth to at least one child, likely more. The cause of death is also blunt force trauma, but she was hit right here," Dr. Scott said, pointing to the temporal bone.

"Can you tell what they were assaulted with?" Quinn asked.

"I can't say for certain, but I think it might have been something that had smooth edges. Possibly an ax or a cudgel. As it happens, death might have been accidental, given that blunt force trauma is more common than you imagine. It could have been the result of a fall or being kicked in the head by a mule or some such creature. Given that both were buried face down, I'd say that you're probably right, and they'd been interfered with. I suppose we'll never know for sure."

Quinn pulled out the plastic bag and showed Dr. Scott the cross. "I found this beneath the woman's body. Can you tell anything just by at looking it?"

"Let's have a look." Dr. Scott carefully took the piece of metal from the bag and placed it on the mechanical stage of a microscope. "I'm amazed that it hasn't crumbled into dust, having been in the ground for nearly eight hundred years," he muttered as he studied the object, adjusting the magnification to get a better look.

"I think it might have gotten caught in the folds of the shroud, but then the fabric would have rotted away after a few years anyway," Quinn said, realizing it wasn't a reasonable scientific explanation.

"No, my dear Quinn, not the shroud, the hair. Hair takes a lot longer to disintegrate, and I think that we are lucky enough to say that we have a strand right here." He reached for a pair of tweezers and lifted a tiny fragment of hair off the knot in the leather. "This little fellow will tell us more than you think. I'll run some tests and ring you as soon as I find anything out."

"I'd be most grateful. Perhaps we can have that cup of coffee to discuss the results."

"You're on. Sarita, please give Dr. Allenby a copy of the results. I'm sure you'll need to refer to the data again before this is over."

Quinn accepted a manila folder, collected the cross, then said her goodbyes and left. It was time to begin her research and glimpse into the past, in more ways than one. She now had one more link to the victims. She never sent the necklace John Myers found at the site to a lab. There was no need. She'd taken it home and cleaned it carefully, stripping away centuries of dirt to reveal the serene faces of Madonna and child. The necklace was made of silver, and must have been an object of value in the Middle Ages, especially since it came with a medal of the Virgin. Someone had placed that necklace there for a reason, and having finally found the courage to hold it in her bare hands, Quinn knew exactly who it had been, except that she didn't yet understand the context.

On first contact, the necklace yielded confusing results. Quinn normally saw visions of the owner of an object, but the necklace seemed to carry more than one set of images. She'd use it later, after the cross, which was a direct line to the adult skeleton and would hopefully tell her story in a sequential manner. For now, it was Quinn's little secret.

Quinn dialed Rhys to give him the preliminary results of Dr. Scott's tests, but that wasn't the real reason for her call, which was why she called him on his mobile instead of trying his office. Rhys answered on the first ring.

"Quinn, I hoped you'd ring today. Anything from Colin?"

"Yes, I'm just at the mortuary now," Quinn replied as she found a quiet corner and perched on the edge of a hard plastic chair. "He needs a bit more time, but our skeletons date just around the beginning of the fourteenth century and were most likely victims of a violent crime."

"Excellent," Rhys gushed. Quinn could almost hear the gears shifting in his head. He was already planning the episode.

"Rhys, actually there's something else I'd like to discuss with you," Quinn began, her heart rate increasing in proportion to the topic she was about to broach.

"Oh yes?"

"Rhys, I'd like you to arrange a meeting with Robert Chatham and Seth Besson. I need to know which one of them is my biological father," Quinn said. Her voice sounded flat, but she was trembling. The idea of meeting her father face to face was as exciting as it was terrifying.

"Quinn, darling, please don't ask that of me. I haven't seen either Robert or Seth since uni. To suddenly look them up and broach the subject of that night…" Rhys allowed the sentence to trail off, hoping that Quinn would appreciate his dilemma, but Quinn wasn't about to back down.

"Rhys, you owe me this much."

"And I'd like to help you out, but you're asking the impossible. You know I'd love to help, but there must be another way."

Quinn considered this for a moment. She supposed it would be terribly awkward for Rhys to do what she asked of him. Perhaps he could help her in some other way.

"Can you track them down for me? Friend them on social media perhaps? I'd like to learn as much as I can before I approach them in person."

Rhys sighed audibly. For thirty years, he thought he was off the hook for what he'd done the night Sylvia Wyatt was raped, but the past was coming to collect its debt, and he had to pay up. "All right. I will do what I can."

"Thanks," Quinn replied and rang off before Rhys could say any more. She had no intention of making this easy for him.

Chapter 5

October 1346

Dunwich, Suffolk

A chill wind blew off the North Sea, bringing with it the smell of brine and wood smoke, coming from somewhere downwind. The needles of a sprawling yew tree moved like tiny fingers in the breeze, the red berries swaying mournfully. Petra lowered her eyes from the ruddy face of Father Oswald and fixated on the tips of her shoes, trying desperately not to smile. She had to play the grieving widow, at least until after the burial. She supposed God saw everything and would take her happiness at the passing of her husband into account, but she'd paid with twelve years of her life for one foolish mistake; she'd served her time.

Petra stole a glance at Edwin, who stood next to his sisters and grandmother, his head bowed in prayer. No, she could never call him a mistake. Edwin was the child of her heart, her reason for being, and the only reminder of the man she'd given her heart to twelve years ago. How different her life might have been had they been allowed to marry. They'd have been a family, and loving parents to the boy who now shed tears for a man who not only hadn't been his father, but who had been cruel and indifferent to the child he believed to be his son.

But now Cyril was dead, killed by the job he so feared losing, and she was glad of it. Petra still bore the scars of his belt on her back, the fresh welts covering the old, faded ones. Tonight, she would lie by herself in a bed that had been the altar of her sacrifice, which led to years of marital abuse. She nearly giggled at the thought of never having to endure Cyril's attentions again, thrusting into her as she lay still as a corpse, praying for it to be over so that she could enjoy a few hours of respite before having to deal with him again come morning.

Father Oswald finally finished the service, and the diggers began to fill in the grave, eager to get the job done and repair to the inn for a well-deserved jar of ale. Petra put a hand on each of her daughters' shoulders and walked from the cemetery, followed by her mother, who was supported by Edwin.

"Are you sad, Mama?" Ora asked, gazing up at Petra with an expression of interest. At eight, there was little she missed, so Petra tried to always be as honest as she could.

"A bit. Are you?" she asked the child.

"No," Ora answered truthfully. "Is that very wicked of me?"

Cyril had spared the girls when they were little, but over the past year, both Ora and Elia had felt the sting of his slap more than once. In time, Cyril would have taken a belt to them for disobeying him, or simply because he could. He took pleasure in punishing them, and went far beyond what was necessary to get his point across.

"No, it isn't. We all deal with death in different ways. It's all right not to feel bereft." Petra noted Elia's look of surprise, but said nothing. Of the three children, she'd been closest to Cyril, and he forgave her more than he would ever forgive the other two. He always remarked that Elia resembled his dear departed mother, so perhaps he even loved her. He hadn't loved Edwin, and made that clear, especially once Edwin's affliction became apparent. Cyril said it was a curse. Edwin was a cursed boy born in a cursed place.

Dunwich had been a prosperous place once, a city that went back to the times of the Anglo-Saxons, known then as Dommoc. It was a place of commerce and trade, a place to which merchants flocked and fortunes were made. It boasted one of the biggest ports in England, with as many as eighty ships at its zenith, and a population of thousands. The town's decline began long before Edwin's birth, even before her own, but Petra heard stories of the great storms that came in 1287 and 1328. They eroded the coastline and destroyed houses and part of the harbor, engulfing it in water, which never receded all the way. The priests said that it was a punishment from God on the wicked people of Dunwich, a pestilence brought on by their greed, but there were those who said that the fault lay not with the people, but with the land. The cliff on which Dunwich had been built was made of sandy soil, easily washed away by the pounding waves and strong currents of the North Sea.

And, of course, there were those who attributed the wrath of the sea to a local legend. Eva, a heartbroken young maiden, had cut out her heart and threw it into the sea after being forsaken by the man who'd taken advantage of her. According to the tale, Eva failed to die and haunted the sea from that day on, wreaking havoc on the place that witnessed her disgrace. Petra's mother had told her of the legend when she was a little girl, and Petra wept for Eva, heartbroken at the thought of a young woman being so ill-used by a man she trusted.

Petra hadn't fared much better than Eva. There was a man who'd made false promises and a child conceived in sin. There had been no time to waste, no chance to find a kind and gentle suitor. Petra had to marry in haste to hide her condition, and the man she married, although kind enough at first, turned out to be a cruel and domineering master. He made Petra's life a living purgatory, especially once Edwin's fits began, and Petra realized that there was something terribly wrong with her precious boy. Perhaps it was a punishment from God, a cross to bear as the wage of her sin. She'd gone against the teachings of the Church, had lied to her husband, and had protected the man responsible for her situation, rather than holding him accountable. She deserved to suffer, and she bore it silently, but why Edwin? Were the sins of the father, or in this case the mother, always visited upon the son?

Petra's labor with Edwin had been difficult. It lasted for several days, with the child lodged in the birth canal for nearly a full day before being forcibly dragged out of Petra's womb by her mother, who feared for her only daughter's life. Edwin had been blue, his heartbeat faint, and his eyes closed to the light of an overcast winter morning. He made no sound, even after being slapped on the rump by his grandmother. Edwin clearly wasn't meant for this world, but Petra cried and cried, and begged to hold her baby. After an hour in the arms of his weeping mother, Edwin rallied, letting out a thin wail that pierced Petra's heart. He lived, and she would do anything to see him thrive. Edwin was never hale and hearty, but he survived, and that was all that mattered.

Edwin grew up to be a kind-hearted boy, who felt deeply for others, especially for the mother who always interjected herself between father and son to protect him from the former's wrath. Fear and anxiety brought the fits on, more often than not, and Petra did everything in her power to shield her son and keep him safe. The fits began when Edwin was only two. They passed as quickly as they came, but the shaking was so violent that Edwin often bit his tongue and nearly choked on the saliva that foamed at his mouth. He usually fell into a heavy sleep after a fit, his body desperate for a period of quiet needed for him to recover. Petra prayed that the fits would stop as Edwin grew, but they only got worse, lasting longer and sometimes resulting in injury. Once, when he was eight, Edwin thrashed so violently that he broke his arm and had to wear a wooden splint for nearly two months. Petra strongly suspected that Cyril was glad of the injury. He would have happily inflicted it himself had Petra not begged him to let the boy be.

"What's to become of him?" Cyril roared as Edwin cowered in the corner, frightened out of his wits. "Who will take him on? Who in their right mind would want an apprentice who's so afflicted?"

"Why can't he work with you?" Petra pleaded, hoping that Cyril would teach Edwin the shipbuilding trade once the boy got older. It was a valuable skill in a port city where new ships were built and damaged ships limped in for repair. But Petra knew the answer before Cyril even had a chance to reply. Edwin couldn't work with his father. He had to be taken on as an apprentice and complete his seven years before applying to be accepted into the Guild, of which Cyril was a member. But just because Cyril was a journeyman, a master craftsman paid a daily wage, didn't mean that the son would get admitted, even if he managed to complete his training. The Church and the guilds ruled the town, as they did every town in England. Edwin was freeborn, the son of a freeborn man, but he might as well have been a serf for all the choices he had open to him. At least as a serf, he wouldn't starve, and be put to work doing a job that would put food on the table, meager as it might be.

"Are you mad, woman?" Cyril carried on. "What do you think he'll do to himself if he's holding an ax in his hand and a fit comes on? He's broken bones without so much as leaving home, and you want to allow him to wield sharp tools in the vicinity of other men? Out of the question. I'd send him to the priory, but even the monks won't take him if they find out about this curse he's been born with. It's the Leper Hospital for him once he's of age. I'd happily take him there now. Why waste good food and clothing on someone who can never repay it?"

"Cyril, you can't mean that," Petra wailed, terrified that her son would become one of the hideously disfigured unfortunates who resided at the St. James Leper Hospital on the outskirts of Dunwich, looked after only by a master who saw to their needs at great risk to his own life. There was no other place for an afflicted person to go. The cripples of the town received alms from the monks, but Petra and Cyril had kept Edwin's affliction a secret, hoping and praying that he would grow out of it in time. Besides, he was of sound mind and body most of the time, so the monks might not see fit to dispense alms to someone who was capable of earning a wage. The alms went to those who were missing a limb or were soft in the head.

"Cyril, please. Surely there's something Edwin can do that isn't dangerous. There's nothing wrong with his mind."

"And what good is a mind?" Cyril taunted her. "He's the son of a shipbuilder, a man destined to work with his hands. Perhaps you'd like to spend all our savings to educate the idiot? Teach him to read and write? Much good it would do him." Cyril had stormed from the house, leaving Petra in tears and Edwin in a comatose sleep. Petra hated Cyril for his cruelty, but deep down she knew he was right. Edwin needed to learn a trade, and most trades involved the handling of dangerous tools and performing under the sharp eyes of master craftsmen who'd not keep Edwin on once they learned of his affliction.

Petra put Edwin's future from her mind as she went about setting out pies and platters of sliced pork for the mourners and refilling their cups with beer or hippocras. She tried to keep the cost of the wake to a minimum, but many of Cyril's guild-mates had come to the funeral, and Petra could hardly keep them from coming to the house. She'd hoped that there'd be some food left over for the following day, but by the time everyone departed, there was hardly a crumb left. She'd have to go to the market tomorrow for supplies. Petra went about clearing and washing the crockery and sweeping the dirt floor, eager to get to bed. The children had retired to their bed in an alcove behind a curtain. They still slept together, despite the fact that the girls were on the cusp of womanhood. Unless Edwin slept on the floor, there was nowhere else for him to bed down.

"Petra, come sit," her mother said as Petra set aside the broom and surveyed the small space.

"I'm for my bed, Mother. We'll talk tomorrow."

Maude nodded and rose to her feet. "Goodnight, child," she said and shuffled toward her own pallet by the fire. Her old bones couldn't take the cold, even on warmer nights. Now that Cyril was gone, Maude could share Petra's bed, but she couldn't climb the ladder to the loft, so had to sleep downstairs.

"Goodnight, Mother."

Petra climbed the ladder and kept her head down as she walked toward the bed. The roof wasn't high enough to accommodate a person at full height, but she only went up there to sleep. Her day was spent either downstairs or outdoors, performing the chores that took up most of her time. Petra removed her barbet, unpinned her hair, and stared at her reflection in the square of beaten metal that served as a mirror and hung on the wall. With her hair down, and by candlelight, she almost looked like the girl she'd been. She knew what her mother wanted to talk to her about, but she wouldn't think of that today. Tonight was her first night of freedom in twelve years, and she would enjoy it as much as she could, since it wouldn't last long.

Chapter 6

November 1346

Dunwich, Suffolk

Petra considered throwing another log on the fire, then changed her mind. She needed to keep the fire going during the day for cooking, baking, and heating water for laundry, but in the evening, she let the fire burn down, huddling under woolen blankets to keep out the cold. She'd always been mindful of practical matters, but over the past month, the need for economy had become more urgent. Cyril had left a bit of money upon his death, but after paying for the burial and the stone cross to mark his final resting place, the wake, and buying some necessary supplies, Petra's funds were greatly diminished. She'd cut down portions and allowed the children only one slice of bread smeared with fat when they broke their fast in the morning, but the savings wouldn't last much longer.

Petra checked on the children, who were fast asleep, and sat at the table across from her mother, glad to be off her feet at last. She was weary, but not quite ready for bed.

"You must remarry, Petra, and soon," Maude said to her daughter, bringing angry spots to Petra's pale cheeks.

"Yes, so you keep telling me, Mother," Petra retorted. "I am well aware of our situation."

"Don't think I don't feel for you," Maude said, reaching out to cover Petra's hand with her own. "I know what it's like to be a woman, my girl. You're not the first to make sacrifices to feed your family and protect your children."

"Haven't I sacrificed enough?" Petra cried, but she knew what her mother was thinking even though she didn't say it. There was no point; it'd been said often enough. She'd made her bed. She'd lain with a man who wasn't her husband, got with child, and had to marry the first person who asked, desperate to avoid disgrace and possible banishment. She had no one to blame but herself. She couldn't even blame the father of her child, since he was a man, and it was practically his responsibility to try to seduce a beautiful young girl, according to her mother. If only Maude knew the truth. Petra had never revealed Edwin's father's name. She had to protect him, and she had to protect herself. She hadn't uttered his name since the day they said goodbye, walking along the beach, seagulls screaming above their heads and the bitter wind drying Petra's tears.

Her lover was being sent away to a place she couldn't follow. If he defied his father, he would be cast out, and unable to provide for a wife and child without a useful trade to rely on. He had to go, and she had to remain behind and find a way to survive. Petra had never laid eyes on him again, but he still lived in her heart, the handsome boy with soulful dark eyes whose slow smile pierced her heart and made her reckless. She'd known the risks, but somehow, when looking into his face, they seemed minor compared to not enjoying those moments with him and not knowing what it was like to lie with a man you loved rather than some suitor-turned-husband who was a stranger in every way.

Petra sighed, feeling like an old woman despite the fact that she was barely twenty-seven. She wasn't old yet, but the flush of youth was long gone. At twenty-seven, she was considered middle-aged, a woman who was no longer expected to bear children for a new husband. Her main purpose would be to look after his comforts and act the parent to the children he already had, especially if they were still young and needed mothering. At this stage, marrying her would be a practical decision for a man, not an emotional one, and for her, marrying again and giving up her hard-won freedom would be a fate worse than death. Would life never give her a break? "I'll sell Cyril's tools," she said.

Maude scoffed. "And how long will the money last? Winter is almost upon us. We'll need extra wood, and Elia's shoes are worn through. I've darned Edwin's hose more times that I can count, and he's outgrown his jerkin."

"Edwin can wear Cyril's clothes. I know he's much thinner and shorter than Cyril was, but you can take in the garments to make them fit. Leave enough room for him to grow into them. And I will go to the cobbler and see if I can trade Cyril's boots for shoes for Elia and Ora. They won't be new, but they'll last through the winter at the very least," Petra said. The cobbler was a good man, and would trade Cyril's worn boots for two pairs of used botes for the girls, Petra was sure of it. Perhaps the laces would need to be replaced, but the leather would still be good, and the botes would come up above the ankle, keeping the girls' feet dry during the winter months. Maude nodded, pleased by her daughter's pragmatic thinking. She'd taught her well.

"I'm for my bed," Petra said, desperate to put an end to the unsettling conversation. It was one of many, and her head ached with tension brought on by constant fretting. They'd never been well-to-do, but she supposed they'd been comfortable enough. They dined on beef or pork at least once a week, and Cyril grudgingly allowed Petra to buy cloth once a year to make a new gown for herself. She even had a cloak trimmed with vair, an extravagance she permitted herself on her twenty-fifth birthday, with Cyril's blessing, of course.

Her old gowns were recut into clothes for the children, but Petra insisted on buying a length of linen to make new undergarments for the family. After a year's wear, the shifts and braies were worn through, and the children did grow, making new garments necessary. Cyril was less generous when it came to shoes, decreeing that the children wear their shoes until there were holes in the soles. Cyril inserted bits of leather to cover the holes, therefore squeezing a few more months of wear before finally agreeing to new footwear. Petra hated those little economies, but now she realized that they had been necessary, and were nothing compared to what she'd have to give up if she didn't find a source of income. There would be no new gown or undergarments this year. Cyril's much-worn and darned hose would have to find new life with Edwin, at least until the winter was over, and the girls would have to make do with their old shifts. They were too short and threadbare, but would have to last a while longer.

Petra climbed wearily to her loft. She would have to find something for Edwin, and soon. He would need a way to support himself once he came of age, and possibly his sisters as well should anything happen to Petra. The girls were still young, but in a few years' time, they would be of marriageable age and would need to be dowered. Where would she find the money to make them desirable to a prospective husband? They were comely of face and docile of manner, but that wasn't enough to secure their future. If Petra hoped to marry the girls off to journeymen, she needed to offer something worth having, something that had value. Everyone was poor, and had no desire to be poorer still. Love was a luxury few could afford. Even the wealthy married to further their family's goals and forge alliances. Children were nothing more than a commodity to be traded for the best price.

Petra removed her headdress and gown and unbraided her hair before climbing into bed in her shift and hose, shivering from the cold. A bitter draft seeped right through the walls, making her blanket feel woefully inadequate. Petra would have been better off sleeping in her woolen gown, but she couldn't afford to put extra wear on the garment, so she hugged her knees to her chest and shivered pitifully until she finally fell asleep.

Chapter 7

January 2014

London, England

Gabe tossed his mobile onto the desk and buried his head in his hands. He was shaking, his mind momentarily paralyzed by what he'd just learned. How was it possible for a person's life to change so drastically in a matter of moments? In his line of work, he dealt with the unraveling of people's lives on a daily basis, but history was academic, not personal. He knew only too well of settlements that had been burned down to the ground, their entire populations slaughtered, but not before the women were raped, the brutality witnessed by their husbands and children who cried in helpless frustration. He'd read of ships sinking, their crews and passengers swallowed by the sea, and, of course, he was well-versed in the casualties of war. But this was his life, and this time the events were happening to him and to Quinn. Gabe growled with despair, startling his PA, who'd just walked in.

"Dr. Russell, are you quite all right? You look a bit peaky," Sherry Lee said as she deposited more paper into Gabe's already-overflowing in-tray.

"Ah, yes. Thank you, Sherry," Gabe muttered as he jumped up and grabbed his coat. "I just need some air."

He strode out of the office and ran down the stairs, desperate to get outside. The cold, smoggy air assaulted him as he exited the building, but it was a welcome respite from the stuffy, overheated fug of his office. Gabe began to walk. He was almost running, but he had no idea where he was going. He didn't want to go home. What he needed was a drink and someone to talk to before he went home to break the news to Quinn. *Oh God,* Gabe thought miserably. *What will Quinn make of all this?*

Gabe couldn't recall exactly when he stopped walking, but he found himself sitting on a bench in Hyde Park. He had no recollection of getting there, or of purchasing a bottle of whisky from the off-license. Gabe unscrewed the cap and took a sip, enjoying the feel of the fiery liquid as it slid down his throat. It had just gone 10 a.m., but he didn't care; he was desperate. What he felt was so convoluted that he couldn't even begin to put it into words. He was shocked, upset, frightened, and very apprehensive, but he was also excited, curious, and filled with a longing that left him nearly breathless.

Gabe lowered the bottle when he saw a young woman with a small girl walking along the path. The woman looked bemused as the little girl bombarded her with questions, not waiting for an answer before moving on to the next topic. The girl had golden hair that escaped from her pink hat and wide blue eyes. She looked like a character from some children's book that he couldn't quite recall. Was it *The Secret Garden*? No, she reminded him of *Alice in Wonderland*. Well, he'd just tumbled down the rabbit hole, so it made perfect sense. Gabe lifted the bottle to his lips and drank deeply.

Chapter 8

January 2014

London, England

Quinn looked up from her book on medieval Dunwich when she heard the scrape of the key in the lock, surprised that Gabe was back so early. It was just past noon, and he rarely got home before six. She cast her mind over the contents of the fridge. He'd be hungry. Perhaps she could make him some pasta or a salad. She'd been planning to pick up some chops from the butcher's down the street, but thought she had a few hours to spend on research before it was time to prepare dinner.

"You're home early," she called out. "Would you like...?" The rest of the question died on Quinn's lips when she noted Gabe's appearance. He looked strangely pale, despite the biting cold outside, and his gaze wasn't focused on anything in particular. Quinn went to kiss him, but drew back when she smelled the liquor on his breath.

"Gabe, have you been drinking?"

Gabe enjoyed the occasional pint or a glass of wine, but he wasn't a serious drinker, not like some who started as soon as the sun was over the yard arm. Gabe was a social drinker who always stopped before he reached his limit. Quinn had seen him tipsy a few times, in his younger days, but never stinking drunk, as he appeared to be at that moment.

"Yes, I have," Gabe replied as he collapsed into a wing chair. "And I'd like to keep drinking, except that I ran out of whisky." He pulled an empty bottle out of his pocket and looked at it in confusion, almost as if he expected more whisky to materialize out of thin air. He shrugged in resignation and set the bottle on the floor before leaning against the back of the sofa and closing his eyes against the bright light streaming through the window.

"Gabe, what's wrong? Is it your parents?" Quinn cried. She couldn't think of anything else that would send Gabe into such a tailspin. His parents were elderly. Things happened. Gabe shook his head, but didn't open his eyes. He didn't want to look at her.

"Mum and Dad are well, as far as I know," he finally replied, slurring his words ever so slightly.

"Did you get sacked?" Quinn tried again. Losing his job would upset Gabe terribly, but she knew of absolutely no reason why that should happen. Gabe was good at what he did, and had the respect of colleagues and students alike.

"Not yet," Gabe muttered, his mouth curling into a mirthless smile. He finally opened his eyes, but refused to make eye contact, staring off into the distance instead.

"Then what is it? What's happened?" she pleaded, now really worried. Gabe was the calmest, most rational person she knew. Gabe didn't drink in the morning or stare into space as if he couldn't quite remember where he was supposed to be. Quinn couldn't begin to imagine what might have driven him to this type of a breakdown.

"I'm not sure where to start," Gabe mumbled.

"At the beginning," Quinn retorted. "But first, you will have some coffee." She raced into the kitchen and turned on the espresso machine, making Gabe a double espresso. He accepted the cup gratefully, took a sip, and grimaced with distaste.

"You could have added some sugar," he complained.

"Never mind the sugar. Talk."

Gabe finally looked at her, his eyes clouded with emotions she couldn't decipher. He looked devastated, but at the same time there was a light in his gaze, and a faraway dreamy look that wasn't completely alcohol-infused.

"You know how the Institute hosts guest speakers every year," he began.

"Yes." What did guest speakers have to do with this? Quinn wondered, but remained silent as she waited for him to continue.

"Five years ago, we had an expert on carbon-14 dating give several lectures. She was a lovely woman named Jenna McAllister, from St. Andrew's. Her lectures were very well received." Gabe paused, his gaze sliding toward the window where a grayish-white London sky was visible through the sheer curtains.

"Go on."

"Jenna had recently lost her husband of twenty years. Brain tumor. She was so sad, and so desperate to find something to smile about. I offered to show her around London, since she hadn't been in nearly a decade and wanted to see the sights."

"Did you sleep with her?" Quinn asked, finally understanding where this was going.

"She invited me back to her hotel room for a glass of wine, and I just couldn't say no. I liked her, mind, but she was much older than the women I normally found attractive, but I couldn't bear to reject her."

"So, you had pity sex with a woman old enough to be your mother?" Quinn asked. She tried not to sound judgmental, but didn't do a very good job of disguising the irritation in her voice.

"Hardly old enough to be my mother. She was forty-six."

Quinn took a deep breath to calm her rising annoyance. Why was he telling her this? He'd had several relationships over the past eight years while she'd been involved with Luke, who'd also been involved in several relationships behind her back. It was all ancient history as far as she was concerned. Quinn never expected Gabe not to have a past, so why this sudden confession? Quinn bolted out of her chair as understanding dawned.

"Oh my God. She's back in town, and you slept with her!" she cried, rounding on him. "That's it, isn't it?" Even as the words left her mouth she was sorry. Gabe would never do such a thing. He was loyal and honest, not a complete wanker like Luke.

Gabe shook his head, his expression one of utter astonishment. Quinn's accusation had done what the espresso failed to do, and he was now fully alert. "You really think I'd do that?"

"No. I'm sorry, Gabe. I just don't understand why you're telling me this."

"The attorney from Scotland who represents Dr. McAllister called. Jenna and her mother died in a car crash on New Year's Eve."

"I'm terribly sorry," Quinn mumbled, stunned by the news. She certainly hadn't expected that. But why would this woman's attorney be ringing Gabe?

"Did she leave you something in her will?"

"You could say that," Gabe muttered. He looked like he was going to be sick.

"Out with it!" Quinn cried, unable to bear the suspense any longer.

"Quinn, Jenna had a four-year-old daughter. She named me as the father and stipulated that the child should live with me should anything happen to her. She had no other family besides her mother. Quinn, I never knew," Gabe exclaimed. "I never saw her after that weekend. She sent me a holiday card every year, but she never mentioned a child. The lawyer said that she was afraid I might sue her for custody or visitation rights, and with her being in Scotland, she preferred to retain full control. She never had any children with her husband, which was something she regretted bitterly. This child was a gift she never expected."

Quinn sank back into her chair, the meaning of Gabe's words finally sinking in. "You have a daughter."

"Yes, I do. Quinn, I'm so angry with Jenna for keeping the child a secret, and heartbroken that she is dead. And so overwhelmed with the desire to see my baby that I can barely think straight. I'm leaving for Scotland in the morning. I completely understand if you wish to call off our engagement," he added miserably.

"*You* are leaving for Scotland?" Quinn echoed. "No, my darling; *we* are leaving for Scotland. Do you really think that I would not support you in this and that I would see a child as an impediment to our marriage? Seriously, Gabe!"

Gabe walked over and put his arms around Quinn, burying his face in her neck. "I didn't dare hope that you'd forgive me. I know it's a lot to ask, but now that I know, I want to be her father more than anything in the world."

"There's nothing to forgive," Quinn replied, kissing Gabe's temple and trying not to breathe in the alcoholic fumes that came off him in waves. "We will go to Scotland and fetch this little girl, and then we will get married and be a proper family. Got it?" she asked with mock severity.

"Yes," Gabe mumbled into her hair.

"Right. Now, go lie down for a bit; you look like you need it."

"Won't you lie down with me?" Gabe asked, smiling sheepishly. He looked so relieved that Quinn instantly regretted her earlier reaction. *Poor man*, she thought, *he must have been really worried about telling me.*

"Well, if I must, I must," Quinn replied with a smile, "but don't expect me to kiss you. You reek of booze."

"Sorry," Gabe mumbled. "I sort of came apart at the seams for a moment there."

"Pull yourself together. You are about to take on a four-year-old. This was the first meltdown of many, and she might have some as well."

Gabe took Quinn by the hand and pulled her toward the bedroom, but Quinn stopped, realizing that she had yet to ask a vital question.

"Gabe, what's her name?"

"Emma," he said, savoring the name on his tongue.

"Emma. Emma Jane McAllister Russell. It has a nice ring to it."

Chapter 9

The drive to Edinburgh was a tense one. Gabe decided to drive rather than take the train or fly for the simple reason that he needed a little time to come to terms with the situation and thought it would be the easiest way to bring Emma home. He was vibrating with nervous excitement as he drove, a faraway look in his eyes as he imagined meeting his little girl for the first time. Quinn, on the other hand, was feeling somewhat more pragmatic as she compiled a mental to-do list.

"Gabe, have you given any thought to the practicalities?" Quinn asked carefully, knowing that Gabe hadn't focused on anything beyond meeting Emma.

"Hmm? Like what?" Gabe asked, giving Quinn a perplexed look.

"Asked the man who never had to take care of a child," Quinn joked. She had no desire to make Gabe feel foolish or unprepared. He was too overcome with shock and excitement to give practical matters too much thought, and that's where she came in. "Well, for starters, where will she sleep? Neither one of us has a spare bedroom. Emma will need a room of her own."

Gabe looked so startled by the question that Quinn nearly burst out laughing. He really had no clue what he was in for. "And what about childcare? We'll need to find a reputable nursery school, won't we?"

"Surely that can wait," Gabe protested.

"For a little while, sure, but someone will have to look after her while we work. And there're other things."

"Such as?" Gabe asked, looking utterly bemused.

"When is her birthday? What does she like to eat? What's her favorite toy? What TV programs does she enjoy watching? Does she have a best friend?" Quinn looked over at Gabe and smiled at him ruefully as she reached out to take his hand. "Oh, don't look so panicked, love. We'll figure it all out."

"Will we?"

"Of course. Where is Emma now? Who is looking after her, and do they know we are coming?" Quinn asked carefully. Gabe had been too much in shock at the news to ask too many pertinent questions.

"Emma is staying with the Lennoxes. They were Jenna's friends. Mr. Lennox, who is Jenna's lawyer, thought that it would be an easier transition for Emma, staying with someone she knew rather than being turned over to the state until the situation was resolved."

Quinn nodded and reached for Gabe's mobile, which he'd plonked into a cup holder. At least now she had a starting point.

"What are you doing?" Gabe asked as Quinn scrolled through the contacts.

"You just drive, Dr. Russell, and leave the rest to me." Quinn pulled out a notepad and a pen and dialed the lawyer's office. After a brief conversation, she then dialed Mrs. Lennox's number. Gabe watched in amazement as Quinn filled page after page with notes, nodding to herself as the other woman spoke, and putting forth questions he would have never have thought to ask.

"And lastly, who's Emma's pediatrician?" Quinn asked, earning a look of respect from Gabe. When she finally rang off, he squeezed her hand.

"That was bloody brilliant, Quinn. I'm in awe. But why did you ask about the pediatrician? Won't Emma's new doctor have access to her records through the NHS database?"

"I would assume so, but we might need to consult someone who knows her. Emma just lost the two people closest to her. She's frightened, sad, and confused. We might need help dealing with her grief, and her doctor might be able to recommend a therapist who specializes in working with young children."

"Do you really think it'll be as bad as that?" Gabe asked, looking even more worried than he had a few minutes before. The excitement was wearing off and anxiety setting in, which, under the circumstances, was perfectly normal.

Gabe had clearly never considered the fact that Emma would be grieving, or that she might be terrified at the prospect of being taken away from everything she'd known up until a fortnight ago.

"Two people she's never even heard of are coming to take her away. She might come along willingly, or she might put up a fight, and who could blame her?"

"I hadn't thought of that," Gabe admitted. "I assumed she'd be happy to meet her dad."

"She's a little girl, Gabe, not a grown woman. You are a stranger to her, and she is to you. It will take time."

"I wish I'd thought to ask Mr. Lennox for Emma's picture. I keep trying to imagine what she looks like, but draw a blank," Gabe confessed. "I keep picturing Jenna instead, but her features are hazy in my mind after all this time. The only thing I truly remember is her hair. It was long, thick, and flaming-red. She was quite proud of it, I think," he added, as a look of sadness passed over his face. "I can't believe she died, and in such a sudden and brutal way."

Quinn smiled gently at Gabe. "Pull over for a moment, love."

"Why? There's nothing here."

"Because I'm one step ahead of you, and I don't want you to crash into a tree."

Gabe obediently pulled over and turned in his seat, his expression one of tense anticipation. He held out his hand and Quinn passed him the mobile. Gabe sucked in his breath as he beheld his daughter for the first time. An expression of pure wonder lit up his face, and Quinn's vision blurred with unshed tears. She'd hoped that the first time Gabe beheld his child would be when their own child was born, but she couldn't begrudge him this. For Gabe, this was a wondrous moment, and her heart nearly burst with tenderness for him.

"I don't think you'll be requesting a paternity test," she said, her voice shaky. "She's the spitting image of you."

"She is, isn't she?" Gabe replied as he used the back of his hand to wipe his damp cheeks.

Chapter 10

January 1346

Dunwich, Suffolk

The children huddled closer to the fire, desperate for its meager warmth. A gale-strength wind was blowing off the sea, leaving the small house barely above freezing. Some of the rich merchants in town had glazed windows, but most houses in Dunwich had nothing besides wooden shutters to stand in the way of the cold, and the draught that was strong enough to nearly put out the fire in the grate. Petra ladled out some broth and handed around slices of bread. The children looked disappointed, but that was all she could manage. She couldn't afford to buy meat, but she had managed to negotiate a fair price for some marrow bones, which she'd boiled for hours with an onion to get the most flavor from them. The money from the sale of the tools was about to run out, and it was time to consider something more drastic.

"I'm still hungry," Ora complained. "I want some more." Petra tore off a piece of bread from her own slice and handed it to her daughter, who reached for it eagerly.

"Here, take mine," Edwin cut in. "Eat, Mama. You've grown thin," he said, his eyes full of concern.

"I'm well, Edwin," Petra replied. "I'm really not that hungry."

Ora accepted the bread from Edwin while Elia held out a hand for her mother's share. Everyone had lost weight, not just Petra, since one could hardly grow stout on broth and water-based gruel. Their diet would grow a bit more varied once the warm weather arrived and there would be apples, peas, and root vegetables to supplement their meals, but the winter months were always lean, even when there was enough to buy food.

"I could go with Alfric and set some snares," Edwin offered. Alfric was his only friend, a boy several years younger and two heads taller, who'd taken on the role of man of the house since the death of his father. Edwin doted on Alfric, and Alfric, in turn, tried to teach Edwin everything he knew. Alfric was mature for his years, and surprisingly enterprising for a boy of ten. He set snares in the woods outside of Dunwich and brought fat rabbits and squirrels for his mother's pot. Alfric sold the fur to merchants of his acquaintance, who paid him less than the going rate because he couldn't sell the fur openly.

"I forbid you to set snares," Petra replied, her tone firm. "That's poaching, and if you get caught, you'll be severely punished. I won't have it. It's not worth the risk."

"But Mother, no one minds if you catch a few squirrels or badgers. Alfric says that lowly creatures are not subject to Forest Law, since the nobles wouldn't stoop to eating their meat. He was caught once, last Michaelmas, but was released immediately, having only been apprehended with two squirrels on him. There was no harm done, and his family ate well for a whole week."

Petra didn't think Edwin would get caught, not if he went with Alfric, who knew every track and hollow in the woods, but the strain might bring on an attack, and Alfric, still being a child despite his maturity, might tell someone. It was too much of a risk, although a bit of meat certainly wouldn't hurt any of them, nor would the extra money from the sale of the skins.

Edwin looked sullen, but didn't argue, taking his mother's word as law. Instead, he used the crust of his bread to wipe his bowl, soaking up every last drop of broth before setting the empty bowl aside. Petra could understand his frustration. At nearly twelve, he was at an age when decisions about his future needed to be made. He was frightened and unsure of what the future held, and Petra's heart went out to him. She had an idea, but would have to give it some more thought before voicing it to anyone. She didn't think Maude would approve, but Petra could make her see the benefits of the arrangement if it came to pass.

"What am I to do, Mother?" Petra asked the older woman as they sat by the hearth after the children had gone to bed. "We have enough food for a few more days, a week at most, if we halve our portions."

"Go see Lady Blythe," Maude said, pinning her daughter with her pale-blue gaze. Maude had been a beauty once, but a life of hardship and loss left her looking haggard and older than her forty-six years. Maude had buried two husbands and three children, all of them sons who might have looked after her in her old age. Petra was the only family she had left, and Maude felt Petra's suffering keenly. She wished only to help, but the mention of Lady Blythe caused Petra to square her shoulders and glare at her mother with defiance.

"Mother, I can't."

"You can, and you will. You've no other choice. Go beg an audience tomorrow. She'll see you. Now, off to bed with you."

Petra climbed into bed and shivered as she curled into a ball. The excitement of sleeping alone had worn off quickly, leaving her wishing that she had a husband to take care of her and keep her warm. Cyril had been a tyrant, but he'd been a good provider and a hard worker who took pride in his labors. Now she was alone, with no one to help her or offer advice. Her mother was right, of course, as always. This was no time for false pride. She had a family to support, and at the rate they were going, they wouldn't last till spring.

Petra barely slept a wink that night. The prospect of having any future dealings with Lady Blythe left her feeling anxious and unsettled; old memories and fears came back to haunt her. Petra had been placed in Lady Blythe's household when she was eleven, having outlived her usefulness at home. Her father died when she was four, leaving Maude in no better position than Petra found herself in now. An opportunity to remarry presented itself quite soon after the period of mourning was over, and Maude seized it with both hands, thankful to have someone who was willing to look after her and her daughter. The man Maude married was a grain merchant, who was well-respected and admired in the community. Alfred Cummings had been recently widowed and needed a mother for his two young sons. His daughter, who was fourteen at the time, was already betrothed, and would be married on her sixteenth birthday. Diana took an interest in Petra, never having had a sister, but their budding relationship was cut short by Diana's marriage. Her husband's family had a fine house on the other side of Dunwich, so Diana rarely visited, especially once she gave birth to her first son.

The marriage was happy at first, Alfred and Maude savoring a period of marital unity and affection. Maude enjoyed being a mother to Alfred's sons, finding the boys to be both respectful and pliable. Within five years, Maude was blessed with three sons of her own, making her happiness complete, especially since Alfred glowed with pride at having five healthy sons. Life might have been very different had Maude and Alfred's children survived infancy. The boys died in quick succession, leaving Maude, who'd always been lively and optimistic, broken and sad. By that time, Alfred's boys were already out of the house, having been apprenticed to a blacksmith and a carpenter, and the house became ominously silent and tainted with misery.

After a time, Alfred's grief turned to anger, which he began to take out on his helpless wife, whom he blamed for the death of his children. It was at that time that his attention turned to his fair-haired, blue-eyed stepdaughter. Petra was on the verge of womanhood, her body blossoming and her allure increasing by the day, a fact that she was completely unaware of. Maude, having noticed the way Alfred looked at her daughter, wasted no time in securing a place for her in Lady Blythe's household, claiming that it was time Petra learned something of the real world and a woman's place in it. Alfred did not object. He was honest enough to admit to himself that having Petra under his roof posed a danger to his immortal soul.

Lady Blythe Devon was a wealthy widow, and a force to be reckoned with. She had taken over her husband's business interests upon his death and vowed to make the family the most successful wool merchants in Suffolk. They had been well-to-do already, but Lord Malcolm had a weakness for gambling, losing much of his profit at dice before it even made it into the coffers. Lady Blythe would tolerate no such set-backs in the future. She ruled with an iron fist, using her sons to do her bidding. Thomas was the elder, and the more practical of the two. Rather than try to fight his mother for control, he allowed her to take the reins and quietly went along with Lady Blythe's plan, part of which was that he marry the daughter of a competitor and consolidate their operation. The girl was no beauty, and didn't have much to recommend her in terms of character, but Thomas did his duty, and their holdings doubled practically overnight.

Thomas spent much time in Lincolnshire and Wales, negotiating the purchase of fleeces and sending sacks of wool back to Dunwich with a team of trusted pack-whackers, who drove the ponies home. The wool was then picked over by pickers, who divested it of any bits of dung, leaves, and vermin, then prepared it for shipment to customers, many of whom were overseas in the Low Countries, making the proximity to the port a valuable asset.

While Thomas was away, Lady Blythe spent her time wooing buyers and securing sales, engaging the services of her youngest, Robert, for those merchants who had no wish to deal with a woman. Robert was only seventeen at the time, but he was wily and smart, qualities that his mother put to good use.

Petra had seen little of Thomas while she was in Lady Blythe's employ, but she had gotten to know Robert a little, since he was still unmarried and living with his mother. Beneath the charming exterior, Robert chafed at his situation and often complained to Petra bitterly about his mother, a habit that earned Petra more than a few stripes across her back from her employer, who was aware of Robert's friendship with the girl. Robert had no wish to spend his life handling greasy fleeces and making deals with fat, greedy merchants. He'd begged his father to secure him a place as a page in some noble house when he was a boy, which would have been a stepping stone to becoming a squire. Robert liked the idea of becoming a knight and performing in tourneys during spells of peace, but most of all, he dreamed of distinguishing himself on the battlefield, earning the respect of his peers and possibly even getting the notice of the king.

Lord Malcolm had been in favor of the plan, but Lady Blythe overrode her husband and squashed Robert's dreams by reminding her husband that he was a drunkard and a fool, so it wouldn't be too long before his sons had to take over his business, and it would take both of them to make it prosperous and secure for future generations. Lord Malcolm didn't bother to argue, seeing the truth in his wife's argument. He might have liked his ale and a few hours of gambling, but he knew good sense when he heard it, and so forbade Robert to mention the subject ever again.

It wasn't long after Petra came into Lady Blythe's employ that Robert was married off as well. He refused several proposed brides, but finally settled on a sweet, comely girl, who came to live at Lady Blythe's house along with Thomas's wife, Mildred. Lady Blythe terrorized the young wives and her servants, and brooked no opposition or backtalk of any kind. She was known for her extreme piety and saw sin behind every bush. Lady Blythe believed that to spare the rod was an affront to God and used it often and with great effect. Not a week went by that Petra didn't earn a beating for a cup of spilled ale or food that wasn't hot enough when it reached the table. Petra bore it all, knowing that she had no place else to go. By that time, she'd understood her mother's reasons for sending her away, and visited only on her afternoons off, which were once a fortnight.

Alfred abandoned Maude when Petra was fifteen, proclaiming his wife to be a dried-up, old crone. He'd taken a mistress who was young enough to be his daughter. The girl's father had been handsomely paid for his blessing and sizable donations to the church coffers kept the priests from condemning the immoral relationship. Alfred retained his position of respect in the community, deserting his wife and step-daughter without any repercussions. The one honorable thing he did before leaving was to designate a sum for Petra's dowry, which he left with Maude.

Lady Blythe released Petra from service after Alfred left, mindful of a girl's duty to her mother, but Petra never forgot her cruelty or lack of compassion. The idea of having to endure her self-righteous claptrap for even a moment left Petra burning with indignation, but short of going begging to her step-father, who was still alive and quite well off, Lady Blythe was her last resort.

Chapter 11

Petra owned two gowns: a serviceable faded brown wool that she wore day-to-day, and a dark-blue gown of lighter wool dyed with woad. Petra wore the blue gown only to church and on feast days, and kept it wrapped in linen and folded neatly in the trunk when not using it. She chose the brown, since it was somber and shabby, and better suited to begging. She braided her hair and pinned it up before donning her barbet. Lady Blythe would notice every detail of her appearance, and she wished to look as docile and impoverished as possible. Petra glanced with longing at her fur-lined cloak, but decided to take Maude's instead, which was made of plain, dark-gray wool. The fur-lined cloak was a relic of more prosperous times, and she had no wish to show Lady Blythe that she owned anything so fine, even though Lady Blythe would not consider vair to be anything more than rodent fur, suitable only for the wife of a journeyman. Petra said goodbye to the children and set off toward the center of town, her demeanor no more cheerful than someone walking to their execution.

Lady Blythe's house was a few minutes' walk from the harbor. It had been further inland, but due to the ever-encroaching nature of the sea, it was now closer to the water's edge, in the busiest part of town. It was a prosperous home, added to over time and built almost entirely of stone. It had real wood floors and a roof laid with slate, not the more-commonly used thatch that rotted and began to leak after a time. Real glazed windows reflected the morning sunshine in their diamond-shaped panes, and smoke curled from several chimneys, proclaiming the owner's ability to light fires in different rooms, despite the cost.

Petra knocked on the door and waited, a part of her hoping that she would be turned away and told never to come back. The door was opened by a young girl, who looked at Petra with surprise.

"What do you want?" she asked.

"I wish to see Lady Devon. I'm willing to wait for as long as it takes," Petra added, since she had no appointment.

"Come in then. I'll tell her you're here."

Petra was ushered into an antechamber that was furnished with only a bench and two tall candles in iron stands. The candles weren't lit since the room was bathed in natural light, which poured through the window set high in the wall. The light made a pretty pattern on the floor, distorting the panes and making their reflection look slanted and elongated. Petra took a seat and folded her hands in her lap, prepared to wait. Even if Lady Blythe was unoccupied, she'd never see her without making her wait first, to remind her of her lowly station.

The minutes slid by, reminding Petra of how hungry she was. She'd barely eaten that morning, too nervous to swallow the thin porridge Maude made several days ago. It had thickened considerably from being repeatedly reheated, but it was still gruel, and Petra couldn't stomach it. Her mouth watered at the thought of an eel pie. What she wouldn't give for a nice, thick slice. If she had coin to spare, she'd go to the market and buy herself a treat, but she couldn't afford to waste even a halfpenny. Besides, it was the first Thursday of the month, the day the monks collected market fees, leaving stall owners feeling disgruntled and angry. *For men of cloth who believe in poverty and charity, they certainly never miss an opportunity to line their pockets*, Petra thought bitterly. The king had granted Greyfriars numerous rights, ranging from collecting market tax to owning all the dung in the town, which they collected street by street and from the town ditch. Anyone who required dung to fertilize their fields had to buy it back from the monks, making the priory wealthier with each passing day. Many in the town praised the monks for their charitable works, but in Petra's view, they owed the people of Dunwich, considering how much they took. *Hunger is making me ill-tempered*, Petra thought as she glanced at the door. *I'd do well to keep my anger in check.*

She wasn't sure how long she'd sat there, but the light had changed from the bright glare of morning to the gentler glow of early afternoon. Finally, the servant appeared, looking a bit flustered.

"Lady Blythe's confessor is just leaving. She'll see you presently."

Petra turned as a tall man in clerical robes came through the inner door. He held a prayer book and a rosary in one hand and his hat in the other, his gaze fixed on the door. He might have walked straight past her had Petra not inhaled sharply and caught his attention. His hair was cut short, his cheeks lean in a clean-shaven face. He looked almost gaunt, and very stern, but his gaze softened when it settled on Petra, his lips turning up the corners just enough to hint at a smile. He was about to say something when he noticed the curious stare of the servant and changed his mind. He bowed stiffly and departed, leaving Petra shaking with shock. She hadn't seen him in twelve years, but the heat that flooded her face was a testament to the fact that not much had changed, at least not for her.

Petra quickly rearranged her face into an expression of bland docility and followed the servant into Lady Blythe's parlor. The old woman was sitting in front of a roaring fire, her hands folded in her lap and her eyes alert. She didn't offer Petra a seat.

Instead, she motioned for her to stand far enough from the hearth so as not to enjoy any actual warmth. Lady Blythe studied Petra for a few moments, as if trying to recall exactly where she'd seen her before.

"How's your mother?" she finally asked, admitting that she knew her visitor.

"She's well, lady."

"Heard about your husband. Shame," Lady Blythe said. She had an abrupt way of speaking, almost as if she couldn't be bothered to waste unnecessary words on those beneath her.

"Thank you, lady."

"Need work, do you?"

Lady Blythe laughed when Petra looked surprised by the question. "Why else would you be here? Not like you harbor any warm feeling for me. And not like you should. I worked you hard. You needed to learn discipline and humility."

"Yes, lady."

"Don't 'yes, lady' me. Just say your piece. You're a grown woman now. Act like one."

Petra bristled at the old woman's tone, but rose to the challenge. She was right; Petra was a grown woman, and the woman in front of her was much smaller and less intimidating than she recalled. Lady Blythe had aged over the past twelve years, her shrunken body small in the massive carved chair. Had she not had a foot stool, her feet would have dangled in the air, like a child's.

"Lady Blythe, my husband's death left me short of means. I have three children and an elderly mother who depend on me. I would be grateful for any work you could offer me."

"That's better. Any work?" Lady Blythe asked with a predatory smile.

Petra wanted to scream that she had no wish to scrub pots, take out Lady Blythe's chamber pot, or pick over wool in the shed, but she was in no position to be choosy. "Any work," she repeated, her tone firm.

"Things have changed somewhat since you were last here. My sons are grown men and no longer feel the need to heed a mother who's in her dotage. Robert established a household of his own years ago, but Thomas has recently returned, having lost his wife and married off his daughter. He's taken over the business from me, so I don't see much of him. I am here alone most days. The only person I see is Father Avery. I have servants to do the lowly work. What I need is a companion." Lady Blythe burst out laughing when she saw Petra's look of shock.

"Is spending time with me more off-putting than scrubbing pots, girl?"

"No, lady. It would be my pleasure to be your companion."

"So, you'll do it just for the pleasure of it?" the old lady cackled.

"No, lady. I don't have the luxury of donating my time for free. I have a family to feed," Petra replied, angry that the old woman was goading her.

"No, you don't the luxury. I will pay you a fair wage. In return, you will sit with me, read to me, pray with me, and eat with me. Can you read?"

"Yes, lady. I know my letters."

"Who taught you?" Lady Blythe demanded. Most women in Dunwich were illiterate, as were the men. They had no need of reading as long as they knew how to count.

"My stepfather. He was taught his letters by his uncle, who was a priest," Petra replied. That wasn't strictly true. She'd been taught by her mother, who'd been taught by her own father, but it wouldn't do to tell Lady Blythe that a woman so far beneath her own station knew how to read, when Lady Blythe probably didn't.

"I will read any book you like," Petra said, instantly regretting her choice of words when she saw the thunderous look that passed over Lady Blythe's features.

"The only book I *like* is the Bible, you dimwit. You will read the Holy Scriptures, and you will treat them with reverence. Is that understood?"

"Yes, lady."

"You may start tomorrow. I will not expect you to live here since you have children, but you will arrive at seven and remain until I'm ready for my bed. Don't look so horrified. I retire early these days. I will pay you once a month and include your meals in the bargain. Here," Lady Blythe reached into the pocket of her gown and produced several coins. "You wouldn't be here if you weren't desperate. Buy food for your family, enough to tide you over until you receive your wages. Now go."

"Thank you, lady," Petra breathed, grateful despite her animosity toward the woman. Perhaps she'd misjudged her.

Petra fled before Lady Blythe had a change of heart, and went directly to the market. She steeled her heart against the eel pie and instead bought a bag of grain, several herrings to fry for their supper, and a jar of lard for cooking. She also purchased several marrow bones, with bits of meat still clinging to the smooth surfaces, and a couple of onions. She would leave the rest of the money with Maude. Her mother enjoyed going to the market and would make the coins stretch further than Petra would.

Petra wished that she'd brought her basket. There was nothing to carry her purchases in, and no one was kind enough to give her a sack or a wooden crate. It was slow going and awkward, but she finally managed to get her loot home, smiling widely as she came through the door.

"Herrings for supper," Petra announced happily as she handed the bones wrapped in flax to her mother and set down the bag of grain.

"She's received you, then?" Maude asked.

"I start tomorrow."

"Praise the Blessed Virgin," Maude exclaimed, crossing herself. "Our Holy Mother is looking after us."

Chapter 12

January 2014

Near Sheffield, England

"Move over and let me drive for a while," Quinn said when they stopped at a petrol station to fill the tank and get a snack. They were about halfway to Edinburgh, with at least another four hours ahead of them. The day was fairly mild, a hazy winter sunshine lighting their way as they sped along. The fields glistened with last night's frost and the trees created intricate designs against the pale-blue sky.

"I'm all right," Gabe protested as he turned toward the driver's side.

"No, you're not. You barely slept last night, and you haven't eaten anything since yesterday. You look like death warmed over," Quinn said, exaggerating a bit to prove her point. "Here, I got you a ham sandwich and a cup of tea."

Gabe smiled ruefully, knowing when he was beaten. "Yes, ma'am. I will eat the sandwich and take a nap. And if you do anything to my beloved Jaguar while I sleep, there will be hell to pay."

"Oh, give me some credit," Quinn protested. "I can drive in a straight line, and as long as some tree doesn't jump out at me, I think I can manage to keep your ride safe."

Gabe's arched eyebrow said it all, but he obediently handed over the keys and settled into the passenger seat where he unwrapped the sandwich, made a face of distaste, but took a bite anyway, chewing obediently. For someone who could barely boil an egg, Gabe was quite a connoisseur when it came to eating out, and a sandwich from the petrol station was not up to his usual standards.

"Just eat," Quinn said, silencing whatever he was about to say. "You don't have to enjoy it."

Gabe took another bite, but his eyelids were already growing heavy, his body desperate for rest. He'd come to bed late last night, and after tossing and turning for several hours was up just after 3 a.m. Quinn found him lounging on the sofa when she woke up, with some awful horror movie from the 1970s playing on the screen.

Quinn reached over and took the hot cup out of Gabe's hand just before he nodded off, his half-eaten sandwich forgotten. She hoped that the motion of the car would lull him into a deep sleep; he needed it. Quinn put on her sunglasses and stepped on the gas pedal. The Jaguar purred and sprang into life, chewing up the miles as she sped toward Scotland. It was still early enough that there weren't too many cars on the road, so Quinn could relax and enjoy the ride. She had to admit that she welcomed a little bit of solitude. Gabe's news knocked her for a loop, and in her effort to support him as he rode his emotional roller coaster, she'd had virtually no time to analyze her own reaction to the sudden change in their lives.

Quinn stared straight ahead as she mulled over the situation. She wasn't upset with Gabe for fathering a child. He was a man in his late-thirties, and had enjoyed his share of relationships over the past two decades. He'd done nothing wrong, and the only one to blame in this situation was Jenna McAllister, who chose not to tell Gabe that he had a child. Quinn could understand her motives, but she was angry on Gabe's behalf, knowing how much he would have cherished time with Emma. He'd missed a crucial part of her childhood, time that he'd never get back. And now he was coming to her a stranger, a man she'd never met rather than a father she loved and could turn to for comfort.

Quinn sighed. She'd indulged in several daydreams over the past two months in which she and Gabe had a baby, but she certainly hadn't expected that the baby would come before the wedding or would be four years old. Quinn's heart went out to the little girl who'd just lost her mother and grandmother, but she wouldn't be honest with herself if she said that she wasn't just a tiny bit resentful. This was her time to obsess over wedding gowns, choose flowers, and bask in the love of her fiancé; instead, she was about to become a stepmother to a child she'd never met, who would probably completely take over Gabe's heart and leave her out in the cold.

Quinn knew she was being melodramatic, but, truth be told, she was scared that Emma would replace her in Gabe's affections. What if he decided to call off the wedding and focus on Emma instead? Would Quinn understand or feel hurt and betrayed? She supposed that if Gabe wanted to put their plans on hold, she would support him in his decision, despite her hurt. She wanted to marry him and begin their life together, not spend a year or more in a holding pattern, waiting for Gabe to get to a place where he felt like he could commit to her without disrupting Emma's life.

Quinn reached for Gabe's mobile and opened the picture Mrs. Lennox sent her. Looking at her from the screen was an adorable little girl, her dark-blue eyes huge in a heart-shaped face, which was framed by dark waves that reached to her shoulders. She looked heartbreakingly like her father, a female version of the boy he had been. Emma was lovely, and visibly traumatized by the events of the past week and a half. Quinn smiled at the picture of

Emma, angry with herself for being such a shrew. This child needed her, and she would love her as if she were her own daughter. And if Gabe needed time, then she would give him all the time in the world because for the first time in her life, she was truly in love and loved in return, and she would do nothing to jeopardize that.

Chapter 13

January 2014

Edinburgh, Scotland

By the time Quinn and Gabe finally got to their destination, a winter twilight settled over the city, casting the skyline in a lovely shade of lavender. It was colder than it had been in London, a dusting of snow blanketing open areas and silvering tree branches. Gabe parked the car and looked up at the light spilling from the first-floor windows. Emma was behind those windows, but they had to attend to business first and see Mr. Lennox in his ground-floor office. Quinn reached out for Gabe's hand, squeezing it in a gesture of support. His hand was freezing cold. He was nervous.

"Come, let's get this done," he said and walked toward the stone steps leading up to the door.

A young woman let them in and asked them to wait while she informed Mr. Lennox that his next appointment was there. Quinn glanced around the office. It was comfortable, somewhat old-fashioned, and completely devoid of any artifice, much like the man himself. When Mr. Lennox came out to greet them, Quinn instantly warmed to him. He was an older man, possibly in his mid-fifties, dressed in a pair of charcoal-gray corduroys paired with a comfortable woolen cardigan over a white shirt. He wore a tie, but still looked relaxed and casual. He was of average height, with sandy hair, warm brown eyes, and a friendly smile. Mr. Lennox introduced himself and shook their hands, treating them like old friends.

"Do come into my office. Would you like a cup of tea? Or perhaps something a wee bit stronger?"

"Tea please," Gabe replied. Drinking hard liquor before meeting his little girl for the first time would not be the best idea, nor would it give Mr. Lennox a very good impression of him. Mr. Lennox must have anticipated Gabe's answer because a tea tray appeared moments later, brought in by the assistant who let them in earlier. She poured out three cups and left as quietly as she had come. Gabe didn't touch his tea, but Quinn added a splash of milk and took a sip. She always found the act of making and drinking tea soothing, and, at the moment, the warmth of the teacup in her hands was pleasantly calming. Mr. Lennox, who took his time adding sugar and milk to his tea, drank deeply, then turned back to Gabe, who was waiting patiently for the tea ceremony to end.

"I know you must be very anxious to meet Emma, but we have a few documents to go over and some papers for you to sign. I will need a picture I.D., Dr. Russell. Just a formality, you understand."

Gabe handed over his passport, which looked well-used and had numerous stamps from all the places Gabe had visited in the last few years. Mr. Lennox studied the photo, then nodded and handed the document back, satisfied. "Now then, I have some documents here pertaining to Emma. Here's her birth certificate, her passport, and a copy of her medical file. I also took the liberty of including this photo album. I thought you might wish to see it, and Emma will certainly need a keepsake once she's older. There are several pictures of Jenna and Emma. You might wish to remove them, but I think Emma will want to have pictures of her mother."

Gabe accepted the album, but didn't look at it, setting it aside instead. Keeping his nervousness in check was hard enough without looking at baby snaps of Emma with her mother. Seeing them together, happy and utterly unaware of what was in store for them both, would probably undo him on the spot. Mr. Lennox clearly anticipated Gabe's reaction because he continued without pause, moving on to the next order of business.

"Dr. Russell, I hadn't mentioned this on the telephone, but there's something else we need to discuss. After Emma was born, Jenna made a new Will and Testament. Her husband left her very comfortably off, and she had several investments and properties of her own, which she inherited from her father, who was divorced from her mother at the time of his death. Jenna left everything to you."

"What? Why would she do that? She hardly knew me," Gabe replied, earning himself a stern look from Mr. Lennox. Jenna clearly knew him well enough to have a child with him, the look said very eloquently, so Gabe's sentiments were unworthy. They diminished the relationship and made Jenna's judgment appear less than sound.

"Jenna had no close relatives besides her mother, who is now deceased, and she probably wished for you to keep the legacy in trust for Emma."

"Did she create a trust?" Gabe asked.

"No. She left it to your discretion. The most valuable asset is Jenna's house here in Edinburgh. The mortgage is fully paid off, so you needn't worry about making payments. You can put the house on the market, if you wish, or you can let it to tenants. I can make the arrangements for you, if you are so inclined. There's no rush to make any decisions. I don't suppose you'd consider moving to Edinburgh?" Mr. Lennox asked, his eyes crinkling at the corners.

"Ah, no. My life is in London, Mr. Lennox."

"Of course. Just a thought. We have several fine institutions that could benefit from your expertise, and yours, of course, Dr. Allenby." Mr. Lennox included Quinn in his smile before returning to the documents spread out before him, leafing through the pages.

"Mr. Lennox, if we are finished here…" Gabe muttered.

"Of course, of course. You're eager to meet Emma. I just need your signature here and here, and we are done."

"Kelly, if you'll just close up for the night," Mr. Lennox called out to his assistant as he locked away the file, handed Gabe his copies, and reached for his briefcase, ready to leave. "It's just upstairs. Very convenient, having an office so close to home. No commute," he joked as he led the way.

Gabe and Quinn followed Mr. Lennox up the stairs. A delicious smell wafted from beneath the door. Mr. Lennox inhaled deeply and smiled. "Mari made shepherd's pie. I do hope you'll join us for supper. You must be hungry after the long drive."

"Thank you," Quinn replied, seeing as Gabe was incapable of speech. His eyes were glued to the door, which opened at the sound of footsteps on the stairs.

"There you are. Come in," Mari Lennox exclaimed, opening the door wider to let them in. "Emma and I have been waiting for you, haven't we, pet?"

Emma, who was sitting on the floor, carefully set down the piece of Lego she was holding and looked up at the two strangers who were staring at her in silent awe. She seemed a bit frightened, her eyes huge in her face as she regarded them solemnly. She looked just as she did in the picture, only more vulnerable somehow.

"Won't you say hello, love?" Mrs. Lennox prompted.

"Hello," Emma whispered.

"Hello, Emma. My name is Quinn, and this is Gabe," Quinn said since Gabe remained mute. "We came all the way from London to see you."

"Do you know the Queen?" Emma asked.

"Not personally, but I hear she's quite nice," Quinn replied. She elbowed Gabe in the ribs, in an effort to get him to speak.

"What are you building?" Gabe asked. His voice sounded shaky, but he managed a quivering smile.

"It's a castle with a tower," Emma replied proudly.

"Is the tower to watch for the enemy?" Gabe asked, taking a step closer.

"No, it's for the princess. It's got the best view," Emma explained, pointing to something just in front of the castle. It was hard to tell what it was since there was a pile of small pieces of different colors littering the carpet.

"Right. Of course. Great view," Gabe mumbled, making Mrs. Lennox guffaw with laughter.

"Is there a prince?" Gabe tried again.

"Well, of course there is. Who else is going to rescue the princess?" Emma asked matter-of-factly. She held up the plastic prince in one hand and the princess in the other. "They are going to kiss," she announced and demonstrated, making a loud "mwah" sound.

"Are they in love then?" Gabe asked, warming up to the subject.

"Yes, but they haven't met yet. The prince has to kiss the princess to wake her from a sleeping spell."

"Right, silly me," Gabe replied with a smile. Emma was talking to him, which was a step in the right direction.

"Mari made shepherd's pie," she announced. "My grandma used to make it sometimes. She died," Emma whispered. Her mood changed dramatically, her eyes filling with tears at the mention of her grandmother. "I miss my mum," she said.

"I know, and I'm sorry," Quinn said, stepping in. "Gabe used to know your mum."

"Did you?" Emma asked, looking at Gabe with new interest. "Did you love her?"

"Yes," Gabe answered without a moment's hesitation. "I loved her very much."

"Did she tell you about me?"

"I'm sure she meant to, but we hadn't spoken in a long time. She was very busy."

Emma nodded wisely, as if she understood how busy grown-ups could be. "I'm hungry," she said.

"Let's wash your hands, pet. Quinn and Gabe will join us for tea. What do you think of that?" Mrs. Lennox asked, her tone jovial. Emma shrugged, as if she didn't care one way or the other.

Quinn risked a peek at Gabe. His eyes followed Emma, and Quinn could see the beginnings of panic in his gaze. Emma had no idea that he was her father, nor would she simply go off with them without a second thought. She felt safe and comfortable with Mari Lennox, which was saying a lot of a child who'd just lost her two closest family members.

"Have you got a place to stay for the night?" Mrs. Lennox asked when she returned and settled Emma at the table. Mr. Lennox had mentioned that they could stay in Jenna McAllister's house since it now belonged to Gabe, but they'd declined.

"Yes, we booked a room," Quinn replied as she took a seat opposite Emma, who was watching her intently.

"I think Emma will need a few days," Mari said quietly as she served Emma and poured her a glass of milk.

"A few days for what?" Emma asked as she lifted a fork to her mouth.

"A few days to make friends with Quinn and Gabe," Alastair Lennox chimed in.

"They are too old to be my friends. Besides, I already have friends. I want to go back to school. I miss Lucy, and I miss my room. I want to go home," Emma added sulkily.

"Will you have that drink now?" Alastair asked as he surveyed Gabe's look of dismay.

"Yes, I think I will."

**

Quinn felt overwhelming sympathy for Gabe as he tossed his coat over a chair, kicked off his shoes, and collapsed on the bed with a groan of misery. "That went well," he mumbled as Quinn snuggled next to him. The meeting with Emma hadn't been a resounding success, but it hadn't gone badly, in her opinion, and she intended to talk Gabe out of his sour mood.

"Come now. Stop feeling sorry for yourself," Quinn said, but tempered her words with a tender kiss so as not to hurt Gabe's feelings. "That went as well as could be expected. Did you think that Emma would throw herself into your arms and call you 'Daddy'? She's never set eyes on you before. Give her time. Make friends with the princess and learn to build Lego castles — that's what dads do. She'll come around. Perhaps we should stop by Jenna's house and pick up some of Emma's things for her new room. She'll want her things around her. I actually think that putting a framed picture of her mother in her bedroom would be a nice idea."

"Yes, you're right," Gabe replied, already feeling better. He'd never been one for sulking, and having something to focus on helped him feel a bit more in control of the situation. "Perhaps one of the pictures from the photo album, or maybe there's already a good photo at the house. We'll have a look tomorrow. Do you think it would be a good idea to bring Emma with us?"

"No, it might be painful for her, but maybe we should take her to the nursery school and let her spend some time with her friends. She's been cooped up with Mari since Jenna died, and it can't have been much fun for her."

Gabe nodded. "I had no idea you were so knowledgeable about children. Perhaps we should start one of our own. Right now!" Quinn giggled as Gabe rolled on top of her and pinned down her wrists, kissing her tenderly. He was still smiling, but she could see a shadow of desire in his eyes as the kiss turned more passionate. Quinn wrapped her legs around Gabe's waist and kissed him back, glad that he was in better spirits.

"Maybe not at this very minute, but you can never have too much practice," she said when Gabe finally came up for air. "I think one child at a time is a good plan."

Chapter 14

January 1347

Dunwich, Suffolk

Petra crept up the stairs, careful not to disturb Lady Blythe, who'd fallen asleep by the fire, and opened the window on the landing. There wasn't much of a view from the ground floor since all there was to see were other houses, but the upper floor offered a vista of the harbor and the sea beyond. Petra inhaled the frigid, salty air and surveyed the scene. The sea was calm today, the smooth surface sparkling in the weak winter sunshine as seagulls screamed and swooped to catch their prey, coming back up with thrashing fish in their beaks. Several ships were in port, their sails furled and the masts piercing the sky like blunt swords. There wasn't as much activity since many ships stopped sailing during the winter due to gales and fear of sinking, but there was still something to see.

Petra turned her head to the left and craned her neck to see if anyone was still in the square. It was market day, and although it would grow dark soon, there were still vendors in the square, taking advantage of the last hour of daylight to sell their wares. Many merchants had already gone, having sold their goods early on. Foodstuffs tended to sell earlier in the day than trinkets, cloth, and tools. Petra wished that she could sneak away and take a walk to the square. She had no desire to buy anything, but she simply wanted to stroll among the stalls, looking at the goods and exchanging a word or two with the merchants who were always eager to engage potential customers in friendly banter. She particularly liked to visit Micah Sills, who worked in bone. Master

Sills was a farmer who never let anything go to waste, not even a bit of bone, shaping and carving intricate pieces while he sat by the fire after supper. He sold everything from dice to crosses displayed on strings of leather. Petra liked the chess sets the best. Not many people understood the complicated game, which was said to have been brought to English shores by traders from Spain, but everyone liked to look at the pieces. The tallest pieces were no longer than Petra's finger, but they were surprisingly lifelike. Kings, queens, and bishops were works of art, each one wearing a unique expression befitting their station. There were rearing horses to represent knights and castle towers, which Master Sills referred to as 'Rooks.' Most vendors didn't permit non-buying patrons to handle the goods, but Micah Sills encouraged people to pick up the pieces and run their fingers over the delicate carvings.

"Makes the bone shine, frequent handing does," he said as he rubbed the face of a black queen. All the pieces were either white or black, the bone dyed black by using a mixture made of ground oak galls, water, and iron salt solution. The black pieces were beautiful, but Petra liked the white ones best. She thought of them as representing good, while the black pieces represented evil. She wished she knew how to play, but the rules of the game were too complicated even for most men.

Petra heard a noise from downstairs and hastily shut the window. Lady Blythe did not hold with opening the windows and letting in the cold and the smells from outside. She would be angry. Petra tiptoed away from the window and descended to the ground floor, ready to make an excuse for venturing upstairs, but Lady Blythe was still asleep. Petra took her customary seat and studied the old lady. She'd mellowed with age, and where before all Petra saw was a tyrant, what she saw now was a lonely old woman who was on the verge of losing everything she'd worked for. Lady Blythe's sons still gave their mother a report once a fortnight, but they did this out of respect since their mother was no longer directly involved in any negotiations with buyers or sellers. Lady Blythe knew that they were humoring her, but took the meetings with all seriousness, asking numerous questions and barking orders that her sons would most likely ignore. There were no other social calls. The days were interminable, with Petra arriving just in time to help Lady Blythe dress and make her way to her private chapel, where she spent an hour on her knees praying to the Good Lord. Petra was expected to join in, and she was thankful for the cushioned kneelers, or she would have simply keeled over.

  After prayer, Lady Blythe took breakfast with Petra, then, weather permitting, ventured outdoors. For Petra, that was the best hour of the day since she at least got a breath of fresh air and an opportunity to stretch her legs. The rest of the day was spent spinning wool, reading the Scriptures, and, in Lady Blythe's case, napping. By the time Petra got home in the evening, she was exhausted from boredom and desperate to have a word with Maude and the children before they retired. She reminded herself every night that she must be grateful to Lady Blythe, since Petra's wages kept the family in food and firewood, but the thought of spending all her time just sitting in near-silence with the old woman nearly made her weep.

  There had been only one occasion when Petra found herself trembling with excitement, but it didn't last long. Father Avery had come to call on Lady Blythe a week ago. Petra's mouth grew dry with nervousness, and she began to perspire, but she didn't get a chance to see or speak to the priest. Lady Blythe sent her away and told her to go buy some fish for her supper. Normally, Petra would have been thrilled to leave the house for a bit and wander along the harbor, but she longed to catch a glimpse of Avery. She hadn't seen him since the day she came to see Lady Blythe, and hoped that they might get a moment to speak privately. But Father Avery was gone by the time Petra returned with the fish, leaving her feeling disappointed and frustrated.

Petra spent the next few days hoping that Father Avery would call again, but he hadn't been back since. After all, what did Lady Blythe have to confess, sitting by the cozy fire all day and reading passages from the Bible before nodding off for an hour or two? Hardly a life of mortal sin that required weekly absolution. Petra forced a smile onto her face when Lady Blythe finally stirred and sat up straighter in her chair, having woken up. She blinked several times and stared at Petra as if she wasn't quite sure why the young woman was there.

"Would you like some hippocras, lady?" Petra asked.

"Yes, I'll take a cup. How long till supper?"

"At least an hour, lady," Petra replied. Thankfully, Lady Blythe dined early, releasing Petra for the day no later than six.

"What have we today?"

"Boiled mutton and mashed turnips," Petra replied. Mutton was the old woman's favorite, and Petra was glad of any meat she could get, not being able to readily afford it for her own household. Petra was grateful to have her meals with Lady Blythe since that made for one less mouth to feed on her wages. Maude purchased some bones and gizzards from the butcher once a week to flavor the stew and supplement the children's diet of pottage and pease pudding, but couldn't afford to splurge on a chop or a shank.

Petra fetched her employer a cup of hippocras and resumed her seat, hoping the time would go by quickly until they supped. Lady Blythe stared into the fire, her mind far away.

"I've asked Father Avery to dine tomorrow," she suddenly said, startling Petra out of her reverie.

"Will you need me to leave early, lady?"

"No, I'd like for you to join us. You could benefit from some enlightened conversation," Lady Blythe said, enjoying her role of benefactress.

"Is Father Avery a new parish priest?" Petra asked carefully. She'd attended St. Leonard's all her life, but there were several other churches in the area, and the parish priests were well known in the community, even if only by sight. A new parish priest was assigned only when the current one died, or was no longer able to perform his duties, but Petra could think of no one who'd lately needed replacing. What was Avery doing in Dunwich?

"Father Avery recently returned from Oxford, where he taught theology for several years after graduating from the seminary. He is a learned and pious man, Petra. A scholar. He's even been to Rome, where he met the Holy Father himself. It's an honor to have him in my house."

"How do you come to know him, lady?" Petra asked, curious as to why such a paragon of scholarly virtue would take the time to visit Lady Blythe. Unless there was a monetary incentive, which was not something most priests were above pursuing.

"Father Avery came to visit me when he returned to Dunwich. He's originally from these parts, you know. My husband and his father were devoted friends before my Malcolm was taken into God's embrace. Father Avery is staying at Greyfriars Priory at the present. He tells me that he's working on a rather difficult translation."

"Is he a monk then?" Petra asked, unable to reconcile the image of the carefree young man she'd known as a girl with that of a Franciscan monk, bent over some ancient manuscript as he tried to decipher the words by the flickering light of a candle.

"Don't be silly, girl. Father Avery is enjoying the hospitality of the monks while he remains in Dunwich. He has grand plans. Hopes to become a bishop one day."

Is that so? Petra thought bitterly. Avery had been heartbroken when his father pledged him to the church. Obedience, celibacy, and poverty were not something he aspired to, but it seemed that he'd changed his tune. Most clerics were happy enough to be a parish priest. It wasn't a life of wealth and privilege, but they did hold a place of respect in the community and enjoyed certain benefits if they found a wealthy patron who was willing to offer coin in exchange for absolution and God's blessing.

Petra never thought of Avery as someone with ambition, but then again, the last time she'd seen him he was only seventeen. He'd been angry and defiant, but most of all, afraid of losing everything he held dear. It seemed that Avery found new ideas to feel passionate about, and chose to make the most of his situation. Petra wouldn't call it a vocation, since it'd never been Avery's desire to enter the church and serve God, but for many, a position in the church was more about advancing their own interests rather than serving the Lord or their parishioners.

Petra was distracted from thoughts of Avery by the sound of an opening door, followed by heavy footsteps coming from the antechamber. Lady Blythe insisted that the front door be kept locked throughout the day, so whoever had just entered the house had a key. Petra exhaled in relief. It was probably Robert, come to check on his mother. He'd been to the house the week before, to give Lady Blythe her usual update on the business, despite his brother's absence. Perhaps this was more of a social call. She turned to Lady Blythe to inform her that she had a visitor, but the old woman nodded off again, her head dipping onto her bosom in slumber.

Petra sat up straight, quickly tucked a stray wisp of hair beneath her barbet, and smoothed down her skirts before reaching for her embroidery. It wouldn't do to look like she was dawdling while Lady Blythe slept. The door opened softly to reveal Lord Thomas Devon. Petra hadn't seen him since returning to Lady Blythe's service and was surprised by how much he'd changed over the past twelve years. Gone was the lanky young man with a mane of dark hair and serious blue eyes. He'd been replaced by a man of late middle years, whose powerful frame nearly filled the shadowed doorframe. Lord Thomas's temples and beard were liberally silvered with gray, and his eyes narrowed in suspicion as he glared at Petra, making her feel like a fish on a hook.

Petra sprang to her feet and curtseyed to Lord Thomas, wishing all the while that Lady Blythe would awake and explain Petra's presence in the house, but she slept on, snoring loudly enough to wake the dead. Lord Thomas motioned for Petra to follow him, and she obeyed, walking behind him on silent feet toward the dining hall. This room was considerably brighter, since Nan had just lit a brace of candles in preparation for Lady Blythe's supper. Lord Thomas turned to face Petra. In the past, he'd favored simple, comfortable garments, but now his dress proclaimed his elevated position. There were stringent laws in place, detailing which fabrics and furs each class was permitted to wear to make their station obvious. A man in Lord Thomas's position could wear the very best, being of noble birth and high standing.

This evening, Lord Thomas wore a traveling cloak of midnight blue, trimmed with miniver and adorned with a silver clasp decorated with gemstones. Beneath, his clothes were just as fine, made of rich velvet and the softest leather. Lord Thomas shrugged off his cloak and draped it over a chair as he studied Petra, his brow furrowed. His gaze was as serious as Petra recalled from before, but there were new lines etched into his face, the grooves bracketing his mouth being the most obvious. Lord Thomas didn't look like a man who smiled often. Petra recalled her recent conversation with Robert as she stared at her toes. Robert should have kept his counsel and respected his brother's privacy, but he'd always been something of a gossip and couldn't resist taking a stab at his earnest older brother.

"Those two just never got on," Robert confided in Petra, referring to Thomas and Mildred. "Cold and ill-tempered she was, refusing Thomas her affections more often than not. She'd birthed two stillborn boys and then bore Thomas a daughter. After that, the marriage bed had grown cold. Covered with a quilt of cobwebs," Robert had confided to Petra with a wicked smile. "Tis a sad thing to say about a woman so recently deceased, but I think my brother was glad to see the last of her. Miserable, she made him. No man should dread coming home to his hearth, not even one as humorless as my brother," Robert added.

"And what of his daughter?" Petra asked, curious what type of child such a marriage produced. Her own children were a product of a loveless marriage, but they were kind and compassionate, unlike their father. Perhaps Lord Thomas's daughter was the same.

"Just like her mother, by all accounts, in looks as well as temperament. I don't see much of her. Thomas had arranged a marriage for Tanith last year. She agreed readily enough. He's a good catch, her husband, and as much of a cold fish as she is, apparently. Married nearly a year and no sign of a babe in her belly. They probably perform their marital duties once a month during a full moon, if it falls on a Tuesday," Robert added, making Petra giggle. "I think Tanith will start leaving offerings to the Pagan goddess of fertility soon if she doesn't conceive. When one god fails, you try another. I hear her father-in-law is none too pleased with her, the old rogue. Sired eight sons in his day, some of them born just months apart, if you get my meaning. But we don't speak of such things."

Robert really did have a vicious tongue, always had, but he spoke the truth, which one heard so rarely. Had Robert been poor and without influence, he likely would have been accused of blasphemy by now and been punished for his sins, but Robert always landed on his feet, like a cat. He might have favored his mother in looks, but his personality was that of his father, who spent his youth carousing and fornicating with other women. There were several young men in Dunwich who bore a striking resemblance to the late Lord Devon, and a few young women as well. Lord Devon looked after all his children, ensuring that their mothers, most of whom were already wed by the time he lay with them, suffered no ill-effects from their association with him.

Robert was faithful to his wife, but that didn't stop him from flirting with any attractive woman who happened to be in his path, and Petra was no exception. She enjoyed his visits, but never took anything Robert said seriously. She didn't expect the reunion with Lord Thomas to be quite as pleasant, if his scowl was anything to go by. Petra raised her eyes to Lord Thomas, recognizing the need for an introduction, when a spark of recognition finally lit up his eyes.

"Petra, it's good to see you again. I was sorry to hear of your husband's passing," Lord Thomas said. "I do hope my mother is treating you well."

"Thank you, Lord Thomas, she is," Petra replied truthfully.

"How are you managing?" he asked, surprising Petra with the unflinching honesty of the question. No one asked her that. No one cared enough to. She was just another widow, left to fend for herself and support her family as best she could.

"We're getting by," Petra replied. The fact that she was back in his mother's household was answer enough. A life of wifely duty had been replaced by a life of subservience. At least Lady Blythe no longer beat her.

"And your children?" Lord Thomas went on, watching her intently.

"They are well, lord. Thank you for asking."

"Have you secured an apprenticeship for your son? He's nearly twelve, is he not?"

"Ah, yes."

"When's supper?" Lady Blythe demanded as she shuffled into the room, saving Petra from answering. She'd been about to lie, but had been spared from having to be dishonest. Petra breathed a sigh of relief and swept from the room under the pretense of checking on supper. It had to be ready by now.

"Nan, please serve the mistress and Lord Devon," Petra instructed the servant. "They're ready to dine."

"Right away," Nan replied. She'd been dozing by the hearth, her head lolling from side to side when Petra walked in. That girl was as lazy as a cat, always finding a warm place to sleep. In the old days, her back would have been striped more often than not, but Lady Blythe had mellowed with age, forgiving domestic negligence that she would never have overlooked in years past. Perhaps she'd been less tolerant then because of her husband's ways, taking out her frustration on her servants, since she could hardly whip her husband or the women who warmed his bed.

Chapter 15

Petra helped herself to some mutton and a slice of bread and sat down to eat in the kitchen. She would normally eat with her mistress, but Lady Blythe hadn't invited her, and Lord Devon would wish to speak with his mother privately. She felt relieved at not having to answer his questions. Why did everyone ask after Edwin? Why were they so concerned with his future? She supposed it was a natural question to ask about a boy who was on the verge of becoming a man, but Edwin's future was a sore subject for her, and she tended to overreact.

And she was tired. She'd spent the day seeing to menial tasks that were really Nan's responsibility, but the girl was asleep on her feet, burning the loaves of bread and nearly setting the hem of her skirt on fire. Petra changed the linens on Lady Blythe's bed, washed her chemise and woolen stockings, hung them to dry in front of the kitchen fire, and took out the chamber pot that Nan should have emptied out first thing in the morning, but hadn't. She'd have to have a talk with Nan first thing tomorrow. At least the mutton wasn't overcooked, or maybe she was just too hungry to notice. It'd been hours since the midday meal, which had been just broth and bread. Lady Blythe ate sparingly throughout the day, saving her appetite for supper, but Petra, who woke much earlier and expended more energy throughout the day, needed more food to sustain her. She looked around to make sure no one was watching and sliced off another sliver of mutton, hastily stuffing it inside the bread to make sure no one was the wiser. Lady Blythe wouldn't miss it, but it would make a difference to Petra, who was still hungry.

Petra was grateful when it was time to go home. Her spirits were low, and she wished only for an hour with her children and her bed. She would have liked to just slip out the door, but it would be rude not to bid Lady Blythe and Lord Devon a good night. Petra knocked on the door of the parlor and entered. Lady Blythe must have retired, but Lord Devon sat by the dying fire, a cup of hippocras in his hand. He set aside the cup and rose to his feet, walking toward Petra, his expression unreadable. Perhaps he wished to reprimand her for something, or maybe just to wish her a good night. Lord Thomas took the cloak from Petra and draped it gallantly over her shoulders, fastening the clasp as he looked down at her. He wasn't that much taller than Petra, so their faces were close, their gazes locked.

"May I walk you home?" Lord Thomas asked, taking Petra utterly by surprise.

"Really, there's no need, lord," Petra replied, but Lord Thomas was already donning his own cloak.

"There's every need," he replied. Had Robert said that, Petra would have smiled and conceded, but Thomas looked so solemn that Petra felt irrationally nervous and eager to get away from him.

They walked in silence for a few minutes, enjoying the fresh air. It smelled of coming snow and wood smoke. The sky was clear, strewn with bright stars that lit their way. All the windows were already shuttered, narrow shafts of light escaping through the cracks and striping the road. Petra could hear the sea, the waves swelling and rolling onto the beach as they'd done for eternity. The ships were nothing more than black smudges against the sky, bobbing gently and creaking like tired old men. Normally, she half-ran, frightened of being out alone, but tonight she felt safe, if not completely at ease. Petra was groping for something to say when Lord Thomas finally spoke, surprising her with the softness of his voice.

"I intended to return sooner, but stayed away once I found out my mother had given you a position in the household."

"Why? Have I done something to offend you, lord?" Petra asked, wondering if he was about to dismiss her on his mother's behalf. Now that he was back, he would be her companion, at least until the spring, when he would be off again, buying newly-shorn fleeces and searching for new suppliers for his ever-expanding wool empire. Robert liked to remain close to home, but Thomas, no longer encumbered by a family, enjoyed his travels and went farther afield every time in search of new prospects. Or so Lady Blythe had said.

"No, not at all," Lord Thomas rushed to reassure her. "It's just that I was very fond of you when you were a girl," he said. Petra couldn't see his expression in the darkness, but he sounded as if he were blushing with embarrassment. *As well he should be*, Petra thought with indignation. When she worked for Lady Blythe twelve years ago, Thomas was newly married to Lady Mildred, God rest her soul, and had no business being 'fond' of anyone, save his wife, no matter how uncomely or unpleasant she happened to be. Of course, Petra could hardly voice her thoughts or say anything to offend Lord Thomas, so she said the next best thing.

"And I was fond of you. And Lord Robert, of course," she added hastily, so as not to give Thomas the wrong impression. That was pure poppycock, of course, since as a lowly servant she didn't so much as speak to the sons of the house without being spoken to first, but what was she supposed to say? They had been kind to her, that was true, but that was just their nature, especially Robert's. Petra never attributed their kindness to any personal feeling.

"Petra, I've fulfilled my duty to my family. I married a woman of their choosing and was a dutiful husband to her, despite the fact that I never grew to care for her. She's gone now, and I'm free to follow my heart."

Dear God, what is he talking about? Petra's mind screamed. She moved away from him, ever so slightly, suddenly very uncomfortable with where the conversation was heading.

"I'm sure any woman would be lucky to have you," she mumbled awkwardly.

"Would you think yourself lucky to have me?" Thomas asked.

"Lord Devon, I don't think your mother would approve of this conversation," Petra said, hoping he'd get the hint and be quiet, or better yet, return home and let her walk on in peace.

"I don't much care if my mother approves. I'm a grown man, and I'll be damned if I allow myself to be dictated to again. I will give my future wife a comfortable life, and will look after her children, if she has any," he added, implying that the future of her children might be uppermost in Petra's mind. It was, but she couldn't imagine that Thomas was seriously referring to her, making the whole point moot. Perhaps he was drunk and wouldn't remember any of this come morning, which would be the most desirable outcome, since it would spare them both awkwardness.

"That's very kind of you, lord. Your future wife is a lucky woman," Petra replied, hoping he'd think her obtuse and change the subject.

Thomas turned to face Petra and took her by the shoulders, forcing her to look at him. "Petra, don't pretend to misunderstand my meaning. I'm not making you an offer of marriage, not yet, but

I would like permission to pay you court. My intentions are honorable, and I would like nothing more than to show you that I can make you happy, if you give me a chance."

"Lord Devon," Petra began, but Thomas interrupted her.

"Please, call me Thomas. I much prefer it. There's no need for titles between us."

Petra nodded. He was lowering himself to her level, so as not to make her feel intimidated or beholden to him, and she appreciated his sensitivity. It would be churlish to refuse.

"Thomas, I lost my husband less than three months ago. I'm still grieving," Petra lied. "I am flattered by your interest, but I need time," she pleaded, hoping that would put him off for a little while. She wasn't against Thomas paying court to her, but she'd been taken completely by surprise and needed to think on his offer. Lady Blythe would not be pleased by her son's interest in her companion. Thomas was wealthy and titled, and she was the poor widow of a shipbuilder. She wasn't worthy of him, and he would see that given time. She wished to spare him the embarrassment of having to withdraw his attentions, and needed to retain her position in Lady Blythe's household. She couldn't afford to risk her livelihood; her family depended on her.

Chapter 16

"Grieving?! Need time?!" Maude exclaimed, her eyebrows virtually disappearing beneath her headpiece. "Are you mad, girl? When a man like Lord Devon shows an interest, you let him know, without being too forward of course, that you are his for the taking. What do you think will happen to you once his mother dies? You will be back where you started, only older and less desirable. I wanted to insinuate you into Lady Blythe's household in the hope that you might catch the eye of an eligible man. Well, you've caught the eye of the most eligible one of all, and he doesn't even have children for you to raise. Just think what this could mean for you, Petra."

"Mother, with all due respect, I'm simply not ready to marry again, especially to a man I hardly know. I'm sure Thomas is a good man, but he's considerably above me in wealth and station. He will regret his choice, and take his anger out on me," Petra replied, fervently wishing that she hadn't shared her conversation with Thomas with her mother. Of course, Maude was right to some degree, and Petra would have given her own daughter similar advice, but the thought of being owned by a man once again scared Petra into caution. She worried about the future, worked long hours to put food on the table, and barely saw her children, but at least no one beat her if the mood took them or if they had a difficult day, or rode her until she was sore and bleeding. Thomas was a big man, like Cyril, a man who had the power to hurt her badly if he chose to do so. She didn't think him a brutal man, but no one really knew what went on between a husband and wife behind closed doors.

And then there was Avery. Petra had kept his return to Dunwich a secret from her mother. Avery had unintentionally ruined her life once, and he had the power to do so again, but the thought of seeing him made Petra smile foolishly. Her hands shook with nervousness as she smoothed down the fabric of her skirt as she stared into the dying flames of the fire, but seeing only Avery's face. He was the only man she'd ever loved, and the only man who'd ever been kind and loving to her in return. He would have married her had his father not sent him away, and he would have cherished her and their son. Perhaps Edwin would have turned out all right had Avery been there to raise him, rather than Cyril who frightened the child with his booming voice and quick temper. Avery would never have raised a hand to either of them, of that she was sure. He might not have desired to take the holy orders, but he did have a predisposition for the priesthood. He was kind and sympathetic, and eager to help when he could. But Avery was as far out of her reach as he ever was, Petra reminded herself as she tore her gaze away from the hearth. He was Father Avery now, a Roman Catholic priest.

Petra smothered the fire and bid her mother a good night before climbing up to her frigid loft and undressing for bed. She would not reject Thomas outright, she decided as she unpinned her hair, nor would she encourage him as her mother suggested. She would simply go about her daily business and see where that took her. She lay awake for some time, worrying about the future, but when she finally drifted off to sleep, it was Avery, not Thomas, who was in her thoughts.

Chapter 17

January 2014

Edinburgh, Scotland

"There are four missed calls from Rhys on your mobile. He just left a message on mine to inform me of that fact and to demand that you get back to him as soon as possible," Gabe announced when Quinn came out of the shower. He was still lounging in bed, seeing as it was too early to call on the Lennoxes and collect Emma for her playdate at the nursery school. Gabe tossed Quinn her mobile and she stared at the call register. All the calls were from the previous evening.

"Oh, no," Quinn moaned. "I had a meeting scheduled at the BBC last night. I completely forgot, what with everything that happened. Rhys won't be pleased with me."

"Better ring him back then and apologize for your unforgivable truancy," Gabe joked as he folded his arms behind his head. Quinn threw a decorative pillow at his head and dialed Rhys.

"We had a meeting," Rhys barked as soon as he answered the phone. "I waited for over an hour. And your mobile was off."

"I'm sorry, Rhys. I should have called, but something urgent has come up. I'm in Edinburgh."

There was a loaded silence on the other end while Rhys absorbed that bit of information. "You don't waste any time, do you?" he said, sounding unusually angry.

"What are you talking about?"

"I'm talking about Robert Chatham. How did you even know he was in Scotland?"

"I didn't," Quinn replied. "That isn't why I'm here."

"There's no need to lie to me, Quinn. I won't try to dissuade you from talking to him; it's not my place. I just wish you'd honor your commitments before running off to Scotland to pursue your own agenda."

"I said I was sorry. It won't happen again," Quinn replied with genuine contrition. She took her work responsibilities very seriously, and although the meeting wasn't to discuss anything urgent, but rather more of a progress report, she still should have remembered to reschedule it, or at least give Rhys a heads-up that she wouldn't be attending. Quinn had a sneaking suspicion that Rhys was a lot more annoyed about her trip to Scotland than her absence last night.

"Why's Chatham in Edinburgh? And how do you know about it?" Quinn asked.

"He's at a business conference for the entire weekend. I saw it on his Facebook page. I looked him up, like you asked me to."

"Where's the conference being held?" Quinn asked, suddenly unable to breathe.

"As if you don't know," Rhys retorted. "It's at the Radisson Blu Hotel." Quinn scribbled the name on a notepad by the phone, doing her best to avoid meeting Gabe's accusing stare.

"Look, Rhys, I'm here on a personal matter that has nothing to do with Robert Chatham. I'll be back in London in about a week; we can reschedule our meeting then. Now, if you'll excuse me, I must go."

Quinn rang off before Rhys could berate her any further and sank down on the bed, a faraway expression on her face. As a student of history, she didn't really believe in coincidences, especially not two at the same time. Not only was Robert Chatham in Edinburgh at this very moment, but now she'd been informed of his whereabouts thanks to forgetting about her meeting with Rhys. Fate was handing her a unique opportunity, one she might not get ever again.

"Do I want to know?" Gabe asked, not having heard Rhys's end of the conversation, but having deduced enough on his own.

"Robert Chatham is here in Edinburgh for a conference."

Gabe sighed with frustration. "Quinn, I know how much it means to you to find out who your father is, but are you sure you really want to know? Will you be able to establish a relationship with a man who forced himself on your mother? You've been punishing Rhys ever since you learned about that night. Instead of finding peace, you've found anger and a thirst for vengeance. Would it not be better to just abandon this quest?" Gabe asked gently. "You have a loving father, who raised you and supported you. He's still there, darling, and he will walk you proudly down the aisle when we get married because he deserves that honor."

"Gabe, you are right in everything you say, and cold, hard logic is on your side, but this is not a cerebral decision. This is purely emotional. I need to know. I need to put a face to the man who fathered me, and I need to find out if he has psychic ability, as I do. I want to know where this gift comes from."

Quinn grabbed her mobile, looked up the number for Radisson Blu Hotel, and dialed before she could change her mind. "Yes, hello. I'm with Chatham Electronics. I seem to have misplaced my itinerary for the conference this weekend. Would you be kind enough to email it to me?"

Quinn rattled off her email address and thanked the helpful person on the other end. She checked her email and nodded with grim satisfaction. "There's a cocktail reception this evening. I hope you can spare me for an hour, Gabe."

"Quinn, don't do this," Gabe pleaded. "Not today of all days."

"I must."

"And what exactly are you going to do? Approach this man and yank out a tuft of his hair? It's not as if you'll be able to tell if he's your father just by looking at him."

"Don't you worry; I will get a viable DNA sample. How hard can it be?"

"I don't know. How hard is it to obtain someone's hair, nail clippings, or a glob of saliva?" Gabe retorted. He meant the remark to be sarcastic, but Quinn could hear the bitterness in his voice. He was upset, mostly because Quinn was doing this at a time when he needed her most, but she wouldn't be swayed by guilt. An hour was all she was asking for. Surely that wasn't unreasonable.

"Am I expected to come with you to this event?" Gabe asked. He no longer sounded annoyed, just resigned. Despite his protests, Quinn knew that he understood, and would support her no matter the outcome.

"No, I prefer to go alone, but thank you for asking."

"Okay, do it your way. I'm going to take a shower. We are picking up Emma in an hour."

Gabe disappeared into the bathroom, leaving Quinn a few moments of solitude to formulate her plan, but her mind was still on Gabe's argument. Quinn could understand his point of view.

She probably would have told him the same thing had the shoe been on the other foot, but she needed to know. The desire to find out who her parents were had been a driving force since she was eight. She didn't expect to establish a relationship with the man who raped her mother, nor did she plan to denounce him to the police after all these years. Sylvia had moved on and had no wish to reexamine the past, but Quinn simply wanted to look into the eyes of the man whose blood flowed through her veins. She needed to know that the man wasn't a monster, and had some redeeming qualities despite doing something despicable thirty years ago. She could have other siblings out there, although she wasn't at all sure she cared to meet them. She had yet to meet Logan and Jude, a prospect that left her nervous and excited at the same time.

Quinn glanced at her traveling case. She hadn't brought anything smart enough to wear to a cocktail reception. She'd have to pop out to the shops and pick up a dress and a pair of shoes, but she'd mention that to Gabe later. He was nervous enough about spending time with Emma, and it was time for her to get ready.

Quinn selected a pair of leggings and an oversized Shetland wool sweater, glad she'd brought something really warm. The day was sunny, but the temperature had plummeted during the night, and the wind had picked up, moving silently through the trees outside the window. Quinn ran a brush through her hair and applied a little makeup while Gabe dried his hair and got dressed. There was a tightness around his eyes and mouth that suggested that he was a lot more nervous than he was letting on. Quinn put on an appearance of calm, but she was anxious as well. Without Mrs. Lennox as a buffer, they would be on their own with Emma for the first time, and the prospect was daunting. What did one do with a child to fill the hours? Emma would visit the school for two hours, but then they'd have to entertain her for the rest of the day.

Quinn sighed and did what any modern-day woman would do. She went online and entered the search: "Things to do with children in Edinburgh." Several results popped up on the screen, listing every possible form of entertainment, including parks, museums, cinemas, and the Edinburgh Zoo. Armed with the information, Quinn felt somewhat less worried.

"Ready?"

Gabe nodded as he reached for his coat. "Yes. I'm sorry, Quinn," he said, returning to their previous conversation. "I have no right to judge. I'd probably do the same if I were in your situation. Let me know if you need me to do anything. I can be the Clyde to your Bonnie."

"Thank you, but I'm not planning on shooting the place up. I just want to talk to the man." Quinn replied. Gabe's support meant the world to her, and to know that he understood made what she intended to do slightly `less shady`.

Chapter 18

February 1347

Dunwich, Suffolk

Petra woke well before dawn, her mind instantly alert. She was as jittery as a bride on her wedding day. Today was the day she was going to see Avery. The thought left her feeling nervous and excited at the same time. He was a priest now, a man of God, but she couldn't help the feelings she'd harbored for him all these years. Perhaps he'd forgotten all about her and embraced his new life, but he didn't have her child to remind him day in and day out of the love they shared when they were young. Did he remember her? Did he ever think of her? Had she been his only experience of physical love? Avery had gone directly to the seminary after leaving Dunwich, so it was entirely likely that she had been the only woman he'd ever lain with.

Petra hastily dressed, climbed down the ladder, and set about lighting a fire in the hearth, so that the house would warm up a little before her mother and the children woke up. There was no need for them to suffer the cold, especially Maude, whose joints ached and swelled during the winter months, slowing her down and making her moan with agony by the end of the day. Maude had painful chilblains on her hands and feet as well. In more prosperous times, Petra rubbed them with lavender oil, but Maude refused to spend their few precious coins on a medicine for herself. "I'll be all right, girl," she said time and time again. "A bit of lard works just as well." It didn't, but Maude would brook no argument.

Petra's hands shook with cold as she tried to get the fire going, but the kindling refused to catch, no matter how many times she struck the tinder and flint. At last, a tiny tongue of flame appeared and began to grow, devouring the dry sticks and giving off some measure of warmth. Petra added two logs once the fire had taken hold, set some water for washing to heat, and sat down in front of the hearth, holding out her hands and feet to the glowing flames. She had a few minutes before the children awoke, and she planned to enjoy them in front of the fire. As she stared into the leaping flames, her thoughts instantly returned to Avery.

Did priests forsake their physical needs without any difficulty? She imagined not. Petra had known only her husband since Avery left, but she had several female friends who spoke frankly of such matters when they were alone, and they all shared a similar experience to that of Petra. Their husbands exercised their rights regularly, never tiring of the act or caring if the woman beneath them enjoyed it. It was a hunger that needed to be fed, day after day, year after year. Did that hunger fade in men of the cloth or did it die down for a time, only to reawaken when they least expected it?

She had no desire to stir feelings of love in Avery. She only wanted to talk to him, to know that he was well, and perhaps to tell him about Edwin. Would it cause him torment to know that he'd fathered a child? Would he wish to see his son? Petra had no way of knowing. The man who returned to Dunwich was a stranger to her.

Petra reluctantly left her spot by the hearth and turned her attention to making breakfast. The children were stirring, and she could hear Maude coughing behind the curtain of her alcove. At least she wouldn't have to wash with cold water, which would aggravate her chilblains. Petra sliced some leftover bread and spread it thickly with fat before setting the slices close to the fire.

By the time they were ready to eat, the bread would be hot, with melted fat soaked into the stale dough to make it more palatable.

Edwin was the first to rise, as usual. He pulled on his breeches and hose as he hopped from one foot to the other on the freezing dirt floor, before stuffing his feet into shoes and donning his jerkin.

"Do you need me to fetch some water, Mother?" he asked.

"There's enough for now. Come and have a wash. I warmed it up."

Edwin smiled gratefully as he washed his hands and face and took a seat at the table, accepting a slice of warm bread and a cup of ale. Petra ruffled his hair affectionately and went to rouse the girls, who tried to remain abed for as long as possible. Petra suddenly smiled to herself, realizing something that had eluded her until now. Edwin had not suffered a single fit since Cyril died. Was it possible that his fits were brought on by fear of his father? If so, he was cured. Petra felt a moment of pure joy when she imagined that that her son might no longer be afflicted. She would monitor him carefully, and if there were no more fits, she'd see to finding him a suitable apprenticeship, perhaps with the help of Lady Blythe.

Petra was in a state of nervous anticipation as she hurried toward Lady Blythe's house. She didn't expect to see Thomas, since he mentioned that he'd be going out with Robert first thing in the morning, and she was glad of it. She was still reeling from their last conversation and needed a bit of time to adjust her thinking to this new, if unlikely, possibility. Thomas and Robert were off to inspect a new location for a wool-picking shed, and wouldn't be back until much later in the afternoon, since the property was some distance from the town. The wool-picking shed they'd been using for the past decade was no longer big enough to accommodate all the wool Thomas was buying, so they needed to expand and hire more wool-pickers as well.

Petra hated to even think about putting the girls to work, but if her income wasn't enough to sustain them, she might have to ask Thomas to take on Ora and Elia as wool-pickers come spring. It was tedious, dirty work, but it was something the girls could easily do. Their earnings would help significantly and maybe they'd have enough left over to put something by for next winter. And, if she could hold off on finding Edwin an apprenticeship for a year, he could work as a pack-whacker for a spell. He was too young to go out on his own, but there were at least two men to every pack of donkeys, and although pack-whacking didn't pay much, there were hidden benefits, according to Robert. Pack-whackers usually followed the same route, so got to know the people along the way and were frequently asked to do small favors which were handsomely repaid in food and other goods. A chunk of cheese, a length of cloth, or a bag of flour went a long way to helping a family cope. Petra smiled as she pulled her cloak tighter about her and bent her head into the wind. She felt more hopeful this morning than she had in months. It was a heady feeling, and one she wasn't accustomed to. She finally reached Lady Blythe's house and knocked on the door, which was locked. When Nan opened the door, her face looked like curdled milk.

"What's amiss, Nan?" Petra asked as she removed her cloak and hung it on a peg by the door.

"Her ladyship is unwell. She was up all night with a bilious attack. Not a moment's rest did she allow me, that old…" Nan wisely refrained from finishing that remark, but Petra was fairly sure she was about to say 'besom', a term remarkably fitting, in Petra's opinion.

"And Lord Thomas?"

"Slept like the dead, thank the Lord for small mercies. At least I didn't have him ordering me about. I know how to look after his mother, been doing it long enough," Nan replied with an eloquent scowl. She'd been in Lady Blythe's service since she was ten, and knew her employer like no one else. Nan looked pale, with dark smudges beneath her eyes — a testament to her sleepless night.

"Why don't you go lie down for a bit, Nan? I'll look after Lady Blythe."

"Thank you, Petra. I owe you. I'm so weary, I can barely see straight."

"You owe me nothing. Get some rest. I'll come and fetch you in two hours." Nan nodded and shuffled off, desperate for her bed.

Petra made her way up the stairs with a sinking heart. She'd pinned her hopes on seeing Avery, but it seemed that Lady Blythe would not be up to entertaining this day. Petra nearly gagged as she stepped into the darkened bedchamber. It reeked of vomit, sweat, and worse. Lady Blythe lay huddled under the counterpane, her face waxy and drawn. She was shivering despite the roaring fire, her teeth chattering loudly when she tried to speak.

"Where's that slattern?" she demanded, referring to Nan. "I told her to take out this chamber pot ages ago, and I need a clean shift. This one is soiled," she added miserably.

"I'll see to everything. Nan's in the kitchen, preparing broth," Petra lied. Lady Blythe would be livid if she knew that Nan was sleeping. Petra took a clean shift from the trunk and helped Lady Blythe change before tucking her back into bed. She needed a wash, but that would have to wait until she felt better and wasn't shivering so violently.

"Just let me be," Lady Blythe croaked. "Need rest."

"As you wish, lady."

Petra fetched an extra blanket, added another log to the fire, and stepped out of the room, leaving the door open to air out the terrible smell. She opened the window on the landing just a crack, sucking in fresh air. Lady Blythe would be furious if she knew that precious heat was being wasted, but the miasma that permeated the entire floor was so awful it nearly made Petra ill. She waited a few minutes, then shut the window and went downstairs to the kitchen where porridge was simmering over the open flame. Judging by the smell emanating from the pot, it was badly burned. Petra carefully moved the pot out of the flames and examined the contents. She'd expected to break her fast with Lady Blythe and was hungry, so she might as well eat. Petra helped herself to a bowl of porridge, careful not to scoop up any burned bits, and a cup of ale. She'd have to let the pot soak once it cooled and have Nan scrub it clean later.

Petra ate slowly, her stomach burning with disappointment. She'd so looked forward to seeing Avery, but now she would spend the day cleaning up vomit and emptying out the filthy chamber pot. She felt sorry for Lady Blythe, but the old lady had the constitution of an ox; she would recover in a day or two. Petra finished her breakfast and filled a bowl for Lady Blythe. Perhaps she would take a spoonful or two. The thick porridge might help to absorb some of the bile in her gut.

Lady Blythe had stopped shivering and had thrown off the extra blanket, her eyes now more alert. "Where's Nan?" she asked again, peering behind Petra. "Did she burn the porridge? I'd beat her blue if I had the strength."

"It's only a little burnt. Will you take some, lady?" Petra asked as she perched on the side of the bed.

"No porridge, but I'm thirsty. Mouth so dry. Bring me a cup of ale."

"Right away." Petra returned downstairs, left the bowl of porridge for Nan, and filled a pewter mug with ale. She held the cup to Lady Blythe's lips, helping her to drink. "Are you feeling better now, lady?"

"A bit. It was that mutton," Lady Blythe grumbled. "I'll have a stern word with that butcher come market day. If he thinks he can sell me rancid meat, he has another think coming, the rogue." Petra had the mutton as well, but she felt quite well, and Thomas slept through the night untroubled by indigestion. Perhaps something else was ailing Lady Blythe, but Petra refrained from suggesting it.

"Shall I send a message to Father Avery and tell him not to come today?" Petra asked with a sinking heart.

"No need. Have Nan make a kidney pie and some peas. Tell her not to skimp on the butter for the peas, and bake a fresh loaf of bread. There are some apples in the cellar. She can make stewed fruit for dessert. The food at the priory is plain and never plentiful. The poor man looks half-starved."

"Is Father Avery to dine alone?" Petra asked, mystified. With Thomas away and Lady Blythe indisposed, he would be left to fend for himself, which wasn't very hospitable.

"No, you foolish girl. You can keep him company. I'm sure you can manage to hold a polite conversation for an hour. You can benefit from Father Avery's wisdom, even if he won't benefit from yours. But at least he'll have a good meal in him. I owe him that much for the kindness he's shown me. Now get me some more ale."

Petra ran downstairs to fetch the ale. She'd give Nan the two hours she promised her, then wake her up in time to make the meal Lady Blythe ordered. She'd help her cook. The thought of spending an hour alone with Avery left her nearly breathless with fretfulness. What would they talk about for a full hour? Would he feel angry at having to dine with her instead of Lady Blythe? Would it be terribly awkward?

Petra glanced toward the stairs, then approached the window and opened it all the way. Father Avery was probably used to all kinds of awful smells, living with monks who weren't known for their fondness for bathing, but she'd be damned if he had to inhale the reek of vomit while dining with her.

Chapter 19

January 2014

Edinburgh, Scotland

"How can one child have that much energy?" Gabe asked as he sank into a wing chair and reached for his coffee cup, taking a healthy gulp. "I'm exhausted," he complained.

"Having second thoughts about fatherhood already?" Quinn asked as she sat down across from him. Gabe offered to pour her some coffee, but she passed. She was jittery enough as it was.

"Of course not. Emma is…" Gabe replied, searching for the right word, but not coming up with one immediately. The smile of awe on his face told its own story, however. "Amazing. An absolute miracle," he added happily.

"She certainly is, but a very energetic one," Quinn laughed.

They'd taken Emma to lunch after her playdate at the nursery school and then made their way to the zoo where they spent several hours walking from one enclosure to another, making a pit-stop at the petting zoo as any self-respecting parent would. Having seen every single animal, Emma demanded to go back to see her favorites, which proved to be nearly all the animals they'd already seen. Since it was too early to bring her back to the Lennoxes after the zoo, Emma had expressed a desire to go to a playground and spent another hour running around manically from the slides to the swing, and back again. Gabe followed her around for the first half-hour, terrified that she'd hurt herself or get abducted by a lurking predator, but he soon exhausted himself and consented to sit on a bench that offered a panoramic view of the entire playground. He never took his eyes off Emma, but quickly learned that he didn't actually have to go down the slide with her.

"And just think; we get to do it all again tomorrow," Quinn teased.

"I think it's time we went home," Gabe replied. "Emma has had time to get used to us. We can't stay here forever, and I think the Lennoxes would like their life back. What do you say we leave tomorrow?"

Quinn considered that idea for a moment. She supposed Gabe was right. Even if they waited another week, it wouldn't be any easier to announce to Emma that she was going to live in England with the two people she'd only just met. Mari asked them not to tell Emma that Gabe was her father just yet. She said the child needed time, but there was never going to be a perfect time. It was time to tear the plaster off and deal with the pain.

"All right. Tomorrow, we go home, but tonight, I attend this cocktail party."

Quinn had left Gabe and Emma at McDonald's after the playdate, Emma enjoying her Happy Meal and Gabe looking dubiously at his own burger. Gabe didn't hold with junk food, but Emma had been adamant that her mum allowed her to have McDonald's once a week, and it was time for her treat. Quinn strongly suspected that Emma was playing them like a violin, but had no wish to argue, not when she needed to escape for an hour to buy a dress. Gabe looked terrified when Quinn waved to him through the window and took off for the nearest shop. She didn't need anything fancy, just a little black party frock that didn't cost a week's pay. Quinn found the perfect dress on a clearance rack, and shoes to match. It wasn't black, but it was too pretty to pass up and priced to sell. The dress was made of satin, in a decadent shade of claret, and had an asymmetrical design that gave it a trendy and unique appearance. Quinn was smitten. She paid for her purchases, grabbed her bags, and raced back to McDonald's where Gabe was beginning to look slightly desperate.

"Thank God you're back," he breathed. "She wants ice-cream." Quinn didn't think this was reason for panic, but recognized Gabe's dilemma only too well. He was afraid to say no and upset Emma, which was understandable, but it was important for them to establish their authority.

Emma looked at Quinn with an expression of pure innocence. "I'd like a cone, please."

The kid was good, Quinn would give her that. "Now, darling, you've just had a good meal. Why don't we leave dessert for later? I'm sure you'll want a treat after the zoo," Quinn suggested.

"No, I want it now. Mum always got me a cone after my meal."

"Well, Mum's not here." Emma's eyes filled with tears, but she knew she was beaten.

"All right. But I want ice-cream at the zoo. They have animal-shaped ones. I like the one that looks like a monkey."

"And you shall have it," Gabe jumped in. Quinn gave him a filthy look, but it was too late. He'd already promised. Now Emma would want the ice cream as soon as she walked through the gates.

"You can have ice cream after we're finished at the zoo. Shall we go then?" Quinn asked.

"I want ice cream first." Emma fixed Gabe with a steely stare. "You promised," she reminded him before pulling on her hat and gloves.

"All right. Ice cream first," Gabe conceded.

Emma smiled coyly. Butter wouldn't melt in her mouth, she was so cool. Quinn couldn't help admiring her negotiating skills. If she got her way so quickly at four, what would she be like at fourteen? Quinn wasn't ready for the answer, and neither was Gabe.

Now, hours later, Quinn was tired and would have liked nothing better than a hot bath followed by an early night. She had no desire to get dressed up and go to a party where she didn't know a soul, but this was her only chance to get close to Robert Chatham, and she couldn't afford to pass it up. She sighed and reached for the shopping bag, pulling out the dress. The sight of it cheered her up marginally, although pajamas would have made her much happier, especially since Gabe was already lounging on the bed and scrolling through the movie selection in search of something that appealed. Quinn applied some make up, twisted her hair into a stylish chignon, and pulled out a few tendrils to frame her face. There, that would have to do.

"You look beautiful," Gabe said from his position on the bed. He had firm plans to watch TV until she got back, and had stockpiled a few snacks in case he got hungry in the process. "You never dress that way for me," he added petulantly.

"No, but I *undress* for you, which is more important," Quinn teased and leaned in to give him a kiss. "Don't wait up."

"Be careful."

Chapter 20

Quinn checked her coat at the cloak room, stole a quick peek at her appearance in the mirror, and walked into the room where the party was being held as if she had every right to be there. She felt relieved when no one challenged her and made her way to the open bar. It was always easier to circulate with a drink in hand. She ordered a glass of Pinot Noir and surveyed the room from her vantage point. The party had been underway for nearly two hours, and the guests were at the stage where they'd consumed a few drinks and were feeling friendly and less inhibited than they would normally be at a work function. Quinn spotted Robert Chatham right away; he was difficult to miss. Quinn had done some research on the man and his company, but seeing him in person still made her mouth go dry.

Chatham was a good-looking man. He was tall and broad, his ash-blond hair lightly silvered with gray, which only made him look more distinguished. Unlike many men of his age, his jowls hadn't gone soft, nor had he grown stout about the middle. He looked trim and fit, and his face appeared very youthful for a man on the cusp of fifty. He was deep in conversation with several people, but even from a distance, Quinn could see that the conversation centered on him. The body language of the other guests made it evident that they deferred to Robert Chatham and valued his opinion, putting him at the center of the discussion.

Several people, mostly men, tried to engage Quinn in conversation, but she replied politely and moved on, her gaze fixed on Robert Chatham. She had no wish to interrupt his conversation, so had to bide her time until he was left on his own for a bit. Quinn wasn't comfortable with what she was doing, since deceit never came easily to her, so she tried to pretend that she was at an Institute do where everyone stood about awkwardly until the alcohol began to flow. A short time later, tongues suddenly loosened and sexual innuendo became the order of the day, not a pretty sight in a roomful of middle-aged archeologists. The day after the party was usually charged with uncomfortable silences and almost palpable regret, pertaining mostly to drunken hook-ups in empty offices. At least there'd be none of that tomorrow, since Quinn would leave as soon as she'd had a chance to speak with Robert Chatham and gather a sample of his DNA. Quinn smiled to herself. Monica Fielding, the only person she could think of whom she genuinely disliked, was the mistress of dissemblance and subterfuge. Tonight, she would be Monica; a woman comfortable with deception and fluid morals. Quinn finally saw her chance and moved toward her target.

"Mr. Chatham?" Quinn asked, a playful smile on her face.

"Yes." The man was even more attractive up-close, but had the air of a warrior surveying a battlefield and weighing the odds. On the outside, he appeared relaxed, but there was a watchfulness in him, and a coiled energy that was off-putting.

"I wanted to congratulate you on your contract with Samsung. You must be very pleased," Quinn said, giving him her most winning smile.

"Indeed, I am. It's was a major coup for the company. Miss?" he looked at her, his eyes full of playful curiosity.

"Fielding. Monica Fielding."

"Who do you work for, Monica?"

"The competition, of course," Quinn replied coyly.

"And *what* are you working on?" Robert Chatham asked, leaning in a little too close.

"I'm not at liberty to divulge trade secrets," she whispered, making him laugh. "All I can say is that I'm on the administrative end of things, rather than technical. Number crunching, and such. Which is why I'm so impressed with your meteoric rise. You haven't put a foot wrong in three years."

"Sadly, my father passed away three years ago. He'd been at the helm of Chatham Electronics since the 1970s, when his own father retired. My father was a shrewd businessman, but like many men of his generation he found himself a little out of step with progress. Things did not move as quickly in his time, so he became fearful of taking risks. I, on the other hand, am all about risk."

"Well, you must be psychic," Quinn teased, "because every risk you take seems to pay off." She watched Chatham carefully, desperate for a reaction. She wasn't disappointed. He leaned forward again, his lips almost brushing her cheek.

"As it happens, I am psychic. I experience visions of the future all the time. Do you know what I'm seeing now?" he asked, casually brushing his hand against her hip.

"Do tell," Quinn said. She knew where this was going, but was still hopeful that he wasn't having her on.

"I see you coming up to my room for a night cap. This party is beginning to bore me."

Quinn looked up at the man. He made her uneasy, but she'd come tonight with the sole purpose of gathering some form of DNA, and at the moment, she had nothing. Chatham's jacket was immaculate, with not a stray hair in sight, and he'd given his empty glass to a waiter a few moments before. She'd go for one drink and then leave.

"One drink," she said.

"One drink," Chatham agreed.

Quinn nearly flinched when Robert Chatham placed his hand on her lower back and steered her through the crowd, out the door, and toward the bank of elevators in the lobby. She wasn't prepared for this, but her plan, although not bulletproof, was relatively basic. Have one drink, ask to use the loo, collect stray DNA, make her excuses and depart.

Robert Chatham stood across from her in the lift, studying her with a small smile. "You remind me of someone," he said, tilting his head to the side as if appraising a painting. "Can't put my finger on it."

Perhaps I remind you of my mother, whom you raped when she was just seventeen and probably haven't given a second thought since, you arrogant wanker, Quinn thought bitterly.

"I know. You remind me of *Destiny*, a painting by John William Waterhouse, particularly because you're wearing that color. Are you familiar with the Pre-Raphaelites? I own a rather priceless Rossetti. I know it's a bit childish, but I keep it in a place where only I can enjoy its beauty. It's one of my most treasured possessions."

How nice for you, Quinn retorted in her head. "I am more of a modern art girl. I like things that are edgy and new," she replied, just to annoy him. She actually didn't care for modern art at all and would have given much to own a Rossetti, but spending millions on art simply wasn't her style. If she had the money to spend, she'd give it to a charity for children or refugees, not on a painting to hide from the world and gloat over.

They exited the lift, and Robert unlocked his room, ushering Quinn inside. It was a suite, with a large, airy bedroom and a cozy sitting room, complete with a discreet minibar. Quinn stepped inside, eager to put some distance between her and Robert Chatham, but she'd barely taken a step before he wrapped his arm around her waist and pulled her close. She instinctively pulled back, unprepared for such intimacy. Robert Chatham leaned in, his lips brushing her neck while his hand moved to her breast. He trailed kisses down her neck, moving downward and running the tip of his tongue along the top of her breast, just above the neckline of the dress. Quinn quivered with revulsion.

"You are so lovely," he breathed as his hand found her buttock and squeezed.

Quinn managed to wedge her hands between herself and the man, pushing him away. She knew he'd make a play for her, but she hadn't expected it to happen that quickly. Most people took a little time to gauge their prospects and allow the sexual tension to build before making their move. Robert Chatham clearly didn't play by those rules. He just assumed that Quinn was game, and didn't seem like the type of man to take no for an answer. Given what he'd done to Sylvia, she should have expected that, no matter how many years had passed. Once a predator, always a predator.

"I need a moment," she whispered and fled toward the loo the second his hold on her slackened. Quinn rushed to the bathroom and locked the door behind her. Her breathing was ragged, and she found that she was shaking as she leaned against the cool tiles of the wall. Robert Chatham was big and strong, and aggressive. She had miscalculated. There would be no flirting over a glass of wine or an opportunity to say no. He meant to get down to business as soon as she emerged from the bathroom, so she had to take what she could and get out before the situation got out of hand.

Quinn looked around the bathroom. It was spotless. There was nothing out of place, not a hair on the sink or the floor, or a used tissue in the rubbish bin. The room must have been cleaned after Chatham showered that morning, the cleaner taking away anything that might prove useful. Quinn found Chatham's razor and turned it over. The blade appeared to be brand new, not a single bit of stubble stuck behind it. She looked around in dismay. There had to be something she could use. Not even his dressing gown, which hung on a hook behind the door, had any hair on it.

Quinn grabbed the rubbish bin and looked inside. It was empty, but on the very bottom, stuck to the trash bag, was a used plaster. She pulled a pair of tweezers out of her bag and carefully removed the plaster. It had a bit of dried blood and several hair follicles stuck to it. Robert Chatham must have nicked himself while shaving, which would explain the new razor. He must have disposed of the old one. Quinn bagged the plaster and hid the evidence in her bag before taking a deep breath and exiting the bathroom. She had to get out of this room, and fast.

"I am sorry, but I must go," Quinn said, smiling apologetically. "Duty calls."

"And what duty might that be?" Robert asked, smiling at her like a cat who was about to devour the canary.

"My husband is expecting me," Quinn lied.

"Is that so? You weren't in too much of a rush before."

"I quite forgot," Quinn said, shrugging in a nonchalant manner.

"Forgot you have a husband, or that he's expecting you? I would hate for a woman to forget about me," he drawled, moving closer to Quinn until she was forced to take a step backward.

"No woman would dare forget about you," Quinn replied inching slowly toward the door.

"No, she wouldn't. And neither will you, if I have anything to say about it."

Quinn gasped as Robert Chatham pushed her roughly against the wall and kissed her hard, pinning her with his body and making it impossible to escape. His tongue invaded her mouth just as his hand invaded her body. He slid his hand up her skirt, pushing his fingers against the silk crotch of her knickers and rubbing urgently to arouse her. Quinn tried to press her legs together, but Chatham wedged his thigh between her own, preventing her from doing anything to stop him.

Quinn tried to break the kiss, but he grabbed her head with his free hand to keep her in place, kissing her hungrily. She felt as if she were being devoured. Chatham's erection pressed into her pelvis, making her cringe with disgust. She had to get away, and there was only one way she could do so now. Quinn gathered all her strength and pushed him away. His eyes were glazed with desire, and his trousers bulged, his intentions clear. He blocked the door, leering at her.

"Aren't you the little cock-tease?" he said, advancing toward her again.

"Will Samsung remain in business with you if you're accused of assault?" she spat out. "It wouldn't be the first time for you, would it?"

That had the desired effect. Her words hit Robert Chatham like a bucket of cold water. He yanked open the door and held it open. "Get out, you bitch. I will destroy you if you say a word against me. You hear?"

Quinn didn't bother to answer. She rushed out of the room and toward the lift, which thankfully came very quickly. Quinn rested her forehead against the cold metal wall of the lift. Her legs shook, and her breath came hard and fast as her brain finally accepted how close she'd come to getting hurt. She'd led him on, that was true, but that didn't give him the right to force himself on her if she said no.

Quinn let out a shaky laugh. He'd done it before, when he was hardly more than a boy, and he'd likely done it since. Few women reported an assault, especially when their story could be torn apart by a clever lawyer, as hers would be if she filed a complaint, had Chatham actually managed to rape her. She would be made to look like a total slag; a woman who flirted with a man, went up to his room, and allowed him to touch her and kiss her before suddenly changing her mind and calling the man's amorous advances an assault. No one would believe her, as no one believed the countless women who'd been raped and were told that it was all their fault and they had it coming. Quinn suddenly understood why Sylvia, being only seventeen, never filed a report. Bringing her attackers to justice wouldn't undo what had been done, but she'd have been dragged through the mud, probed, examined, and humiliated, and that's even before the trial began. Quinn managed to calm herself by the time the lift reached the lobby. She collected her coat, settled into a taxi, and closed her eyes, grateful beyond words to be going home to Gabe.

Chapter 21

The room was dark when Quinn let herself in. Gabe must have fallen asleep, which was just as well, since she was in no mood to discuss the night's events. She kicked off her shoes, then took off the dress and threw it on a chair. She didn't think she'd want to wear it ever again. It felt tainted, stained with deceit and shame. Perhaps she'd give it to Jill and ask her to sell it in her vintage clothing shop. Someone else might enjoy it, not knowing its brief, but unpleasant history. Quinn pulled on Gabe's t-shirt and inhaled its comforting smell. It smelled of Gabe's aftershave and his own unique scent and felt warm and soft against her skin. Gabe's arm instantly encircled her when she climbed into bed, his lips brushing her temple in the darkness.

"Go back to sleep," Quinn said, but Gabe was suddenly wide awake, his eyes blazing with anger as he rolled her onto her back and loomed above her, his face bone-white in the moonlight streaming through the net curtains.

"What's the matter?" Quinn asked, alarmed. She instinctively pressed her hands against Gabe's chest to push him off, realizing that this was the second time that night that she felt physically threatened by a man, and hating the feeling of helplessness. She knew Gabe wouldn't hurt her, but there was something in his eyes that scared her nonetheless.

"You reek of another man," Gabe spat out. Quinn could see the fury building within him. He was jealous.

"Stop carrying on like some primal Alpha Male," Quinn retorted. "Chatham tried to kiss me. I pushed him away."

"Really?" Gabe growled as he pulled down the t-shirt and lowered his head to her breasts. Quinn felt a twinge of panic, realizing that Chatham's aftershave lingered on her skin. He'd been all over her, and she was as tainted as the dress she longed to be rid of.

Gabe looked up at her. His expression was one of incredulity and shock. Quinn opened her mouth to say something, but the pain in his eyes shut her up. He didn't believe her. Quinn knew she should be angry, but she could hardly blame him. The physical evidence spoke for itself.

"Gabe, nothing happened. I couldn't get a sample from him at the party, so I went up to his room to see if I could find something in the bathroom. He tried to get it on, but I pushed him off and left before things could get out of hand."

"And he just allowed you to walk away?" Gabe asked. His eyes were narrowed in speculation. He doubted her explanation, and with good reason.

"Not exactly. I had to threaten him," Quinn confessed.

"With what?" Gabe spat out.

"With the truth. I implied that I knew what he'd done to Sylvia, and that it wouldn't go well for him if I leveled an accusation of assault against him. I threatened to expose him in front of his business associates."

Gabe looked stunned. He got out of bed, pulled on his jeans, shirt, and shoes and strode from the room, slamming the door behind him. Quinn felt as if he'd slammed the door in her face. She hadn't betrayed him in any way. She explained what happened. Why was he so angry? Quinn threw off the blanket and stormed into the bathroom. She needed to wash the stink of Robert

Chatham off her body. She hoped the hot shower would help her calm down and get to sleep. She just wanted this day to end.

Two hours later, Quinn was still wide awake and alone. She'd hoped that Gabe would go outside, walk until his anger cooled, and come back feeling penitent, but Gabe hadn't returned. She'd called him, but his mobile began to vibrate on the bedside table, rendering him unreachable. Quinn turned on the bedside lamp and padded over to the closet. Gabe's keys were still in his coat pocket, so he couldn't have gone far, not on foot, and not without a coat.

"It's two in the morning, Gabe. Where are you?" Quinn moaned miserably as she attempted to beat her pillow into submission. "Come back."

Quinn reached over to the nightstand and took Petra's cross out of the plastic bag. Perhaps focusing on someone else's troubles would make her own seem less significant. It was a callous thought, but Quinn was past caring.

Chapter 22

February 1347

Dunwich, Suffolk

Petra nearly dropped the bowl of buttered peas when she heard the sound of the iron knocker. She took a deep breath, set the bowl on the table, and nodded to Nan to go and open the door. She thought she could do this, but suddenly, her knees turned to jelly, and she felt as if she were breathing, but the air wasn't quite reaching her lungs.

Get a hold of yourself, Petra thought savagely as she smoothed down her skirts and checked that her headdress was on straight. She walked out of the kitchen, looking as serene as she could manage while her heart hammered painfully in her chest. She tried to focus on trivial domestic tasks to distract herself from her impending meeting with Avery. The vile smell had been aired out, the meal was nearly ready, and Lady Blythe was asleep, having somewhat recovered from her bilious attack. Petra had swept away the old rushes and replaced them with new, sweet-smelling ones at the last minute. She hoped that her employer would not reprimand her for being wasteful, since the old rushes might have lasted another fortnight or so, but the scent of sweet flag mixed with herbs was pleasant and comforting.

Father Avery was in the parlor, his back to her as he warmed his hands by the fire. His shoulders were slightly stooped, and he looked thinner than the last time Petra had seen him. Her heart contracted with affection for him, and she felt a tell-tale blush creeping up her cheeks despite all her efforts at remaining aloof.

"Good day to you, Father," Petra said. Her voice shook, but Father Avery didn't seem to notice. He whirled about at the sound of her voice and stared, open-mouthed, for just a moment before composing himself. He seemed to recognize her, but Petra couldn't be sure.

"Good day. I was invited by Lady Blythe. Are you her companion?" he asked as he drew closer. Petra was about to reply when she heard Nan coming up behind her and reconsidered her answer. Nan was a good girl, but fond of idle gossip and lurid tales. It was best to pretend that Petra and Avery had never met, at least until later.

"Yes, Father. Mistress Ordell is the name," Petra replied, bowing respectfully to the priest. "I'm afraid Lady Blythe has been taken ill, but she bid me to welcome you and join you for dinner."

"I do hope it's nothing serious," Father Avery said, looking concerned.

"A bilious attack. She's on the mend, but still weak. Won't you join me in the dining hall?" Petra asked, giving Nan a stern look. The girl was too nosy for her own good. She should have been in the kitchen, instead she was standing behind Petra, gawking at Father Avery like a love-stricken tavern wench.

Father Avery followed Petra into the room, which was dominated by a long, wooden table made of dark wood. Twenty hardback chairs stood at attention, waiting to receive guests, but only two places were set. There was a time when Lady Blythe's husband held lavish dinners for his friends and associates, but it'd been a long while since the dining hall had been used for its original purpose. Petra and Father Avery took their seats and made polite small-talk while Nan set food on the table and departed with a modest curtsy.

Petra kept her head bowed while Father Avery said grace, but her thoughts were not on God's bounty. Thankfully, Avery was brief and to the point. Petra waited until he finished, then poured him a cup of ale. Avery nodded thanks and took a sip, his long fingers holding the cup gracefully. She'd forgotten what beautiful hands he had. Avery opened his mouth to say something, but Nan bustled in again, bringing the pie and setting it on the table. The heavenly aroma filled the air, and Petra suddenly realized that despite her nervousness she was hungry.

"That looks wonderful," Avery said as he helped himself to a slice. "The monks at Greyfriars don't dine on such fine fare. It's all boiled mutton and stewed fish. I must admit that I crave a bit of variety from time to time. One gets spoiled in Oxford," he added with a small smile. Avery glanced at the door and satisfied that Nan seemed to be nowhere in sight, turned his gaze to Petra.

"Petra, how wonderful it is to see you," he said, his voice low and silky. "I heard you've been widowed. I'm sorry for your loss."

"Don't be. My husband was a brute, who'd sooner hit than talk," Petra replied honestly. Looking at Avery's beloved face, she couldn't bring herself to speak to him as she would to a priest. The years melted away, erasing Avery's clerical robes and filling in the tonsure, the young man she'd known sitting across from her.

"Why did you marry him?" Avery asked gently.

"Because I didn't have much choice. Time was of the essence," Petra replied meaningfully, watching as Avery's eyes widened in understanding. She hadn't meant to tell him so abruptly, but she couldn't keep this from him. She might never get another chance to speak to him privately, and he needed to know that he had a son. It was a sin for a man of God to have a child, but

Avery had fathered Edwin before he went off to the seminary, so perhaps it wasn't quite as bad.

"Tell me," he begged, his composure shattered.

"We have a son. His name is Edwin. He's nearly twelve."

"A son," Avery whispered, his eyes misting over. "Please, tell me about him."

"He is a lovely boy, Avery; good and kind. He's been a great help to me since Cyril died."

"Did your husband know?" Avery asked. "Is that why he abused you?"

"No, he believed Edwin was his, but he was never kind or loving to him. He berated him cruelly and beat him often."

Avery shook his head in disgust. "I'm so sorry that you both had to endure that. I would have never left you had I known," he breathed. "I loved you so much, Petra. Not a day went by at the seminary that I didn't think of you and prayed that you were well. I had no idea," he said, shaking his head. "My father wrote to me and told me that you married. I was pleased for you, but heartbroken that you had forgotten me so quickly."

"Forgotten you?" Petra echoed. "You thought I loved my husband?" she asked. She hadn't meant to sound bitter, but she couldn't keep the derision out of her voice. How naïve men were sometimes, how blind. She'd suffered for twelve years because she'd given herself to a young man she loved, and all this time he thought that she'd been enjoying a marriage where she was cared for and treated kindly. She supposed he had no reason to believe otherwise, but how could he think that she'd cut him from her heart so completely? Hadn't he known how she adored him?

"Can I offer you another slice of pie?" Petra asked, needing the momentary diversion to compose herself. What was the use of talking about the past? What was done, was done. Cyril was safely in his grave and couldn't hurt her or Edwin anymore, but there were other pressing concerns which needed to be addressed, and this was as good a time as any.

"Avery, I need to ask something of you, and this might be my only chance," Petra whispered, glancing at the door. Nan could come back at any moment. They had no need of her, but she was too nosey to stay away for long.

"Please ask," Avery invited. "I will do anything I can to help you."

"Edwin is a fine boy. He's smart and capable, but he has an affliction. He's had fits since he was hardly more than a babe. I think they're brought on by fear and anxiety, but sometimes they happen for no reason."

Avery stilled and looked at Petra with concern. "Does anyone know? Has anyone outside the family witnessed these fits?"

"I've managed to keep it a secret thus far, but Edwin is getting older. He needs a way to support himself, Avery. He needs to learn a trade."

Avery nodded, acknowledging the truth of this. "Do you require funds for an apprenticeship?"

"I haven't had him apprenticed for fear that he will hurt himself or others and bring the wrath of his master upon him, or worse, the attention of the Church. You of all people know what that could mean. I had something else in mind."

"Such as?" Avery asked. He'd stopped eating, the food getting cold on his plate as he grappled with his feelings.

"Edwin can read and write. My mother taught him," Petra confided. Avery nodded, appreciating what this meant. The vast majority of folk were illiterate. Few men were educated, and even fewer women. Petra's mother had come from a family that had been noble once and had taught her letters, but Cyril Ordell had been illiterate, as were most craftsmen and tradesmen. Only those with noble titles were taught to read and write, and the clergy, of course.

"You wish to send him to the seminary?" Avery asked, his voice laced with doubt. "How would that keep him safe? He'd be more exposed than ever."

"I wasn't thinking of sending him to the seminary. I'd like him to become a scribe. I heard it said that there are monks who copy texts at Greyfriars Priory. Edwin can do that, surely. The priory is a quiet, peaceful place. Perhaps Edwin would be cured of his affliction in a place where he felt safe," Petra explained.

"And how would Edwin feel about becoming a monk?" Avery asked. "As a priest, I should encourage a young man to devote his life to God, but as a man, and as his father, albeit an absent one, I would not recommend a life in Holy Orders for someone who doesn't wish for it. I remember how hopeless and bitter I felt when my father announced to me that I had been pledged to the Church. I wouldn't force that on anyone."

"I haven't mentioned it to him, but I think he would welcome it. Edwin is frightened by his condition. At times, the fits are so severe that he breaks bones. He suffers terribly, Avery. I must help him in any way I can."

Avery shook his head in consternation. "He breaks bones?"

"He is your son. You must help him. You have influence," Petra hissed.

Avery sighed. "Petra, there's something I must tell you."

Avery was about to say something when Nan entered, carrying the stewed fruit. She set about clearing away the empty crockery while stealing quick glances at the priest. She was nervous around him, as if he would condemn her for eternity if the pie hadn't been to his liking. Petra suspected that Nan couldn't reconcile Avery's good looks with his calling. She was torn between her growing attraction to him and her fear of repercussions for her impure thoughts.

"The meal was superb," Avery said kindly, noting Nan's nervousness. "I ate more than I should have."

"I'm glad you liked it, Father Avery," Nan said, blushing.

"Your cooking can lead a man to gluttony," Avery said. He meant it as a joke, but Nan paled visibly, nearly dropping the carafe she was holding.

"I'm sorry," she stammered. "I meant no harm."

"I was joking, my child," Avery said, smiling at her. "I only meant to compliment your skill."

"I have no wish to lead anyone into temptation," Nan whispered and fled.

Avery looked after her with consternation. He'd meant to put her at ease, but instead made her flustered and confused.

"Is it safe to have some fruit, or will she think she's paved my way to Hell?" Avery asked as he reached for the steaming bowl.

"Pay her no mind," Petra replied. She'd have a word with Nan later assure her that Avery hadn't meant anything sinister by his comment.

Avery finished the fruit and pushed away the bowl. "I haven't had fruit in weeks. It's such a welcome change from the gruel the monks normally eat. I must return to the priory though, no matter how much I wish I could stay. It's been such a joy to see you, Petra."

Avery got to his feet and began to walk toward the door with Petra hot on his heels. She could hear the sound of crashing crockery coming from the kitchen, and hoped Nan wouldn't overhear over the din.

"What about Edwin?" she demanded. She couldn't let Avery leave without some sort of reassurance, but Avery seemed reluctant to commit to any sort of action.

"We'll speak again soon. I must think on it. Give my regards to Lady Blythe. I will call on her tomorrow," Avery said as he walked out of the house, leaving Petra feeling more unsettled than before he arrived.

Chapter 23

Father Avery hurried down the street, eager to get as far away from Petra as possible. Seeing her after all this time, and actually speaking to her, brought back memories he'd tried to suppress for twelve long years, and his soul was in turmoil. Petra knew how much he resented being packed off to the seminary, but she never knew how much he'd really had to sacrifice. It wasn't just the emotional void of never having a family of his own or a woman to hold, but much more than that. As a priest, he wasn't entitled to a single thought that wasn't controlled by the Church. His every hour was accounted for, his every action scrutinized. He thought he found an outlet when he'd been invited to teach at Oxford, but what he meant to tell Petra, but never got the chance, was that he'd left Oxford under a cloud.

Staying at Greyfriars Priory was not a choice, but a penance. He'd been sent to the monks as a warning, and offered a glimpse into what his life would be if he failed to mend his ways. Avery had great respect for the monks, and admired their dedication and lack of personal ambition, but that wasn't the life he wanted for himself. Spending his days behind the walls of the monastery, his every hour filled with either work or prayer was not an existence he could tolerate. He'd been his happiest at Oxford, exposed to learned men and new ideas, surrounded by students, not only of theology, but of general knowledge — a knowledge he craved. The world was changing, people's ideas evolving, but he was eternally trapped in an institution that feared change and peddled ignorance and fear.

The monks at Greyfriars assumed that he was doing penance for an inappropriate relationship with a woman.

Thankfully, the bishop saw no reason to enlighten them as to the nature of Avery's transgression, but it didn't really matter. Penance was penance, and locking Avery away from the world was the harshest punishment the bishop could think of. Avery was by no means a prisoner at the priory, but he was on a short leash, his activities outside the walls of the monastery noted and reported to the bishop. Bringing an afflicted child into the monastery as an apprentice scribe would draw scrutiny from above and raise questions about his relationship with the family. His father was not the only one who knew of Avery's devotion to Petra when he was a young man. Questions would be asked. Judgments would be passed. He would be putting himself at risk.

Avery left the town behind and entered a lonely stretch of road that led to the priory. The wind picked up. It howled and moaned, reminding him of that silly legend his mother always went on about, about the fair maiden who'd thrown her heart into the sea. Today, he could almost believe that a woman's cries carried on the wind. Perhaps that woman was Petra. How could he deny her plea for help when he'd left her pregnant and alone, forced to fend for herself in a world where a woman was nothing more than the property of her father or husband. Petra had been forced to marry in haste and submit to a man who treated her cruelly. And their poor son. The boy suffered at the hands of his brutal step-father, and it was Avery's duty to help him make his way in the world.

Avery stopped, the wind whipping the skirts of his clerical robe as he stood in the middle of the road. He had to see him. He had to see his son. Despite his father's handiwork, Avery had managed to leave a part of himself behind, and the thought made his heart soar. He wasn't just an empty vessel, a useless husk gutted by the Church; he was a father, and a man, and he had to help his boy.

Chapter 24

January 2014

Edinburgh, Scotland

Gabe set down his empty glass. It was time to go, but he had no desire to return to the room he shared with Quinn. He was still angry and upset, despite the three glasses of whisky he'd just downed. The alcohol took the edge off, as it usually did, but Gabe's mind was still crystal clear, his thoughts swirling around in self-destructive patterns. Truth be told, he was upset long before Quinn even came back, which was why he'd decided to go to bed and not drive himself mad while he waited for her. He wasn't so much worried for her safety as for her state of mind. Like so many adopted children, she'd fantasized about her birth parents and had elevated them to God-like status in her mind, having no real character flaws to pin on them. No child wanted to believe that their parent had been a prostitute, or a junkie, or just someone who couldn't get rid of their infant fast enough. They chose to believe that their parents had been beautiful, idealistic, and in love when they were conceived, and that insurmountable obstacles prevented them from keeping their beloved child.

As far as birth mothers went, Sylvia Wyatt certainly wasn't the worst candidate, but her story had broken something in Quinn, and now she was determined to find the man who fathered her through an act of violence. Given the circumstances, Gabe couldn't imagine that Quinn genuinely hoped for a relationship with the man, so what exactly would bring her a sense of resolution? She hadn't been herself since finding out about the night she was conceived, and the force that drove her to seek out these men was more destructive than healthy.

Gabe understood Quinn's desire to look her biological father in the face, but this wasn't the woman he knew. His Quinn would have confronted the man head-on, instead of going to his room when she knew exactly what he was after, and then threatening him with exposure when things didn't go her way. She was allowing her emotions to get in the way of personal safety and good sense, and Gabe was worried about what this would do to her in the long run.

If Robert Chatham turned out to be a match, Quinn would still not be satisfied, especially since she disliked the man so intensely. Perhaps, in time, she might have reconciled herself to Rhys Morgan, who seemed to be a good man despite the mistakes of his youth. Robert Chatham was an entirely different article, and a nasty one at that. And if Chatham proved not to be a match, then Quinn would move Heaven and Earth to find Seth Besson, who at this point could be anywhere. Just knowing that he was the last man standing would not appease Quinn, but she'd need to meet the man and evaluate him for herself.

Gabe sighed and seriously considered ordering another drink, but they were picking up Emma in a few hours, so he had to be sober and alert. The thought of Emma instantly put a smile on his face. He wished with all his heart that Emma hadn't lost her mother, but now that he knew she was his, he couldn't imagine a life without her. He'd known her for only a few days, but she'd already kindled something within him that was so powerful that it fascinated and scared him in equal parts. He still had to keep reminding himself that this was real, and once they left Edinburgh, Emma would be his responsibility. The thought sobered him, but the joy he felt when imagining her in his life forever took his breath away. How could he not have known that he was a dad?

How was it that his subconscious did not alert him to the fact that a part of him was out there in the world, going about her childish business and spending day after day without knowing of his existence?

And now Quinn, who was going through this existential turmoil, had been cast in the role of mother without any warning or choice, and had to deal with life-altering circumstances at a time when she should have been enjoying her time as a bride-to-be. He knew it wasn't fair of him to spring parenthood on her or to expect her to simply step into the role of mum without any reservations, but part of him wished that Quinn would just give up this quest of hunting down her father and concentrate on the situation life had handed them. The next few months would be crucial, and, selfish as it sounded, he needed her support.

Gabe got to his feet and walked out of the dimly lit bar. There had been at least a dozen people when he'd come in a few hours ago, but now the bar was almost empty, the bartender wiping down the counter and collecting used glasses in preparation for closing. It was later than Gabe had realized. He walked the few blocks back to the hotel and entered the lobby, which was deserted. The night porter had snuck off to the back office and was watching television, a cup of coffee in his hand. Gabe walked quietly past and, instead of taking the stairs to the second floor, continued on to the guest lounge at the back of the building. There were several wing chairs arranged in front of the cold fireplace and a comfortable sofa bracketed by end tables piled with magazines and newspapers. It would have to do. He'd have to be up in a few hours anyway. Gabe stretched out on the sofa and fell into an uneasy sleep, dreaming of leering men and giggling little girls.

Chapter 25

When Quinn woke up, ribbons of salmon-colored sky were already unfurling above the tree tops, just visible through the net curtains at the window. The sound of passing cars could be heard from outside, and somewhere nearby, a door slammed. The water was running in the bathroom, and Gabe emerged a few minutes later with a towel wrapped around his waist and smelling of aftershave.

"Good morning," Quinn said, striving for normalcy. "Where did you go last night?"

"Out," was Gabe's curt reply. He prepared his clothes for the day and began to toss everything else into his traveling case in preparation for departure. Normally, Gabe would fold his shirts and separate clean clothes from the items he'd already worn, but this morning, he just threw everything in randomly, clearly still angry.

"Gabe, I was really upset last night," Quinn said, hoping to draw him into conversation and clear the air. This wasn't the first time Gabe had been angry with her, but normally, his anger melted away once they talked things out, and he'd had a chance to explain his point of view. But Gabe wasn't taking the bait.

"That makes two of us," he spat out and turned his back on her.

"Why are you so angry?" Quinn cried. He was replying to her, but just barely, and the rigid set of his shoulders and the muscle working in his jaw were obvious indications that he was furious. Gabe turned to face her and threw her a look of utter incredulity.

"Why am I angry?" he asked, his voice dangerously low. "Well, let's see. Could it be because you lied to me? You said that you would be in a crowded room surrounded by other people at all times. You promised me you'd be safe. Clearly, that wasn't the case. You knowingly went to the room of a man who's raped before, a man who could have overpowered you with one hand tied behind his back," Gabe retorted, his eyes narrowed and his jaw clenched in anger as he ran his fingers through his damp hair in agitation.

"You pushed him off? You pushed him off because he allowed you to. He could have done anything he wanted to you, and no jury would convict him. You gave your consent simply by going to his room with him. No woman goes to a man's hotel room without realizing that she's been invited there for sex."

"Do you honestly think that I went there to have sex with him?" Quinn cried, outraged.

"No, I don't. That would be rather twisted, given that he might be your father. I think that you knowingly put yourself in danger to collect a few worthless DNA samples, and by doing that, you put me and Emma in danger as well, because if he hurt you, I would have killed him with my bare hands, and Emma would lose her one remaining parent, since I'd be spending the rest of my life in prison."

Quinn just stared, open-mouthed. She'd never seen Gabe this angry or heard him speak this way.

"Gabe, you're overreacting," she replied, which was exactly the wrong thing to say to him. Gabe's eyes glinted with fury, and he advanced on her, making her back away from him toward the bed.

"Am I? I've always believed myself to be a rational, civilized human being, but I realized something last night when I smelled that bastard on you. I'm no different from any other man who's been driven to extreme measures in a moment of passion and acted on instinct rather than sense. For the first time in my life, I wanted to do someone harm, and I would have, had he given me reason to. I would have killed him without a second thought if he raped you, and would have lost everything I hold dear in the process. I would have lost Emma and you," he whispered.

"Gabe, I'm sorry. I really am. I wasn't thinking," Quinn pleaded. She went to him and tried to wrap her arms around his neck, but Gabe stepped back, leaving her standing there like a fool.

"No, you weren't. Now, get dressed and pack your things. We are picking up Emma in an hour."

"Well, at least we'll be home by dinnertime," Quinn said, her voice flat. When she left for the cocktail party last night she couldn't have imagined the fallout she'd have to deal with this morning. Perhaps Gabe was right. She'd been stupid, reckless, and inconsiderate. She never gave Gabe a second thought when she went up to Chatham's room, focusing only on herself and her need to know the truth.

"We are not going home," Gabe replied.

"Where are we going?"

"We are going to Berwick. My parents are desperate to meet Emma, and I think we need a few days alone to sort things out and prepare my flat for Emma. Now, are you just going to stand there?" he asked, giving her a hard look.

Quinn turned away from Gabe, so he wouldn't see the tears that sprang to her eyes. Gabe's anger was worse than the fear she felt last night when Chatham pinned her against the wall, making her feel helpless and vulnerable. Gabe's anger cut deep because the thought of losing his love left Quinn feeling utterly gutted and lost. She never felt this kind of pain when Luke left her. It had been hurtful and shocking, but not visceral. Quinn turned back and threw herself at Gabe, nearly knocking him off his feet. She wrapped her arms around him, sobbing into his chest.

"I'm sorry. I'll never do anything so stupid again," Quinn cried. "I didn't realize. I never considered the consequences."

Her lips found Gabe's, and she pressed them to his, willing him to kiss her back as she held on to him for dear life. She felt his body tense against hers and thought that he'd push her away, but instead, he lifted her to her feet and carried her to the bed. Gabe tossed his towel to the floor and was on top of her in seconds, his mouth devouring hers and his knee pushing her legs apart. There was no foreplay, just the raw, all-consuming collision of two people who were overcome with emotion and need for each other. It didn't last long, and they were both panting by the time it was over, but they had made their peace and forgiven each other. Gabe rested his forehead against hers, his breathing ragged.

"It scares me how much I love you," he whispered. "I'm lost."

And I am found, Quinn thought as she allowed the last of her protective barriers to crumble.

Chapter 26

When Quinn and Gabe presented themselves at the Lennoxes an hour later, there was no trace of their earlier conflict. They were united as a couple, excited and apprehensive about the journey they were about to embark on. In a few minutes, they would become full-time parents, and it was both daunting and exhilarating. Gabe knocked on the door and squeezed Quinn's hand in silent support.

"Everything is packed and ready to go, except for young miss here," Mari said, leading them into the front room. Emma was stretched out on the sofa, lying perfectly still with her eyes closed. She was wearing a pink princess dress, and a plastic tiara was askew on her head.

Gabe looked at Mari in panic. "Is she sick?" He was prepared for tears, and a possible temper-tantrum, but not this unnatural silence from his daughter, who still hadn't so much as opened her eyes despite their presence in the room.

"It's nothing that a kiss from a prince won't cure. We are playing Sleeping Beauty. Alastair offered his services, but was rejected on the grounds of being too old. Gabe, you're up."

Gabe looked a bit bemused, but walked over to Emma and sat down on the side of the sofa, leaning toward her to kiss her.

"Kneel, Prince Gabe," Emma whispered out of the side of her mouth.

Gabe complied, kneeling on one knee and taking her hand in his as he bent over Emma and kissed her gently on the cheek.

Emma's eyes fluttered open, and she proceeded to reenact the scene from the Disney movie, smiling at Gabe serenely and blushing.

"Shall we away to my father's castle?" Gabe asked, still acting princely, to the delight of Emma.

Emma considered this for a moment. In the movie, she was already in the castle, but this was an interesting development, and she wasn't about to pass up an opportunity to be spirited away.

"Do you have a horse waiting?" she asked.

"No, but my carriage is at your disposal, Princess," Gabe improvised.

"My shoes," Emma said regally. Gabe accepted a pair of pink trainers from Mari and solemnly put them on Emma's feet, as if she were Cinderella.

"The glass slippers fit," he proclaimed, making Emma laugh.

"That's a different story," she chided him. "I'm Aurora."

"Sorry, Your Highness. I got my princesses mixed up. Are you ready to go?" Gabe asked. Quinn could hear the worry in his voice. If Emma refused to leave, they would have to cajole her somehow, but Emma was ready.

"Take me to your castle, Gabe," she said dramatically as she allowed Mari to help her on with her coat.

"Sweetheart, could you possibly call me Dad?" Gabe asked. His voice caught a little as he made this request, but Emma was oblivious to his fragile feelings.

"No," she said simply. "I like calling you Gabe."

Gabe looked crestfallen, and both Quinn and Mari gave him sympathetic looks. Emma didn't recognize Gabe as her father. To her, he was just a nice man with whom she'd stay for a while in England. Being only four, she couldn't really imagine any kind of long-term future, which was probably for the best, given that neither her mother or grandmother would be a part of it, a fact she hadn't quite accepted yet. She liked Gabe, but felt more comfortable with Quinn, since she was used to being around women. Emma jumped off the couch and walked over to Quinn, taking her hand shyly.

"There's time yet," Mari said to Gabe as she handed him Emma's cases.

"I know. Thank you for everything, Mari," Gabe said and kissed the older woman on the cheek.

"Call me if you need anything, or even if you just want to talk. The first few weeks won't be easy. Alastair wanted to be here, but he had a client waiting," she said as she walked them to the door.

"Give him our regards," Gabe said, his mind already on the journey ahead.

"Bye, Mari," Emma called out over her shoulder. She didn't feel sentimental about leaving Mr. and Mrs. Lennox, which was probably a blessing. Losing her mother and grandmother was enough of a blow without feeling as if she was being torn from the Lennoxes as well.

Quinn buckled Emma into the child seat they'd installed and sat next to her in the back while Gabe stowed her cases in the boot. Quinn had prepared several books and games for the trip, and Emma was already holding her favorite stuffed rabbit, appropriated named Mr. Rabbit. She smiled at Quinn, but her smile was a bit wobbly. She was as nervous about her new life as her four-year-old self could be and craved reassurance. Quinn patted her hand.

"Don't worry. Everything is going to be wonderful. Gabe's mum and dad are really nice, and they can't wait to meet you."

"But I don't even know them," Emma protested. "Mum never said I had other grandparents."

"No, I don't suppose she did, but I think you are going to really like them. And did I tell you that they have a puppy?"

"They do?" Emma asked, her fears forgotten.

"Yes. His name is Buster, and he's really sweet."

"What does he look like?"

"Well, he's kind of yellow, I suppose, with big, kind, brown eyes. He loves to play, but Gabe's dad is getting too old to run around with him, so it will be up to you to keep him entertained. I hear he loves playing fetch. Will you play with him?"

"Yes," Emma replied happily.

Gabe finally got into the driver's seat and turned to smile at Emma and Quinn. "Are you two ready?"

"Yes," Emma said again. She waved to Mari, who was standing on the stoop with Alastair.

"And off we go, Princess Emma," Gabe said as the car slid away from the curb.

"Off we go," Emma cried regally, Mari and Alastair already forgotten.

Chapter 27

January 1347

Dunwich, Suffolk

Avery woke up with a start, unsure of what woke him. His cell at the priory was as dark as a tomb, and just as cold. An icy draft seeped through the shutters, and the wind outside sounded like the howling of a wolf. Avery shifted on his narrow cot, suddenly aware of what it was that jolted him out of sleep. He was aroused. The feeling was so unexpected that he nearly laughed out loud at the irony of it. He'd spent the past twelve years learning to deny every desire. It had been hard at first, especially since he thought of Petra often and couldn't help remembering the weight of her breast in his hand or the silky skin of her inner thighs. Those first two years had been torture, but eventually, the physical memories faded, and Avery applied himself to suppressing his every physical need. He fasted for days, spent hours on his knees, and looked at every comely woman as if she was nothing more than God's vessel and not an object of desire. He thought he'd won his battle against emotion and lust, but one hour with Petra, and he was undone. His body throbbed with need, and his mind whirled with thoughts, images of Petra as bright and beguiling as a stained-glass window depicting the Virgin Mary herself.

Avery flipped onto his stomach with a groan. He was in agony. His body had betrayed him, and so had his mind. All he wanted was to go to Petra, tell her how much he still loved her, and take her in his arms. He wanted to remove the barbet that hid her hair and run his fingers through the golden tresses that had been like a field of ripe wheat the last time he'd seen it. He wanted to cup her breasts and slip his hands beneath her skirts. He wanted to feel her arousal and know that he was in a position to satisfy it.

Petra had changed since he'd last seen her. How could she not have? Her figure was fuller after carrying three children. It was no longer the coltish body of her girlhood, and her breasts looked larger than the pale, firm globes he'd suckled so long ago. But to him, she was even more beautiful. She was no longer a willowy girl, but a grown woman ripe for the picking. He could smell her scent when they'd dined together. She had that intoxicating womanly smell that drew him in like a moth to a flame. He wanted her so badly it hurt, and he groaned with frustrated desire, knowing he wouldn't be able to get back to sleep.

Avery got out of bed and sank to his knees. The stone floor was icy and hard, and his knees cried out in protest as he put all his weight on them and began to pray for forgiveness, guidance, and strength. Avery prayed for nearly an hour, but God in his wisdom did not see fit to hear him. Instead of devotion and purity of thought, all he felt was molten desire coursing through his veins. It would not abate, and he couldn't get the image of Petra out of his mind.

Avery finally gave up and lay back down. He hadn't touched himself in twelve years, not even when bathing. He avoided any physical contact which would remind him what it felt like to feel pleasure. He thought he'd won, his body becoming nothing more than a hollow husk belonging to God, but at this moment it belonged to Petra, even if she didn't know it. Avery trembled as his hand slid downward, his fingers closing around his shaft. The feeling was exquisite, and he went to work, exploding in a storm of sensation, his body going limp with release, his mind blessedly empty of remorse.

Chapter 28

February 1347

Dunwich, Suffolk

Petra smiled to herself before she even opened her eyes to the new day. She felt wickedly decadent for staying abed for an extra hour, but it was Candlemas, and her employer had given her the day off. Petra hadn't had a full day off since she started working for Lady Blythe, and she relished the prospect of spending it with her family. Candlemas had always been her favorite feast day, not only for religious reasons, but because it came at a time of year that was dark, cold, and barren. Candlemas, or the Purification of the Virgin, was a time of rebirth, a turning point between the waning of winter and the approach of spring and the start of the new planting. Petra didn't give much thought to planting, but she did associate Candlemas with the coming of spring. Ever since she was a little girl, her mother always said,

> If Candlemas be fair and bright,
> Winter has another flight,
> If Candlemas brings clouds and rain,
> Winter will not come again.

Petra couldn't see what type of day dawned for Candlemas, since there was no window in her loft, but she hoped it was a cloudy one. She would gladly sacrifice this feast day to rain if spring made an early appearance this year. The children would be bitterly disappointed though. They had been looking forward to this day since their bleak Christmas celebration and hoped to enjoy all that Candlemas had to offer. They'd been chattering and making plans for the past week, and Petra encouraged them in their planning, glad to see them happy and animated after several months of subdued acceptance.

Even Cyril had enjoyed Candlemas when he was alive. He didn't much care about the candle-blessing at the church or the procession afterwards, but he did enjoy the games on the green and the performances by the mummers and minstrels. Cyril was a powerful man, and always eagerly participated in hammer-throwing contests and wrestling, proud to show off his brute strength. For the past two years, he'd even felt benevolent enough on Candlemas to allow Edwin to try his hand at throwing the hammer, despite the fact that Edwin was still too young to officially enter the contest. The hammer didn't fly far, but Cyril was so pleased with his own results that he almost praised Edwin for his efforts and promised that he'd help him practice so that he could enter the competition once he was of age. Edwin had been desperate to win Cyril's approval, and Petra was pleasantly surprised when he didn't mention the competition at all this time, no longer worried about making Cyril proud.

Petra slid out of bed with a sigh of resignation, dressed hastily, and made her way downstairs. Maude already had the fire going, and it was pleasantly warm and snug. Fragrant broth bubbled over the open flame, and yesterday's pot of porridge stood off to the side, the pot heating without the contents burning or overcooking. Maude poured Petra a cup of broth and busied herself with setting out the bowls and spoons on the table in preparation for breakfast.

"Get the children up," Maude said as she hefted the pot of porridge out of the hearth and set it on the table. "We have much to do this day."

Petra didn't argue. Her mother had her own set routine for most feast days, and Petra allowed her to take the lead. Maude had so few things she enjoyed and looked forward to. Petra knew exactly why Maude was in a rush for the children to rise. She already had the cooking stone warming by the hearth and would begin to mix the batter for the pancakes as soon as they'd eaten, eager to have them finished before they left for Mass. Using flour for Candlemas pancakes was an extravagance this year, but Petra didn't object. The flat, round pancakes represented the sun because of their shape and golden color, and she couldn't bear to deny the children this special treat. Perhaps they wouldn't make as many this year, just enough to mark the occasion. They'd eat a pancake each as they came off the stone, still hot and fresh, and then have one more after they came back in the evening, having spent the day outdoors enjoying all the entertainment that Dunwich had to offer.

When the children were small, they all went to the green together, but now that the children were older, they'd been hatching their own plans, so Petra and Maude would most likely be on their own, at least until supper. Petra gulped down the last of her broth and went to wake the children.

Ora jumped straight out of bed, eager for the day to begin, and hopped from foot to foot on the cold floor as she pulled on her hose and stuck her feet into her shoes before stepping into her skirt and lacing her bodice. Elia, always the last to wake up, pulled the blanket over her head, hoping for a few more minutes of sleep. Edwin rubbed his eyes and ran a hand through his hair as he sat up in bed, his eyes going straight to his grandmother as he reached beneath his pillow.

"Don't even think of putting that on," Maude growled at Edwin, who was studying a bear mask with ill-hidden glee. "Tis a Pagan rite, and you won't be participating in it. Not now, not ever."

"Oh, come now, Grandmother. Tis nothing Pagan about it," Edwin protested as he set aside the mask. "All the lads have one. And it's just to mark the awakening of the bears, nothing more. Alfric made this for me. Just look how lifelike it is." Edwin held up the mask, showing off to all proudly.

Maude frowned and was about to say something when Petra cut in. "There's no harm in it, Mother. What's Pagan about bears leaving their dens? Let the lads have their fun this day. They've earned it."

Maude clearly didn't agree, but said no more about it. There were those who lit bonfires and prayed to the goddess Brigid to purify and bless the land before planting in celebration of Imbolc, but wearing a bear mask was hardly the same thing. Petra knew that what her mother was really worried about was Edwin drawing attention to himself in any way. She feared for him, and wished to keep him by her side where she could look after him.

"Let him go," Petra insisted, earning a look of gratitude from Edwin.

"I'll stay out of harm's way, Grandmother," Edwin promised as he set aside the mask. "We'll only wear the masks for a short time anyway. Alfric and I wish to see the contests and watch the mummers. I hope they have the same mummers as last year," Edwin said as she pulled on his breeches. "I nearly split my sides laughing."

"Me too," Elia put in as she finally consented to rise. "And there was that old man with the dog who did tricks. Remember?"

"The dog danced while he played his lute," Ora chimed in. "I felt sorry for it."

"Why, you silly goose? The dog got his reward in the end," Elia said, always eager to annoy her sister.

"Yes, I suppose he did, but it looked so skinny and sad," Ora replied.

"Much like its master," Edwin said. "It can't be an easy life, always traveling from place to place and living off people's charity. Imagine never having a place to lay your head or anyone waiting for you at the end of the day."

Petra smiled at Edwin as she spooned porridge into the bowls. Of the three children, he was the most sensitive to people's suffering, and felt a kinship with anyone who was different. Neither Ora nor Elia would give much thought to the old man who'd likely been on the road for years, depending on his aging dog for his bread.

"Come have your breakfast, then see to your chores. Ora, collect the candles to take to church for the blessing. And Elia, help your grandmother mix the batter for the pancakes once you're finished. Edwin, bring more wood for the fire and fetch some water."

"Yes, Mother," the children answered in unison.

Petra climbed back up to the loft and applied herself to braiding her hair and pinning it up beneath her headpiece. She had two spare veils which she would lend to the girls for the day since it was customary to wear white on Candlemas. They didn't have white gowns, but white linen veils would do. They could wear them for the procession.

Petra sat down on the bed and folded her hands in her lap. The friars usually joined the townspeople for the celebration after conducting their own Mass at the priory. Petra couldn't help wondering if she would see Avery this day. He used to love feast days when he was a boy, always opting for the mummers and minstrels instead of contests of strength. He loved the music and plays, especially if they were bawdy in nature. Would he be there today to enjoy the performances or would he avoid the revelry as most of the friars did since it was unseemly for a priest to indulge in such entertainments?

Petra sprang to her feet when she heard church bells. It was almost time to go. Mass would begin shortly. She grabbed the veils for the girls and climbed down, her mouth-watering as the aroma of sizzling dough enveloped her. Petra accepted a warm, golden pancake from Elia and inhaled the heavenly smell. The pancake was lightly spread with butter, and it melted on the tongue as Petra took her first bite. The children had already had theirs and were looking at her with envy, but the pancake wasn't enough to share four ways, so they would just have to wait to have the rest later.

Maude had removed the shutters, and Petra gazed at the brilliant blue square of sky visible through the unglazed window. Winter wasn't ready to release its grasp on this part of the world, but this didn't upset Petra. She had a whole day to enjoy herself, her family was thriving, and the sun shone brightly, lifting her spirits. She would put both Avery and Lord Thomas from her thoughts and make the most of this gift. Tomorrow and its worries would come soon enough.

Chapter 29

Petra stood at the edge of the crowd, content to trade a better view of the play for a bit of space. She had no wish to be jostled by overexcited onlookers who'd been at the ale and were growing rowdier by the minute. The mild winter sunshine felt warm on her shoulders, and she could hear seagulls screeching in the distance even over the din of the audience. She would have preferred to take a walk, but needed to keep an eye on the girls, who were at the front with their two friends, enjoying the performance.

Petra could hardly see what the mummers were up to, but the bursts of laughter were a testament to their skill. They'd done a somber play about the presentation of Jesus at the Temple forty days after his birth to mark the occasion and then moved on to what they did best, which was bawdy comedy. The subject matter wasn't appropriate for Ora and Elia, but Petra couldn't deny them this rare entertainment. She suspected that the lewd meaning, which infused nearly every line of dialogue, went over their heads, innocent as they were. Instead, they focused on the physical comedy, laughing joyously as the cuckolded husband spied on his errant wife and wound up stepping on a hoe, which promptly hit him in the face, giving the wife's ardent lover time to escape.

Petra gave up on the play and looked around, hoping to spot Edwin. He'd gone off with Alfric right after Mass, leaving Petra and the girls to participate in the candlelight procession. Maude had decided to return home. She claimed it was to bring back the blessed candles, but Petra suspected that she was just too tired to spend hours on her feet as they made their way from one entertainment to another. Petra watched Maude hobble away, her feet raw with chilblains and her lower back aching from the cold and damp that seemed to seep through the walls of the house and be an ever-present reminder of their reduced circumstances.

Petra finally spotted Edwin by the wrestling ring that had been erected on the green. He stood off to the side with three other boys, all of whom were Alfric's friends. Several men had already tried their luck, and several more were awaiting their turn as two brawny lads went at each other at the center of the makeshift ring. There was much booing and hissing when the crowd favorite went down, but he managed to spring back to his feet and get his opponent into a headlock, effectively ending the match. A roar of approval went up from his supporters, likely members of his guild, and the judge pronounced the match over.

The next pair of contestants were already entering the ring. Their friends clapped them on the back and offered words of advice, but neither was listening. They were fixated on each other, teeth bared and fists curled as they prepared for the fight ahead. Edwin was mesmerized. He'd pushed up his bear mask onto his head and was watching the match, Alfric at his side. If Petra knew Alfric, he'd try to enter the contest, despite his age, but unless he could find an opponent close to his own height and weight, he would be denied a chance to fight. Alfric bent down and said something to Edwin, who shook his head, his eyes never leaving the two men in the ring. They were evenly matched, and their supporters were split down the middle, yelling insults and jeering every time one of them lost his footing and seemed about to lose.

Petra looked away. Seeing the two men going at each other, their faces feral and their eyes narrowed as they searched for any hint of their opponent's weakness reminded her too much of Cyril. He never missed an opportunity to enter the ring, winning nine out of ten times and strutting around afterward as if he'd done something miraculous. He usually hurt his opponent more than was necessary, and basked in the cheering of the crowd after the win, preening like a jackanapes. Cyril always rode her extra hard on a feast day, needing to get his aggression out before going to sleep. Sated at last, he would leave Petra crying into her pillow as her tender parts throbbed with unbearable pain.

Petra was just about to check on the girls when she saw Edwin shift from his spot. The two men in the ring were finished. They were donning their jerkins and joking with their friends, the loser not sore at all about being defeated. He clapped the winner on the shoulder and they shook hands, all animosity forgotten as the organizer called for the next set of volunteers.

"Edwin, no!" Petra cried, but it was too late. Edwin was already in the ring, his bear mask tossed to the side as he faced Alfric. It wasn't a fair match-up since Alfric was a head taller and at least a stone heavier, but the men were hungry for entertainment, and the disparity in the boys' size didn't seem to bother anyone. Edwin had removed his jerkin and was wearing just his shirt, which was the only one he had. Maude would be furious if he tore it, but Petra couldn't be bothered about the shirt. She was too worried about Edwin getting hurt.

Alfric was smiling and jeering as he danced around the ring, taunting Edwin in a friendly manner. Alfric would never hurt Edwin, but Petra couldn't bear to see her boy engage in physical combat, not even with a friend. He had that look on his face, the kind he had whenever the subject of his future came up. He felt defiant, scared, and outraged by the unfairness of his lot. This was his chance to prove something, to show the world that he was a man, and not some invalid who couldn't be trusted with sharp tools or other men's welfare.

Edwin let out a roar and charged Alfric, nearly knocking him off his feet. Alfric laughed and righted himself, grabbing

Edwin and pinning his arms to the side as he brought his foot behind Edwin's ankles. Edwin's legs went out from under him when Alfric moved his foot, and Edwin went down hard, Alfric on top of him. The crowd cheered, and Alfric gave his fans a winsome smile as he held Edwin down on the grass. Edwin struggled like a landed fish, but Alfric was too heavy and had the advantage of position. Alfric finally released Edwin and helped him to his feet, inviting him to have another go. Edwin had no chance, but he wouldn't slink away in shame. He resumed his defiant stance and glared at Alfric, now genuinely angry. This was no longer a game to him, but a fight to the death.

Edwin began to circle Alfric, who was still enjoying the approval of the spectators. Edwin charged again, this time knocking Alfric off his feet and jumping on top. Alfric wrapped his arms around Edwin and flipped him onto his back, straddling him and holding him prone. It took him mere moments to reverse their positions, and the crowd booed Edwin, calling him a milksop and a weakling. Edwin's face was puce with rage, and his mouth opened as he was about to say something. Petra stifled a scream of panic when she saw Edwin's eyes roll into the back of his head and his body begin to jerk. If Alfric didn't release him, Edwin could choke on his tongue. Petra tried to push her way through the crowd, but the men closed ranks, watching with interest as Edwin's teeth began to chatter and foam appeared at the side of him mouth.

Petra was wailing with fear and helplessness. There was no way she could get to Edwin, and even if she could, what could she do? Everyone was watching, craning their necks to get a better look at the boy who was having a fit right in front of them. Alfric was still sitting on Edwin's chest, his mouth open in shock. Petra cried out for someone to help Edwin, but no one moved, not even the organizer, who just stood off to the side, watching the show. Someone pushed through the crowd from the other end, shoving men aside as if they were nothing more than stubborn sheep. Someone yelled out an insult to the newcomer, but was instantly shushed by his friends. This man wasn't one of them, he was someone who commanded respect and awe. His fine dress proclaimed his status, but he would have been known to the men even if he wore a leather jerkin and breeches.

Lord Devon entered the ring and physically lifted Alfric off the ground, tossing him aside like a sack of wool. He covered Edwin with his own body and held him until the fit passed, leaving Edwin shaking and sputtering, his eyes wild with incomprehension as he finally came to. The men were muttering among themselves, trying to understand what they'd just witnessed.

"He's possessed," someone cried, and the rest of the men surged forward, driven by ignorance and fear. "The Devil must be driven out before it comes for the rest of us."

Thomas glared at the men at the front and they hesitated, afraid to offend a nobleman. Thomas held up a flat stone and showed it to the crowd. "The boy hit his head on a stone when he went down," he said, loudly enough for everyone to hear. "He's been knocked senseless. Step aside. He needs to lie down somewhere quiet until he recovers."

Thomas lifted Edwin gently. The crowd parted, allowing Thomas to walk through unchallenged. Some were still muttering, but didn't dare to say anything out loud. Lord Devon had the power to ruin their lives if he chose to do so, and it wasn't worth the risk to anger him. Alfric trailed behind Thomas, whining that he never meant to hurt no one, and it was all just a bit of fun.

"Go home, boy," Thomas growled as he cleared the crowd of onlookers. "You've done enough damage for one day."

Petra stumbled toward Thomas. Her heart pounded with fear, and her legs felt like jelly. She reached out for Edwin and touched his face. It was flushed, but cold to the touch. "Edwin," she whispered.

"I'm all right, Mother."

"Come, let's get him inside," Thomas said. He carried Edwin to the house and set him down in front of the fire where Lady Blythe was dozing up until that moment.

"What's this then?" she asked, staring at the boy seated across from her.

"Nan, bring Edwin a cup of hippocras," Thomas ordered. "And some bread and cheese."

"Mother, Edwin hit his head and was taken ill," Thomas explained. "He needs to rest for a moment."

He grabbed another chair and set it by the fire, pushing Petra into it before she collapsed. Petra felt as if all her insides had been scooped out and dumped on the hearth. This was what she'd dreaded for the past ten years. Their secret was out. Edwin's fit would be the talk of Dunwich tomorrow, and soon enough someone would set the priests on them. What would they do to Edwin?

Thomas knelt by Petra's chair and took her hand. "Mistress Ordell, all will be well. Edwin was taken ill, that's all. No one will say a word about this, if they know what's good for them."

Lady Blythe gave her son a shrewd look, but refrained from saying anything. She'd find out what happened later, probably from Robert. Thomas wouldn't say a word; she was sure of that.

"I thought you went to a tourney," Lady Blythe said, watching her son. "What were you doing on the green?"

"I got bored," Thomas replied, his tone curt.

"Is Robert still there?"

"How should I know?" Thomas replied without looking at his mother. He was saved from more questions by the arrival of Nan, who brought wine, bread, and cheese. Thomas poured a cup of hippocras and handed it to Edwin.

"Drink it all."

Edwin took an experimental sip. He'd never had hippocras. It wasn't the drink of poor people. He appeared to like it and drained the cup, clearly hoping for a refill. Thomas obliged, but told him to eat some bread and cheese first. He then poured wine for Petra and placed the cup in her hands.

"I think it's time for me to retire," Lady Blythe said. "I would have had Nan prepare something for your supper, but you said you wouldn't be home, and I just had some broth and bread," she added reproachfully.

"Sleep well, Mother," Thomas said. He barely noticed his mother's pique, and seemed relieved when she shuffled off to bed.

"Petra, are you all right?"

"Yes, of course. Thank you for your help, Thomas." She didn't know what else to say. Perhaps Thomas really believed that Edwin had hit his head and the shaking and foaming at the mouth was the result of that trauma. It was best not to disillusion him and let him draw his own conclusions. Thomas poured himself a cup of wine and took a long sip.

"I must go get the girls," Petra said, springing from her chair. Edwin never had more than one fit at a time. He was safe now, and needed to go home. Elia and Ora were still out there on the green, and it was growing dark and dangerous. Men had been drinking for hours, their blood up after watching contests of strength and bawdy plays. They were still young girls, but old enough to draw the eye of someone who was bent on mischief.

"Go on then. I will walk Edwin home once he's fully recovered," Thomas offered. "You've no need to worry about anything, Petra," he added softly. "I will look after you."

"Thank you, Thomas," Petra whispered and fled. She should have felt relieved to have the protection of Lord Devon, but instead she felt indebted and trapped by his good intentions.

Chapter 30

February 2014

Berwick-upon-Tweed, Northumberland

The day was mild for the beginning of February, the approach of spring just discernible in the air. The wind of the previous day had died down, and the sun that played peek-a-boo with the clouds held just the tiniest bit of warmth. Gabe gazed out the library window, his eyes never leaving Emma, who ran around happily with Buster. Graham Russell did his best to keep up with his granddaughter as he threw the ball across the lawn and cheered Emma to get it before the puppy did. Emma was laughing, her cheeks rosy with cold and her yellow wellies flashing by as she ran after the puppy who barked happily. Buster hadn't had this much fun since arriving from the kennel just before Christmas.

"Fancy a cuppa?" Phoebe Russell asked as she came into the library, carrying a tray with two mugs of tea and a plate of freshly-baked scones.

"Thanks, Mum," Gabe replied and took the tray from his mother, setting it on a low table in front of the hearth. A cheery fire burned in the grate, making the room feel snug and welcoming, and Gabe felt that wonderful sense of belonging that he experienced whenever he came home.

Phoebe settled herself in her favorite chair and took a sip of tea before reaching for a scone. It was still warm, with fresh strawberry preserves spread in the middle and a dollop of clotted cream to complete its perfection. Delicious. Phoebe pushed the plate toward Gabe, urging him to take one. She loved elevenses. It was the perfect time of the day to take a break, enjoy a cup of tea, and have a little something to tide one over until lunch, which was usually at one. Phoebe took a bite of scone and chewed thoughtfully.

The past two days had been a revelation and a joy. Meeting Emma had been one of the happiest moments of Phoebe's life, and the spark the little girl lit in her aging husband was remarkable. Phoebe hadn't seen Graham this animated in years, possibly never; he hadn't been very hands-on with Gabe, preferring to read the paper or work on the estate instead of playing games with his son. Seeing Graham running around after Emma was almost surreal, and wonderful.

The child, who looked so much like their son, walked into their stuffy old pile and filled it with sunshine, illuminating every dark corner and murky corridor. Ironic how terrible tragedy often led to unbearable joy. A granddaughter. Phoebe still couldn't say the word out loud, thinking it secretly to herself and smiling as if it were a delicious secret. *A beautiful granddaughter*, she thought and grinned into her mug.

She'd known Emma for only two days, but thought her heart would burst with the love she felt for the child. She'd tell her siblings and friends soon enough, but for the moment, she wanted to keep this miracle all to herself. She'd be even happier if she wasn't so worried about Gabe. He wasn't himself. True, he'd just gotten engaged to the woman he'd loved for eight years and, within two weeks, his world turned on its axis, and he got full custody of the daughter he'd known nothing about, but it was more than that. Something was troubling her boy.

"Where's Quinn this morning?" Phoebe asked. Her tone was light, but her gaze fixed on her son, accessing his expression.

She noted that he hadn't taken a scone, and that was alarming within itself. Gabe never passed up on homemade goodies.

"She's having a bit of lie-in. She has a headache," Gabe replied.

"Everything all right between you two?" Phoebe asked. Graham always told her that she was too nosey and should leave Gabe to sort out his own problems, but Phoebe thought that to be absolute nonsense. To ignore your child's pain was paramount to admitting that you didn't care. She cared; she cared a lot, and she'd be damned if she let her boy suffer without trying to help him.

"Of course, Mum," Gabe replied, but the tightening of the jaw and the defensive stance weren't lost on Phoebe. Even the way he held his mug of tea showed tension.

"Gabe, are you all right?" Phoebe asked. "I don't mean to pry, but you've been here for two days, and the only time I've seen you smile was when you look at Emma. What is it, son?"

"I don't know, Mum," Gabe replied, exhaling loudly. He slumped into a chair across from Phoebe and set down his mug, his hands gripping the armrests as if he were experiencing turbulence on an airplane. "I can't put it into words."

"Try," Phoebe encouraged. "It helps to talk."

Gabe shook his head and shrugged in frustration. He'd always been articulate and straightforward, but at the moment, he seemed to have trouble expressing his feelings, possibly because he was having so many of them all at once. He was also a British male, and therefore not someone accustomed to wearing his heart on his sleeve. There were times when Phoebe envied the Americans their penchant for oversharing. There was such a thing as giving too much away, but at times, it was probably very liberating to just say what one thought without fear of appearing weak or worrying about the reaction of others. It was too late to change Graham, who never volunteered anything of a personal nature without being threatened with bodily harm by his frustrated wife, but Phoebe still had high hopes for Gabe, especially since Quinn wasn't the type of woman to shy away from difficult conversations and would never think less of Gabe for having fears or succumbing to momentary bouts of weakness.

"Well, if you're not ready…" Phoebe said, going for reverse psychology. It used to work when Gabe was an adolescent and getting anything out of him was like pulling teeth.

"It's not that," Gabe replied, giving her a weak smile. He knew exactly what she was up to, and a spark of understanding passed between them before Gabe's gaze slid toward the roaring fire, the connection broken.

"It's just that…" He let the sentence trail off, clearly lost for words.

"What?" Phoebe pressed.

Gabe tore his eyes away from the fire and faced her, having made up his mind to talk. "I've dreamed of Quinn for eight years, Mum. I thought that if I ever had her love, I'd be invincible. I knew exactly how I'd feel and what I'd want," Gabe began, spreading his hands as if trying to grasp the idea he was trying to convey. "I thought I'd be so happy."

"Aren't you?" Phoebe asked. Perhaps Gabe had put Quinn on a pedestal for so long that the reality didn't live up to the fantasy, but Phoebe had known Quinn for years and couldn't imagine a woman more perfect for her son. What had gone wrong between them in the short time they'd been together?

Gabe nodded. "I am. I'm happy, but I'm also…" his voice trailed off again. "And now with Emma…"

Gabe stared behind his mother's shoulder for a moment, lost in thought. He had a look of intense concentration just like he used to when he was little and tried to explain something that was beyond him. Phoebe's heart turned over with love for this man-child who seemed to be struggling with his feelings so much.

"I thought I was strong, Mum. I thought I was in control, and that I had some say in what happened to me. I believed myself to be able to handle anything that life threw at me, but at this moment, I feel as if I'd been cleft right down the middle, my innermost fears and thoughts tumbling out and getting the better of me. I'm scared, and my fear makes me feel helpless," Gabe confessed. He turned back toward the hearth, reluctant to see his mother's reaction to such weakness. He'd never admit any of this to his father, who would likely just clap him on the shoulder and tell him to man up.

Phoebe set down her mug and came up behind Gabe's chair. She wrapped her arms around him and kissed the top of his head like she did when he was a boy and knew that he wouldn't welcome a full-on cuddle from Mum. Phoebe pressed her cheek against his temple and smiled to herself. He was shaken by his feelings, but she finally understood exactly what he was going through.

"Gabe, I liked your father very much when we first married, but I'd be lying if I said that I was madly in love with him. In my day, girls didn't look for love the way they do now, nor did they give much thought to sexual compatibility; we didn't know such a thing even existed, not until it was too late to do anything about it. Your father was my first and last, and we rubbed along well enough together all these years," she said. Gabe didn't interrupt to ask what on earth she was talking about. He was used to her round-about way of making a point.

"It wasn't until you came along after the disappointment of two miscarriages that I experienced what you're feeling now. I held you in my arms, you looked at me, and I felt the kind of all-encompassing love that took my breath away. The knowledge that you were mine to love and protect made me tremble with fear. I was the only thing that stood between you and anything that might hurt you, the only line of defense. I was strong before you were born, but after only a day, I was a bundle of nerves. I couldn't stop crying. I suppose they'd call it post-natal depression these days, but it was just overwhelming fear that I would let you down somehow, and you would suffer through my incompetence."

Gabe turned to face his mother, taking her hand in his. "Mum, I don't understand," he said gently. His mother never spoke to him like this, never shared so openly. He hadn't even known about the miscarriages. It wasn't a subject his parents would deem appropriate, and the fact that she was telling him now baffled him.

Phoebe came around and sat across from him again, leaning toward him in her eagerness to explain. "Son, you've finally won the woman you've worshipped for nearly a decade, and then a short while later you were presented not only with a child, but with the sole responsibility for that child. For the first time in your life, you love so deeply that you are undone by your vulnerability. The thought of losing either Emma or Quinn is so frightening that you feel helpless and confused, unsure of what to do to keep them safe, and to keep yourself safe for them."

Phoebe reached out and cupped Gabe's cheek, smiling at his bewilderment.

"You're experiencing what every new parent feels, only you also have a new love on top of that. You want to be the best possible parent to Emma, but you're also worried about what this will do to your relationship with Quinn. She seems genuinely fond of Emma, but Emma is your child, not hers, and this is a time in her life when she thought she'd have your undivided attention. You're walking a fine line right now, and you must make sure not to alienate Quinn as you work to find your footing with Emma. Try not to complicate the situation any further by adding more variables to the equation."

"Variables? Mum, what are you talking about?" Gabe asked, gaping at Phoebe as he tried to figure out where she was going with this mathematical reference. Phoebe sighed with impatience. Why did men, even highly intelligent ones like her Gabe, always need things to be explained to them? Any woman would have instantly taken her meaning.

"Gabriel, when you have a baby, it should be a joyful event for you both, not something to be juggled along with everything else you have going on in your life at the moment. Right now, you need to focus on your daughter. You need to work out the delicate balance between bride and child before you add another child into the mix."

"What makes you think there'll be another child?" Gabe asked, coloring slightly. He still felt awkward discussing his sex life with his mother, but Phoebe's matter-of-fact tone made it easier to believe that they were just two adults discussing a run-of-the-mill matter.

"Being in love generally leads to babies," Phoebe said with a smile. "Especially when you are too distracted to think about practicalities," she added meaningfully, making Gabe groan as he rolled his eyes in mock horror.

"Listen to your mother. I know a thing or two about life," Phoebe said, hands on hips.

"Mum, how did you get to be so wise?" Gabe asked as he tried to keep the grin off his face.

"I don't know. It's a gift," Phoebe joked, making Gabe chuckle. It was nice to see him laugh. "Does this mean I've helped?" Phoebe asked.

Gabe nodded, smiling into her eyes. "Yes, Mum, you've hit the nail on the head, as you always do. I never realized that loving someone so completely leaves you so vulnerable. I keep thinking of all the things that can go wrong, and I'm paralyzed with fear, terrified that I won't be able to fix it."

"Something happened with Quinn while you were in Scotland, didn't it?" Phoebe asked. Gabe paled visibly, so she waved her hand, dismissing the question. She no longer required an answer; Gabe's reaction was enough.

"Son, go upstairs and spend some time with your fiancée. We'll look after Emma. Show Quinn some affection, but remember what I said," Phoebe said, giving Gabe a stern look.

"Yes, ma'am," Gabe chuckled. "No more grandchildren for you."

"Let me enjoy this one first," Phoebe said as she rose to her feet. "I think I'll join them outside. They're having way too much fun without me."

Chapter 31

Quinn left her case by the door, shrugged off her coat, and walked straight to the sink to fill the kettle. She was desperate for a cup of tea after the long drive. Quinn set the kettle on the hob and looked in the fridge. The milk had gone bad, so she poured it down the sink. She'd drink the tea black. Quinn opened the kitchen cupboard and had a quick rummage. A couple of biscuits would have been nice, but the ones she found had gone stale, so she tossed them into the rubbish bin, annoyed with herself for not thinking ahead. She should have asked Gabe to stop at the petrol station where she could have stocked up on milk, a packet of fresh biscuits, and a newspaper. Gabe always read the news online, but at times, Quinn liked to sit down with a newspaper, the way her father used to do every day after work, a cup of tea at his elbow. He used to read interesting bits out loud to her mum while she prepared supper.

Quinn's stomach growled with hunger. She hadn't eaten anything since the full English Phoebe had made for them before they left, and she needed something to pick on. There was some pasta in the cupboard and a hunk of Parmesan cheese in the fridge. That would have to do. Quinn set the water to boil for the pasta and poured herself a cup of tea. She'd missed her little chapel. Not many people would enjoy living in a refurbished church, but Quinn loved its aura of serenity. It enveloped her every time she came home, like a balm to the soul, and she welcomed its peace and drew strength from the very walls, where so many had prayed and shared their hopes and dreams. The house was blissfully quiet, but cold.

Quinn set aside her tea and took out a box of matches, lighting the kindling, which was already in the hearth. The flame flickered and sputtered, but eventually came to life, the logs slowly catching fire and the room filling with the pleasant smell of burning wood. The chapel didn't have central heating, so the fire was a necessity as well as a luxury. The room began to slowly warm up. Quinn drained the pasta, dumped it into a bowl, and grated some cheese over it. She took her meal to the sofa and got comfortable in front of the fire, debating if she should have a glass of wine to go with her meal, but decided against it. She glanced at the clock. Gabe would be close to home by now. She hoped he'd pick up a takeaway for himself, since his refrigerator was probably even emptier than hers. Gabe got grumpy when he was hungry, she remembered with an affectionate smile.

Gabe had dropped her off at home on his way to London. He would have stayed the night, but he had to be in London first thing in the morning to prepare for a departmental meeting that was scheduled for nine o'clock. Quinn supposed she could have gone with him, but she'd meet him in London tomorrow instead. She needed a day to herself, and Gabe understood. Perhaps he needed a little time to himself as well to make sense of the past few weeks and come to terms with the drastic changes that rocked his well-ordered life to the core.

Leaving Emma with Phoebe and Graham for a few days had been a good idea. Emma took to her grandparents instantly, and the presence of Buster, who was as cute as a puppy could be, helped a great deal. There was much to be done over the next few days, and Gabe would need Quinn's help, which she was more than happy to offer. Organizing the life of a little girl was like planning a trip to the moon as far as Gabe was concerned, and although he was usually very good with practicalities, in this case, he was completely out of his depth.

Quinn took her empty bowl to the sink and refreshed her tea before going back to the sofa where she curled her legs beneath her and leaned her head against the back of the sofa. Despite the welcoming peace of home, her feelings were in turmoil, and the messages from Rhys and Dr. Scott hadn't helped. Rhys threatened to sue her for breach of contract if she didn't present herself at his office on Friday, and Colin said that he had something to share with her and asked if they could meet at her earliest convenience. Quinn had overnighted the plaster from Robert Chatham's room to Dr. Scott, so it was possible that he had the results already. Quinn wasn't quite sure that she was ready to deal with the outcome.

Now that she'd had the dubious pleasure of meeting Robert Chatham, she realized that had Rhys proved to be her father, she would not have been devastated. There was no excuse for what Rhys had done in his youth, but he'd regretted his actions and tried to atone for them in his own way. Rhys would spend the rest of his life trying to make it up to her, and she would let him. Robert Chatham, on the other hand, was a totally different entity. He was a born leader, a man who could easily get others to do his bidding. Quinn could see how Rhys would have been bullied into taking part. He'd been insecure and sensitive, something his friends would have used against him. Chatham probably did not regret a single thing he'd ever done, and even if he learned of the consequences of that night, he wouldn't have cared.

There was a time when Quinn thought that not knowing who her parents were was the worst thing that could happen to a person, but now she knew better. She was coming round to the idea of having Sylvia in her life, but if Chatham was her father, she'd never share that with him. The man was hateful. Quinn could still feel his lips on her neck and his hand between her legs. The memory of those moments made her shudder with disgust. Even if they weren't related, his touch made her feel violated and threatened. He was a brutal man, a bully who took what he wanted. Of course, she'd intentionally put herself in his path and went to his room knowing full well what he expected, but a woman still had the prerogative to change her mind. Chatham wouldn't have allowed her that. He would have forced her, and not felt an ounce of remorse after the fact.

    Quinn set aside her mug and practically ran toward the bathroom. She'd taken numerous showers since that night, but she still felt dirty. She turned on the taps and added some scented oil to the bathwater. A nice soak would help her relax, and perhaps wash away the memory of Chatham's hands on her body. She stripped off her clothes and climbed into the tub, resting her head against the porcelain as the hot water lapped over her breasts. She'd hoped to feel peaceful, but suddenly experienced a wave of loneliness. She missed Gabe and Emma. She'd known the little girl for just over a week, but found herself longing for the sound of her voice and the peal of her laughter. Quinn smiled as she closed her eyes. Despite everything, they were becoming a family, and it hadn't been as difficult as she might have expected. She wondered if her own parents felt the same when she came into their lives.

    Quinn extended her hand from the tub and reached for her phone. She had an overwhelming desire to speak to her parents, to hear their voices and share her news. Perhaps she would have told them sooner had they still been in England, but they'd retired to Spain several years ago, and although they spoke every day, the closeness they'd enjoyed her whole life had suffered. Her parents had a new life, which they were enjoying immensely, and Quinn no longer felt the urgent need to share news with them as soon as something happened. Perhaps that was a side-effect of growing up, or maybe now she had more to hide. It'd taken her months to tell her parents about Sylvia. She meant to tell them right away, but somehow every time she heard her mother's voice on the phone, she simply couldn't bring herself to shatter her sense of security. To tell her that the birth mother of whom she'd dreamed ever since she was a little girl had shown up on her doorstep and that her father was a rapist would not be something that would sit well with the Allenbys. And then, of course, there was Emma.

Quinn's parents adored Gabe and had been thrilled to hear that they were planning a future together, but to suddenly announce that Gabe had a four-year-old child he'd known nothing about would not endear Gabe to them. Her parents would raise all kinds of objections, mostly to protect Quinn, but also because deep down they still had a rather old-fashioned set of values. Gabe would be forever tarnished in their eyes, and that was something Quinn wished to avoid. But she'd waited long enough. Her parents had a right to know, come what may. Quinn dialed her mum's number and waited for her to answer. As the phone rang, she smiled wryly, imagining that the apprehension she felt was something akin to waiting for the guillotine to drop. The call went into voice mail and Quinn exhaled in relief. She was reprieved for one more day.

Chapter 32

February 1347

Dunwich, Suffolk

Petra pulled on her hood and wrapped the folds of her cloak tighter about her body, but the wind still sliced through her, making her shiver. She couldn't see the sea, but she could hear it. It was like a living, breathing thing lurking in the shadows. On some days, it was mellow and compliant, and on others, it was vicious and cruel, ready to pounce and devour everything in sight. The waves crashed against the shore with unrestrained brutality, making the ships at anchor bob on the water like flotsam, the light from the lanterns on deck rising and falling like a secret signal.

Petra had always disliked this time of year, when the night was so much longer than the day. When Cyril was still alive, she was busy from dawn till dusk, but at least she got to see the sun while she went about her chores. Now, she arrived at Lady Blythe's just after sunrise and left well after sunset. The only daylight she saw was through the window on the landing or when Lady Blythe sent her out to buy some fish for her supper. Petra savored those moments of freedom and took as long as she could despite the cold that left her feet and hands numb. Perhaps tomorrow, she'd offer to run an errand for the old lady, or she'd go mad. She hadn't been out in days, and hadn't had any time off since Candlemas, the memory of which still made her shudder.

Thomas hadn't mentioned the incident with Edwin, but a kind of kinship sprang up between them. He saw himself as her protector, her knight, and she was his chosen lady. Thomas was solicitous of her, even in front of his mother, and sought Petra out whenever he was at home. Twice this past week, Thomas had invited her to share a cup of hippocras with him before she left for the day, and Petra was too timid to refuse, despite the fact that she was tired and wished only to go home. Thomas behaved as if things were settled between them, but Petra had never given her consent.

Oh, she knew she was being foolish, and she should seize this opportunity before Thomas came to his senses and changed his mind, but some small part of her refused to yield. Had she not seen Avery, spoken to him, and told him of Edwin, she would have thanked her lucky stars for having a man like Lord Devon pay court to her, but although her sensible side knew what must be done, her heart just wouldn't listen, wouldn't comply. Avery was no more hers for the taking than he had been twelve years ago, but she couldn't accept that after having found him again. Her soul ached for him, as did her body. After years of being dormant, like a bear in its den, her desire had come awake, yearning for a man's touch.

Thomas had brushed his hand against hers on several occasions. His hand was warm and strong, a man's hand, but it didn't excite her the way the sight of Avery's slender fingers and narrow wrists had. Avery had the hands of a scholar and the eyes of a poet. He used to play the lute when he was young, shyly performing for Petra and waiting for her to clap her hands in approval. Did he still play, or had he given up music along with everything else? He must have. Petra couldn't reconcile the seriousness of Avery's gaze with someone who amused himself by playing the lute and reciting poems about valiant knights and the beautiful, unattainable ladies they loved. Avery had sacrificed every part of himself that mattered, including his love for her.

Petra looked up at the sky. It was shrouded in thick, low clouds that completely obscured the moon and the stars. There was hardly any light to see by, and suddenly, she was scared. Most respectable folk were already at home, sitting by their hearths after supper and spending a bit of time with their kin before retiring for the night. Petra longed to be by her hearth with her family. She felt like she hadn't spent any proper time with them in weeks, particularly the girls, who having taken on some of Petra's chores, fell into bed right after supper. She missed them, and she missed Edwin, who'd been withdrawn and silent since Candlemas. He wasn't yet twelve, but he understood the consequences of what occurred and knew that life wasn't going to be kind to him, one way or another.

It'd been nearly a fortnight since she'd seen Avery, but Petra hadn't heard from him nor spied him at any of the Candlemas celebrations. She'd looked for him too, despite her promise to herself not to. There'd been several friars from the priory and Knights Hospitallers dressed in their black capes and tunics with the white cross emblazoned on the front. At least they hadn't been wearing their chainmail hauberks or helmets, or carrying any weapons besides their swords, it being a day of celebration. All the parish priests were there as well, tending to their flock, but she hadn't seen Avery anywhere.

Lady Blythe was long recovered and eager to see her confessor. She'd even sent a message to the priory, but still Avery stayed away. Had Petra offended him in some way, or had she overstepped her bounds by asking him to help their son? Of course, finding out he had a son must have come as a shock to Avery, but she'd had no choice. She had no one else to turn to, no male relatives to offer protection or guidance or much-needed funds. Had she spooked Avery enough to send him running back to Oxford? Or perhaps he'd been ill, shut up at the priory as the brothers tended to him. These questions went round and round in her head, but she was no closer to an answer. Avery seemed to have vanished.

Petra bent her head into the wind and hastened her step. Every sound startled her and forced her to walk faster. She suddenly felt very alone and very vulnerable. A woman walking on her own after dark was a target for rowdy seamen, and being so close to the port, she was at risk, especially since most of them had been in the taverns for hours and were well lubricated with ale by this point. She could never be mistaken for a whore, but when drunk enough, the men didn't care; they just wanted a warm body to hold and a willing, or unwilling, wench to slake their lust on. It happened often enough, but the perpetrators were never taken up by the constables or brought before the sheriff. The woman was accused instead if she dared to make a complaint, blamed for being out alone or told that her wanton behavior justified the assault.

Petra cried out in terror when a hand closed about her upper arm. She whirled about, but couldn't see the face of her assailant, who was wearing a dark cloak, the hood pulled low over his face. His hand was strong, the fingers like a vice around her flesh. Petra whimpered with fear. She prayed the man might be a Knight Hospitaller, but couldn't see the white cross. The knights were good men, and protectors of women. They would never assault a woman in the street, so why was this man gripping her arm unless he was bent on an act of violence against her?

"Shh, it's me, Petra," the man hissed. "Don't be frightened." He pushed his hood back enough for Petra to see his face. She let out the breath she'd been holding and pulled her arm from Avery's grasp, taking a step back to regain her composure.

"So, you've taken to skulking in the shadows?" Petra demanded, trying to sound outraged to cover up her initial fear.

Her heart was still racing, and her breath came fast and hard, but her fear had turned to excitement at seeing Avery.

"I can't be seen with you," Avery explained as he steered her toward a clump of trees. The trees were old and had thick trunks, completely obscuring Petra and Avery from prying eyes, had there been any at this time of night and with a storm coming on.

"Won't you be missed?" Petra asked. Avery looked to be in good health, so he must have been intentionally staying away, avoiding her.

"I usually return to my cell for solitary contemplation between Vespers and Compline. No one will comment on my absence," Avery explained.

"Did you come to see me about Edwin?"

"In a manner of speaking," Avery replied. Petra could just make out his face in the darkness, his eyes drinking her in, his lips slightly parted. "Oh, Petra, I thought I was immune," Avery breathed.

"Immune to what?"

But Avery didn't respond. His arm came about her waist and he pulled her close, his lips covering hers with a familiarity that made her weak in the knees. The years slipped away, and they were young again, drunk on the heady emotions of first love. Avery pushed her up against the tree, his kiss becoming more demanding as he pressed his body against hers. There were layers of fabric between them, but she could still feel his heat and his solid strength as he held her in his arms.

Somewhere in the back of Petra's mind, she knew she should stop him, but her heart had been frozen for twelve long years, her body used regularly by a man she despised, who'd left her physically bruised and emotionally humiliated. Avery's kiss made her feel desired and wanton. She could feel his arousal through the fabric of her skirts, and instead of feeling repulsed and frightened as she had since her wedding night, she felt mindless longing and a need to surrender.

Avery pushed her up against the tree. Petra supposed it was rough and hard, but she didn't feel anything except searing heat that warmed her to the core. She gasped when Avery's hand slipped between her legs, his fingers bringing her the kind of pleasure she hadn't experienced since he left. Avery lifted her up and covered her with his body, his cloak making them one with the dark. He swallowed her cry of rapture with a kiss as he entered her, their bodies joining together as if suddenly remembering something they'd forgotten long since. Petra clung to Avery, every thought and objection obliterated from her mind as he impaled her on his shaft.

She cried out softly as he moved within her, thrusting again and again until she thought she'd die with the joy of it. Petra began to tremble as convulsions of exquisite pleasure erupted somewhere deep inside her, reminding her of what love was supposed to feel like when both people gave themselves up completely and willingly. Avery lowered her to the ground, but held her until she regained the use of her legs, which felt like stalks of grass in the breeze. He rested his forehead against hers and closed his eyes, taking a moment to allow his breathing to return to normal.

"I never stopped loving you," he whispered. "Not for a moment."

"What shall we do?" Petra asked, the practical side of her already asserting itself. She thought her longing was one-sided, but now she knew better. Avery must have done a lot of soul-searching before allowing himself to break his vow of celibacy. If he was willing to do that, perhaps there might be a future for them after all.

"I don't know. I need time to think."

"I must get home, Avery. I will be missed."

Avery brushed pine needles off her cloak and adjusted her headpiece. He leaned forward and gave her the gentlest of kisses, making her feel not only desired, but loved. "Give me a little time, my sweet."

"I have all the time in the world," Petra replied. *But now it has meaning*, Petra thought as she walked alongside Avery. He escorted her as far as he could, then melted into the shadows, needing to return to Greyfriars in time for Compline. He would get a few hours of sleep before the Midnight Office prayer and then be up again before dawn for Matins. The monks are not only denied physical pleasures, but they aren't allowed uninterrupted sleep either, Petra reflected as she let herself into the house and smiled happily at her family. Her mother threw her a curious look, but she refused to meet her gaze, greeting the children instead and asking about their day as they sat down to a supper of pease pudding.

Petra excused herself as soon as she could and climbed up to her loft, desperate to wash all traces of Avery from her body. She wasn't too old to get with child, so measures had to be taken. She knew her mother had smelled a man on her, but she probably thought it was Thomas, and her narrowed eyes and pursed lips screamed her disapproval as loudly as any words. Petra avoided her gaze all through supper. She was experiencing a strange emotion, and it was only once she'd gone to bed and lay awake reliving her reunion with Avery that she was able to put a name to it. She was happy.

Chapter 33

January 1347

Dunwich, Suffolk

Prior Jacob led the monks out of the chapel after the midnight prayer and watched the men disperse as they shuffled off to get a few hours of sleep before the next prayer service. He knew he should get to bed as well, but although physically tired, his mind was teeming with thoughts and ideas. Prior Jacob walked to the tiny cell that served as his study and lit a candle, his hand automatically going to the letter he'd received earlier in the day. The prior unrolled the scroll and read it again, although he already knew the contents by heart. He finished reading and held out the paper to the flame of the candle, watching in fascination as the paper caught, and the letter began to burn and shrivel, turning into black fragments that eventually blew off the desk by the draft from the window.

The prior opened the shutters, and a blast of frigid air burst into the cell, making him shiver. He could light a fire, but he relished his suffering, seeing it as penance for anything he might have done wrong throughout the day. He was a conscientious man and liked to feel that he was first and foremost one of the brothers and deserved no special treatment. There were no hearths in the cells. The brothers slept on straw mattresses spread on narrow wooden cots. The windows of the cells were unglazed, the cold kept out only by wooden shutters that did little to keep the cells warm. Creature comforts were not a part of monastic life, and Prior Jacob didn't seek them for himself.

He turned his chair toward the window and looked out at the night sky, which was aglow with the light of the moon. Wispy clouds floated over its buttery surface, casting darker shadows over the landscape before finally gliding past and revealing the full glory of the nearly round orb. Countless stars glittered in the heavens, twinkling at the prior and making him momentarily forget the cold. The draft from the window extinguished the candle, plunging the cell into near darkness, but Jacob didn't mind. He needed to think, and he thought best when he was alert and physically uncomfortable.

Prior Jacob had been the prior of Greyfriars Priory for only four months. He'd succeeded Prior Francis, who died quite suddenly of apoplexy, leaving the friars to choose his successor. Prior Francis had been at the helm of the priory for nearly a decade and was very popular with the friars. Having ascended to the position of prior when already in his late fifties, Prior Francis took on the role of father-figure for many of the younger members of the order, who were still secretly homesick and were in need of a bit more patience and guidance than the older friars.

Prior Francis had been short of stature, thick-set, and possessed of a ruddy round face that always wore an expression of attentiveness and understanding. He'd been kind, fair, and humble, a combination of traits that inspired loyalty and devotion among the members of the order. Surprisingly, not many of the friars seemed interested in the office of prior, and only two candidates had been put forth: Friar Jacob and Friar Martin, a man in his late seventies, who was stooped and had a hacking cough that could be heard coming from his cell during the night. Friar Martin was pious and humble, but he had a certain peevishness of character that made him unpopular with the rest of the friars, who weren't interested in petty slights or keeping score of worthy deeds.

Friar Jacob was in his early fifties. Tall and whippet-thin, he was in good health and possessed of great physical strength. He no longer had to shave his tonsure since he'd gone bald on top years ago, with only a fringe of light brown hair remaining to encircle his head. He had a lean, almost gaunt face, with light gray eyes and a long, thin nose that dominated his face and nearly obscured his small mouth, one that rarely stretched into a smile. Although somewhat humorless, he was known for being devout, hard-working, and scrupulously honest.

The vote was twenty-two for Jacob, and four for Friar Martin, whose advanced age and general unpopularity worked against him. The friars wished for continuity, and chose a younger man to fill their beloved prior's sabots. Jacob had been overcome with gratitude at being chosen and vowed to himself to be the best prior Greyfriars had ever had. He instantly regretted this act of vainglory and asked God for forgiveness, spending several hours on his knees as penance for the sin of pride. He wasn't there to elevate himself, but to serve God and the other friars who relied on him to communicate with the abbot and see to the smooth running of the priory while they dedicated themselves to hard work and prayer.

When Father Avery arrived six weeks ago, Prior Jacob had no qualms about welcoming him to the priory. Father Avery was not a Franciscan, nor was he looking to enter a monastic institution. He needed a place to stay while he enjoyed a period of reflection and recovered from an illness which had left him weakened in body and spirit, or so the prior had been told. Prior Jacob was happy to help, seeing it as his duty to offer hospitality and a place of peace to anyone seeking it. Father Avery was gracious, humble, and surprisingly charismatic, and unwittingly reminded the friars of the prior they'd lost so recently. Father Avery had that type of inherent charm that attracted women and gathered men to his side. He was a natural-born leader, a man who had only to speak to someone to gain their allegiance.

Prior Jacob thought nothing of Father Avery's presence at first, but after a fortnight, he began to notice the priest's popularity with the rest of the friars. He wasn't very well-liked himself, despite his best efforts at being strict but fair. He simply wasn't the type of man who inspired that type of loyalty. If, for whatever reason, Father Avery decided that he wished to join the order, he would be a rival and a threat, so Prior Jacob decided to find out what he could about the man who could unseat him if he chose to do so. He wrote to a parish priest of his acquaintance who was based near Oxford. The letter that arrived yesterday had been something of a surprise.

Living in near-seclusion, Prior Jacob had little contact with the outside world. He left the priory rarely, going only to meet with the abbot and to occasionally buy supplies that the friars couldn't produce themselves. The priory did not have a fish pond or a mill, so Prior Jacob purchased barrels of fish and sacks of flour, as well as beer for the men to drink. He kept the transactions as impersonal as possible, refraining from indulging in gossip or idle curiosity. Perhaps now he would be more open to hearing the latest news, given what he'd learned. As prior, he had a responsibility to his men, and in his self-imposed ignorance, he'd exposed them to a heretic and a radical. Father Roan wrote:

Dear Prior Jacob,

I'm glad that you came to me with your concerns, as they are, indeed, valid. Father Avery is well known to me, as is his good friend and colleague John Wycliffe. As you might not be familiar with the name, allow me to warn you about this very dangerous man. He's a graduate of Merton College here in Oxford and a seminary professor, as was Father Avery before he was sent away.

John Wycliffe is, in my opinion, a heretic who should be excommunicated and exiled, but he is under the protection of those who tend to agree with his ill-conceived views. He has many followers, who call themselves the Lollards.

Wycliffe speaks openly of reforming the Church, and wages a war against the ideals that have sustained us for centuries. He has dared to openly criticize the sacraments and rituals synonymous with our faith, and even went so far as to question the existence of the papacy. One of his greatest follies, however, is the notion that the common man should be privy to the word of God. It's said that he has begun working on a translation of the gospels into the vernacular, and means to translate the New Testament with the express purpose of making it accessible to the masses.

Father Avery has expressed similar opinions to several of his students and has been suspended from teaching for a period of one year. It is your duty as a man of God to help him see sense and prevent him at all cost from spreading his vile influence to the holy men entrusted to you. Maintain your vigilance where this man is concerned.

Your brother in God,

Father Roan.

Prior Jacob pinched the bridge of his nose, as he was prone to do when deep in thought. He liked Father Avery and believed him to be a trustworthy and learned man, but this changed everything. It was Prior Jacob's duty to protect his men and the community of Dunwich from this heretic. He would keep an eye on his movements and report anything untoward to the abbot, who would be of a similar mind on the matter. In the meantime, Prior Jacob would do nothing to alert Father Avery to his investigation.

If anything, he would cultivate his good-will by granting his request of taking on a young boy of his acquaintance as an apprentice scribe. They did not need another scribe, but the boy, who was surprisingly literate, could mix pigments for ink, sharpen quills, and assist the scribes in any other way they required. At the very least, the child would be removed from the influence of the man who had the power to damn his soul.

Chapter 34

Petra's feet barely touched the ground as she made her way to Lady Blythe's house the morning after her encounter with Avery. She didn't know what the future held, or if there would ever be another opportunity for them to come together, but over the years, she'd learned to take a moment of happiness and make it last, since they didn't come around often. She'd committed a sin, again, but all she felt was an all-encompassing joy and a sense of being alive such as she hadn't felt in years. Her body was still aflame, her hunger for love awakened with a start after years of being suppressed and ignored.

Petra hung her cloak on a peg by the door and walked to the kitchen to check on her mistress's breakfast. Nan was hard at work, having been up for hours. She slept on a narrow cot in an alcove behind the kitchen and rose well before dawn to get the fire going, bake fresh bread, and get a start on the day's chores. She looked harassed as always, her hair escaping from her linen hood and clinging to her sweaty brow. This was laundry day, which was a monthly ordeal that took most of the day. Doing the laundry left Nan shaking with fatigue, the muscles in her arms and legs aching and sore by the time she finally fell into bed. It wasn't a job for one person, but Lady Blythe, always intent on economy, was too tight-fisted to hire an additional servant, and Thomas, being a man, was oblivious to what was expected of the poor girl.

"The bread's nearly done," she huffed as she stepped away from the hearth. "And there's hot broth if you'd like a cup before waking Lady Blythe."

"Thank you, a cup of broth would be most welcome. Is Lord Devon in?" Petra asked carefully.

"Oh, aye. He's still abed. Came in just before dawn. Drunk he was, and disorderly," Nan complained. "Scared me half to death when he stumbled into the kitchen by mistake. Then he took a piss into one of the pots," Nan added with distaste.

"Does he come in in that state often?" Petra asked, realizing how little she actually knew about Thomas. Cyril didn't drink himself into a stupor often, but when he did, it didn't bode well for Petra or the children. Drink mellowed some men, and awakened a rage in others, provoking them to violence against those who were to hand and had no means of defending themselves.

"No," Nan replied as she poured Petra a cup of broth. "He's a good man, Lord Thomas. Kind. I think he's just lonely, and last night he'd had a blazing quarrel with her ladyship. He really put her in her place; I'll tell you that. Told her to mind her own business, or he'd send her to a nunnery. Imagine, Lady Blythe in a nunnery," Nan giggled. "Now that's a sight I wouldn't mind seeing."

"What did they argue about?"

"How should I know? Not like I was listening at doors, was I?" Nan retorted, suddenly defensive. "And no refreshments were called for," she added sarcastically. "Now, get on with you. I have things to do."

"Is there any hot water for me to take up to her ladyship?"

Nan nodded, her mind already on something else. She was as easily distracted as a child, her mind flitting from one thing to the next. Petra took a sip of her broth and mentally reprimanded herself. Nan was a child. She was only thirteen, hardly older than Elia, and already forced to make her way in the world. She was an orphan, and had little chance of a respectable marriage since there'd be no one to provide her with a dowry, unless Lady Blythe decided to be charitable, which was unlikely.

"I'll come and give you a hand with the laundry while her ladyship naps," Petra promised, glad to see a hint of a smile. The poor girl really was overworked and underpaid, since all she got was a roof over her head and her meals. She wouldn't earn a wage until she was older and considered to be properly trained.

"I would be most grateful," Nan replied as she began to carefully extract the hot loaves from the oven niche in the hearth. They looked perfect, which didn't happen often. Usually Nan got distracted and burned the bread a little, invoking the wrath of her employer.

Petra finished her broth, poured some hot water into a pitcher, and headed upstairs to wake Lady Blythe. The old woman was already awake, sitting up in bed, propped up by several pillows. Her gray hair hung in two limp plates, and there was noticeable puffiness beneath her eyes, a testament to a night spent tossing and turning.

"Shall I help you dress, lady?" Petra asked as she set the pitcher down.

"Hmm, look at her," Lady Blythe said, as if speaking to a third person in the room. "So cool, so aloof. When all the while she's been laying plans, and looking to take my place."

"I'm sorry, but I don't take your meaning," Petra replied, confused by the venom in Lady Blythe's voice.

"Don't you?"

Petra remained silent. Lady Blythe was not one to hold back. She would vent her anger on Petra no matter what she said, so it was safer to remain quiet and keep her distance. She still remembered the sting of Lady Blythe's belt when she was a girl. Lady Blythe didn't beat Nan as often, simply because she lacked the energy, but she made up for it with scathing tongue-lashings that left the girl in tears and trembling with fright at the thought of being thrown out with only the clothes she stood up in.

"It seems that my son wishes to marry you. "You are a fool," I told him. "An ungrateful wretch, who wants to throw away all that had been done for him." But he won't listen. His mind is made up. What have you done to bewitch my Thomas?"

"I've done nothing, lady. I have given him no encouragement."

"You better not have, or your back will be striped like a tiger's. Ever see one of those? No, I thought not," she answered herself. "My Thomas can have any girl he wants. A girl of breeding and means, a virgin whose womb is fertile and ripe for planting. He could still have sons. Instead, he wishes to marry a lowly nobody. And not just a nobody, but a nobody who is too old to bear children and has three whelps of her own to support. You are of low birth and advanced years. You have nothing to offer a man of his stature."

"No, lady, I don't," Petra agreed. Lady Blythe's bluntness was cruel, but everything she said was no more than the truth.

"You will refuse him, you hear?" Lady Blythe demanded. "You will not give him any hope."

"And if I refuse to refuse?" Petra asked, taunting the old woman despite the consequences. She couldn't afford to lose her place, but even a woman of her station was entitled to some pride.

"Then I will convince him to wait until June to wed. He will change his mind by then, you can be sure of that, my girl. He's no fool, but it's been a long time since he's had a woman in his bed. He's not thinking straight. I will tell Robert to bring Thomas a whore, a dozen whores, if that's what it takes to cool his lust. He'll forget all about you then, you'll see."

Petra looked at the old lady and let out a giggle, which she immediately stifled by clamping a hand over her mouth and pretending to cough. The notion that it would take a dozen whores to turn Thomas away from her was laughable. She was no great beauty, nor was she young and pure. She was a mother of three; married, widowed, and battered by life. Surely there was no need for such extreme antics.

"Am I dismissed from my position, Lady Blythe?" Petra asked, not wishing to suffer any more abuse if she were to be let go anyway.

"No, you are not! You will continue with your duties, and remain by my side where I can keep an eye on you. Keep your friends close, but your enemies closer, they say," she replied, her eyes narrowed with dislike.

"Am I your enemy then?" Petra asked. Lady Blythe was clearly more threatened by her chances with Thomas than Petra previously imagined. Was it possible that Thomas truly loved her? What a strange and unexpected turn her life had taken since Cyril died. Lady Blythe didn't reply, her silence signaling that the conversation was at an end for the time being.

"I'd like to wash now. Take out my blue gown and woolen stockings. I'm cold."

"Yes, lady," Petra replied. She was as distracted as Nan while she helped Lady Blythe dress and escorted her down to break her fast. She had to talk to Thomas, but for the life of her, she didn't know what to say. The sensible thing to do would be to accept his proposal and get on with her life, but her encounter with Avery made accepting Thomas seem like a betrayal of all of them.

Chapter 35

"The master wishes to see you," Nan announced as she shuffled into the kitchen with an empty basket on her hip, having finished hanging out the laundry in the yard. Her normally sallow cheeks were rosy with cold, and her hands were nearly blue after handling wet bed linens and Lady Blythe's underthings. She set down the basket and held her hands out to the fire, sighing with contentment as they began to regain their normal color. "I saw him coming out of the stable," she added.

"How did he seem to you?" Petra asked, wondering if he regretted the argument with Lady Blythe and was perhaps already reconsidering his intentions toward her.

"Sore-headed and shame-faced," Nan replied. "Serves him right for drinking like a peasant."

"Don't let him hear you say that," Petra laughed. Nan really was too outspoken at times, a trait that earned her the back of Lady Blythe's hand at least once a week.

"Tis the truth," Nan shrugged. "I saw him being sick behind the stable. If I ever marry, I'll find a man who has an aversion to drink. Nasty, it makes them, and violent."

"Was Lord Devon violent toward you?" Petra demanded. Nan shook her head, and Petra suddenly wondered what Nan's life had been like before she came to serve Lady Blythe. Nan had her opinions and was always up for a gossip, but she never talked about herself. Petra always assumed that there wasn't much to tell, but perhaps she was wrong. Some memories were too painful to share. Could be that this place was a refuge for her as much as it had once been for Petra herself.

"Lord Devon is the exception. He gets maudlin when he drinks, but not belligerent, like some. You know how men can get when their blood's up. They need to kick and punch someone, someone who's too weak to defend themselves and won't put up much of a fight. Can't have their manhood challenged. Can they?" Nan asked with disgust. "That's about the only thing I recall about my father — his fists, and how often he used them."

Nan wiped her hands on her apron and reached for the hunk of venison she planned to make for supper. She skillfully impaled it on a spit and positioned it above the flames, where it would roast until suppertime, filling the house with its appetizing smell. If Thomas was too unwell to eat, Nan would get a nice portion for her own supper, since she ate whatever was left over from the mistress's table.

"You'd best go see him now. He said he'd be waiting in the parlor. Likely wants to say his piece before his mother wakes from her nap, the old sow."

Petra couldn't help smiling at the girl. Nan had spirit; she'd give her that. It might not serve her well when it came to staying in Lady Blythe's good graces, but perhaps saying what was on her mind made her feel a little less downtrodden. "All right; I'm going," Petra replied and left Nan to her work.

Petra tried to push aside a feeling of apprehension as she hurried toward the parlor, but she couldn't help worrying. If Thomas still wished to marry her, she'd feel beholden to him, and if he'd changed his mind, she might lose her position. Neither outcome would bode well for her. Petra entered the room and approached slowly, not wishing to disturb Thomas, who sat staring into the flames, his expression pensive.

"Ah, Petra, come in. Sit down," he said, getting to his feet as a sign of respect. He reached out, as if to caress her cheek, but snatched his hand back, recognizing the intimacy of the gesture. Thomas held out his hands instead, enveloping Petra's in his own. His hands were large, warm, and calloused. Thomas wasn't a man who enjoyed idleness, despite his wealth. He often worked right alongside his men, loading sacks of wool, driving the ponies, and delivering shipments to the waiting ships, unlike Robert, who preferred not to get his hands dirty and conducted most of his business in taverns.

Petra took a seat and waited for Thomas to speak. He looked tired and upset, his face pale, and his eyes bloodshot from overindulgence in drink the night before. Petra wished he'd look away, but his gaze never wavered as he studied her face.

"You are a sight for sore eyes," he finally said. "Today of all days."

"Is something wrong, Thomas?" Petra asked. She didn't think an argument with Lady Blythe would leave Thomas this unsettled. He used to argue with her all the time in days past, standing his ground despite his mother's ire. Thomas had always been dutiful, more so than Robert, but he resented his mother's bullying ways and preferred to decide for himself, even when the outcome was a foregone conclusion, much as his betrothal had been.

These days, Lady Blythe had little power over her sons, who ran the family business and controlled the Devon wealth. She liked to pretend that she still held sway over them, but in truth, they had no need of her counsel or her sharp tongue. They indulged her desire to feel involved, and gave her the respect sons owned their mother, but their personal choices were no longer any concern of hers. They were grown men, and masters onto themselves.

"Petra, I'm leaving tomorrow. I must visit the sheep farmers before the shearing starts. I'll be gone a fortnight, possibly longer."

Petra nodded, wondering what the urgency was. Normally, the sheep weren't sheared until the spring, allowing the animals, especially lambs, the extra protection of their fleeces during the winter months. Once the shearing began, the wool came in continuously for weeks, the pack-whackers and pickers working practically non-stop to prepare the fleeces for shipment.

"There's trouble a-brewing," Thomas said, shaking his head in dismay, or maybe disbelief.

"What kind of trouble?"

"There's a wool merchant in Lavenham. Walter Nevins is his name. I've never met the man myself, but have heard him mentioned. He's ambitious and shrewd," Thomas said. "And ruthless. He seems to have come into a sum of money. An inheritance from a relation, no doubt. He's putting that money to good use. Nevins has been visiting the sheep farms, and offering men who've worked with us since the days of my father a higher price per sack of wool in an effort to cut us out."

"How much more is he offering?" Petra asked. She had no notion of what a sack of wool went for, but to buy as much fleece as Thomas and Robert did would require a fortune, even without paying more per sack.

"Enough to make the farmers think twice about refusing. If he buys up our share of the fleeces, our profits will suffer, and we might not have enough put by to buy fleeces next year, opening the way for Nevins to pay the farmers less, since he would have eliminated the competition."

"Would the Guild not have something to say about that?" Petra asked.

Thomas shook his head. "The Guild cannot be expected to eradicate competition among its members. That would harm everyone in the long run. We all negotiate our own terms and prices. Nevins is within his rights."

"What will you do?" Petra asked. She never imagined that the wealthy worried about their income, and just assumed that they led comfortable, well-provided for lives. This was a glimpse into a world she knew nothing about.

"I will visit all the farmers and remind them of their commitment to us. We've treated them fairly and guaranteed their annual income for decades. Nevins might be paying more this year, but that doesn't mean that this price will apply in the future, or that he will return to buy from them in the coming years."

"And what if they refuse?" Petra asked. Her mother always said that a bird in the hand was better than two on a branch. More money this year might outweigh the fear of making less in the future.

"If they refuse, then I will renegotiate the terms and offer them a higher price. I cannot allow Nevins to steal my livelihood from me, nor will I."

"Then I wish you Godspeed, Thomas, and hope that you will put this Nevins in his place."

"Thank you, my dear." Thomas finally smiled, his eyes filling with gratitude and hope.

"Petra, I know that you are recently bereaved and need more time to consider my proposal, but I'll have you know that I told my mother of my intention to marry you."

"So, I've heard," Petra replied, smiling back. "Your mother is none too pleased."

"She'll come around," Thomas replied, dismissing Lady Blythe with a wave of the hand. "I won't press you for an answer now, but I would like to settle things between us when I return. Please, think about my proposal most carefully. I really am very fond of you, and I will give you and your children a good life, regardless of what happens in the coming weeks. You have my word."

"You shall have my answer when you return, Thomas."

Petra rose to her feet and was about to leave when Thomas came up behind her and took her by the arm. He pulled her close and bent down to kiss her, his lips gentle against hers before he deepened the kiss, his desire for her obvious. Petra didn't resist, but neither did she return his kiss. That would have been a promise of sorts, and wouldn't be fair.

"Something to remember me by," Thomas said as he released her. "I hope I didn't offend you."

"Not at all. Safe journey, Thomas."

Petra fled the parlor, eager to get away and think. Thomas's kiss hadn't been unpleasant, and had she not seen Avery again after all these years, she would have welcomed it. Only an utter fool would refuse a proposal from a man like Lord Devon, especially when Avery was in no position to offer her a future.

But the heart wants what it wants, Petra thought as tears welled in her eyes. *Oh, why did Avery have to come back?*

Chapter 36

February 2014

London, England

A cold, miserable rain fell in sheets as Quinn dashed across the street and into Freestate Coffee, a cozy café chosen by Dr. Scott. The aroma of freshly-ground coffee beans overlaid by the smell of pastry made Quinn pause and inhale deeply. It was heavenly, especially on such a filthy morning. She ordered a cappuccino and an almond croissant and weaved her way between the tables toward the back where Colin Scott was sitting in the corner. He gave her a friendly wave and moved his coat from the chair that he'd been saving for her.

Seeing Dr. Scott outside the mortuary was a revelation. Gone were the green scrubs and surgical cap, replaced by black jeans, combat boots, and a designer hoodie. Colin's hair, which was normally bound at work, hung to his shoulders, its sandy waves framing his face. Several women were giving Colin no-so-discreet looks of appreciation, their eyes drawn by his chiseled features and beautiful eyes. It always struck Quinn as odd that a man who looked as trendy and artistic as Dr. Scott would choose to dissect cadavers for a living.

"Mornin'," Colin drawled as he waited for Quinn to get settled and stow her dripping umbrella beneath her seat. "Awful out there."

"Better than snow, I suppose," Quinn replied and took a sip of her coffee. "This place is a bit out of the way for you, isn't it?"

"Not really. I live just around the corner. And I love their coffee. Best in London, in my opinion."

"It really is good," Quinn agreed, although at the moment, she would probably have enjoyed vending machine coffee in a Styrofoam cup as long as it was hot.

"So, which do you want first, information on your mysterious fourteenth-century remains or the results of the paternity test?"

"The remains please," Quinn replied. She didn't think she'd be able to concentrate on what Colin had to say after hearing the results of the DNA test. The answer seemed to surprise Dr. Scott, but he didn't question it. He pushed his empty coffee cup out of the way and leaned forward, resting his folded hands on the table. The look on his face underwent an instant transformation, going from casual friendliness to one of barely-restrained enthusiasm. This was a man who was passionate about his job, someone who saw a body on a slab as more than just a corpse, but a puzzle to be solved, a story to be told. Quinn understood only too well. Her decision to become an archeologist was rooted in exactly the same desire. Every bone and artifact had a story to tell. They gave a voice to someone who was long gone, whose life might not have been extraordinary or rewarding, but worth remembering all the same.

"I'm sorry to report that the hair we found lacked a follicle, so we weren't able to obtain any nuclear DNA. The only test we can perform on a hair shaft is the mtDNA test, which shows genetic information passed down the maternal line, and we didn't run the full mitochondrial genome because it's very costly and requires authorization," Colin said, smiling apologetically.

"The only thing I can state with any certainty about your lady is that she was of Anglo-Saxon descent and was fair-haired and light-eyed. She was predisposed to seizures, cortical blindness, and sideroblastic anemia, which doesn't mean that she suffered from any of those conditions. These predispositions would have been passed on down to her children, and her female children would, in turn, have passed them on to their own offspring."

Quinn nodded. What Colin was saying fit right in with what she knew of Petra and her children already. Petra didn't suffer from seizures, nor did her daughters, but she had passed on the predisposition to her son, Edwin. Quinn thought that Colin had finished, but he smiled at her triumphantly, having saved the best for last.

"The only real thing of interest that I can share with you is that based on the DNA sequencing we've done on the teeth of the child, we've been able to ascertain, with about ninety-percent accuracy, that the remains are those of mother and child. So, they weren't two random people buried next to each other; they were related," Colin concluded. "And whatever unforgivable sin the mother had been accused of, the son was likely party to the act since he'd been condemned to a prone burial in unconsecrated ground."

Colin leaned back, the excitement fading from his face as he remembered the limitations imposed on him despite his desire to know more. "Unfortunately, given the historical obscurity of these people, we don't have the funding to perform a full panel of genome and DNA sequencing. Someone would have to foot the bill, and your Mr. Morgan doesn't have the authority to pay for this from the coffers of the BBC."

"Thank you, Colin. I understand. Every little bit helps. I'm sure Rhys will find a way to spin this into a story his audience will love. The episodes of *Echoes from the Past* are rooted in reality, but are, for all intents and purposes, a work of fiction. We take a few basic facts and create a reenactment of what might have happened to our victims. At this stage, no one can say with any certainty what actually did happen to them, so it's less documentary and more historical fantasy."

"I'm glad I could help," Colin replied. "I'm a scientist; I don't feel comfortable dealing in speculation, but I suppose you don't require cold, hard facts in this case. One theory is as good as another when it comes to how they died. They were definitely murdered, but we'll never know why or by whom. Given the circumstances of their burial, the Church was clearly involved in some way."

"Perhaps not in the murder itself, but in the events that led up to it," Quinn agreed. An image of Petra and sweet-faced Edwin popped into her mind, but she pushed it back, unable to reconcile their living, breathing selves with the two dried-up skeletons in Colin's lab. Now that the tests were complete, their bones would be boxed up, labeled, and stored in some back room, where no one would ever look at them again. Petra and Edwin Ordell wouldn't even get a proper burial or a headstone, since as far as everyone was concerned, no one knew exactly who they were.

"Now, are you ready for the other set of results?" Colin asked, his eyes twinkling with ill-concealed curiosity.

"As ready as I'll ever be," Quinn replied. She pushed away her croissant, having suddenly lost her appetite. She could feel the onset of a headache and her stomach clenched in anticipation of the news, her mind screaming that perhaps she didn't want to know after all. Ignorance was bliss, or so some believed, and in this case, that just might be true.

Colin shook his head, his eyes never leaving Quinn's face. "Not a match. I hope you're not too disappointed."

Quinn let out the breath she'd been holding and smiled at Colin. "On the contrary, I'm giddy with relief. The man is odious."

"Quinn, please forgive my curiosity, but how many candidates are there?"

Quinn's eyes slid away from Colin's face as her cheeks colored with embarrassment. She would have resented the intrusive question from anyone else, but not from Dr. Scott. She liked this man, and felt she could trust him with the truth. Quinn lifted her face, meeting his gaze head on.

"My mother was raped by three men at a party when she was a teenager. I'm the product of that night." Quinn tried to sound light-hearted, but she could hear the bitterness in her voice. Sylvia might have moved on, but Quinn hadn't. Not yet.

"So, now you have your answer," Colin said. "It was the third man."

"Yes, I suppose it was."

"What will you do now? Will you track him down?" Colin asked.

"To be perfectly honest; I don't know. In theory, I'd like to meet him and possibly get to know him, but given the experience I've had with the first two, I'm not sure that would be wise. Besides, he's not as accessible. He is American."

Colin nodded. "I never knew my father. He left when I was two. I've seen photos, of course, and heard stories, but I never actually saw him after he left."

"Did you never try to find him?" Quinn asked, curious. She would have tried.

"No. I always felt that if my father didn't care enough to maintain a relationship with his children, he didn't deserve us. I saw no reason to hunt him down. My sister tried when she was going through her rebellious stage, but didn't get very far. He left the country shortly after walking out on us. Immigrated to Australia, of all places. He might be dead for all I know."

"Perhaps you have the right attitude. I can't imagine that meeting my birth father will make me happy. The dad who raised me is a wonderful man. I couldn't have asked for a better father."

"Then you are luckier than most."

Quinn was about to reply when Colin's face lit up with a joyful smile. His eyes were on the door of the café, so Quinn turned to see who hijacked Colin's attention from her. A dark-haired man made his way toward their table, a matching smile on his face. The man was wearing scrubs under his coat, and a camouflage cap was pulled low over his face. Quinn noticed the tattoos snaking up his arms as he shrugged off his coat. They started at the wrist and covered his forearms, making him look surprisingly macho.

"This is my partner," Colin said, accepting a warm kiss from his boyfriend and scooting over to make room at the table. "Dr. Quinn Allenby, meet Logan Wyatt."

Quinn and Logan stared at each other, the penny dropping simultaneously. Logan held out his hand, smiling widely and revealing straight white teeth. "A pleasure to meet you at last, sister dear."

Chapter 37

Quinn settled herself on a white leather sofa outside Rhys's office and declined an offer of coffee from his assistant, who informed her that Mr. Morgan was in a meeting and would see her as soon as he was available. The rain outside the plate-glass window still came down in sheets, and it was gloomy, even in the brightly lit office. The PA ignored Quinn while she tapped away at her keyboard and periodically answered the telephone, but Quinn didn't mind. She was in no mood to make small talk. She reached for a well-thumbed magazine, and immediately returned it to the rack, realizing that she had no desire to read. Instead, she looked out the window, barely noticing the hazy skyline of the city as her mind returned to the encounter at the coffeehouse.

Meeting Logan had been a surprise, but it wasn't nearly as awkward as it might have been. Logan didn't miss a beat as he added sugar to his coffee, spread strawberry jam on his scone, and prattled on about the awful weather for a few moments, giving his boyfriend and newly-discovered sister a moment to compose themselves. Despite his fierce tattoos and spiky hair, he was easy-going and entertaining, a man who was clearly comfortable in his own skin and expected everyone to respond to his charm, which was considerable.

"I just got a new tat last night," he shared as he took a bite of his scone. "And you will be the first to see it, after my honey, of course."

Logan set down his coffee cup, leaned toward Quinn and pulled up the sleeve of his shirt. The skin around the tattoo was reddened and a bit swollen, but the image of a little bear cub was perfectly executed and fit neatly between the older tattoos. Colin blushed furiously and looked into his cup. Logan smiled at his partner and covered his hand with his own larger one.

"It's a tribute to Colin," he explained. "Colin comes from the Gaelic name Cailean, which means little cub. Isn't it sweet?" he joked as he cut his eyes at Colin.

"It is, rather," Quinn agreed. She suddenly wondered how Gabe would react if she got a tattoo of the archangel Gabriel to honor him. He'd probably be shocked, but secretly pleased, depending on where she got it, of course. "Do you have any tattoos, Colin?" Quinn asked.

"No, but I do find them sexy on others," he replied. "Especially on Logan." Quinn smiled at the two of them. They were clearly in love and very comfortable with each other, which was heartwarming to see in an age when many people broke up as soon as they hit a bump in the road.

"How long have you two been together?" Quinn asked, wondering if this was a new relationship or an established one.

"Oh, going on three years now," Logan replied. "You know what they say about doctors and nurses," he said, grinning wickedly. "Shagging in broom cupboards at the hospital, and all that. Actually, Colin and I are moving in together," Logan informed her.

"Just as soon as you tell your mother," Colin cut in.

"Doesn't Sylvia know about you two?" Quinn asked. Sylvia had mentioned that Logan was gay, but perhaps she wasn't as accepting of it as she'd made it sound. It wasn't easy to adjust your expectations of your children and accept their dreams for the future, even when they were already adults.

"She does," Logan said and leaned back in his chair, having finished his breakfast. "I went through a 'girl phase' in my late teens. I thought I'd try on being bisexual. You know, have the best of both worlds, but it just didn't feel right. Mum's still hoping that I might rediscover my love of women. Not that she doesn't love Colin, but she's getting to that age where she's starting to long for grandchildren, and I can't imagine that Jude will oblige any time soon."

"Is he still on tour?" Quinn asked, curious what the other brother was like.

"He'll be back soon. Mum can't wait. He's still her baby boy. Of course, now there are new possibilities for satisfying her granny lust." Logan smiled seductively at Quinn, his gaze skimming over her engagement ring and making Quinn blush.

"I'm just joking, love. Mum is real excited though. You're all she talks about. I never realized what a gaping hole you left in her life. Shame you didn't find each other sooner."

"We're just getting to know each other," Quinn replied, a little unsettled by the intensity of Logan's gaze.

"Give her a chance," Logan said as he began to gather his things. "She doesn't want to put pressure on you, but she really does long to be a part of your life. Well, gotta dash. Work is calling," he added, the smile back in place. "See you later, little cub… and big sis," he added with an impish grin. He gave Colin a lingering kiss and took off, leaving them to finish their breakfast.

"Logan told me all about his long-lost sister, but I honestly never made the connection," Colin said. "He never mentioned your name, or I would have known immediately. How many Quinns could there be in London?"

"Not many, I should think. What an extraordinary coincidence that Logan and I met like this."

Colin suddenly laughed, rolling his eyes as if he'd finally understood the punch line of a joke. "This wasn't a coincidence at all. That wily rascal," he said, shaking his head. "I told him last night that I had a meeting with Dr. Quinn Allenby. He knew it was you all along."

Quinn smiled. She wasn't sure if Colin was annoyed with his boyfriend for crashing their meeting, but she was glad he had. Meeting Logan had been an unexpected gift, and she suddenly felt more hopeful about her relationship with Sylvia. Perhaps, in time, they could become family after all.

"Dr. Allenby, Mr. Morgan will see you now," Rhys's PA cut across Quinn's thoughts as several exec-types walked out of Rhys's office.

Chapter 38

Quinn gathered her belongings and walked into Rhys's office, ready to face his displeasure. He'd been brusque on the phone, and she expected a full-on bollocking for missing their meeting and not keeping him up to date on her findings. Rhys had a schedule to meet and the functions of various departments to coordinate. Quinn had never realized what went into making a television program, or how many people were actually involved in the production of each episode.

"Nice of you to show up," Rhys said, pushing aside a memo he'd been reading and glaring at Quinn across his ultra-modern desk. "Scotland, was it? You could have given us a heads-up."

"Rhys, I already told you; it was a personal matter of great urgency. And that's all I'm willing to give you. Do what you will," Quinn challenged him. Her attitude had the desired effect on Rhys, whose bark was worse than his bite.

"Have a seat," he said and extracted a plastic container from the drawer of his desk. He pushed it toward Quinn with an air of someone making a peace offering. "Have a madeleine," he said, his expression sheepish. Rhys enjoyed baking, and did it often and well.

"That's a lot of madeleines," Quinn observed as she took one to be polite. She was still full, but to refuse would have been churlish. Rhys took his hobby very seriously. The container held at least two dozen golden, shell-shaped biscuits.

"I was stressed," Rhys replied. "Anyhow, let's make a start. I have an appointment in half an hour." Rhys looked furtive for a moment, but Quinn paid him no mind. Whom he met with was none of her concern. She'd really liked him once, but since finding out about his role in Sylvia's life, she scaled their interaction to a minimum, keeping things as impersonal as possible. When sitting across from Rhys, it was hard to forget that he might have been her father.

"Right. We are due to start filming the first episode next week. I'll have my PA forward you a schedule. Now, what have you got for me on this new case?"

"Not much," Quinn countered, annoyed by Rhys's demanding tone. Quinn had every intention of telling Petra's story, but she would do it on her own terms, and when she was ready.

"Come now, you must have something for me. It's a fascinating business. Is it not?" he asked, his voice now silky and cajoling.

"Rhys, at this stage we are dealing with pure conjecture. According to Dr. Scott, our victims were mother and son, who died of blunt force trauma to the head. They were buried on the fringes of a leper cemetery, face down as a sign of disrespect. Their remains date back to early- to mid-fourteenth century, and those are the only hard facts we have."

"Have you been able to locate any parish records?" Rhys asked. Quinn's eyebrows lifted in surprise, and Rhys smiled and shook his head, instantly realizing the futility of his question.

"There *are* no parish records. Were you hoping I'd go deep-sea diving and see what I can salvage from a church that was claimed by the sea six hundred years ago?" Quinn asked.

"Sarcasm doesn't become you," Rhys retorted and reached for a biscuit. He leaned back in his chair and chewed thoughtfully as he considered the situation. "Actually, that's perfect."

"Is it?"

"There's not a shred of evidence as to who these people were or why they died. Any story we decide to tell is as valid as any other. Since there are no records, no one can disprove our version of events, and I know that our version will be the truth, won't it?" he asked, watching Quinn intently. "Come now. What have you seen, Quinn?"

Quinn sighed with resignation. Telling Rhys about her gift seemed like a good idea at the time, but now she wished she'd kept it to herself. Rhys had every intention of exploiting her to get his story, and nothing would stand in his way. Rhys Morgan gave the phrase 'creative license' a whole new meaning.

"The cross I found belonged to a young woman named Petra Ordell. She was a widow with three children, the oldest being a boy named Edwin. Edwin suffered from debilitating seizures which seemed to be brought on by stress. He might have been epileptic, but I can't say for sure. That's all I know so far."

Rhys looked disappointed, but tried to make the best of the situation. "Well, I'm sure something of interest will crop up. This Petra didn't get herself buried face down in the dirt by being a model citizen. So, the child was her son?"

"It would seem so," Quinn replied. She had no desire to tell Rhys about Petra's relationship with Avery or the details of Edwin's true parentage. She needed to know more, but her stomach twisted with anxiety every time she thought of what awaited Petra and Edwin. They were ordinary people, the type of individuals who rarely made a mark on history, their lives of interest only to their descendants. What happened to them, and why had they been punished even in death?

"I'll keep you posted," Quinn said as she sprang to her feet, eager to put an end to the conversation. Rhys hadn't asked about the silver necklace found at the site, and Quinn saw no reason to bring it up. She had yet to unlock its secrets, so there was nothing to tell.

"Wait, what happened with Chatham?" Rhys asked as he rose to his feet and reached for his coat. His next meeting clearly wasn't at the office.

"Not a match."

"Did you speak to him? What did you make of him?" Rhys asked, his curiosity getting the better of him.

"I thought he was a right old wanker, if you must know. A bully and a misogynist. Nice company you keep."

"Come now, I haven't spoken to the man since I was a teenager. Are you ever going to let me live this down?" Rhys asked, his expression petulant.

"Probably not," Quinn replied, but without genuine heat. Continuing to stay angry with Rhys was pointless and counter-productive. "What can you tell me about Seth Besson?"

"Absolutely nothing. He was a friend of Robert's. I'd only met him a few times. Have you searched for him online?"

"Not yet. I'm doing one potential dad at a time," Quinn joked, but the truth was that she wasn't ready to face the man who'd fathered her. She needed time.

"If there's anything I can do to help," Rhys offered without any enthusiasm. "Come, I'll walk with you to the lift."

"Thanks, I'll let you know," Quinn replied as she followed Rhys out of his office toward the bank of elevators.

"Quinn, I'm meeting Sylvia," Rhys suddenly blurted out. "She's finally agreed to see me."

Quinn nodded, unsure of what to say. She wouldn't tell Rhys this, but she had a newfound respect for him. Facing a woman you raped three decades ago was not for the faint of heart, and Rhys deserved some credit for taking that step toward forgiveness.

"Good luck," Quinn said and meant it.

Chapter 39

Quinn stopped in the lobby, rummaged in her handbag for her Oyster card, which still had enough of a balance for several tube rides, and stepped out into the overcast morning. The rain had slowed down to a drizzle, but it was cold and damp, and a chill wind blew off the river. Quinn huddled into her coat and began to walk down the street toward the nearest tube station. She had to get home; there was much to be done. Gabe had dismantled his office and cleared the room, but they still had to paint it before the furniture arrived in two days' time. More importantly, they needed to find a suitable nursery school before bringing Emma to London. There was a stack of brochures on the counter waiting to be perused. At least now they had an idea of what to look for.

Gabe invited Pete and Brenda McGann round for dinner the night before. Pete was Gabe's best friend from university days, and Quinn knew and liked the McGanns. They were kind, down-to-earth people, who didn't act shocked or judge Gabe for fathering a child out of wedlock, despite their staunch Catholic views. Instead, they instantly offered help, in whatever form it was needed. Quinn hadn't had much time to cook, so they got a takeaway and a couple of bottles of wine, opting for a relaxing evening that required no serving or clearing up. After dinner, Pete helped Gabe take apart the furniture, and Brenda sat with Quinn on the sofa and answered her ever-growing list of questions. The McGanns had two teenage boys, and Brenda was the only close friend who had any knowledge of raising children in London, where the choices were numerous and overwhelming.

"So, what do I look for in a nursery school, Brenda?" Quinn had asked. "Besides the obvious, I mean."

"Make an appointment to see the school. Of course, they will tell you only positive things and steer you toward what they want you to see, but don't be shy. See how clean the toilets are; that's always a good indicator of how sanitary the place is. Ask about the ratio of teachers to students, and inquire about their security measures and response time to an emergency. Do they have a nurse on the premises? Are parents allowed inside?" Brenda added as an afterthought.

"Why is that important?"

"It's much safer when parents are not allowed on the premises and meet their children by the gate. This way no strangers are ever in the building, and everyone is accounted for. There are always cases of custody disputes, and at times abuse, and it's best to keep those issues out of the schoolroom and let the individuals and the courts deal with them. There have been cases of parents kidnapping their own children or even their children's friends. People don't think rationally when they are under great strain."

"I see," Quinn said, pondering this. "That would never have crossed my mind."

"And it shouldn't, but we live in strange times, when people seem to snap all too easily. You'll be amazed at what you'll have to consider as Emma gets older. Becoming a parent changes your life inside out. You have to know where your child is and with whom at all times. Never take anyone's word for it. There are too many cases of children being snatched off the street or from the park, and sometimes even from their homes. You must be vigilant, Quinn."

"Now you're scaring me," Quinn said. Emma was so trusting, so sweet. She'd had reservations about leaving Edinburgh with Gabe and Quinn, but accepted the situation because adults she trusted told her that she must. What if someone tried to steer her wrong or lure her away?

"I don't mean to scare you, but you need to understand the reality of the dangers around you. My boys are teenagers, but I still worry all the time. There are so many negative influences out there and situations we have no control over."

"It must be easier with boys," Quinn said, thinking of all the things that could happen to a little girl, especially in this age of child trafficking and sexual predators.

"You would think that, but that's not necessarily the case. Nowadays, boys are just as vulnerable as girls. If a girl makes an accusation of sexual assault, whether it actually happened or not, the boy is guilty until proven innocent, not the other way around. Many girls cry foul because they can. It's a very effective way to hurt someone who rejected them, and it's difficult to prove that it was consensual if intercourse took place. I worry about my boys all the time. They don't understand how underhanded some girls can be. In the old days, girls trapped boys into marriage. Today they just send them to prison."

"That's an awfully grim view," Quinn said, wondering if Brenda was being a bit biased, having only boys. Her birth mother never sent anyone to prison, when she should have. Girls were just as vulnerable, if not more so, because it was equally difficult to prove that an assault had taken place instead of a consensual act.

"It is, but it's the grim reality of the Internet Age. Kids don't realize how much ammunition can be gathered against them from social sites. They post inappropriate pictures, make careless comments, and engage in cyber-stalking and bullying. Sometimes things get out of control."

"Thank God Emma is only four," Quinn breathed. "I'm utterly unprepared for the world of parenthood."

"Neither am I, and I've been a parent for sixteen years," Brenda sighed. "Things were so different in my day. Today, kids hook up before they even ask each other's name. Sex is casual and frequent. Many kids have dozens of partners before they even leave school," Brenda said bitterly. "Sometimes, I honestly can't wait for my boys to go off to university. I just can't handle the pressure of having two teenagers with raging hormones in the house."

"Does Pete feel the same way?" Quinn asked carefully.

"He doesn't really talk about it, but he worries. We were each other's first, you know," Brenda added with a sad smile. "We were such innocents."

It was only after the McGanns left and Quinn and Gabe had gone to bed that night that Brenda's comments finally made sense.

"They're going through a difficult time with Michael," Gabe said after Quinn shared with him what Brenda had said. "He got involved with a girl at the start of term. They were happy for a few weeks, but then Michael started to lose interest. The girl got her feelings hurt and accused Michael of assaulting her. She's since taken the accusation back, admitting that she only did it to hurt him, but Brenda and Pete have been to Hell and back. And it damaged their relationship with their son, since they had to keep asking him point blank if he'd done anything that might be construed as an assault."

"You can't blame them for asking. Can you?"

"No. Nor can you blame Michael for being upset. It's taken a toll on everyone. Michael is angry and silent these days, hurt that his parents didn't support him when he needed them most. He wants to switch schools and then join the military immediately after graduation, but Pete and Brenda hope they can still talk him out of it. Pete is riddled with guilt, and Brenda is angry. She's not a woman who deals well with having no control over a situation."

"We really are woefully unprepared, aren't we?" Quinn asked as she snuggled closer to Gabe.

"We'll get there," Gabe replied. "One thing at a time. Was Brenda helpful about the nursery school?"

"Yes, very. I have a list of things to look for, and a list of things to avoid."

"Then we are already ahead of the game," Gabe muttered as he began to drift off.

"Right," Quinn agreed, but she wasn't convinced. She hadn't asked for any of this, and after her conversation with Brenda, she felt more unprepared than ever.

Chapter 40

Quinn was just about to go down into the station when her mobile rang. It was her cousin Jill, and Quinn felt a pang of guilt as she stared at the caller ID. She hadn't been in touch with Jill since sending her a text on New Year's Day, wishing her a Happy New Year and announcing the engagement. Jill was Quinn's closest friend, and the only person besides her parents and Gabe in whom she confided, but lately Quinn just didn't feel like talking. After finding out about the night she'd been conceived, Quinn found herself turning inward, as if not telling anyone might retroactively change what happened. She had told Jill, of course, but had no wish to keep returning to the subject, not until she was in possession of new facts.

Quinn had finally worked up the courage to tell her parents about Sylvia a few weeks ago, but they hadn't been ready to discuss the news until they'd had some time to deal with the shock. Quinn understood. This was the call they never expected to receive since Quinn had been found in a church pew when she was only a few days old and turned over to social services until an adoption could be arranged. Since no one knew who Quinn's birth parents might be, there was no danger of Quinn ever tracking them down. An extraordinary chain of events led Sylvia to Quinn a few months back, and now Quinn knew, and understood, why Sylvia chose to give her up, but she still had to lay out the facts for her parents.

The conversation had gone much as Quinn anticipated. Susan and Roger Allenby loved her too much not to feel outraged on her behalf and eager to soothe the hurt, which allowed them to vent their anger, but left Quinn feeling upset and unsettled. She saw their point of view only too well. They wished they could turn back the clock and prevent Sylvia from showing up on Quinn's doorstep. It was always better to cherish a dream than be faced with the reality, which was sometimes unexpected and cruel, and Sylvia's version of events was just that.

"Darling, we will support you in whatever you decide to do," Roger said when he managed to get a word in edgewise.

"Quinn, you don't owe this woman anything," her mother cut in. "She found you by chance. It's not as if she was even searching for you. And to think that your father…" She sucked in her breath, still unable to accept the truth. "Please, let this go. Can't we be enough?"

"Mum, you and Dad are enough, and always have been, but I need to know where I come from. I'm a historian. I spend my life uncovering people's stories. How can I not know mine?"

"Sue, she needs to do this," Roger Allenby said. "She'll never rest until she finds out. And the sooner she does, the sooner she can put this behind her and move forward with her life. Isn't that right, sweetheart?"

"Yes, Dad," Quinn said, grateful for his understanding. He had always been the more open-minded of the two, although Quinn knew that her mother's stubbornness was born of a fierce love for her, and the desire to protect her from pain.

"Please tell me this woman will not be invited to the wedding," Sue pleaded. "There will still be a wedding. Won't there?"

"Yes, Mum," Quinn said gently. "There will be a wedding, and I would like to invite Sylvia. She's no threat to you. Just think of her as another guest."

"As if I could. The thought of her there…"

"Mum, Sylvia has two sons. I'm going to invite them as well."

"Must you?"

"They are my half-brothers."

Quinn heard the sharp intake of breath, followed by a loaded silence from her mother, who was no doubt rummaging in her pocket for a tissue. She felt betrayed, which was exactly what Quinn had feared all along. How could she explain to her parents what it meant to her to have siblings after all these years? It was a dream come true, a fantasy come to life. She'd prayed for siblings when she was little, asking God to bring her a brother or a sister in lieu of birthday or Christmas presents. She wouldn't mind sharing her parents with a baby, she'd assured God. She would be good, and helpful, and loving. It was her dearest wish to be a big sister. But, there was never a baby. Her mother was infertile, a word Quinn didn't understand until much later, and the Allenbys didn't have the financial resources to go through another adoption. Quinn was destined to be an only child. She had Jill; that was true. Jill was her honorary sister and closest friend, but it wasn't the same, since they weren't biologically connected in any way.

"We look forward to meeting them. Don't we, Sue?" Roger said, his tone gentle, but full of warning. He rarely got between Quinn and Susan when they disagreed, but he realized that this situation would require serious diplomatic negotiation, especially once the wedding drew nearer. "Now, tell us about Emma," Roger invited.

Quinn ignored the sniffle that came over the line. Her mother hadn't taken the news well, but to her, Gabe having a child was still the lesser of two evils. Of course, that hadn't stopped her from expressing her opinion about men who indulged in casual sex with women they barely knew and didn't prevent her from voicing her disappointment with her future son-in-law, who would have to work very hard to get back into her good graces.

"Lord only knows how many more children there might be," Susan said dramatically. "I hope you know what you're getting into, Quinn."

"Mum, Gabe is hardly a serial lothario who's had a string of meaningless affairs. I trust him."

"So you say," Susan countered. "You trusted Luke as well. And look how that turned out."

Quinn groaned. "Mum, I don't want to talk about Luke."

"Neither do I," Roger said firmly. "You were about to tell us about Emma."

"Oh, she's lovely, Dad. She's so sweet and funny, and she looks just like Gabe."

"Hmm," her mother interjected, still sniffling.

"She's lucky that she will have you for a mum," Roger said.
"How's Gabe handling fatherhood?"

"Like most new fathers. He alternates between joy and panic, with panic prevailing," Quinn joked.

"To think that he never even knew about her," Susan said, joining the conversation again. "I can understand a woman depriving her child of a father because he's a danger to her, but Gabe was hardly a threat. She must have been very selfish, this Jenna," Susan added.

"Let's not speak ill of the dead, Sue," Roger suggested. "Gabe's a good man, Quinn. Please, don't hold this against him.

He might not have planned this, but life has its own plan, and he's taking responsibility, which is all that matters. So many men wouldn't."

"Gabe is so in love with his child, Dad. He grieves the time he missed with her, but he will be the best father Emma could have wished for."

"I've no doubt he will be," Roger agreed.

"So, when can we meet our granddaughter?" Sue asked, her voice no longer laced with the bitterness of a few moments ago. Quinn smiled. At least this portion of her news didn't cause a nuclear meltdown, at least not a full-blown one.

"As soon as you return to England. I'd like your help planning the wedding, Mum."

"Try and stop me. You are my only daughter, and I will be a mumzilla of gigantic proportions." Quinn chuckled. Clearly, someone had been watching American reality programs.

"Looking forward to it. You will have to fight Phoebe for the privilege. She's already making plans. You two can go head to head," Quinn joked.

"Will Emma be a flower girl?" Sue asked. "Oh, she will look lovely walking down the aisle with her basket of petals."

"Emma would like to be a bride's maid," Quinn replied. "She was quite clear. She said that being flower girls is for babies."

"Clever girl," Roger said. "I like her already."

"Have you set a date?" Sue asked, moving on to practicalities.

"It'll be this summer, but we don't have an actual date yet. We have yet to decide where we want the wedding to be."

"I thought it'd be in London. And we'll have the reception at a nice hotel," Sue said, adopting her newly-acquired mumzilla voice. "Quinn, you must set a date and book something as soon as possible. All the best places get booked years in advance."

"Gabe's parents have a beautiful garden. I thought it might be nice to put up a tent and have a reception there after we get married at the local church."

"Darling, this is England we are talking about," her mother retorted. "Chances are it will rain."

"Sue, don't you have your book club meeting to get to?" Roger asked. Quinn could hear the amusement in his voice.

"Hmm? What? Oh, yes. Sorry. We'll talk about this later."

"I've no doubt we will," Quinn replied as her mother hung up her extension.

"I have to go too, Dad. Nice save, by the way. I'll talk to you tomorrow."

"Anytime, love."

**

Quinn pressed the answer button on her mobile. She really wasn't in the mood to talk and briefly considered sending the call to voicemail, but guilt won out. "Jill, hi."

"Hello," Jill replied. Quinn could hear the hurt in her voice and tried to diffuse the awkwardness by jumping right in.

"I'm sorry. I know I haven't called, but something's come up." Quinn inwardly cringed at her choice of words. In the past, had something come up, she would have called Jill right away to discuss the situation, but things had changed, at least for her.

"Can you come over?" Jill asked. Her voice sounded small and desperate. "I know you must be very busy, but I need someone to talk to."

"Are you all right?"

"I've been better," Jill replied. "Oh, and if it's not too much trouble, bring a bottle of Malbec. Or two."

"I'm on my way."

Quinn sent a quick text to Gabe to tell him that she'd be home in a few hours, dropped the phone into her handbag, and descended into the station. Jill sounded very upset, and it was only while Quinn paced the platform as she waited for the train that she realized that it was Friday, and Jill wasn't at work. Jill loved her vintage clothing shop in SoHo and never took time off, primarily because she ran the business single-handedly. Jill had given up a lucrative career in forensic accounting to follow her dream, and had been very content with her life the last time Quinn visited her back in November. She had a new boyfriend, and the shop seemed to be doing well. What could have happened since they last spoke?

Of course, much could change in the life of an unmarried thirty-something small business owner in two months. Quinn briefly reflected on her new venture with the BBC and the breakup from Luke, which happened by text, and was later followed by the revelation that her partner of eight years was already in a relationship and making plans for the future with someone else. Luckily for her, things had worked out for the best, but that wasn't always the case. Jill was sensible and insightful when it came to the choices of others, but she was something of a hothead when it came to dealing with her own life. She was surprisingly impulsive for a woman who used to spend her days crunching numbers, but her decision to quit her job, invest every penny she'd saved in a new business, and turn down a proposal of marriage from her long-term boyfriend had still come as a surprise to those who knew her, especially her parents, who'd spewed dire warnings about decisions made in haste. Quinn hoped that whatever happened could be easily resolved with a cozy chat and a few glasses of wine. Jill had always been supportive when Quinn needed her, and Quinn had every intention of being there for her best friend, no matter what crisis Jill was facing.

Quinn picked up two bottles of wine at the off-license shop on the corner and walked up to Jill's flat on the third floor. The apartment was small, but fashionably decorated with eclectic pieces of furniture and Eastern-inspired accents. Jill referred to her style as 'shabby chic.' Jill herself looked shabby, but not particularly chic. She was wearing an oversized jersey and leggings, and her hair looked unkempt and unwashed. Her face was devoid of any makeup, a sign in itself that something was wrong, and her feet were attired in strange fuzzy socks in an alarming shade of magenta.

Jill plopped herself down on the sofa after letting Quinn into the flat and thrust out her chin in the direction of the kitchen, silently inviting Quinn to get wine glasses and a corkscrew. Jill swallowed half a glass of wine in one gulp, then set it down and turned her red-rimmed eyes on Quinn. Her fingers plucked nervously at the Indian throw-pillow she hugged to her body like a life-preserver.

"Jill, what's happened? Why aren't you at work?" Quinn asked, imagining every conceivable tragedy.

Jill shrugged. "I just couldn't face it today."

"Is something wrong at the shop, or with Brian?"

"Yes and yes," Jill said as tears filled her eyes. "Oh Quinn, everything has gone wrong so quickly. I was really happy. Finally, I was doing something I loved, and I thought I'd found a new love in Brian. We were getting on so well. And then it all went tits-up, as Brian likes to say."

"Why don't you tell me what happened," Quinn invited as she set down her own wine glass. She normally liked Malbec, but the wine made her feel queasy. Perhaps she should have eaten something before drinking. She hadn't had anything since the madeleines Rhys made, and it was well past lunchtime.

"I must close the shop," Jill replied, sounding broken. "I've tried, I've really tried to keep it going, but I simply can't continue hemorrhaging money. I get about a dozen walk-ins during any given day, and maybe one of them, two if I'm really lucky, make a purchase. There are days when I sell nothing at all. Business picked up a bit just before Christmas, so I got my hopes up, but it's been practically nonexistent for the past two months. I'm seriously in the red, Quinn."

"Is there nothing to be done?" Quinn asked. She knew what this meant to Jill. She'd been so happy when she quit her job and threw herself into setting up her business. And now, less than a year later, she was talking about chucking it all in. "Can you not advertise, utilize social media?" Quinn asked, knowing the answer already. Advertising cost a lot and didn't necessarily bring in customers. Jill catered to a particular type of customer, women who liked vintage and one-of-a-kind pieces, not mass-produced ready-to-wears peddled by all the major chains and priced to sell.

Jill shook her head. "I can't compete, Quinn. I'm spending way more than I'm earning, and if I stay open for a few more months, I will get heavily into debt. I'm an accountant, for the love of God. I can't allow that to happen. I made a bad decision. I miscalculated, and now I'm paying the price."

Quinn poured Jill more wine and sat back, thinking. There was something niggling at her, but she couldn't quite remember what it was. Something she'd read. Quinn took a sip of her wine and closed her eyes, trying to envision what it was she was trying to recapture, but nothing came to her.

"And what happened with Brian?"

Jill's fingers started plucking at the pillow again, pulling out bright red threads and tossing them to the floor, which was already littered with colorful fibers.

"Things were good. At least I thought they were. And then I found out that his ex has been stalking him on social media. I don't go online much, but with business being so slow, I started spending more time on Facebook, searching for groups where I might promote for free. I never knew how many groups there were," Jill said, shaking her head in wonder. "There are so many devoted just to Victoriana. I've joined several and posted some photos of my merchandise. A lot of people responded, but many of them are not actually based in London, so no joy."

"And the ex," Quinn prompted.

"She started commenting on all of Brian's posts and sending him daily messages, asking him to come round. Seems that she's no longer keen on the bloke she left Brian for. He appears to have a wife and two children that he forgot to mention for nearly a year."

"Yes, that would put a damper on the proceedings," Quinn replied, disgusted. She couldn't help thinking of Luke, who most likely forgot to mention that he'd been living with Quinn for the past few years to his new love, Ashley, until he was sure that he wanted to pursue a future with her and give up Quinn. "What a wanker."

"He is, and it did. I confronted Brian last week, and we had a blazing row. I accused him of wanting to get back with Denise and stringing me along until he knows for sure that things are back on between them."

"And does he want to get back with her?"

"He claims that he doesn't, and that he never replied to any of her messages, but I don't really know. Do I? He could have gone to her flat if he wanted to, and I wouldn't be any the wiser. What bloke can resist a woman who's gagging for him? He's probably shagging her right now," Jill added dramatically.

"What exactly did he say?" Quinn asked, suddenly feeling sympathetic toward Brian. Jill was being a bit irrational, even for Jill.

"Other than that I'm controlling, mistrustful, and generally insane? He said he loves me and would never go back to Denise, not even if things didn't work out between us."

"But you don't believe him? Has he given you reason to doubt him?"

Jill started crying softly, and buried her face in the much-abused pillow. "No, he hasn't, but I was so upset about the shop and so stressed about my financial losses that I took it out on him. I haven't heard from him since."

"Has he heard from you?" Quinn asked carefully.

"No. Complete radio silence."

"Do you think you might want to shoot him a text? Tell him you'd like to talk."

"Why should I, when he hasn't reached out to me? I'm the injured party here," Jill retorted, tossing the pillow angrily across the room and splashing the rest of the wine into her glass.

"Jill, if you love Brian, then give him the benefit of the doubt. You are the one who accused him of cheating and lying. If you think he is, then grieve and move on, but if you think that he really does love you and wants a future with you, then you are making a mistake. Text him, call him, send a carrier pigeon. Whatever. Just make the first move. Talk things out. Clear the air. It's never too late to end a relationship, but it might be too late to salvage one. I bet he's desperate to hear from you."

"Do you really think so?"

"I do. Here," Quinn picked up Jill's mobile off the coffee table and handed it to her. "Do it now, before you change your mind."

"Oh, all right," Jill mumbled and began to type. "I asked him if he'd like to meet for a drink tonight. Nice and neutral."

"Good girl. Now, there's something I just thought of." The elusive idea that Quinn had been chasing a few minutes ago finally crystallized in her mind since she was no longer trying so hard to grasp at it.

"Jill, I read something a few weeks ago. A small blurb online, really. It talked of how a dress worn by Kate Middleton sold out in days after she was photographed wearing it to a charity event."

"So?" Jill asked, gazing at Quinn in confusion.

"So, that's what women want. They want to look like a princess. Kate has a very particular style, and every time she wears something, it flies off the racks, no matter the cost. If you want to remain in business, you have to cater to a different type of customer. I know you love the vintage pieces, but that's not what the general public desires. You must reinvent yourself in order to survive."

Jill took a gulp of wine and looked at Quinn, her eyes brightening. "You know, you might be onto something there. I tend to think that women want unique, timeless pieces, but marketing trends say otherwise. They obviously prefer to fit in rather than stand out. They might admire an Edwardian frock or a beaded flapper dress in a magazine, but would never actually splurge on one, thinking they'd have no occasion to wear it. They want practical, classic garments that make them feel like royalty. Who would have thought?"

Quinn smiled. "Things never work out quite as you expect them to, do they? But you can still offer vintage dresses and accessories as long as you also invest in more practical stock. You have a good location, and high potential for foot traffic. All you need are some high-profile items that will draw the more conservative shoppers in."

"I reckon it's worth a try. I will contact some of the manufacturers of Kate's dresses on Monday. They're probably swamped with orders, but I can hang on for a few more weeks, maybe even as long as two months."

"You said there was some interest on Facebook. Why not create a website and offer an online catalogue? Or post some of your merchandise on Pinterest, especially the vintage jewelry. Some of those pieces are stunning and quite eye-catching. You might have to hire someone to set up the website for you, but if you get some online orders, the website design will pay for itself."

"You know, for an archeologist, you have a pretty keen business mind," Jill replied, finally smiling.

"You'd be amazed at how enterprising our ancestors were when it came to selling their wares. Modern-day people didn't invent commerce, we simply took it to cyberspace, which is the biggest marketplace of all these days. Use it to your advantage."

"It honestly never occurred to me. I guess I'm not as business savvy as I imagined myself to be. Oh," Jill said as her mobile buzzed. "It's from Brian."

Jill's face split into a happy smile. "He says that he blocked Denise from all his accounts. He sent her a message telling her that it's over, and he wants nothing more to do with her. He is asking if he can pick up a take-away and come round tonight. You know what that means. Make-up sex," Jill said, her hand instantly going to her greasy hair. "I need a bath."

"I'll leave you to it then. I have to get back."

"Wait, have you set a date?" Jill asked, her mind already on the question Quinn had yet to ask. "Have you chosen your bridal party?"

"Jill, there is only one person I want by my side when I marry Gabe, but the wedding is currently on hold."

"What? Why? Did you two fall out?"

"No, but you're not the only one who must reinvent herself to survive. Gabe and I went to Scotland just after the New Year."

"Why? What's in Scotland?"

"Gabe's daughter."

Jill forgot all about her hair and stared at Quinn, her eyes round with surprise. "Gabe has a daughter? And he never told you?"

"He didn't know. Emma's mother was killed in a car crash on New Year's Eve. She left instructions in her will to contact Gabe in case anything ever happened to her."

"Oh dear," Jill breathed. "So, Gabe now has full custody?"

"Yes. We went from being friends to getting engaged to becoming parents within a space of two months. To be honest, I'm reeling. Emma is lovely, but I'm still coming to terms with the idea of being her mother. It all happened so suddenly."

"Blimey," Jill said. "Your problems are much bigger than mine."

"You don't know the half of it," Quinn replied. "I think I know who my father is."

"How?"

Quinn shook her head in disgust. "Let's just say that I was able to obtain DNA from the second candidate. He's not a match, thankfully. So, that leaves only the American – Seth Besson."

"And you are going to hunt him down," Jill said, a mischievous smile lighting up her pale face. "I almost feel sorry for the man."

"There's a part of me that wants to meet him, to see the kind of person he turned out to be. I need to know that the man who fathered me is not a monster, but rather someone who made a terrible mistake that he regrets. But after meeting Robert Chatham,

I realize that might not be the case. He might be an arrogant, self-satisfied ass who hasn't given the girl whose life he ruined a second thought. I'm not sure I can live with that, Jill."

"Either way, you won't rest until you find out," Jill said, hitting the nail on the head. "You've come this far; you can't stop now. We don't get to choose our parents, Quinny. Plenty of people have fathers they don't love or respect. Just look at the news. Not a day goes by that you don't hear about some unfortunate child being abused by the person they trust most in the world. Becoming a parent is not synonymous with becoming a saint, it's not even synonymous with becoming a decent human being."

Quinn nodded. "You're right, but it's still terribly disappointing to know that you come from someone whom you can't respect, or even like."

"I know, but since you won't just abandon this, you have to let the chips fall where they may."

"That I do," Quinn replied as she got up to leave. Jill sprang to her feet as well, and wrapped her arms around Quinn. "Thank you," she whispered. "For everything. This morning my life was a train wreck, but now everything's changed. It might still come to nothing, but you have shown me a way to regain control, and for that, I'm truly grateful. What happens now is up to me."

"And up to me," Quinn agreed, secretly wondering if it was. Her beloved Grandma Ruth used to say, "We have no control over what happens to us, but we can control how we deal with it." What happened in the next few months would sorely test that theory.

Chapter 41

February, 1347

Dunwich, Suffolk

Edwin tried not to gawk as he followed Friar William, who instead of walking at a sedate pace, as Edwin would expect a monk to do, practically sprinted down the vaulted corridor. Edwin had seen Greyfriars from a distance and knew that the clifftop priory was vast, but now that he was inside, he'd realized exactly how extensive it was. The church alone took his breath away. It was bigger than any church in Dunwich, with rows of tall, arched windows. The diamond-shaped panes were arranged in an alternating pattern of blue, green, and red, and the morning sunlight that streamed through the windows cast a rainbow of color onto the flagstones beneath his feet.

The ceiling soared toward the heavens, carrying the prayers of the devout to the rafters and possibly straight up to God. Even the merest whisper sounded like a shout, so Edward refrained from saying anything as Friar William showed him the church and just nodded in appreciation. There was a long cloister that ran along all four sides of the inner courtyard and served as a walkway from one building to the other. Friar William pointed out the main features to Edwin as they passed. There was an infirmary, kitchens and refectory, a guest house, and a chapter house. There were also several outbuildings and a barn for the animals. The friars were busy with their morning chores, going about their business in a quiet, efficient manner.

Friar William ushered Edwin into a large, high-ceilinged room inside the chapter house. Here too, the windows were glazed, but the glass was clear, allowing bright light to fill the chamber. Four friars sat at individual workstations, their heads bent over the manuscripts they were working on. The friars looked up as one, nodded in greeting, and continued with their work, too involved in what they were doing to display much curiosity about a boy who gazed about in wonder.

Edwin wasn't sure why Father Avery, whom he'd met after Candlemas, had taken it upon himself to help him. Father Avery had come to their house for Sunday dinner just over a week ago. His mother fussed more than usual, and even purchased a good cut of pork, which she boiled with peas and onions and served with mashed turnips. Grandmother Maude scolded Petra, her anger incomprehensible to the children, who salivated with hunger as the divine smell filled their small house. They'd been sent up to the loft, so as not to be underfoot, but they could still hear the hissed argument between their mother and grandmother as they awaited the arrival of Father Avery.

"That pork was too dear," Maude complained, when she found out how much Petra had spent. "You are not a lady yet, so don't go getting ideas above your station. You had your chance to settle matters, but you passed it up. Again. I don't know how a daughter of mine can be so foolhardy. And now you've invited that priest into our house."

Edwin and his sisters exchanged glances, but knew better than to comment, even between themselves, for fear of being overheard. They hadn't had pork since their father was alive, so if their mother got it into her head that she wished to carry on as a lady, and they got a nice, thick slice of meat for their dinner, they would not be the ones to complain.

"I don't like this scheme of yours, Petra," Maude continued. "Why involve the priest, when all you have to do is ask Lord Thomas to find a place for our Edwin? He'd keep him out of harm's way. He's proven that at the fair."

"Mother, it's never too late for Edwin to become a pack-whacker. Any daft fool can lead a donkey or load sacks of fleece onto a cart. I want better for my son. Edwin is smart, and has some learning. He can have a position of respect and a skill that will serve him throughout his days. If Thomas dies, Lord Robert will be under no obligation to me or my children, and Edwin might find himself without an income or a roof over his head. Father Avery can offer him a future, whereas Thomas can only provide him with temporary employment. Edwin is not his son, so will never attain an important position, not when Robert has sons to take over the business."

"I suppose there is logic to your argument, but I worry, Petra. It's a risk."

"I know, Mother, but Edwin is getting older, and something must be done. And it's up to me to see him settled in an occupation that will provide for him. Besides, as long as he remains calm, there's naught to fear, and what can be more calming than copying letters?"

"What occupation?" Elia mouthed.

Edwin shrugged. He wasn't sure what his mother had in mind, but he had no wish to become a friar. He'd rather run off and join the crew of a ship. Come spring, there would be many more ships in the harbor, so someone was bound to take him on. He could sail off to Flanders or Spain, or even the dark continent of Africa, which Alfric had told him about as they sat around a fire one night roasting a hedgehog. Edwin didn't have any, since his grandmother would say that only heathens would eat such unclean fare, but Alfric swore that it tasted as good as any rabbit. Alfric enjoyed his meat as he spun wild tales about the men of Africa, who had skin as black as ebony and walked around dressed only in loincloths and feathers, with beads hanging around their necks for decoration. Edwin didn't believe a word, even though Alfric swore that his uncle, who'd been a sailor, had visited those distant shores before his ship went down in a storm a year since. The stories passed the time and spurred on Edwin's imagination. There was a whole world out there, a world he would never see if he was locked behind the walls of a monastery or spent his youth leading donkeys loaded with wool.

When Father Avery arrived, Edwin and the girls were presented to him with great ceremony. Father Avery took the time to speak to each one in turn, and treated them as if they were adults, something no one ever did. He was a stern, studious-looking man, who'd recently come down from Oxford, according to his mother, but his face relaxed when he smiled, and his dark eyes held no judgment as he conversed easily with the family, asking questions and regaling them with tales of life in Oxford. His mother seemed to like the priest, and talked to him in a familiar fashion, which seemed to upset his grandmother, whose eyes darted from Father Avery to Edwin in a way that almost made Edwin laugh. What did she expect to see?

Father Avery stayed longer than expected, but no one seemed to mind. The conversation flowed easily, and the hearty meal and spiced wine made everyone feel contented and relaxed. Even Grandmother Maude seemed to enjoy the priest's company, warming up to him despite her earlier reservations. Petra seemed disappointed when he finally rose to his feet and announced that he needed to return to the priory in time for Evensong.

Father Avery said goodbye to each of them in turn, then took Petra's hand, which was unusual for a priest, and bowed over it. "Thank you, Mistress Ordell. It's been many years since I was welcomed into a family as a friend and not a man of the church. This was most pleasant. I hope we might do it again some time."

"You are very welcome, Father. It was our pleasure to have you in our humble home," Petra replied modestly as she walked him to the door.

It wasn't until the remnants of their meal had been cleared away and the crockery washed and dried that Grandmother Maude and the girls finally retired to their beds. Edwin wished them a good night and climbed up to the loft.

"I think I left my lute up here," he said to his mother. It was a small lie, given that his lute was safely beneath his pillow, but he wanted to talk to her privately.

"Mother, why was Father Avery really here?" Edwin asked. He noted his mother's look of surprise, but she smiled up at him and patted the space on her bed, inviting him to sit down.

"Edwin, I knew Avery before he became a priest, which was why I've appealed to him for help. I've asked him to help you get a position as an apprentice scribe."

"I don't want to be a scribe," Edwin replied. "I want to do man's work."

Petra didn't reply. Instead, she put her arm about Edwin and pulled him close, kissing the top of his head as she did when he was little. Edwin felt a flutter of fear in his belly. The incident at the Candlemas Fair brought all his mother's fears out into the open, and now he might be relegated to the priory for the rest of his life, sent to a place where he couldn't do much harm, to himself or others. He should have been more careful and remained on the sidelines during the matches, but he wasn't a cripple, was he? He only wanted to do what any other boy would have done at a fair. He was no longer a child. He was a young man, and he wanted to behave as a man would, and have some say in his own life.

Even Alfric was already preparing for the future. His mother had arranged for an apprenticeship with Master Carney. Alfric was young, but he was big and strong, and the blacksmith, being short of help, was willing to take him on a year earlier. Alfric would serve eight years, instead of the usual seven, working long hours and earning nothing, but at the end of his term, he would become a journeyman and a member of the Guild. He would be a man in every sense of the word, and earn an honest wage, one that would support him and his future family.

"Edwin, Father Avery is a good man and has a mind to help us. Please, don't throw this chance away."

"I will NOT become a friar. You hear me? I'd rather die," Edwin shouted and bolted toward the ladder, leaving his mother staring at him, white-faced and frightened. He yanked off his boots and threw himself face-down on the bed, tears soaking the pillow as he gave in to despair. He hadn't allowed himself to consider what would happen to him, but he could no longer deny the truth.

He'd prayed and prayed, begging the good Lord to cure him and make the affliction go away, but the fit at the fair had been a bad one, and according to his mother, lasted longer than the ones in the past. The rush of fear as he faced his opponent and the burst of aggression he experienced during the fight brought on an attack, and he'd collapsed to the ground, drooling and convulsing for all to see. Edwin thought the Lord had forsaken him, but perhaps he was offering him a way out by bringing him into the fold. Or was he? In either case, the time to decide had come. He'd be twelve come April.

Edwin sat up and angrily wiped his tears. His head throbbed, and his stomach hurt something bad. He needed to go to the privy. Edwin pulled on his shoes and stepped outside. His breath made white puffs in the air as he hurried toward the privy, which was dark and smelly enough to make his eyes water. Edwin felt marginally better after emptying his bowels. The cramps had subsided, and his head cleared somewhat once he was out in the fresh air, looking up at the starry heavens. A three-quarter moon rode high in the sky, its glow bathing the town in a silvery light. There was no one about, but the silence and the sound of the sea in the distance were strangely comforting. Edwin leaned against the wall of the house and gazed at the vast glittering darkness stretching above him. He was cold, but not quite ready to go inside. He knew he wouldn't sleep.

He wasn't angry with his mother, only with the situation. She was doing her best, and he loved her for it. He would tell her in the morning that he would accompany Father Avery to the priory when the time came and thank him kindly. Perhaps accepting your circumstances was part of becoming a man.

**

Edwin mumbled a greeting to the friars and smiled uncertainly as he followed Friar William into the room. This was what he'd really come to see, and now that he was here, his heart gave a leap of apprehension. This could be his life. Forever. But, in truth, it wasn't as awful as he'd expected. His mother was right. A scribe was respected and valued, not to mention comfortable. The scribes were warm and dry, got three meals a day, and each had a cell to call his own. If Edwin became a pack-whacker for Lord Devon, as his grandmother thought he should, he'd spend most of his days out in the open, eating whatever he could get and sleeping rough until he returned home. Also, the wages would be minimal, since any idiot could do the job. Edwin mentally thanked his mother for making him promise that he keep an open mind.

"This is where the manuscripts are copied," Friar William explained, lowering his voice so as not to disturb the friars. "It's delicate, painstaking work that requires great concentration, so the friars work only in the morning, when the light is strongest and they are well rested. They then go on to midday prayer and to dinner at the refectory, after which they proceed to their other, more physical chores."

Friar William motioned for Edwin to follow him toward the back of the room where a long, wooden table occupied most of the wall. "This will be your work area for the time being. You will assist the scribes in whatever they need. Namely, you will make ink and mix paints, replenish the inkwells, sharpen quills, and prepare the gold leaf. You will also measure and cut the vellum to the specifications the scribes give you."

Edwin reached out and carefully touched some of the earthenware jars and glass vials lined up toward the back of the table by the wall. "What are all these?" he asked.

"Those are the various pigments used for mixing the paints. The scribes use many colors, ranging from vermillion to ochre, to woad, and to verdigris. There's also silver and gold, which needs to be hammered into very thin sheets or ground into powder and mixed with egg to produce shell gold."

"What is it used for?" Edwin asked, fascinated.

"The paints are used for the images and the gold and silver for providing an illuminated background. The end result is quite beautiful. Here, let me show you. Come."

Friar William walked toward a row of shelves and lifted a heavy, leather-bound volume, which he carried to an empty desk. He opened it reverently and motioned for Edwin to come closer. Edwin gasped in wonder. The text was written in beautiful, even lines, but the design that bordered the page and the inset image of a saint were like nothing he'd ever seen in his life. The brilliant colors and gold background made the miniature practically leap off the page. Once Edwin looked closer, he saw that it wasn't only the bright colors that made the image so extraordinary; it was the exquisite detail and flawless execution. It was perfect.

"How do they manage it?" Edwin asked, unable to find the proper words to phrase his question.

"It's a long process, my boy, and takes a great deal of precision. You will learn everything in due course, but for now, you will start with the basics. Come, let's not disturb the scribes any longer than necessary."

They came back out into the cloister and then crossed the courtyard toward the massive arch in the stone wall through which he'd come earlier with Father Avery. Edwin hadn't seen the priest since Father Avery introduced him to Friar William and rushed off, but Edwin was sure that they'd meet again soon. Father Avery seemed to have a keen interest in his future, which was odd, but also comforting. God knows, his own father never did. Edwin felt as if a heavy load had been lifted off his shoulders since his father died. It was a disloyal thought, especially in this holy place, but it was the truth. No one ever spoke of it, but Edwin was sure that they all felt the same, except Elia, who'd been closer to their father than anyone else in the family. Edwin glanced up when he realized that Friar William was speaking to him.

"Edwin, since you are not a member of the order, you will continue to live at home. You will arrive in the morning and leave after the midday meal, which is included as part of your apprenticeship. You are, of course, welcome to join us in prayer, and should you decide to join the order, Prior Jacob will be most happy to speak with you. Father Avery has indicated that you are considering dedicating your life to God. No one here will pressure you into making a decision, but we will all tell you, as one, that there's no greater glory than devoting yourself to the Lord and spending one's life in his service. I will see you tomorrow. God be with you," Friar William said as he placed his hand on Edwin's shoulder in a gesture of benediction.

"Tomorrow then," Edwin replied, raising a hand in farewell.

He passed beneath the arch and started back toward town. This part of the road was deserted, since few people came out to Greyfriars Priory on days when the brothers weren't giving out alms. Edwin enjoyed his solitary walk, using the time to mull over what he'd learned. Edwin had envisioned the work of a scribe as tedious and mind-numbing, which it probably was, but seeing that beautiful text made him see their labors in a whole new light. To create something so splendid had to be very gratifying, perhaps even divine. It was certainly more rewarding than sweating in a forge or cutting one's hands to shreds as a carpenter's apprentice. Those beautiful books would remain behind long after the scribes were gone, their legacy to the world surviving for years, maybe even centuries.

Had Edwin been offered this apprenticeship outright, he'd have no reservations, but there was a condition attached to Edwin's tutelage. He had to consider joining the Franciscan order by the time he turned thirteen. The prospect of becoming a friar was enough to make Edwin want to walk into the sea, but seeing the splendor in which the monks lived and worked and experiencing the serene atmosphere of the monastery had been a revelation.

Edwin liked solitude. He wasn't someone who had many friends or longed to spend an evening drinking in a tavern. And now that Alfric was starting his apprenticeship with the blacksmith, he wouldn't have time for Edwin anymore. He'd make friends with the other apprentices, and his life would revolve around the forge, now and forever. Edwin would be left alone, but although he'd miss Alfric, he didn't really mind. Perhaps it was his affliction that set him apart, but he enjoyed his own company. Dwelling and working in a place that encouraged that, but still provided a comfortable living and companionship didn't seem so dire now. Perhaps becoming a friar wasn't as far-fetched of an idea as it had been only that morning.

Edwin stopped and sat down on a fallen log, looking out over the cliff toward the placid sea. It was as still as glass today, the water sparkling in the winter sunshine and stretching as far as the eye could see. It was cold sitting there on the log, but Edwin hardly noticed. He was used to being cold. He closed his eyes and inhaled the brine-scented air, filling his lungs to capacity. He hadn't felt so peaceful in weeks, and it was all thanks to Father Avery. Edwin had no idea why the priest took such an interest in them these days, but whatever motivated him to want to help was much appreciated. A few tasty tidbits appeared on the table on the days when his mother was at home, and there was plenty of firewood to keep them warm.

Grandmother Maude didn't seem pleased by Father Avery's visits, throwing him stealthy looks as he tried to engage Edwin in conversation and teased the girls. Edwin couldn't understand his grandmother's displeasure. Father Avery was a man of God, a priest of the Church. What harm could his presence do? Edwin looked to his mother, who seemed lighter somehow. She even looked younger these days, the groove between her eyebrows gone, and the dead look in her eyes replaced by one of hope and humor. His mother could use a friend, and after today's tour of the priory, it was clear that so could Edwin. He'd refused to come to the priory for nearly two weeks, but his objections had been for nothing.

Edwin got to his feet and began to walk quickly to ward off the chill. He looked forward to returning to the priory tomorrow to begin his training. Sure, he'd be making ink and sharpening quills, but he'd also learn about mixing paints and grinding gold. It was the first step to creating something wonderful, and the prospect made him smile.

Chapter 42

"Mistress Ordell, won't you join us?" Thomas asked as Petra set down a platter of honey-roasted pork on the table. He gave her an expectant look, willing her to agree.

"I have much to do, my lord," Petra replied as she caught a look of disapproval from Lady Blythe.

"Surely it can wait, and you must eat. Come now," he said, patting the chair next to him in invitation. "Nan, set another place," Thomas called out to Nan who'd gone back to the kitchen to get a flagon of wine.

Petra obediently sat down and accepted a slice of pork accompanied by stewed apples. She took a small bite of pork, uncomfortable under Lady Blythe's unwavering gaze. She could almost hear what the old woman was thinking. *You are beneath my son, and there's no place for you in this family. Do the right thing and reject his proposal, or I will make your life a living Hell.*

Petra averted her eyes and stared into her plate, wishing that she'd declined his invitation to dine. Thomas finished his wine and refilled his cup. He had a hearty appetite and ate with relish, oblivious to the undercurrents passing between the two women.

"I hope your trip was a success," Petra said. Thomas had returned only last night and hadn't had the chance to tell her what happened during his travels.

"It was very successful," Lady Blythe interjected. "Thomas talked circles around those dumb farmers. Didn't you, Son?"

Thomas seemed annoyed with his mother, but rearranged his face into an expression of civility and replied. "Yes, it was a success. I was able to retain most of our suppliers, save for two, who thought that selling to Master Nevins this year would be worth the risk. I wished them good fortune in their endeavors, and we parted ways on good terms."

"More the fool, you," Lady Blythe cut in again. "You should have taken them to task, and reminded them how much this family had done for them. Your father lifted those peasants out of abject poverty when he offered them decent prices for their wool and made good on his promise to purchase from them year after year. They owe us not only their livelihoods, but their very lives."

"I think that's overstating it a bit, Mother," Thomas said. "Anyhow, I have no wish to talk business at the dinner table. I've done enough of that during the past three weeks. Mistress Ordell, how is your family? I hear your son is to be apprenticed to the scribes at Greyfriars. What a marvelous opportunity."

"A man should do man's work," Lady Blythe grumbled, her mouth full.

"Not if he can do God's work, Lady Blythe," Petra retorted, thoroughly annoyed with the woman.

"Sharpening quills is God's work now, is it?"

"Well, I've eaten my fill," Thomas said and pushed away his plate. "Mistress Ordell, would you join me for a walk? It's a fine day, and I think my mother is ready for a rest. She seems unusually snappish today. Due to fatigue, no doubt," he added in response to his mother's sharp glance.

"Do not presume to shut me up, boy. I don't pay Mistress Ordell to go prancing about with my son," Lady Blythe countered, but was ignored.

"Come, let's put some color in those cheeks," Thomas said as he took Petra's hand. "Nan, see to my mother until Petra returns," he ordered the servant, not even sparing her a glance.

"I think she hates me," Petra said as Thomas helped her on with her cloak.

"Don't give it another thought," Thomas replied, smiling into her eyes.

Easy for you to say, Petra thought, but smiled back and tied the cloak's strings beneath her chin before accepting Thomas's arm and stepping out into the mild February afternoon. It felt wonderful to be outside during the day. She'd almost forgotten what it was like to be out during the daylight hours. Petra inhaled deeply, enjoying the tang of the sea and the brisk spring air. The normally-gray waters of the North Sea sparkled in the afternoon sunshine, seagulls wheeling overhead as they dove for fish. The docks bustled with activity. Several ships were in the process of being outfitted for the first voyage of the spring, and men called out to each other cheerfully as they went about their business. Several women passed by, chatting easily as they returned from the market, baskets slung over their arms. Some merchants lowered their prices toward the late afternoon, eager to sell off their daily inventory, so many thrifty wives waited until later in the day to do their marketing. The leftover produce and cuts of meat were not as fresh after sitting in the stall since the early hours, but in the colder months, it was safe enough to wait.

Thomas turned Petra away from the center of town and began to walk in the direction of Blackfriars. The street grew less crowded, allowing them to have a private conversation.

"Petra, which church do you attend?" Thomas asked, as they walked past the harbor. He did not take her arm, since that wouldn't be proper, but he walked closer to her than was strictly necessary, inviting the curious looks of passersby.

"St. Leonard's," Petra replied, wondering why he wished to know.

"I thought I might join you for Sunday Mass. Meet your family," he suggested. He was still smiling, but his eyes were anxious, waiting for her to reply.

"If you wish it, Thomas. My mother and children would be honored to make your acquaintance," she replied. This was it. If she refused to allow him to come to Mass and meet her family, he'd take it as a rejection of his proposal, leaving her at the mercy of Lady Blythe, who would instantly dismiss her and probably spread the word that she'd stolen something, or gave offense in some other way, therefore preventing anyone else from giving her honest employment.

"I've asked my mother to accompany me on Sunday. That's how hopeful I was that you wouldn't object," he said, grinning broadly. "I'd even offered to hire a litter for her, since it's too far to walk."

Petra smiled. "I fear to ask what her reaction was. She's very openly against our union."

"I am perfectly capable of using my legs," Thomas said, doing a credible impersonation of his mother. "And, why should I attend a different church after decades of praying at St. Martin's?"

Petra laughed, and Thomas laughed with her, his happiness making him look a decade younger as he gazed at her. He was amused by his mother's rebuke, and indifferent to her opinion.

He'd married a woman of her choosing once, and he wasn't about to do so a second time. And marry he would.

"Petra, I brought you a small gift. I hope you will accept it as a token of my affection," Thomas said as he reached into the pocket of his breeches. He drew out a small leather pouch and held it out to Petra, like a child bringing his mother a spring flower that he picked just for her.

Petra accepted the pouch and held it in her hand for a moment before opening it, enjoying the feel of smooth leather and the promise of the solid object within. Her heart thudded with nervousness and excitement. No one had ever given her a gift before. Cyril had paid for things that were necessary, but he'd never bought her presents. He thought that trinkets were frivolous and a waste of good money, which could be spent on more important things, such as tankards of ale at the tavern. Petra opened the pouch with trembling hands and drew out a small bird. It was crafted of silver, the detail so exquisite that it looked as if it might spread its wings and take flight. The eyes were made of sapphires and there were several tiny rubies twinkling in the plumage of its tail.

"It's a clasp for your cloak," Thomas explained. "May I put it on for you?"

Petra nodded as tears pricked her eyes. He was so kind, and so generous. But would it last?

"It's exquisite," she breathed. "Thank you."

"A bird is a symbol of freedom," Thomas said, as he deftly pinned the clasp to her cloak. "I wanted to reassure you that you will not lose yours if you agree to marry me. I have no wish to own you, Petra. I'm at a point in my life where I wish for companionship and affection, not blind obedience."

"Did your wife give you blind obedience?" Petra asked, curious about Thomas's marriage. He never spoke of his wife, or even his daughter, who expressed little desire to see him since her marriage.

"She did. She never questioned my judgment or argued with me. My word was law."

"How fortunate for you," Petra mumbled as they resumed their walk.

"It was very dull, if you must know. I enjoy a spirited argument."

"Would you not have beaten her if she challenged you?" Petra asked. Cyril beat her mercilessly the few times she dared express an opinion different from his.

Thomas's eyebrows lifted in surprise. "Of course not. A wife should respect her husband and defer to him, but that doesn't mean she isn't permitted an opinion of her own. God knows my mother always had something to say on every subject," he said, the corners of his mouth lifting in mirth. "My father always said that my mother was twice as cunning as any man. He heeded her counsel on many an occasion, and was never ashamed to admit it."

"Sadly, my husband did not share your view of matrimony," Petra replied.

"I'm sorry for that. You mustn't fear me, Petra," Thomas added. "I have no wish to hurt you."

"I know, Thomas."

No, Thomas had no wish to hurt her, but she was hurting nonetheless. Thomas could offer her not only a comfortable life, but a safe and prosperous future for her children. He would provide a dowry for her daughters when the time came, and perhaps school her son in the business and make him a partner. Wool-trading would be a safe enough occupation for Edwin. Maybe Edwin would even be able to take a bride. He'd need someone to look after him once he was a man grown. Marriage to Thomas would solve Petra's every problem, but having Avery back in her life changed everything.

She was tempted to throw away a gilded future to spend time with a man who could never give her a life. After twelve years of denial, the passion had come back like an insatiable hunger, one that wouldn't be satisfied with a few stolen hours. Petra ached for Avery every hour of the day, counting the moments until she could finally escape the mind-numbing boredom of Lady Blythe's company and meet Avery for a brief rendezvous before returning to her own hearth. Avery had discovered an abandoned house close to the beach. The house was a one-room hovel with a packed dirt floor and a leaky thatch roof, but it served its purpose — it kept them safe from prying eyes.

In fact, there were quite a few empty dwellings in town, since the more cautious inhabitants of Dunwich moved further inland after the last big storm. Even the monastery had been moved from its original location at the end of the last century, the friars fearful that their house of worship would get swept out to sea. It would be too risky to meet in town, but the house by the beach was far enough from the nearest neighbor to guarantee privacy and lack of curious passersby.

Avery waited for Petra at their secret place twice a week, and Petra nearly howled with frustration when Thomas chose those days to escort her home. Having him away had been a blessing of sorts, but now he was back, and he wanted an answer. The rational part of Petra wished that Avery would just return to Oxford. The longer he remained in Dunwich, the greater the chance that they would be discovered, but the emotional part of her wished that he'd stay forever. She was truly happy for the first time since she was fifteen, and the thought of giving Avery up once more made her heart contract with sorrow. But there were dangers, and not only from without. She'd fallen pregnant once, and she might do so again. How would she explain away a pregnancy when she was a window meant to be in mourning for her husband? The risk was too great.

Thomas stopped walking and turned to face Petra. His lean cheeks were ruddy with cold, and his eyes shone with hope as he gazed down at her. "Petra, I promised myself when we set out on this walk that I would just give you your present and not demand an answer from you, but truly, I can't wait any longer. I think you already know what your decision will be, so there's no sense in putting this off. You either wish to share your life with me, or you don't. No amount of waiting is going to change that. What say you?"

"I say yes, Thomas," Petra replied, her voice firm and clear despite the turmoil raging in her heart. Had she been free to choose, she would have thanked him for his kindness and gently rejected him, but what choice was there? Refusing Thomas meant poverty, uncertainty, and possible disgrace. She'd had a few weeks of joy, now it was time to face real life again and think of her children.

Chapter 43

February 2014

London, England

Quinn smiled happily as she walked toward the Institute. It was warm for February, and the rain of the past few days had given way to pleasant sunshine, reminding her that spring wasn't far off. She was due to meet Gabe in a half hour to register Emma for the nursery school they'd chosen. It was close to the Institute, which was convenient since Gabe would be able to drop Emma off and pick her up on his way home. The school was charming, and the staff left a very favorable impression on both Quinn and Gabe. Now that they had chosen a school, Quinn felt more at ease. It seemed utterly overwhelming at first, but things were starting to come together, and the initial panic of suddenly having to raise a child was slowly giving way to a sense of order.

We can do this, Quinn thought as she strolled along. Perhaps she could even talk Gabe into having a celebratory dinner at that Mediterranean place they both liked, since it might be their last for a while. They were going to pick up Emma from Gabe's parents tomorrow. Phoebe and Graham were a little forlorn at having to part with Emma. She'd brought a ray of sunshine into their lives, but they saw the necessity of Emma being with her father and settling into a life in London. They called every night and put Emma on the phone to speak with Quinn and Gabe. Gabe dutifully reported on the progress of Emma's room, and Quinn told her about the nursery school, describing it in the most favorable terms possible.

"I want my old school," Emma wailed. "I miss my friends."

"You will make new friends," Quinn promised.

"What if no one likes me?" Emma breathed.

"Of course, they'll like you," Gabe assured her. "Why wouldn't they?"

"Because I have a funny accent," Emma replied. "Mrs. Edwards at the post office said so. She said I sound like a proper little Scot, and she can barely understand me."

"Ah, Mrs. Edwards," Gabe replied, clearly annoyed. "You pay no attention to her."

"That's what Granddad said," Emma said. "He said she has a face like a smacked bottom."

Quinn covered the mouthpiece, and snorted with laughter. Leave it to Graham to make the most inappropriate observation in front of a four-year-old. Quinn was sure that Emma would store that phrase and use it at the first available opportunity, most likely at nursery school. Quinn expected Gabe to say something very correct, but instead he burst out laughing and said, "She certainly does, and that's on a good day."

Emma's tinkling laugh came over the line. She felt better, and that was that mattered. "All right. I'll give it a go," she promised. "Would Mum have liked this school?" she suddenly asked.

"I really think she would have," Gabe replied.

"All right," Emma said again, more subdued now. "I'm going to have my bath now. Bye."

"I have to go," Phoebe said after Emma ran off. "But, just so you know, Mrs. Edwards has been dealt with."

"Right. Thanks, Mum."

"What exactly does she mean by 'dealt with'?" Quinn asked after they hung up the phone.

"I dare not ask," Gabe replied, still chuckling. "But I never underestimate my mother. If Mrs. Edwards is suddenly banned from doing flowers for the church or isn't invited to the next book club meeting, we know who to blame. My mother can be ruthless."

"I better behave then," Quinn quipped.

"Yes, you'd better. And speaking of spanked bottoms…" Quinn squealed as Gabe lightly smacked her bum, leaving her in no doubt as to his immediate plans.

**

Quinn glanced at her watch. She was a bit early. She could go in, but she had no desire to see any of her colleagues, so she decided to wait outside instead. She found an empty bench and settled in to wait for Gabe. She needed to ring Sylvia and check in with Jill. Jill seemed in better spirits the last few days, fueled by Quinn's idea and looking for suppliers who might help her implement it. And Sylvia had left a message, asking Quinn to ring her back. Quinn was just rummaging in her handbag for her mobile when someone sat down on the bench next to her.

"Don't even think of leaving," the man said as his fingers closed around her wrist as she tried to flee. "I'd like a word."

Quinn threw Robert Chatham a look of defiance and prayed that Gabe would come out early and rescue her. Chatham looked angry, and given that he'd found her despite her giving him a false name, she could understand why. That whole episode left her cringing with shame, both at the memory of Chatham's advances and her own behavior. Perhaps it was best if Gabe didn't see them talking to each other.

"How can I help you, Mr. Chatham?" Quinn asked, striving for composure. She wasn't really scared since they were seated in the middle of a public park filled with passersby, but the man made her uneasy.

Chatham turned toward her and studied her for a few moments, his gaze filled more with curiosity than hostility. "I'm not going to hurt you. I just want to talk." He finally let go of her wrist once he was satisfied that she wasn't about to run off.

"I had a pleasant chat with Monica Fielding yesterday. She had a lot to say once your name came up. Did you think I wouldn't find out who you are, Dr. Allenby?" he asked, amused by Quinn's startled expression. "Once I Googled Monica Fielding, I had no trouble finding your profile on the institute website. So, let's skip the polite chit-chat and get to the point. Why would a well-respected archeologist seek me out? And you did seek me out. You targeted me."

Quinn pinned Robert Chatham with her gaze, impressed by how quickly he caught up to her. The man clearly didn't make idle threats. He gave her a pleasant smile, raising one eyebrow to emphasize that he was waiting for an answer.

"Do you really want to know?" Quinn asked. She sounded calmer than she felt, but would not run from a confrontation with this man. She had nothing to lose, not anymore. "Thirty-one years ago, you invited a girl to a party at your house where you and two of your mates drugged and assaulted her. I was born nine months later. I targeted you because I thought you might be my biological father."

"So, you accepted the invitation to my room to see if you could find any DNA?" Chatham asked. He looked amused, which annoyed Quinn, who had hoped for some expression of remorse.

"Yes. I wanted to know for sure."

"And do you?"

"Not a match." Chatham looked momentarily relieved, but then burst out laughing.

"You're a lot feistier than your mother ever was; I'll give you that."

"Don't you talk about my mother," Quinn cried, furious at his levity. Robert Chatham tilted his head to the side and studied her, his mouth twitching with suppressed humor.

"Oh, let me guess. Poor Sylvia spun you a grim tale in which Snow White gets drugged and shagged by the evil dwarfs. Well, let me tell you, Princess, that's not how it happened. Your mother had a reputation for being a slag, which is why I invited her in the first place. I wanted to have a merry Christmas, if you know what I mean. She could have refused the champagne, but she didn't. She drank glass after glass, until she could barely stand. The other two girls offered her a ride home, but she decided to stay. She wanted to stay. She was so far gone, there was no need to drug her, not that I would have. That's simply not my style. I like my women conscious. I kissed her and she kissed me back. She let me touch her and put my hand down her jeans. She liked it. She got a bit upset when Seth joined in, but she never asked us to stop. She was flattered by the attention. Surprised?" he asked, grinning at Quinn who looked mutinous.

"You're a liar," Quinn hissed.

"Am I? Are you sure?" Robert Chatham chuckled. "Rhys was a bit reluctant. He always was something of a coward, but by the time Seth and I were finished with Sylvia, one more bloke wouldn't have made any difference. She just lay there, legs spread, just begging for it. We egged Rhys on; I admit that, but he didn't need much persuading. It was his chance to lose his virginity at last, and with someone who was too piss-drunk to laugh him out of the room."

Chatham caught Quinn deftly by the wrist when she tried to slap him. "And that's not the worst of it, Sunshine. Sylvia clearly never told you that there was a fourth man."

"What?" Quinn breathed. "You are saying that just to be cruel."

Chatham shook his head. "No, I'm not. Ask Sylvia. There's a reason why she never breathed a word of this to anyone."

"Who was he? Was he a friend of yours?" Quinn demanded.

"No, he wasn't, and he wasn't there that night, but he'd shagged her, repeatedly; you can be sure of that."

Quinn looked away as tears of anger and betrayal stung her eyes. She wanted to believe that Chatham was lying, but something in his eyes told her that he was telling the truth. Sylvia had lied to her, had omitted information for a reason. It was her word against Chatham's on whether she was raped or had sex with the boys willingly, but she'd clearly chosen not to tell Quinn the whole story.

Quinn yanked her hand away when Robert Chatham took it in his. His expression had softened, and he looked at her with an expression of compassion and admiration.

"You could have just asked me, you know," he said, his voice low.

"And would you have agreed to be tested?" Quinn retorted. She was trying not to cry, and it was easier to keep a rein on her emotions if she were angry.

"I'm not a good man, Quinn; I freely admit that. I've made mistakes, and I've hurt people intentionally, but had you been honest, I would have gladly given you a swab with my saliva."

"Why would you do that?" Quinn asked, her eyes narrowed as she finally met Chatham's gaze.

"Because I've learned that you must pay for everything in this life, and if the bill for that night came in the shape of a daughter like you, then I would have been proud that something good came out of it. I know that you are relieved that I'm not your father, and you probably have every right to be, but I must say that I'm a bit disappointed."

Quinn gaped at Chatham. She hadn't expected such a dramatic change in his attitude, nor did she think the man had any redeeming qualities, but perhaps she'd judged him too harshly. She still didn't know the entire truth of that night, and until she did, she would reserve judgment.

"Tell me about Seth," Quinn asked.

"There's not much to tell. I lost touch with Seth years ago, after he went back to the States. He was a good bloke. He had that sense of fun that Americans so often have. No inhibitions, no reservations, and no apologies. I'm sure you'll have no trouble tracking him down; it's easy enough these days, but I'd talk to Sylvia first. I think you need to be in full possession of the facts."

Robert Chatham gave Quinn a rueful smile as he got to his feet. "It was a pleasure to meet you, Princess. Perhaps life will throw you in my path again one of these days. Good luck with your search."

Quinn watched as Robert Chatham walked away, his shoulders squared and his stride purposeful. She glared at the mobile that glinted in the sunshine in her open handbag. She would have to hold off on calling Sylvia until she felt calmer.

Quinn looked up and saw Gabe emerging from the building. He must have been rushing to meet her because his coat was unbuttoned, and his scarf was slung carelessly around his neck. He was patting his pockets to check if he'd taken his mobile and wallet. Gabe smiled and waved, and Quinn promptly burst into tears.

Chapter 44

March 2014

Lingfield, Surrey

Quinn threw another log on the fire and settled on the sofa with her glass of wine. It felt good to be home. She'd missed her little chapel. It was the place where she felt most at peace, despite all the turmoil in her life. The flames licked and stroked the logs, filling the room with a pleasant smell of wood smoke. Quinn took a sip of wine, but it brought her no pleasure, so she set it aside. Perhaps she'd have a cup of tea instead. She went to put the kettle on and looked in the fridge. The milk had gone off, again, so she poured it down the sink, wrinkling her nose at the smell. She'd have to drink her tea black, but there was a half-full tin of biscuits in the cupboard, left over from her last shopping spree, which was a fortuitous find since she was feeling peckish. She was always hungry these days.

Quinn glanced at her mobile. Gabe remained in London with Emma, since this was something Quinn needed to do alone, and she preferred to do it in a place where she felt in control and expected no interruptions. And there was another reason. Quinn wanted to give Gabe time alone with Emma. He was still nervous about being on his own with her, and this would be a good opportunity for Gabe to prove to himself that he was perfectly capable of taking care of his daughter. It would take time for Gabe to get comfortable with his new role, but he had to start somewhere and look after Emma without using his parents or Quinn as a crutch.

There was a text from Gabe, assuring Quinn that everything was just fine. They had plenty of snacks and were about to watch Cinderella on DVD. Emma was already in full Disney regalia, wearing her Cinderella gown and tiara. Quinn smiled at the photo Gabe sent of the two of them sitting side by side, matching smiles on their faces. Emma had been sorry to leave her grandparents and Buster, but she seemed to be settling into her new home, and her new bedroom was a big hit.

Quinn set aside the phone when she heard the crunch of tires on gravel followed by the slamming of a door. She was nervous and suddenly wished that she hadn't requested this meeting. Did she really want to know? Gabe tried to reason with her and talk her out of confronting Sylvia, but Quinn needed to know. As someone who spent her life unearthing the past, she felt compelled to examine her own. She got to her feet and went to the door, opening it just before Sylvia had a chance to knock. Sylvia stood outside, an eager smile on her face. Quinn only told her that she wanted to meet, so Sylvia assumed that Quinn wanted to spend some quality time with her.

"Quinn, it's wonderful to see you," Sylvia gushed as she leaned in to give Quinn a peck on the cheek. "I heard you met Logan. What a coincidence. It's such a small world, isn't it? And Colin is such a lovely boy, not like the thug Logan was seeing before. Every mother wants a doctor for her son," she added with a smile, "even if he only doctors the dead."

"Colin searches for answers," Quinn replied. "Closure is important."

"Of course, it is. Is that Chardonnay?" Sylvia asked as she hung up her coat and scarf and accepted a seat on the sofa. "I love the smell of burning wood. We used to have a fireplace in the house where the boys grew up, but I don't have one in my flat."

Quinn poured Sylvia a glass of wine and refreshed her own tea before joining her on the sofa. She knew she had to say something, but Sylvia's excitement at seeing her made her even more reluctant to broach the subject.

"I was so happy when you called. I know you've been busy, but it's been over a month since we last saw each other. Jude will be home next week, so I thought perhaps we can put something on the calendar. I so want you to meet him. And I would love to finally meet Gabe," Sylvia added, her eyes sliding to Quinn's engagement ring.

"Sylvia, I asked you here because I wanted to speak to you in private," Quinn began. Her mouth was dry and she wished that she could just forget the whole thing and spend a pleasant hour chatting with Sylvia, but she needed to know the truth, no matter how distasteful. Sylvia was her biological mother, and Quinn needed to know that she could trust her before she could begin to get involved in a relationship with her.

"What about?" Sylvia asked, sipping her wine.

"I saw Robert Chatham a few days ago," Quinn said, her eyes never leaving Sylvia's face. Sylvia paled slightly, but tried to smile nonchalantly.

"Oh? And how did that come about?"

"I had a paternity test done. He's not my father."

"I see," Sylvia said. She was no longer smiling, her expression closed and her hands folded in her lap. "You don't waste any time, do you?"

"Sylvia, I want to ask you a question, and I need you to give me an honest answer. There can be no future for us if we can't be honest with each other."

"All right."

"Chatham said that there was a fourth man who might be my father. Is that true?"

Quinn expected Sylvia to deny the accusation, but she seemed to shrink into herself, staring into the fire as if she could find an answer in the flames. She suddenly looked older than her forty-eight years, her expression one of utter defeat. Quinn hadn't realized how badly she wanted Sylvia to deny the existence of a fourth man until she saw the slump of her shoulders and the sudden pursing of the lips, giving Quinn the answer she needed.

"Yes, there was a fourth man," Sylvia finally admitted, pinning Quinn with her gaze. "I didn't tell you about him because I didn't want you to think badly of me. Telling you that you had three possible fathers was hard enough."

"Who was he, Sylvia? Was he a friend of Robert Chatham?"

"No."

Sylvia reached for her glass and finished the wine in one long gulp before reaching for the bottle and refilling her glass. She was clearly upset, but Quinn felt surprisingly calm. Now that it was out in the open, she felt a strange sense of detachment instead of the pain of betrayal she expected to feel. She was there simply to learn the facts.

"I told you that my father and I moved after my mother left us," Sylvia began.

"Yes."

"I was new to the village, and it's not easy to make friends when you are a teenage girl. You know how cliquey women can be. I was lonely, especially at the weekends, since no one included me in their plans. I spent a lot of time reading and watching television to pass the time."

Sylvia stole a peek at Quinn then carried on with her story. "My father hired Steven to make deliveries for him since he couldn't leave the shop unattended, and I was too young to drive. There were several deliveries each week, and sometimes Steven took me along with my father's blessing. He said I needed to get out of the house, so I did. At first, I didn't really want to go, but as I got to know Steven, I began to enjoy spending time with him. He was easy-going and made me laugh. One thing lead to another," Sylvia said, shrugging her shoulders.

"Were you in love with him?" Quinn asked, wondering why Sylvia had been reluctant to talk about him.

"I suppose I was infatuated with him for a time, but he was married, you see. He had two children. I was nothing more than a plaything for him, an amusing diversion. When I told him that I was pregnant, he told me to sort it out on my own and stopped taking my calls. He was afraid I'd destroy his marriage."

"And how did Robert Chatham know about you two?" Quinn asked.

"Steven did some work on the Chatham estate, as gardener and handy man. He must have let something slip."

Which was why Robert Chatham thought Sylvia was easy pickings when he invited her to his house that night, Quinn thought, but didn't say anything out loud.

"Is there a possibility that he's my father?" Quinn asked.

"I hadn't been with Steven for several weeks before that night at Robert Chatham's house. His wife had the flu, so he was otherwise engaged, taking care of his girls," Sylvia said, her tone bitter. "I suppose it's possible, but you were born exactly nine months after that night. You could have come late, of course. I never even thought of that."

"So why did you tell him you were pregnant if you didn't think he was responsible?" Quinn asked, probing for holes in Sylvia's story.

"I was young and scared, and I hoped that he would help me, or at least offer me some support. I never expected him to leave his wife and children; I just wanted to know that he cared. But he cut me dead instead. I was too much of a threat to his home life."

Sylvia angrily wiped away the tears that had begun to slide down her cheeks. "I'm sorry, Quinn. I'm not the mother you deserve. I royally cocked things up, but I paid for my stupidity, and I continue to pay for it. That night has haunted me my whole life, and it will be the undoing of any relationship I might hope to have with you. I better go," Sylvia said as she sprang to her feet.

"Sylvia, wait," Quinn said. She'd been angry after speaking to Robert Chatham, but now all she felt was pity for this woman who'd allowed a bunch of callous, cruel men to ruin her life. She'd be damned if she allowed them to continue to cause damage.

"Sylvia, I don't think badly of you. We all make mistakes, and you've paid for yours. I don't care what you did and with whom. I only wanted to know the truth."

"Thank you," Sylvia said as the tears began to flow again. "Quinn, I know that you feel driven to know who your father is, but for God's sake, please, let it go. Nothing good can come of it. These men are not worthy of having you for a daughter, and whether you were fathered by Steven Kane or Seth Besson, you are the person that you are, and nothing will change that. Learning the truth will only cause you pain."

Quinn walked over to Sylvia and put her arms around her, hugging her mother for the first time in her life. "I know you are right, but I won't be able to rest until I find out. Sylvia, I need to know where I come from and who my ancestors were. I need to fill in the blanks so that I can move forward."

Sylvia nodded. "I know. And I hope you find the answers you seek. I just don't want you to be disappointed with the people who've created you."

"I'm not," Quinn replied and meant it. "I'm glad that you found me, and nothing I learn from this point on will change that."

"I hope you're right. I would hate to lose you all over again."

"You won't. Now, let's pick a date for our get-together. I want you to meet Gabe… and Emma," Quinn added, gratified by Sylvia's hopeful expression.

Chapter 45

Twin beams of light bisected the darkness as a car passed outside. There was little traffic at this hour. The house was quiet, with only the occasional creaking of settling wood and the rustling of bedsheets disturbing the silence. It was almost 2 a.m., but Gabe couldn't get to sleep, his conversation with Quinn replaying in his mind. She'd been angry with him, but relented before she fell asleep, her head resting on his shoulder and her arm about his waist as he held her close. She'd moved away since, lying on her back, her hands folded across her stomach like a medieval effigy.

Gabe studied Quinn's face in the darkness, smiling at the sweep of dark lashes across her pale skin and the lift of her mouth as if she were about to smile. She'd been wound up before speaking with Sylvia, but their talk had gone well, and perhaps even served as a step forward in their fragile relationship. Quinn believed Sylvia's version of events, but Gabe wasn't convinced. He had no wish to be one of those people who blamed the victim for the tragedy that befell them, but Sylvia Wyatt puzzled him. True, she had been very young when she got pregnant with Quinn, but even a girl of seventeen had to have some notion of what she was getting herself into.

Gabe folded his hands behind his head and stared at the ceiling, his mind still on Sylvia. Sylvia was either a woman prone to catastrophically bad judgment or a liar who was manipulating Quinn's emotions to get into her good graces. She'd gotten involved with a married man, with whom she carried on for months, and then went to a party at a house of an older boy she barely knew. She drank too much and refused to leave when the other girls decided it was time to go, remaining behind with three college-age lads who'd been drinking heavily and likely made their intentions clear. Surely, she understood the possible consequences of both situations. Could she really have been that sheltered and naïve? Yes, she could have been. Many girls, and women, found themselves in situations beyond their control and realized the danger when it was already too late, but Gabe didn't think that happened with Sylvia, not given what she chose to do after.

Sylvia didn't tell anyone about the assault, not even after she found out that she was pregnant. She didn't see a doctor or tell her father that she was expecting a baby. Instead, she concealed her pregnancy till the end of the school term, then left home, found a place to live and a summer job, and prepared for the birth of her baby. She found an advert for a midwife in the newspaper and called her once she was already in labor, avoiding going to the hospital and having her condition recorded in the NHS database. Sylvia had formulated a plan of action, carried it out, and then left her newborn in a church, returning home to her father as if nothing had happened. These were not the actions of a sheltered girl. These were the actions of a survivor, who was no stranger to strategic thinking.

Perhaps Robert Chatham was telling the truth when he claimed that Sylvia had been a willing participant that night, and perhaps she'd been the one to seduce Steven Kane, and not the other way around. Getting pregnant had not been part of the plan, so she got rid of her baby as soon as she could, not even bothering to go through the normal adoption channels and turning Quinn over to social services. She'd thrown Quinn away like a bag of rubbish. Leaving her baby in a place of safety rather than just dumping her somewhere where she might not have been found right away had been Sylvia's only act of maternal love.

Gabe stole a peek at Quinn, who no longer looked peaceful. Her eyelids were fluttering, and her breathing quickened, as if she were having a bad dream. Gabe reached out and took her hand, holding it until she began to calm down. He wished that he could turn back the clock and prevent Quinn from getting assaulted during the break-in that led to Sylvia finding her. Quinn had dreamed of finding her biological parents, like most adopted children, but meeting Sylvia and learning of her true parentage had done more harm than good. Quinn was hell-bent on finding Steven Kane and prepared to turn her focus to Seth Besson if Kane proved he was not a match. She was obsessed with finding her father, a quest that could bring her nothing but bitter disappointment.

Gabe shot to his feet as a wail pierced the silence of the flat, startling him out of his reverie.

"Mummy! I want my mummy!" Emma screamed.

Gabe hurried into the other room and gathered Emma in a warm embrace. "I'm here, darling. There's nothing to be afraid of."

Emma pushed him away, her eyes huge in her face. "I don't want you, Gabe. I want my Mum. I miss Mum," Emma screamed. "I want to go home."

Quinn walked into the room and sat down next to Emma and Gabe. "Would you like a story?" she asked.

"No!" Emma cried, but she moved closer to Quinn, leaning into her, desperate for comfort.

Quinn wrapped Emma in her arms and rocked her gently, humming the waltz from Cinderella. "Would you like to come to our bed?" Quinn asked, giving Gabe a stern look when he shook his head.

"All right," Emma mumbled. "But I still want my Mum."

"I know, Emma. I know. She would be here if she could, but she's entrusted you to us, so please, give us a chance. Can you do that?"

"I suppose," Emma said as she trailed after Quinn, climbing into bed and pressing her back to Quinn's belly. Emma took Gabe's hand as she closed her eyes, her breath still shaky from crying.

"I'll never leave you, Emma," Gabe said as he kissed the top of her head. "I'll always be your dad."

"I don't want a dad. I want my Mum back, and my Gran," Emma mumbled and turned her face away from Gabe.

After a time, she quieted down, but her breathing was still shaky as she continued to sniffle. Quinn spoke to Emma quietly, telling her the story of Goldilocks and The Three Bears until Emma finally drifted off to sleep, still clutching Gabe's hand despite rejecting him earlier. Quinn gently laid her hand over Gabe's and Emma's, her gaze meeting Gabe's in the darkness. He gave her a pained smile, and she smiled back, wishing that she could say something to make him feel less dejected. Gabe was hurt by Emma's outburst, but who could blame a child for missing her mother?

"How do you cure a four-year-old of a broken heart?" Gabe asked, his voice barely audible.

"With love," Quinn replied. "Endless, unconditional love that never wavers."

"Well, I've got plenty of that. For you both," Gabe replied.

Quinn gave Gabe's hand a reassuring squeeze. "You're a good man, Papa Bear," Quinn said, making Gabe smile.

Chapter 46

March 1347

Dunwich, Suffolk

Prior Jacob stood on the cliff and looked out to sea. Today it was still, the gray expanse flat and lifeless. A few boats dotted the surface, eager fishermen taking advantage of the calm to catch some fish to sell at the market. It was difficult for the poor during the winter months when they couldn't supplement their meager diets with produce from their vegetable patches. Some were fortunate enough to have a fruit tree that yielded free apples or pears in the autumn. There were a few apple trees growing on the priory grounds, and Prior Jacob always enjoyed an apple or two while he picked the fruit for stewing and making jelly. The crisp sweetness filling his mouth made him feel almost guilty, as if he were doing something wrong. But surely it wasn't wrong to enjoy God's bounty, not when it would only go to waste if not harvested.

The prior was distracted from his thoughts by the approach of one of the younger friars. Friar Matthew had joined the order only a year ago, and was still more boy than man. Sandy fuzz covered his cheeks and upper lip and his hazel eyes shone with purpose. Unlike some of the other friars who still viewed Prior Jacob with suspicion, Friar Matthew was full of loyalty and a desire to prove himself useful.

"You wished to see me, Prior?" Matthew asked as he joined Prior Jacob on the clifftop.

"Have you done what I asked?"

"Yes."

"And have you learned anything?" Prior Jacob asked. Matthew was unusually tight lipped, his gaze scanning the horizon as if he were searching for something.

"Father Avery leaves the grounds after Evensong on Tuesdays and Thursdays. He walks into town, toward the harbor. I think he visits someone."

"Whom does he visit?"

"I don't know. The house looks abandoned. He stays for about an hour, then leaves."

"I want you to get closer, Matthew. I need to know whom he is visiting and why," Prior Jacob said, wishing the boy would show some initiative rather than wait to be told what to do. Father Avery was not a parish priest, so would have no reason to visit the sick or dying. Father Avery wasn't doing anything outwardly wrong, since he wasn't one of the friars and was free to come and go, but something about his behavior was furtive and suspicious. And then there was the boy, Edwin. What was Father Avery's connection to him? Why bring Edwin to the Priory? Father Avery said the boy expressed an interest in joining the order, but Edwin had not approached Prior Jacob as of yet, and seemed happy enough to leave after his work was finished and return to his family.

"I saw a woman," Friar Matthew suddenly said. His eyes never left the sullen vista in front of him, but his voice changed. He wasn't comfortable spying on a man of God, and with good reason. The friars were loyal to each other, their trust in their brothers absolute. Father Avery wasn't of their order, but he was still one of them, a man who chose to serve God above all else. He'd forsaken his parents' hearth and the promise of a wife and children and chosen the often-lonely path of holiness. The camaraderie and loyalty of like-minded men made the burden a little easier to bear at those times when a man craved more than divine sustenance, and they all did, even if they chose not to admit to it. Their longing made their devotion to God all the more meaningful and sacred.

Prior Jacob rearranged his face into one of bland patience. "Friar Matthew, the reason I asked you to follow Father Avery is because I'm worried about him. He seems distracted, conflicted even. I only wish to help him, but I can't do so unless I know what's troubling him. Can you tell me about the woman?"

Friar Matthew shrugged. "She wears a hooded cloak, so I've never seen her face. Sometimes she comes, and sometimes she doesn't. Father Avery waits for a while, then leaves. He looks disappointed when she doesn't show."

"I'd like you to continue watching Father Avery. It's our duty to bring him back to God if he has strayed," Prior Jacob said.

"Yes, Prior Jacob. It makes me feel better knowing I'm doing God's work," Matthew said, smiling for the first time. "I know in my heart that Father Avery is devout, but if you think he has doubts, then of course, we must help him find his way back to the Church."

"God will reward you for your diligence, Friar Matthew. He values every member of his flock. Now, go back to your chores, or you will be missed."

Friar Matthew turned and wordlessly walked away, disappearing through an arched doorway in the wall surrounding the priory. It was his job to tend the animals, and that's what he liked doing best. Perhaps it reminded him of his father's farm, and brought a little piece of home to the priory, offering the young man the best of both worlds. Prior Jacob clasped his hands behind his back and began to walk along the cliff. He'd grown cold standing still for so long, and could do with some exercise. Besides, walking helped him to think more clearly and he still had a half hour before Sext.

So, Father Avery has a lover, Prior Jacob thought as he strode along, paying little attention to the gathering clouds on the horizon. They looked like bales of dirty wool, but the air was fresh and invigorating, and Prior Jacob increased his pace as his mind picked apart this new information. He imagined that he'd be happy to learn something disparaging about his rival, but all he felt was a deep sense of unease. For a man of the cloth to take a lover was an affront to God. Prior Jacob knew that there were many, especially those higher up in the Church, who kept not only lovers, but secret families. The thought infuriated him. How could God allow such debauchery to thrive? These men had sworn their allegiance to the Church, had devoted themselves to the service of God, and all the while they were indulging in carnal pleasures, sacrificing nothing and showing a false face to the world. It was a sin to lie with a woman, a sin that should not be ignored.

Prior Jacob had never known carnal love. He'd joined the order when he was fifteen and had still been pure of heart and body. It was wrong to offer yourself to the Lord if you'd been soiled by fornication. His brothers tried to take him to a brothel once, but Jacob refused, disgusted by their base needs, which they satisfied at every opportunity. Jacob loved his mother and the Virgin Mary, and those two women were more than enough for him. He found women to be repulsive, truth be told. Their smell and wanton sexuality unsettled and disgusted him. He approved of marriage of course, for the purpose of procreation and propriety, but relations outside of the holy bounds of matrimony were not to be tolerated.

Jacob had chosen to join the Franciscan monks rather than pursue the priesthood because he wished to be shuttered away from the real world and not have to deal with the sordid lives of parishioners, who indulged in sinful behavior and thought that confessing their sins to a priest could wash away their guilt. The priests gave them penance, but Jacob thought that wasn't enough. People had to suffer for their sins, not just say a few Hail Marys and consider themselves absolved. No, he didn't have the temperament to deal with a congregation. He wished only to live in peace, his days structured and uncomplicated, devoted to worship and work. But ambition had its price, and in gaining the priorship, he'd lost the peace and simplicity of monastic life. Now he had to safeguard his position and protect his men from unholy influence. Father Avery was proving to be a worm in Jacob's apple, a snake in the Garden of Eden.

Prior Jacob turned his face into the wind, watching as white caps appeared on the surface of the sea, the placid water suddenly coming to life and beginning to rock the boats on the horizon. The clouds had grown darker, their underbellies swelling with unshed rain. Was this a sign of God's displeasure?

"I won't let you down," Prior Jacob spoke into the wind. "I will eradicate all sin."

Chapter 47

Petra pulled the threadbare blanket over her naked breasts and snuggled closer to Avery, desperate for every bit of warmth she could get. Avery didn't light a fire in the grate, fearful that someone would become alerted to their presence in the abandoned house if smoke began to rise from the chimney into the frigid night. A candle stub burned bright in the darkness, its little flame struggling to stay alive in the drafty space. Avery reached for his woolen cloak and spread it over them, pulling Petra closer to him and nuzzling her ear lobe.

"Better now?"

"Yes," Petra breathed. She closed her eyes and allowed herself to drift. Being with Avery felt so right, so safe. She wished they could spend the whole night together and wake with their limbs intertwined, their bodies warm and flushed from their lovemaking. Instead, Avery had to rush back to the priory, and Petra had to return home where she had to act as if she'd just returned from spending the evening with Lady Blythe and hide all signs of her happiness from her all-too-perceptive mother. It wasn't until she climbed into her loft beneath the rafters that she washed all traces of Avery from her body and lay in her cold bed, reliving the precious moments she'd spent with him. It was then that the doubts came. She knew she had to speak to Avery sooner or later and tell him her news, but she put off the inevitable, desperate to seize whatever happiness she could.

Petra turned onto her back and gazed up at Avery, who seemed miles away as he twirled a lock of her hair around his finger, his head resting on one arm. "Avery, what will happen?"

she asked, regretting the questions as soon as it left her lips. She knew the reality of the situation, but knowing it and hearing it were two different things, and she wasn't prepared to hear the truth.

"How do you mean?" Avery asked, his eyes sliding reluctantly back to Petra's face.

"With us," Petra clarified. She could still end things with Thomas and tell him that she'd changed her mind. They weren't to be wed until June, so she still had a few weeks before any wedding plans were set in motion. Oh, how happy Lady Blythe would be if Petra backed out and left Thomas to seek a more suitable bride, and how happy Petra would be if Avery decided to leave the Church and build a life with her.

"What *can* happen?" Avery asked and smiled down at her as if she were a silly child.

"I love you, Avery," Petra whispered. She'd said it in her mind a thousand times, but it felt strange to hear the words spoken aloud after all this time. The last time Petra had confessed her feelings to Avery was twelve years ago, on the night Edwin was conceived. Avery had said it first then, had sworn undying devotion and promised a lifetime of happiness, but he was gone less than a fortnight later, off to the seminary against his will.

This time he has a choice, Petra thought stubbornly as she watched emotions passing across Avery's face like clouds across the sun. *This time he can choose me. He can choose us.*

"I love you too, sweetheart, but I'm an ordained priest. I cannot marry. Once my transgressions are forgiven, I will return to Oxford and resume my teaching post," Avery said. His eyes slid away from Petra's searching gaze, telling her all she needed to know, but she persisted, desperate to change his mind.

"You can leave the priesthood," Petra pleaded, her heart in her throat. "We could marry if you did."

"And do what?" Avery asked. He was smiling down at her, but Petra could hear the note of reproach in his tone. "I have no inherited wealth, and no skill that could earn me a living. Would you have me do menial labor when I have a place in Oxford, the seat of learning?"

"So, you are content to leave me?" Petra asked.

"Petra, I have no choice. Being with you has brought me such happiness, and knowing that you bore my son fills me with great pride, but I have nothing to offer you beyond what we have here and now."

"And if I get with child?" Petra demanded, a note of anger creeping into her voice. He'd left her pregnant once, he could do so again. Did he not care what happened to her?

Avery's smile was condescending as he shifted away from Petra, just enough that their bodies were no longer touching. He was putting a distance between them, physical as well as emotional, and letting her know that any future between them was out of the question. His answer, when it came, was as sobering as a bucket of icy water, leaving Petra in no doubt about Avery's feelings for her.

"Then you accept Lord Thomas and pass the child off as his. He will be over the moon, having just the one daughter, and you will enjoy a life of comfort and security. It's the perfect solution for all involved."

"Is it?" Petra asked nastily as she sat up and reached for her clothes. Avery made no move to stop her. He was more than willing to let her leave. Petra pulled the shift over her head and began to roll on her stockings, her movements jerky and rushed. She suddenly saw Avery in a whole new light. She believed him to be incapable of falsehood, a man of God who struggled between his devotion to the Church and his love for her, but suddenly she saw him for what he was. He was a man who took what he wanted and left others to deal with the consequences of his actions. He'd left her with child once, going meekly where his father ordered him, and now he would leave her again, only this time of his own free will.

Avery would not sacrifice anything for her or their son. Not now, or ever. He had lofty ambitions of his own. He'd been sent to Dunwich as a punishment for his unorthodox views, so he decided to make the most of his exile, safe in the knowledge that Petra would never betray him. Regardless of what happened between them, he would walk away unscathed, the consequences of his actions no longer his to bear.

Petra quickly braided her hair and stuffed it beneath her headpiece, tucking in stray tendrils carefully. There was no mirror or any metal surface where she could see her reflection, but she couldn't go home looking disheveled or angry. Maude would not give her a moment's peace if she thought something was amiss. Petra suspected that her mother knew the truth of her relationship with Avery already, but hoped and prayed that Petra would come to her senses and see the error of her ways without having to give voice to her concerns.

"Sweetheart, please don't be angry," Avery cajoled as he looked up at Petra from their makeshift bed. "Surely you didn't think that I would leave the priesthood?"

"The possibility did cross my mind," Petra retorted. She was about to say something more, but didn't. There was nothing she could say that would alter Avery's plans. He'd never intended for them to have a future. He simply took what was given to him and made the most of it. "I won't be coming here again."

"Yes, you will. I know you will," Avery replied, reaching for her hand and pressing his lips to her palm. "I will wait for you on Thursday, and then on Tuesday. You will come," he said again, as if trying to convince himself.

Petra threw on her cloak and stuck her feet into her shoes. "I have to go," she said and fled into the night without a backward glance. How sure Avery was that she would come back, she fumed. How secure in her love. Petra brushed away tears of hurt and hurried home, her hand clasped around the silver bird Thomas had given her. She'd hidden it in her pocket before meeting Avery, not wishing to upset him with evidence of Thomas's affection, when she should have worn the gift proudly, displaying a token of love from a man who was willing to give her everything, not just a part of himself the Church had no use for.

All was quiet and still, everyone's shutters closed against the chill of the March night. The sky was full of stars, the twinkling dots forming strange patterns in the sky, and the moon hanging low over the sea, its yellow surface reflected in the pitch-black waters. A pathway of light shimmered on the surface, like a magic walkway, beckoning to unsuspecting travelers. Petra stopped walking and stared out over the moonlit sea. She felt hollow and unbearably sad, but the beauty around her marginally lifted her spirits, reminding her that every situation was made up of light and dark.

Petra pulled on her hood and rushed home, her head down and her steps brisk. She didn't notice the hooded figure that stepped out of the shadow of the abandoned hut, nor did she pay any attention to the stealthy footsteps that accompanied her home.

Chapter 48

London, England
March 2014

Quinn set aside Petra's cross and stared out the window. A light rain fell from a leaden sky, and a stealthy wind moved through the trees, but all she saw was the pitch-black stillness of the North Sea as it lay in wait, lulling the inhabitants of Dunwich into a false sense of security. The town was dark and silent by night, as any medieval town would be, but by day, it was a bustling metropolis with a busy harbor and numerous shops that did a brisk business during daylight hours. How much longer before the next devastating storm struck the town? Quinn wondered. She knew the years, but not the exact dates of the crippling storms.

But Petra didn't die in a storm. She was murdered, and buried face down on the fringes of the leper cemetery next to her young son, whose skull had been bashed in. Petra had been gone for centuries, but Quinn couldn't help feeling a sense of dread as she watched her go about her daily life, desperately trying to find that elusive balance between love and duty. Surely, she made the wrong choice, but was one mistake enough to get her killed? And how did Edwin's death fit into the puzzle?

What happened to you, Petra? Quinn asked the darkness. *What went wrong?*

"Can't sleep?" Gabe asked as he turned to face Quinn. He was a light sleeper at the best of times, but since Emma's arrival, he seemed to always be dozing rather than sleeping soundly.

"Sorry, did I wake you?"

"No, I wasn't sleeping. Were you thinking about Petra? You really mustn't let her get to you, Quinn. It happened ages ago. It's ancient history."

"She died hundreds of years ago, but she seems so real, so alive," Quinn replied. How could she explain to Gabe how seeing Petra made her feel? He loved history as much as she did, but the past didn't live inside his mind, nor did the images march across his eyelids every time he closed his eyes. He could keep a sense of detachment and view history from the perspective of an academic, but the people Quinn saw were real, likable, and flawed. They loved the wrong people, struggled against the constraints society placed on them, and made grave misjudgments, which often lead to tragedy. Petra wouldn't live out the year, Quinn knew that, but still she couldn't quite see where the danger lurked, or predict what would lead to Petra and Edwin's violent end.

"What was Dunwich like?" Gabe asked as he turned onto his side and propped his head on his hand, sleep forgotten. "I wish I could see what you see. It must be fascinating to experience things as they really were and not as we imagine them. What I wouldn't give to see the town as it was before it was swept out to sea."

"It was vast for that time period. It looked like any other large medieval town, with people going about their business, merchants selling their wares, and women minding their children and running their households. Most houses were built of wattle and daub, with thatched roofs, but there were many stone structures, and some houses were quite grand. Lady Blythe's home was spacious and comfortable, with rich furnishings and glazed windows. There were several parish churches and two chapels of ease."

Gabe pulled Quinn closer and rested his head against hers. "Describe Petra to me as if she were still alive — someone you know."

"She's alive in my mind, Gabe. She's as real as you and I. Those bones on a slab are not the person I see," Quinn added. She couldn't reconcile those ancient remains with the lovely, vibrant woman she saw only a few minutes ago. In Quinn's mind, Petra's face was rosy with cold as she hurried down the deserted streets of Dunwich, her heart contracting with disappointment as Avery's cruel words churned in her head over and over, chipping away at her dream for the future. Quinn felt reluctant to talk about Petra, but she supposed it would help her to accept Petra's fate if she talked things through with Gabe.

"When I look at Petra, I see a woman who hasn't got long to live, and my heart breaks for her. She's so young, and has so much to live for. She's hurt and disappointed in the man she loves, but her troubles are universal. People have been disappointed in love since the beginning of time, but most of them do manage to move on and build a life for themselves, given time. But that's the one thing she doesn't have. I don't know the exact date of her death, but I believe that it's imminent," Quinn said, silent tears sliding down her face.

"Could her death have been accidental?" Gabe asked. He was well aware of Dr. Scott's findings, but was prepared to explore every possible scenario in order to help Quinn come to terms with Petra's untimely death.

Quinn shook her head. "I don't think Petra and Edwin died during a storm. Their injuries might have been caused by something falling on them and fracturing their skulls, but the manner of their burial suggests that the insult was deliberate and malicious. Why would someone do that to victims of an accident?"

"They wouldn't," Gabe agreed. "Petra and Edwin would have received a Christian burial in hallowed ground, and their graves would have been washed away shortly after, leaving us nothing to find."

"Exactly. I do think, however, that they died before the outbreak of the Black Death in 1348," Quinn continued, testing out her theory on Gabe.

"Why makes you say that?" Gabe asked.

"I could be wrong, of course, but since the outbreak of 1348 essentially wiped out sixty percent of European population, I can't imagine that in the midst of all that, someone would take the time to bury Petra and her son with such malicious intent. Most people were tossed into plague pits and left to rot. Had Petra and Edwin died as a result of the plague, their remains would not have been singled out, as they so clearly were."

"So, you believe that Petra and her son died either before the Great Storm or soon after, but before the outbreak of the plague?"

"Essentially, yes."

"You like Petra, don't you?" Gabe asked. "Tell me more about her."

Quinn frowned in concentration. How did you describe a woman who died eight hundred years ago? She was nothing more than a wisp on the wind, an echo across the ages, but, to Quinn, she was as real as any woman she knew, and in some ways, not so different. The world had changed drastically since Petra walked the earth, but women still fought similar battles, if on slightly different battlefields, and dreamed the same dreams. What woman's heart didn't crave love, and how many women had to make the difficult choice between dedicating themselves to their children versus pursuing their own goals and putting their family in second place? Petra was faced with a similar dilemma, only her choices were somewhat more limited.

"She was lovely," Quinn began. "She had beautiful, expressive eyes and a sweet smile, which she bestowed often and with great sincerity. She had beautiful hair, rippling golden waves that made her look years younger when worn loose, but being a married woman and then a widow, Petra's hair was always pinned up beneath her headpiece. The last time Petra would have worn her hair loose might have been on her wedding day to Cyril, when she was fifteen." Quinn sighed. What a cruel fate for a young, innocent girl to marry a man who'd been as brutal as Cyril Ordell.

"In today's day and age, Petra would be just starting out on her life, pursuing a career and starting a family, but in her time, she was someone whose choices were limited to struggling to survive or marrying a man who'd look after her and her children."

"Was there such a man?" Gabe asked.

"Yes, there was. And a good man, by the looks of it. Petra's mother, who was shrewd and pragmatic, schemed to place Petra in the household of a noblewoman for whom Petra had once worked as a scullion. The mother rightly assumed that with being in the house of a wealthy matron, which was situated at the center of town, Petra might come into contact with some eligible men. She no doubt knew that Lady Blythe's son was widowed, and hoped that Petra might catch his eye. Lord Devon was smitten with her, and if Petra shared his feelings, her life might have taken a very different course."

"I take it she didn't fancy him?" Gabe asked, making Quinn smile.

"She might have, had she not been blinded by her feelings for Avery. Despite her *advanced* years and life experience, Petra was still something of an innocent. She believed that she could hide her son's illness and thought that she might reclaim the love she lost when she was a girl. I suppose Father Avery, who'd gotten her with child before he went off to the seminary at his father's bidding, cared for her and his son, but not enough to sacrifice his own ambitions. He'd suffered a setback to his goals when he was sent to Dunwich to *enjoy* a period of reflection. Namely, he had to either renounce his radical ideas about making religion more accessible to the people or spend the rest of his life cooling his heels in some remote parish where he'd have no chance of advancement, not a scenario Father Avery relished. He had his eye on a bishop's miter, and Petra, no matter how desirable, was not going to stand in his way. He told her as much, which was probably the only truly honest thing he did since coming back to Dunwich."

"Father Avery wouldn't have been the first priest to pick and choose which vows to obey. There were quite a few clergymen who had families on the side, keeping them in luxury at the expense of the Church and enjoying a double life," Gabe remarked.

"I don't think Avery was interested in taking on the responsibility of Petra's family. He helped Edwin secure a position at Greyfriars as an apprentice to the scribes, but that was as far as he was willing to go. Petra was a lovely distraction, a belated chance to enjoy the physical pleasures he'd been denied in his youth, but he wished to remain unencumbered in order to pursue his own ends."

Gabe smiled and trailed a line of kisses down Quinn's neck. "So, Petra had to choose between a player, who had no intention of committing himself to her, and a good, reliable man, who failed to ignite her desire, since her feelings were already engaged elsewhere? Sounds like a very modern problem," he murmured.

"Some things never change, do they?" Quinn replied, thinking that she herself had gone for the player instead of the good man when faced with the same choice, and it had been the wrong decision.

Quinn pulled Gabe down on top of her, hoping that the tender kisses were a prelude to what was to come. Emma was fast asleep, so they had a bit of privacy until it was time to get up and begin their day. Gabe's kisses were becoming more demanding, when a quivering voice called from the other room.

"Quinn, I lost Mr. Rabbit. He's gone," Emma cried tearfully. She appeared in the doorway, clutching her favorite blanket to her chest like a drowning man holding on to a bit of flotsam.

"Coming, darling," Quinn replied, leaving Gabe looking after her with undisguised longing.

"Get used to it," Quinn whispered over her shoulder, chuckling as she went on a hunt for the elusive rabbit, who seemed to have wedged himself between the wall and the mattress, one long protruding ear being the only clue to his whereabouts.

"Here he is, the rascal," Quinn said as she tucked Emma back into bed and placed the rabbit securely next to her. Emma wrapped her arm around the rabbit and sighed in relief.

"You don't need to be up for two hours. Think you can go back to sleep?" Quinn asked, hoping that Emma would nod off now that the rabbit had been found.

Emma shook her head. "I'm hungry. I want a soft-boiled egg with toast, so I can make soldiers and dip them in the yolk."

"Right now?"

"Right now."

Quinn left Emma in bed and padded into the kitchen, yawning. She was about to fill the kettle, but changed her mind and turned on the espresso machine instead, then put the water for the eggs to boil and took out a slice of bread. She was just about to make her first cup of coffee when Gabe came in and looked around in surprise.

"I thought you were coming back to bed."

"Emma wants breakfast."

"It's 4:30 in the morning," Gabe protested.

"Don't remind me," Quinn said and took a sip of the bitter coffee. "Want one?"

"I might as well."

"Why don't you go get Emma while I make your coffee? Make sure she brushes her teeth."

Quinn set the egg in a holder, buttered the toast and cut it into strips, and poured a glass of orange juice. She was just getting the cutlery when Gabe returned to the kitchen — alone.

"Where's Emma?"

"Asleep," Gabe replied, a bemused smile on his face. "Oh, that looks good," he said as he eyed Emma's breakfast.

"You're welcome to it," Quinn said. "Too early for me."

Gabe shrugged and reached for a strip of toast. "I haven't had soldiers since I was a little boy," he said as he took a bite of toast and deftly sliced the top off the egg, dipping the left-over piece in the yolk and popping it into his mouth. Quinn smiled at him and handed him a cup of espresso.

Chapter 49

March 1347

Dunwich, Suffolk

Edwin tied the strings of the apron behind his back and took a seat at the wooden table. The room was quiet, only the scratching of quills on vellum puncturing the silence as the four scribes worked, completely absorbed in their task, their heads bent over the manuscripts. One holy text was nearly finished. Friar Anselm was just putting the finishing touches on the colorful borders framing the pages before pronouncing the book complete. The manuscript was a thing of beauty, a document privately commissioned by an earl as a gift for his devout wife, who would value such a treasure above any material possession.

Friar William explained to Edwin that some of the manuscripts were copied for the priory library, but the lion's share of the scribes' work was for commercial purposes. The illuminated manuscripts were put on display by wealthy nobles, not only to showcase their devotion to God, but to flaunt their wealth and status, since the manuscripts cost a fortune to commission and could be purchased only by those for whom money was no object. They were a symbol of wealth and power, and a testament to the piety of the owner. Or an expression of love, as was clearly the case with the earl. The texts created by the friars of Greyfriars Priory were highly valued and sought out by many, which meant that the priory was never short of orders.

Edwin reached for a covered stoneware bowl in which gallnuts had been soaking in white vinegar for several days. The concoction had been left by the fire to facilitate the necessary reaction, but now Friar William pronounced the gallnuts to be ready. Edwin lifted the lid and instantly drew back. The evil smell made his eyes water, but it quickly evaporated once left open to the air. Today, Edwin would stir in the copperas and then add a bit of ground gum Arabic to thicken the ink to the proper consistency, just as Friar William taught him to do. He had to be sure not to add too much gum, or the ink would be unusable, and Friar William would be cross with him. Edwin loved to watch as the light-brown liquid began to change to black and thicken before his very eyes, forming the ink that looked so bold and bright upon the page.

Edwin motioned to Friar William, who came over and tested out the ink on a piece of vellum before nodding his approval. Edwin's chest swelled with pride. This was the first batch of ink he'd made all by himself. His handiwork would live on for centuries once it was used by the scribes. Edwin left the bowl on the worktable and went to collect the inkwells used by the scribes. They would take a short break from their labors while he refilled the pots. The friars stood up from their desks, grateful for a few minutes' respite. Friar William went to answer a call of nature, while Friar Anselm stretched his back and shook out his hands.

"The cramping is worse when it's cold," he complained, splaying his fingers and then opening and closing his hands.

"You're just getting old, Anselm," Friar Gregory replied.

"Indeed, I am, but I thank the Lord for every day he grants me, cramp or not. He has seen fit to ease the headache I've been suffering from these three days."

The friars nodded their agreement. "Praise Him."

"Praise Him," Edwin mumbled, feeling a little self-conscious. The friars spoke of God as if he was always there, completely aware of every word, gesture, and complaint. Perhaps they found the thought comforting, but Edwin found it frightening. He didn't want God to watch him or be privy to his thoughts. But surely, he had better things to do than examine the actions of one boy, especially one as insignificant as himself. Friar William returned, and the friars resumed their seats, their eyes on Edwin as he carefully filled each inkwell and carried it to the work station of each scribe, setting it in the proper place. The friars thanked him and returned to their work, break over. Edwin filled the last pot and carried it to the station of Friar Gregory. He'd filled the inkwell a little too high, and the ink reached almost to the very top. Edwin considered taking the pot back and pouring a bit off, but it seemed unnecessary, so he proceeded to set the inkwell on the desk. He wasn't sure what caused the tremor in his hand, perhaps it was nervousness, but the inkwell toppled and spilled its contents all over the manuscript Friar Gregory had been working on, black splotches covering the open pages, dripping down the rest of the manuscript, and soaking into the vellum.

"You clumsy oaf!" Friar Gregory screamed. "Look what you've done. Get out, you imbecile. I told Friar William not to allow you near the manuscripts. This is months of work ruined by an ignorant clod like you."

Edwin's heart began to pound, making him short of breath. His normally-pale face flamed with shame, the heat spreading from the cheeks to his neck and beyond. He gasped for breath, but his lungs failed to fill with air, deflating like the sails of a ship on a too-calm sea. It was all his fault. He'd been clumsy and careless. He ruined everything. Edwin's hands shook violently as he backed away from the desk, his eyes glued to the black puddles soaking the pages and swallowing the words and images so painstakingly produced by Friar Gregory. The ink dripped to the floor, droplets plopping down on flagstone tiles like black tears.

Edwin fought to stave off the familiar blackness that began to descend on him. *Please, no!* he cried inwardly during the few seconds of awareness he had left before it swallowed him up and he hit the stone floor with a sickening thud, his muscles convulsing and making his limbs jerk uncontrollably. There was a roaring in his ears, and he felt a stab of pain as he bit his tongue. He could no longer see or hear anything besides the blood rushing through his veins. The pain would come later, once he returned to normal, but during the fit all was jumbled, dark, and otherworldly. That was what the moments before death must be like, Edwin thought after every episode. All he could recall was fear, and a sense of not being tethered to this world, his soul torn apart from his body as it fought to return. Someday it wouldn't, and then the blackness would have won.

Edwin gasped for air as his senses began to return to normal. The left side of his face was covered with foaming spit, and his left shoulder hurt dreadfully, having taken the brunt of his weight when he fell. Edwin experimentally moved his arms and legs, praying that he hadn't broken anything this time. He'd broken bones before, when he was a small child. He supposed his bones were stronger and not as easily splintered now that he was almost an adult, but the danger was always there. Edwin wished he could keep his eyes closed forever, terrified of what the brothers' reaction would be when he fully came to.

"Edwin, are you all right, son?" Friar William asked as he bent over Edwin's prone form on the floor. He laid a cool hand on his forehead. "Get me a damp cloth," he said to someone.

"I'm not going near him," Friar Gregory replied. His voice sounded strangled, as if he were terrified. "He's possessed by the devil."

Edwin opened his eyes just in time to see Friar Anselm genuflecting three times in a row. "Be sober, be vigilant; because your adversary the devil, as a roaring lion, walketh about, seeking whom he may devour," Father Anselm mumbled and was joined by Friar Gregory. "Lest Satan should get an advantage of us: for we are not ignorant of his devices," they chanted.

Friar William used the damp cloth Friar Owen had handed to him to clean Edwin's face. "Sit up slowly," he said, his voice kind as he slid an arm beneath Edwin's shoulders to help him up.

"Don't touch him, brother," Friar Gregory warned. "Not if you value your immortal soul."

"I fear Satan as much as you do, Friar Gregory, but I don't see him here. All I see is a frightened boy who was momentarily unwell. Now, get back to your manuscripts and stop spewing nonsense."

Edwin was surprised to see that the friars seemed duly chastised. They crossed themselves again before returning to their work, but their gazes followed Edwin's progress as Friar William helped him to his feet and settled him on a bench where he could lean against the wall. Friar Owen held a cup of ale to Edwin's lips. "Here, have some. It will make you feel stronger. Does that happen often?" Owen asked once Edwin finished the ale.

"No," Edwin lied. "I was overcome with remorse," he added.

"It's all right, son," Friar William said. "Don't blame yourself for what happened. It was an accident. Are you well enough to return to work or would you prefer to rest awhile?"

"I will return to work," Edwin said, although he felt as if all strength had been sapped from his body. His legs felt as soft as jelly, and his head seemed to weigh ten stone, his thinking still muddled. He would have given anything to lie down for a short while in one of the brother's cells, until he felt well enough to resume work, but he was afraid to admit that he was still unwell. Friar Gregory and Friar Anselm were still watching him, their eyes narrowed with speculation and suspicion.

"All right then. You'll feel much improved after dinner," Friar William said. "It's only an hour till Sext."

Edwin nodded. He didn't object to joining the monks in midday prayer. Their singing and chanting made Edwin feel at peace, his soul instinctively recognizing something that his conscious mind didn't, but today, he wished only to be excused. The friars would be keeping an eye on him, waiting for him to confirm their worst suspicions.

Edwin suddenly sat up straighter. He'd been experiencing these fits since he was a babe-in-arms, but he never thought that they were a manifestation of the devil, but what if the friars were right? Surely, they knew more about the ways of good and evil than his mother and grandmother did. Perhaps that was why they tried so hard to keep Edwin safe. Did they believe that he was possessed? Edwin stared into the bowl of ink, his thoughts as black as the substance he'd made. What would become of him? Was he beyond redemption? Perhaps he should speak with Father Avery. He was a man of God after all, a priest. He would know what to do.

Edwin felt marginally better by the time he accompanied the friars to the chapel. Friar Gregory and Friar Anselm kept well behind, but Friar William put a reassuring hand on Edwin's shoulder, silently offering his protection. Friar Owen walked behind Edwin, like a vanguard. Edwin smiled in relief when he saw the kind face of Father Avery, whose smile quickly faded as he read the signs of distress coming from Friar Gregory and Friar Anselm. He noted the defiant set of Friar William's shoulders and Friar Owen's silent show of support.

"Is all well?" Father Avery asked as he looked from one face to the next.

"Yes," Friar William replied before the others could comment. "Edwin felt unwell, but he's since recovered."

"Edwin, would you like me to accompany you home?" Father Avery asked, his brows furrowing with concern. "You can rest in my cell while I'm at Sext, and then I'll walk with you."

"Thank you, Father Avery, but I'm quite all right. I look forward to joining you for Sext," Edwin replied.

Father Avery looked unconvinced, but didn't argue. He simply turned and walked into the chapel where the majority of the monks were already assembled. Edwin stood at the back, glad to have the brothers' focus shift to the service. He closed his eyes and prayed fervently that the fits would stop so that he could reclaim his soul from the devil. It couldn't be too late; it simply couldn't. Surely, he would know if all was lost. Or would he?

Chapter 50

"Enter," Prior Jacob called out, secretly glad to take a break from the accounts he'd been going over. He hated doing the accounts. Despite all his penny-pinching, the priory was not as prosperous as he would have liked, which would displease his superiors. The lion's share of the income came from the production of sacred texts, but with only four scribes, the priory could only accept a few commissions per year. Prior Jacob exhaled angrily when he recalled the damage Edwin had done to a nearly completed manuscript. Friar Gregory had been able to salvage three-quarters of the manuscript by trimming a few millimeters off the top of the vellum pages where the spilled ink had tainted the manuscript. Thankfully, the ink had not penetrated any deeper since the pages were stacked and Friar Gregory had the good sense to immediately turn the manuscript upside-down to prevent the ink from running between the vellum sheets, dripping down onto the wooden table instead. Still, it would take an additional month, at the very least, to replace the pages that had been damaged beyond repair. Friar Gregory had complained bitterly and demanded that Edwin not be allowed anywhere near his work table again.

Prior Jacob looked up as Friar Matthew entered the study and shut the door firmly behind him. His expression told Prior Jacob everything he needed to know. Matthew looked upset, guilt-ridden, and excited at the same time. He was too young and innocent to even consider concealing anything from his prior, and not devious enough to warn Father Avery in advance, in exchange for some future favor. Prior Jacob hated to think that any of the brothers would, but he had to take human nature into account. Father Avery had the ear of the bishop, and to have favor with Father Avery might come in handy for a friar who wished to lodge a complaint or stand for the position of prior should Jacob either take ill or be ousted for any reason.

"Sit down, Friar Matthew," Prior Jacob said, softening his voice. He didn't relish upsetting the young man, nor did he hope to hear anything negative about Father Avery. What he wished was that the good father would simply take his leave and allow them to get on with the business of worship and work, with Prior Jacob at the helm of the priory as he was meant to be.

"Would you care for some mead?" Prior Jacob asked. Friar Silas brought a jug of mead not an hour since, eager for Prior Jacob to sample the latest vintage. A few barrels would remain in the cellars for the brothers' personal use, but a good portion would be taken into town come market day, to be sold at a handsome profit. The funds would buy a new milk cow and several sacks of flour, which would be used to bake extra bread and make cheese for the poor, who came to the alms gate in record numbers this winter. Prior Jacob pinched the bridge of his nose and resolutely put the running of the priory out of his mind, focusing on Friar Matthew instead.

"Thank you, Prior," Matthew replied, gazing with longing at the jug of mead. Prior Jacob poured him a cup, and took one for himself. He rarely drank mead, since it dulled his senses and made him feel pleasantly somnolent, but he suddenly longed for something to take the edge off and ease the tension building up between his shoulder blades. Prior Jacob took a sip, and then another, enjoying the deceptive sweetness of the drink. The alcohol content of Greyfriars' mead was strong enough to fell an ox, if it got at an open barrel, so Prior Jacob resolutely pushed his cup aside and turned his attention to Friar Matthew, who'd finished his drink and was clearly hoping for a refill.

When none was offered, Matthew's normally earnest gaze slid away from his prior toward the open window, where twilight had tinted the sky a dusky purple and the first stars were just beginning to twinkle in the darkening heavens. A soft breeze blew through the window, the ever-present smell of the sea dispelling the greasy stink of the tallow candle. Prior Jacob looked at the lad expectantly.

"I take it you saw something you wish to report?" he prompted when Matthew failed to speak.

"Aye, I did, Prior. Father Avery meets a woman twice a week."

"To offer her spiritual guidance?" Prior Jacob asked, his lips twitching with amusement. That was the usual excuse priests gave when caught in the act. Besides, this wasn't news. Friar Matthew had reported as much before.

"Tis not any guidance I'd ever seen offered by a man of the Church," Matthew muttered.

"Does he lie with her?" Prior Jacob asked, needing to hear the words spoken out loud.

"Yes, he does."

"And does he seem contrite afterwards?" Perhaps that was a foolish question, but it would make Prior Jacob feel better about Father Avery's character. A man who was repentant was always worth saving. And now that he knew of Father Avery's weakness, he could rest easy, since the troublesome priest would never be a threat to his position again. Prior Jacob could afford to be generous and understanding, even magnanimous in his forgiveness of the other man's sins.

"No, Prior. He seems content, and woefully unashamed."

"How can you tell?" Prior Jacob asked, genuinely curious as to why Matthew would make such a statement.

Matthew blushed to the roots of his hair and glanced toward the window again. "Father Avery is not shamed by his nudity, nor that of the woman. He likes to gaze upon her as she lies before him. He stands before her fully unclothed while he…" Friar Matthew nearly choked on the words.

"While he interferes with himself?" Prior Jacob offered helpfully.

"I suppose you could call it that."

"And does the woman take pleasure in it as well?" Prior Jacob asked, suddenly uncomfortably aware of his own urges. He rarely felt aroused, but the image Friar Matthew was painting was surprisingly erotic.

"The woman is filled with sinful lust."

"Do you know who she is, Friar Matthew?"

"I followed her home. She lives in one of the less prosperous sections of town."

"I see," Prior Jacob said. "Thank you, Friar Matthew. You were most diligent in your task. You need spy on Father Avery no longer, and I hope I can rely on your discretion."

Friar Matthew nodded, but made no move to leave. Instead, he clasped the wooden cross hanging about his neck with both hands and fixated on the tips of his well-worn shoes, his head bowed. His tonsure glowed in the candlelight like the bottom of a newborn babe, and he muttered something under his breath, forcing Prior Jacob to lean forward to hear what he was saying.

"What is it, Matthew?" Prior Jacob asked, surprised by the young man's behavior.

"There's more, Prior."

"What more could there be?" Was Father Avery seeing more than one woman? Prior Jacob wondered. It wouldn't matter really, since although his sin would be compounded in the eyes of God, Prior Jacob had what he needed on the priest and wished to hear no more of his transgressions.

"The boy, Edwin, is this woman's son, Prior. I heard Father Avery and the woman speaking of him when he escorted her home last week. Father Avery is the boy's natural father."

"What?" Prior Jacob cried. He'd suspected that Avery was succumbing to lustful urges, something that wasn't all that unusual among members of the clergy, but to find out that he'd known this woman all throughout his priesthood and had fathered a child by her, a child who seemed to be afflicted with possible demonic possession, was news indeed.

"Are you sure, Friar Matthew?"

"Yes. I distinctly heard the woman say, 'but Avery, he is your son, and you have a duty to him.'"

"Thank you, Friar Matthew. You have done me and this priory a great service. It is a sordid task you've had to perform, but you have done your fellow friars an inestimable service, and God will reward you for your honesty and devotion to his glory."

"Yes, Prior," Matthew mumbled. "May I go now?"

"Of course. And Friar Matthew, please make no mention of this revelation to the others. I must carefully consider a course of action before making this information public."

Matthew looked as if the very last thing on earth he wished to do was discuss Father Avery's proclivities with the other friars. He bowed his head, genuflected as he gazed upon the crucifix on the wall, and fled.

Prior Jacob reached for the jug and poured more mead into his cup. He brought the cup to his lips and drank deeply, his reservations about strong drink forgotten in view of Matthew's confession. He'd hoped for something he could use against Father Avery should the priest wish to challenge the prior's position, but he hadn't bargained on a secret of this magnitude. Father Avery was clearly corrupt, and had been since the day he entered the seminary, and now his sins had been visited on his son, who was possessed of the devil. Prior Jacob didn't need to consult the Scripture, the passages came to his mind unbidden, and were frighteningly appropriate.

"And they brought him unto him: and when he saw him, straightway the spirit tare him; and he fell on the ground, and wallowed foaming. And he asked his father, How long is it ago since this came unto him? And he said, Of a child." Mark (9:20-21).

"Thou shalt not bow down thyself to them, nor serve them: for I the Lord thy God am a jealous God, visiting the iniquity of the fathers upon the children unto the third and fourth generation of them that hate me; And shewing mercy unto thousands of them that love me, and keep my commandments."

Prior Jacob finished his mead and hurried from the study, heading straight for the church. He needed to pray on this before he shared this foul knowledge with the other friars. He needed guidance and the light of God's grace.

Prior Jacob's head was bent in prayer as he knelt before the altar, speaking to God as if he were an understanding father. The prior never regarded conversations with the Lord as being one-sided. What many people failed to understand was that if one stopped talking and truly listened, God provided an answer. It didn't always come immediately. Sometimes the answer came in the middle of the night — a rustling whisper in one's mind — but as clear as a bell. At other times, the response came as an action or a comment from another person which seemed to directly answer the question Jacob had asked only a short while ago.

"Dear Lord," Prior Jacob whispered. "It is my duty as the prior of Greyfriars and as a man who has devoted his life to your service to denounce Father Avery, but is it my duty in this case to accuse the child and condemn him? Is it not my holy responsibility to try to offer him protection and salvation? Can his soul be redeemed, or has evil taken root, the devil now in full possession of his soul?"

If that were the case, there would be only one path open to Prior Jacob. He would have to drive the devil out, and purify the priory which was now tainted by association. Prior Jacob hoped that God, in his mercy and wisdom, would allow him to save Edwin. He was hardly more than a child, an innocent vessel of evil, and an unwitting product of carnal sin. Prior Jacob's head snapped to attention as he heard the slapping of leather against stone as several pairs of feet made their way down the nave toward him.

"Prior," Friar Gregory cried out. "Prior Jacob, the boy Edwin has had another fit. It's lasted longer this time. He's possessed of the evil spirit, and something must be done at once."

Prior Jacob rose laboriously to his feet. He assumed that Edwin had left for the day and no decision would need to be made tonight, but it was no later than five in the evening, and Edwin was evidently still at the priory.

"Thank you," he said quietly and crossed himself as he gazed up at the serene countenance of Jesus Christ. Jacob had his answer.

"Where is Edwin now?"

"Father Avery offered to take him home. They left not five minutes ago," Friar Oswald spat out. He was angry, his face florid with indignation. "We should go in pursuit."

Prior Jacob raised his hand, palm out, signaling for the friars to calm down. "We will hold a meeting and decide on the best course of action together. There's some information I must share with you all. Friar Owen, please advise the brothers that there will be a meeting after the evening meal tonight. Father Avery will be in the chapel, taking his turn at Perpetual Adoration, so we will be able to speak freely. I will remain at prayer until then."

Prior Jacob returned to his cell and sank to his knees in front of the wooden crucifix affixed to the wall. He would have preferred to remain at the church, but knew that he would not be able to pray without interruption, and he needed to marshal his thoughts and give his full attention to the Lord. This was a serious matter, and even though God seemed to have made his position clear, Prior Jacob still wished to handle this matter with the utmost diligence. He remained immobile for over an hour, then genuflected and got to his feet. His knees were sore, and he was stiff with cold, but his conscience was clear. He knew the way forward, and would put his proposal to the friars directly after supper.

Prior Jacob waited until the monks finished their meal then took his place at the pulpit from which the scripture was read before every meal. He quickly but thoroughly outlined what he'd learned and then waited patiently for the uproar to die down. Some of the brothers were riled, their faces flushed with anger and disbelief. They called for drastic measures, which they wished to see carried out immediately. Others, like Friar William, remained quiet, their eyes downcast. Prior Jacob sympathized with their feelings.

"Brothers," Prior Jacob called, raising his hands to ask for silence. "I have prayed on this matter, and I feel that it would be the right thing to turn this matter over to the diocese. The bishop can investigate the allegations and decide on a course of action. As an order of friars, I don't believe it's our responsibility to mete out any punishment to Father Avery or try to exorcise the demons that plague young Edwin. I ask for your support in this decision."

Prior Jacob knew there would be dissent among the brothers since some would take a hard line, while others would plead for clemency, but hoped that common sense would prevail. They were an order of Franciscan Friars, not bishops, cardinals, or even priests. It wasn't their place to hold a trial and condemn the accused. And he had no wish, perhaps selfishly, to take responsibility for what happened to father and son.

"And what of the woman?" Friar Gregory cried out. "Is she to avoid punishment for her sorcery? She bewitched a man of the cloth, and she belongs in Hell, as the Scriptures clearly tells us.

"Revelation 21:8: 'But the fearful, and unbelieving, and the abominable, and murderers, and whoremongers, and sorcerers, and idolaters, and all liars, shall have their part in the lake which burneth with fire and brimstone: which is the second death,'" he spat out, eyes blazing.

The hall exploded into chaos, friars quoting the scriptures at each other to support their points of view. Prior Jacob allowed them a few minutes before calling for order. He expected this kind of reaction to the news, but the vehemence with which some of the friars called for punishment surprised even him.

"Those in favor of turning this matter over to our superiors, raise your hands," Prior Jacob said, praying that rational thinking would prevail.

"Those in favor of taking action against Father Avery, his woman, and their son, raise your hands."

Prior Jacob breathed a sigh of relief. The vote was fifteen to eleven in favor of turning the matter over to the diocese.

"And so, it has been decided. I will write an account and deliver it in person to Bishop Harrington. Friar Matthew, I would ask you to write down what you saw, in your own words. The bishop will find it most helpful, I think. Now, let's all return to our cells. I believe we can all benefit from a period of quiet prayer and contemplation."

The friars filed out of the refectory hall. Some appeared to be relieved, while others grumbled beneath their breath, dissatisfied with the decision. They dared not say it out loud, but they thought Prior Jacob weak and ineffective. Perhaps Prior Jacob's predecessor would have handled the matter differently, but as far as Jacob knew, he'd never had to tackle anything of this magnitude. Prior Jacob walked briskly back to his cell, all too conscious of the angry stares boring into his back. If this was a test of his ability to lead the brothers, then so be it. He would accept whatever the good Lord, in his infinite wisdom, saw fit to do.

Chapter 51

Petra accepted Thomas's arm as she stepped carefully on the icy path leading from the church to the lych-gate. Thomas had joined them for Sunday Mass just as he'd promised, and Petra invited him to dinner. She'd been careful with her wages and made economies whenever possible, but yesterday she splurged on a seat of mutton and purchased a small bag of fine, white flour rather than the coarse brown kind she usually used to make bread. Maude made some mushed peas to accompany the mutton, dipping into the store of dried peas Petra kept on hand. She used bits of fat from the mutton and added hyssop, leaves of sage, and old bread to make the dish thicker and more filling. Thomas would not be terribly impressed, but at least he wouldn't leave hungry.

Petra rose before dawn to bake a seed cake, which would be served with prunes stewed in wine and honey, for added sweetness. She'd been terribly nervous on the way to St. Leonard's, but once she saw Thomas waiting for her just outside the church porch, she began to relax. He was dressed simply, not wishing to stand out next to Petra's modestly-dressed family, and made much over the children after offering a deferential greeting to Maude.

"Just watch your step there," Thomas said, and turned to Edwin who had his arm linked through that of his grandmother. "Keep a tight hold of her, Edwin. Tis slippery over yonder."

"Yes, my lord," Edwin replied, gripping Maude so hard she cried out. Edwin slowed his pace to match that of his grandmother, who took tiny steps, fearful of falling. At her age, bones were as fragile as twigs, and took ages to heal if broken. One of the neighbors took a fall two winters ago, and had been limping ever since, her leg not having healed properly. Maude sighed and continued forward carefully. She had no wish to become a burden to Petra, or to her future husband. Lord Thomas would be taking on enough as was, what with three children to support. *He does seem besotted,* Maude thought as she watched the couple. *I hope Petra doesn't frighten him off. Coyness is for young maidens, not middle-aged women, widowed, and thrice brought to child bed. It would be a rare blessing if Petra could give Lord Thomas a son,* Maude mused as she finally reached the end of the path and released Edwin's arm. A man like Lord Thomas needed a son to carry on his legacy and inherit his wealth. Maude glanced at Edwin. Perhaps he would benefit from this union if Petra failed to conceive.

You're jumping ahead of yourself, old woman, Maude chided herself mentally. *First, let's get these two to the altar.*

Her reverie was interrupted when Elia, who brought up the rear with her sister, laughed uproariously and clapped her hands with glee. Ora lost her footing and landed on her backside beside the path, her expression of embarrassment and outrage almost comical. "Serves you right," Elia chuckled. "You needed taking down a peg or two, you stuck-up cow."

Ora got to her feet and pushed her sister into the nearest puddle, which was just beginning to thaw in the noonday sun. Elia cried out in shock as the freezing water instantly soaked into her skirts. Ora planted her hands on her hips and glared at her sister. "Stuck up cow, is it? Well, at least I don't look like a sow rolling in muck."

"Girls, please," Petra cried out, embarrassed by their unseemly behavior. Her daughters normally got along, but something had gotten into them these past few weeks, making them snipe at each other incessantly. Maude said that girls often became moody and irritable before the onset of their courses. Elia and Ora were still children at heart, but their young bodies told a different tale. Already they were changing, evolving from girls into young women, and with Petra not there to supervise and advise them, they were getting out of hand.

"Sorry, Mother," they said in unison, their eyes downcast. It was bad enough to behave like feuding fishwives at home, but to carry on like this in front of someone of higher station was inexcusable. "Please forgive our bad manners, my lord," Ora said, including her sister in the apology, despite the fact that she had been the one to push her into the snow. Petra gave Ora an evil look, but didn't say anything more. She'd say her piece later, when Thomas wasn't there to overhear it. The girls were told to make a good impression on him, and they'd just ruined everything. *Perhaps that's what they intended to do*, Petra thought as she glanced at Thomas to see his reaction. If he became their stepfather, he'd have the ultimate say in everything affecting the girls, and since their experience of male authority was based only on their father, who was unjust and harsh at the best to times, they could be frightened of how their lives would be altered.

"They're only children," Thomas said, noting Petra's mortified expression. "Pay them no heed. They'll be grown women all too soon, and you'll miss their playfulness."

"Yes, I suppose you're right, Thomas. Perhaps we expect them to grow up too quickly."

They resumed their walk, the girls now quiet and contrite as they ambled behind. Edwin was still walking with Maude, solicitous as ever, but noticeably distracted. He'd been quiet and withdrawn for the past few days, and seemed awfully eager to attend church this morning. Petra might have asked Avery if

Edwin's apprenticeship was going well, but she hadn't seen him in over a week and was determined to maintain her resolve. Today's dinner was crucial to her plans, since her flow was several days late. She had been late before, especially during periods of great strain, but this time it was different. She was an unmarried woman who'd lain with a man; she had every reason to worry. Petra supposed that, in a way, this was the push she needed to fully commit to Thomas. She planned to speak to him after the meal, but the children had fallen behind, and they had a few minutes of privacy before they reached the house.

"Thomas, forgive my impatience, but I have given our union much consideration and thought that perhaps we should bring the wedding forward," Petra mumbled. She'd rehearsed her speech many times in her head, but now that the words were out, she felt embarrassed and vulnerable.

Thomas stopped and turned to face her, putting his hands on her shoulders. "Is that so?" he asked, a smile lifting the corners of his mouth. "I thought myself lucky to be invited for a meal at your house, but now I see you had a celebration of a different kind in mind all along. Shall we set a wedding date today then?"

Petra blushed furiously. Now that the deed was done, she felt an immense sense of relief. Thomas hadn't thought her forward, nor did he hesitate in his reply. "I would like that," Petra replied shyly.

"And when shall we marry, my sweet? I know you're still in mourning for your husband, but I'm no longer a young man, so time is of great value to me. The sooner the better, I say," he said, smiling into Petra's eyes.

Had Petra genuinely mourned her husband, she would have preferred to wait the usual period of a year, which would be up in the autumn, but given her trysts with Avery, she wasn't sure she could afford to bow to the dictates of propriety. If her courses arrived within the next week, she could wait, but if they didn't, a speedy wedding would be best.

"Perhaps we should decide on a date once we've shared our intention with your family, but I think early next month would suit me very well," Petra replied, hoping that this would be soon enough to mask a pregnancy, if there was one. Many children came early, so a seven-month baby wouldn't raise too many eyebrows, but if they waited to marry until the end of April she would be taking too much of a risk.

"How very considerate you are," Thomas said, linking his arm with hers once again. "I think my mother would love an excuse for hosting a feast. It's been a long time since the house saw any merriment, and Robert would like nothing more than to toast our future happiness, again and again," Thomas added. Robert liked his wine, and became even more boisterous with every additional cup.

Petra's nervousness began to ebb as Thomas continued to speak of the future. She knew that Lady Blythe was not pleased with his choice of bride, but Thomas seemed certain, and that was all that mattered. An image of Avery sprang into Petra's mind, his body silvered by moonlight as he lay next her, his face serene in repose. How happy she'd been just to gaze upon him, and drink in his beloved features, but now it would be Thomas who would be lying next to her. She did not love him, nor did her body flush with desire at the thought of sharing a bed with him, but he was an attractive man in his own right, so Petra hoped that the intimate side of the marriage would not be repulsive to her. At any rate, it couldn't be any worse than it had been with Cyril.

Thomas had to stoop to walk beneath the low lintel, but he straightened as soon as he entered Petra's modest home and gave her a formal bow. "Thank you for inviting me into your home, Petra. It's an honor to be here."

Petra playfully bowed back. The honor was hers. What had she done to deserve such a good man?

Chapter 52

March 2014

London, England

Quinn set aside the cross, not wishing to see any more. Petra was happy, her future secure as long as she didn't allow Avery to interfere with her plans. She'd made the right decision, as far as Quinn could tell, but something was lurking just out of sight, something that would lead to her death. It was at moments like these that Quinn truly hated her gift. It wasn't a gift at all, but a curse, designed to suck her into the lives of people she couldn't help. As an archeologist, she dealt with death every day, but the people she dug up were long gone, their bones dusty and brittle. Few of them had died of natural causes or reached old age, but dying of an illness or being slain on a battlefield wasn't the same as being murdered, and Quinn had no doubt that Petra and her son had been murdered.

Her heart went out to Petra, but it was Edwin who made her wish she could just call Rhys and tell him that she'd changed her mind and didn't want to do this anymore. She thought she could retain a sense of professional detachment, but how did you keep your feelings in check when you watched the emotional and physical suffering of a child and knew that he would never grow up to become a man or experience all the things that made life worth living? For some reason, it would have been more bearable had Petra and Edwin died during the coming storm. It would have been tragic, but not personal.

Someone had targeted those two, and not only killed them, but made sure that they would not have peace even in death. To bury them face down just beyond hallowed ground was cruel and unforgiving. What could someone as ordinary as Petra have done to invite such malice? And what of Edwin? Had he been in the wrong place at the wrong time when someone attacked his mother? Had he tried to protect her? He thought himself a man, but his cheeks had still been rounded and smooth, and he had yet to experience the growth spurt that usually came with puberty. His eyes were full of innocence and trust, and the understanding of what life could inflict on one was still years away.

Of course, there were other factors at play, and other people. Quinn could only see what happened to Petra, and experience her point of view, but other forces were gathering 'off-screen,' as Rhys liked to say. A part of Quinn wished she could just lose the cross, accidentally-on-purpose, and never find out what happened to mother and son, but she supposed, being a historian, that she needed to know how the story ended. It went against everything she learned to leave a job unfinished, and of course, she was still under contract with the BBC. There was one more episode after this one scheduled for the program, and then she would be done. Rhys might wish to renew her contract, if the ratings were satisfactory, but she wasn't open to the idea. This job was proving to be one of the hardest tasks she'd ever undertaken, and one of the most emotional. Perhaps, now that Emma had come into their lives, Quinn was even more sensitive to the feelings of a child and a mother's need to protect them from harm.

Quinn sighed and replaced the cross in a drawer. Gabe was sound asleep next to her, having read Emma three stories and sworn that Mr. Rabbit would be there when she woke up. Tomorrow was Monday, and Emma was feeling a bit anxious, as she did before each new week at nursery school, which was still new to her. Quinn was feeling anxious too, but for somewhat different reasons. She'd been feeling unwell the past few days, and her moods seemed to be swinging from one end of the spectrum to the other, like a pendulum. One minute she was wonderfully happy, and then suddenly she was barely holding back the tears that threatened to flow for no apparent reason. The smell of bacon, which she normally found appetizing, nearly drove her out of her favorite cafe only that morning, and her breasts felt tender and swollen.

She often felt a bit weepy and achy before her period, but she was a week late, and that was worrying. She had been late several times before, but it happened mostly on foreign digs. The time difference, change of climate, and hours of painstaking labor sometimes threw off her cycle, but she was at home now, enjoying all the cold and damp that an English spring had to offer. She'd never really worried about pregnancy. Luke had been fanatical about using protection, knowing full well that if Quinn found herself pregnant, she'd plead with him to keep the baby, and he had no wish to find himself in that position. Babies had never been at the top of Luke's list of priorities, and neither was she, as she discovered.

Gabe was always careful as well, but there had been that one time in Edinburgh, when they'd both been too overcome by their emotions to think of practical matters and just went at each other like two sex-crazed ferrets. Quinn counted the weeks in her mind. It was just over six weeks ago, or maybe seven, so this would be just about the time a pregnancy would make itself known. Her period in February had been unusually light and short, but she hadn't given it much thought, being preoccupied with settling Emma into her new life in London and her new school.

Quinn stole a peek at Gabe. He looked tense, even in sleep. These past weeks hadn't been easy on him, and he was just beginning to settle into the role of fatherhood, which had been thrust upon him so unexpectedly. Gabe, being the stoic that he was, would embrace the idea of another child and make things work, but was he emotionally ready? He'd proposed only two months ago, and at a time when most men secretly battled a case of cold feet, he was learning to become a dad, doing his best to support Quinn in her ill-fated quest to find her father, and running the institute with the help of his PA and the other department heads, who, being archeologists, were not the most practical bunch, or the most budget-minded.

Quinn stared into the darkness. She wasn't ready for this. Any of it. Everything seemed to be happening backwards, her carefully thought-out life plan going up in flames. She could almost hear the cackling of the Three Fates, laughing at her as they spun, measured, and cut the thread that was her life. It was an occupational hazard for her to deal with people's failed plans and truncated lives. What made her think she was any different? Life came at you, like a great storm, and you did your best to prepare and weather it, hopefully coming out on the other side stronger and wiser, if a little worse for wear in some cases.

Not everyone weathers the storm, Quinn thought drowsily as she began to drift off, images of Petra and Edwin filling her with dread.

Chapter 53

March 2014

Leicester, Leicestershire

Quinn boarded the London-bound train and settled in a window seat, plopping her handbag in the adjacent seat to prevent some socially-minded stranger from sitting next to her and talking her ear off for an hour-and-a-half. She was in no mood to make small talk. In fact, she was in no mood to do anything more than stare out the window. When she'd arrived in Leicester several hours ago, the day had been sunny and dry, but at the moment, a steady rain fell from the lowering sky, and despite the early hour, it looked like night was fast approaching.

The train began to glide out of the station, the houses alongside the track sliding past as Quinn stared miserably out the window. She reached into her bag and pulled out a roll of mints. She suddenly felt lightheaded and nauseated and hoped the mints would help combat the rising bile. Thankfully, the feeling passed quickly, and she leaned her head against the back of the seat and closed her eyes, shutting out the rain-drenched scenery. She just wanted to go home, change into comfortable clothes, make a cup of tea, and curl up on the sofa, preferably alone. She'd tell Gabe what happened, but first she needed a little quiet time to process what she'd learned. They had a mighty row about today's outing, but in the end, he reluctantly gave her his blessing. He wanted to come along, but Quinn resolutely refused the offer, explaining to him once again that she needed to do this alone. One thing she had promised him — willingly — was that there were going to be no games of deception. She would be honest and see where it took her.

Quinn arrived in Leicester just before noon and walked to the High Street. It had taken nearly a half hour, but Quinn didn't mind. She used the time to prepare herself for the meeting that was about to take place. She'd been determined to do this, but now that she was there, all she wanted was to turn around and go back home. It wasn't too late to change her mind, but she knew that she'd find herself right back in Leicester, maybe not tomorrow, but next week or next month. For better or worse, she had to find out the truth.

The Queen's Arms Pub looked like countless other pubs all over England. The façade was old-fashioned and quaint, the interior dim and somewhat oppressive. The blackened beams dissected the white plaster walls like veins, and the brown carpet on the floor had seen better days and much spilled beer. There was a fireplace directly across from the bar, where a merry fire crackled in the grate. Several patrons occupied the tables closest to the fire, enjoying the warmth and the comfortable atmosphere. An attractive middle-aged woman, her blonde hair silvered with gray, came out of the kitchen with a tray loaded with food, and Quinn suddenly felt hungry. The fish and chips smelled divine, and so did the steak and kidney pie. For the past two weeks, she'd been alternating between nausea and all-consuming hunger, but lunch would have to wait, and if she still had an appetite, she'd treat herself to something nice.

Quinn approached the bar, which was manned by a man of late middle-age. He wore a dun-colored sweater vest with matching corduroy trousers and a pair of rimless specs, which gave him a professorial air. His sandy hair was thinning, and there were deep grooves running alongside his mouth. He was in the process of drawing pints of Guinness, but looked up as Quinn approached and gave her a friendly grin.

"Good day to you, love. What can I get you?" he asked. Quinn would dearly have loved a glass of wine to steady her nerves, but alcohol didn't seem to agree with her these days.

"Orange juice, please," Quinn said. She knew she sounded nervous, and the man had realized it as well.

"Are you okay?" he asked as he set the glass of juice in front of her. Quinn nodded, took a sip to wet her mouth, since it'd suddenly gone completely dry, and plunged in.

"Are you the Steven Kane who used to reside in Dunston?" she asked softly. She didn't want to sound like she was interrogating the man, but she had to make sure he was the right Steven Kane before stating her business. She was fairly sure that he was.

"Yes. Who's asking?" he asked, suddenly wary of her.

"My name is Quinn Allenby. I would like a moment of your time, Mr. Kane."

"What's this about? It's nearly lunchtime and we're busy. Are you selling life insurance or some such nonsense?" he asked, squinting at her and pursing his lips.

"I'm not selling anything, Mr. Kane. I would like to speak to you regarding a personal matter," Quinn explained. He shook his head in irritation and swept the payment for the juice off the counter with a practiced motion.

"What possible personal business can you have with me?" he asked. His steely gaze bored into her, daring her to tell him what she wanted, so that he could dismiss her and send her on her way. The façade of the friendly pub-owner had been replaced with the countenance of a man who'd have no problem with evicting her from the premises if she persisted in harassing him.

"My mother is Sylvia Wyatt, but you would have known her as Sylvia Moore," Quinn replied, hoping that Sylvia's name would pique his curiosity enough to at least hear her out.

Steven Kane paused in the act of filling a glass and stared at her, his expression almost comical. Hearing Sylvia's name seemed to have that effect on people, but his attitude thawed somewhat as he studied Quinn with a newfound interest. He finished his task, pushed the glass across the bar toward a customer and scanned the dining room, clearly looking for someone.

"Rhoda, would you mind the bar for a spell?" he called out to the blonde woman. "I just need to have a word with this young lady."

Rhoda gave Steven Kane the gimlet eye before placing several dirty glasses on a round tray and coming back toward the bar. She looked at Quinn with undisguised interest, her head tilted to the side as if she were trying to decide if Quinn was friend or foe. She seemed to judge her harmless and finally smiled and gave a wave of the hand.

"Go on, then," she said, her attention already on the next customer to approach the bar with an order.

Steven Kane gestured for Quinn to follow him and led her to an office tucked away between the bar and the entrance to the toilets. The room was square and small, with a window that looked out into the alleyway behind the pub. A scarred wooden desk dominated the office, leaving just enough space for two chairs. There were bits of paper everywhere: invoices, receipts, post-it notes, and cuttings from newspapers. Steven Kane invited Quinn to sit in the guest chair and took a seat behind his messy desk.

"So, what is it you're after?" he asked, his voice as flinty as his gaze.

"Mr. Kane, I was adopted as an infant and only met my birth mother a few months ago. In some respects, our reunion was a dream-come-true, but in others, it turned out to be something of a nightmare. It seems that I might have as many as four possible fathers, and I am here to ask you for a paternity test. You have every right to refuse, of course, but I would very much appreciate a swab. It would put my mind to rest."

"And what about my mind?" Kane asked, leaning back in his chair and observing her. There was a hint of amusement in the depth of his eyes. When Quinn didn't reply, he permitted himself a ghost of a smile, making her feel a little less awkward.

"Ms. Allenby, I will give you your swab, or whatever it is you need from me. You seem like a nice lady, and I feel for you; I really do. However, having said that, I will also tell you that the paternity test will not be a match."

"Do you deny having a relationship with Sylvia?" Quinn asked. She knew from doing online research that Rhoda was Stephen's wife of nearly thirty-five years. She inherited the pub when her father died nearly twenty years ago, and her husband went from doing odd jobs to becoming the owner of a successful business. Suddenly discovering a thirty-year-old daughter would do no favors to his marriage or his business prospects since his wife could divorce him and keep the pub that had been in her family since 1912.

"No, I don't deny it. Nearly ruined my marriage, it did," Steven Kane said, his eyes glazed with memories. "Your mother was a beauty. You have the look of her, actually, only she was more… What is the word I'm searching for? Aware."

"Aware of what?" Quinn asked, unsure of his meaning.

"Aware of herself; her sex appeal. She knew what she was about, even at sixteen."

"Are you saying that you didn't seduce her? You were quite a bit older than she was, were you not?" Quinn asked. She had no wish to sound judgmental, but it seemed likely that Steven Kane had made the first move and not Sylvia.

"I'm saying that it was mutual. No one seduced anyone. We both went into it with eyes wide open, only I was married, so of course, I was the cad in that scenario. It wasn't my finest moment; I'll tell you that."

"So, why are you so sure that the test will not be a match?" Quinn asked carefully. Truth be told, she hoped he was right. She couldn't imagine Stephen Kane being her biological father. Of the three contenders she'd met so far, Rhys Morgan was the only one with whom she'd felt a connection, until she found out the truth, that is. She'd felt comfortable with him, and they shared common interests and a passion for telling people's stories. Robert Chatham repelled her with his aggression and over-inflated ego, but something about Stephen Kane smacked of disappointment and failure.

"Mind if I smoke?" Kane asked as he extracted a pack of cigarettes from his desk and felt in his pocket for a lighter.

"I do, actually," Quinn replied.

"I'll open the window."

Stephen Kane took a drag of his cigarette, then held his hand out toward the window, allowing the smoke to curl outward and dissipate into the frosty air. Thankfully, the smoke didn't blow back into the office. Kane stared out the window at the brick wall opposite the pub, his gaze misty with reminiscence.

"I have no wish to talk about this, but I suppose you have a right to know, and I might as well tell you the whole truth," he began. "I had a younger brother, Jack. Jack was everything that I wasn't, or so I was frequently told by our mother. He always knew exactly what he wanted and went for it. There was never any hesitation or regret. He met Rhoda when he was just eighteen and proposed to her within weeks. "She is the one," he said, "and there'll never be anyone else." They married and had two girls in quick succession. They weren't well off, but they were all right. Jack worked on a construction site as a welder, and Rhoda stayed at home with the children. They were happy," Stephen added, blowing out another puff of smoke.

"What happened?" Quinn asked softly.

"Jack couldn't afford a car, so he rode a scooter to work. One day, on the way home, he was hit by a lorry. The driver had been drinking and crashed into a tree after he sideswiped Jack. Jack might have survived had someone gotten to him sooner, but by the time the ambulance arrived, he was gone. Rhoda was left on her own, with two small children and no source of income. She might have been entitled to damages had the driver survived, but he died, so she had no claim, and Jack never bothered to get insurance."

Stephen took a deep drag on his cigarette and stared at the curling smoke before continuing.

"Rhoda had to give up the flat and move back in with her parents. They helped as much as they could, but they were elderly, and minding two toddlers all day while Rhoda worked was too much for them. Rhoda was struggling, so I stepped into the breach. I always fancied her, and I knew that Jack would want me to look after his family."

"So, you married her," Quinn said, wondering what this had to do with the paternity test.

"I did. She didn't love me. Not in that way. I was a poor substitute for Jack, but Rhoda was desperate, and marrying me seemed like the best way out of a bad situation. I knew it, but I had an agenda of my own. I am sterile, you see. I was married before Rhoda, and when my wife and I failed to conceive, she sent me for a test. I found out then. Jack's kids were the closest I'd ever come to having my own children, and I've been a good father to them. They love me, my girls," Stephen said, a trifle defensively.

"I'm sure they do," Quinn agreed, eager for Stephen Kane to get to the end of his story.

"We didn't get on, Rhoda and I. Sex is the glue that holds a marriage together, but Rhoda just wasn't interested. We stayed together for the children, and for financial reasons. Rhoda poured her love into the children, but I strayed from time to time. I needed to feel wanted and desired, and I wasn't about to get that at home. That's where Sylvia came in. We had a good time, she and I, but when she got pregnant, I knew it couldn't be mine," Stephen Kane said as he stubbed out his cigarette.

"Actually, my affair with Sylvia brought things to a head with Rhoda. She was angry and bitter when she found out, so I told her that she should either be a proper wife to me or agree to a divorce. We're still together, as you can see, so it's not all sour grapes."

"Is that why you turned Sylvia away when she came to you for help?"

"What else was I supposed to do? If I helped her, I'd be as good as admitting to the whole village that I shagged a minor and that her child was mine. I told her to ask the real father for help. It wasn't my problem."

"Right."

"Let's get this over with then, if you've no objection. I have a pub to run."

Quinn took the package out of her handbag and extracted the cotton swab. She handed it to Steven Kane and asked him to scrape the inside of his cheek, which he did. Quinn sealed the swab in a tube and replaced it in the package. She was more than ready to leave.

"Thank you, Mr. Kane. I appreciate your candor and your willingness to help me."

"I'm sorry, lass. It's not a pleasant thing, traipsing all over the country, asking strange men if they are your father, is it?"

"No, it's not."

In fact, it's quite demoralizing. There are days when I wish that I could go back to not knowing anything about my true parentage. I think I was actually happier then, Quinn thought bitterly.

Steven Kane got to his feet, signaling that the interview was over. "Would you like a spot of lunch? Rhoda just made the steak and ale pies, and they're delicious. You look like you need a bit of time to just sit quietly and think."

Quinn's stomach growled at the mention of food, but she shook her head. She had no wish to spend any more time in Leicester. She felt disappointed and angry. She knew what happened with the other three men, but Sylvia had actually had a relationship with Stephen Kane. Quinn had hoped that the man cared for her somewhat, but he'd simply taken advantage of her, using her to satisfy needs that weren't being taken care of at home. Sylvia might have been 'aware' as he put it, but she was still a girl, and he'd been a grown man; a man who refused to help her when she came to him. The baby might not have been his, but he still could have been a little less indifferent, a little less selfish.

Quinn walked out of the pub without sparing Rhoda, who was staring at her from behind the bar, a glance. She wished the two of them joy of each other. They might have remained married, but the downward turn of Rhoda's mouth suggested that she wasn't a happy woman, or a fulfilled one. Quinn was in no position to judge, but she simply wanted no part of these people. She wanted to go home and throw her arms about the man who loved and desired her. She knew she was lucky, but hearing about the Kanes' loveless marriage made her that much more aware of her own good fortune.

Quinn sat up and looked out the window as the train approached London. It was nearly dark outside, the rain coming down in a torrent that made the houses along the tracks look like dark, fuzzy blobs. Now that she'd had a little time to think, she felt marginally better. The meeting with Stephen Kane hadn't been a complete waste. She'd still give his sample to Colin Scott, just to make sure that Kane had been telling the truth. If he was, then there was only one man left on the list — Seth Besson, if Sylvia could be believed. She'd proven herself to be less than honest, and Quinn wondered if there were going to be any more surprises. Her rational side told her to let go of her hopes and terminate her relationship with Sylvia. The woman had done nothing but mislead her, but she was her birth mother, and as Gabe pointed out, we didn't get to choose our parents.

Quinn grabbed her bag and made her way toward the door as the train eased into St. Pancras station. She'd forgotten to bring an umbrella, so she would get soaked by the time she got her turn at a taxi. Quinn stepped onto the platform and began to walk toward the nearest exit. Her mobile vibrated in her pocket, reminding her that she'd forgotten to call Gabe. He was probably worried sick. Quinn took out the phone and looked at the screen. There was a picture of Emma, wearing her yellow wellies and a matching raincoat. She was holding a Disney Princess umbrella over her head, which she appeared to be twirling happily. The caption said, "Your carriage awaits." Quinn smiled, her melancholy forgotten. No day could be described as being bad if Gabe and Emma were waiting for her at the end of it.

She found the exit Gabe indicated in his text and spread her arms out to Emma, who catapulted into her, a huge smile on her face. Gabe kissed Quinn over Emma's head, his eyes searching her face for a hint of how her day went.

"All right?" he asked, and she nodded, thankful that he hadn't uttered a word of reproach about her not calling.

"You two wait here, and I'll get the car," Gabe said. "It's really coming down."

"Do you want my umbrella, Gabe?" Emma asked.

"No, I'm all right, sweetheart," Gabe replied, smiling at the little girl. "You hold on to it."

"Ok," Emma said, clearly relieved not to have to give it up.

"Did you have a good day at school?" Quinn asked once they were in the car, and Emma was strapped into her seat.

"We had *Show and Tell*," Emma replied.

"So, what did you show?"

"I brought Mr. Rabbit and told them that my mum bought it for me when I was a baby," Emma replied sadly. "I didn't tell them she died."

"You don't have to tell anyone if you don't want to," Gabe said. "What did the other children bring?" he asked in an effort to distract Emma from her sadness. She went into a litany of items, describing each one in detail. Quinn's mind began to drift as she rested her hands on her handbag. Stephen Kane's DNA was inside it, but there was also a pregnancy test that she'd picked up at Boots before boarding the train. It was time to confirm her suspicions and share the news with Gabe if the test was positive. Maybe she'd even do it tonight.

Chapter 54

"So, what was Stephen Kane like?" Gabe asked after reading Emma a story and tucking her into bed. He sat down next to Quinn on the sofa and pulled her into his arms. They hadn't been able to talk about Quinn's visit to Leicester with Emma in the room, but Quinn felt Gabe's gaze on her all through the evening, gauging her mood and offering silent support.

"He was all right. More forthcoming than he needed to be, actually. He said that he's sterile and couldn't possibly be my biological father."

"Do you believe him?" Gabe asked.

"He gave me a sample readily enough, which leads me to believe that he was telling the truth. I'll verify it with Colin, of course. He also said that Sylvia had been a willing participant in their affair. He called her 'aware'. Said she knew what she was about," Quinn said.

"Not an innocent victim then, as she'd like you to believe?"

"Well, it's his word against hers, as it is with all of them. I don't think anyone would readily admit to taking advantage of a young girl. And people do tend to rationalize their actions in their minds, turning the facts this way and that until they fit with what they wish to believe of themselves."

"That's certainly true." Gabe nodded and looked away, his gaze fixated on nothing in particular. She knew him long enough to recognize it as a gesture of avoidance. He was bursting to say something, but was desperately trying not to influence her one way or the other, and if she stared him down, he'd crack.

"Gabe, I know what you are thinking, so you might as well look at me," Quinn said.

"Do you?" Gabe asked, still not making eye contact.

"Yes. You are thinking that Sylvia lied to me again and again, and that she might have manipulated the facts to gain my sympathy."

"Well, it is possible, is it not?" Gabe replied, turning to face Quinn, eyes narrowed in speculation. Someone who didn't know Gabe would think that he disliked Sylvia and chose to blame the victim, as many would, but with Gabe, it was nothing personal. He believed in facts which could be supported with solid proof. And, more than anything, he wanted to protect Quinn from getting hurt.

"Yes, it is. Rhys didn't dispute what happened that night, but then again, he is still guilt-ridden by the whole thing because he was ashamed about being coerced by his friends into doing something he clearly hadn't been comfortable with, with a girl who was too drunk, or drugged, to put up much of a fight."

"Look, Quinn, Sylvia might have been pure as the driven snow, or she might have been the village slag; you'll never know the truth, and ultimately, it's for you to decide if you want to judge her or just chuck it all up to ancient history. She is, without question, your biological mother, and somewhere out there is your father. Of course, whether Seth Besson raped her or shagged a girl who was a willing partner makes a big difference to any possible relationship you might have with him. So, if or when you meet him, perhaps you should give him a fair chance, since you don't actually know if he's guilty."

"So, now you approve of me meeting him?" Quinn asked, trying to hide her amusement.

"I know that you won't rest until you do, so I will keep my opinions to myself and follow you to the ends of the earth, or to the United States, in this case. I will help you see this to the bitter end."

"Thank you, Gabe. That means the world to me."

"You don't need to thank me. I want you to be happy, and I know that finding out the truth about your heritage and your gift will bring you peace. And whether you choose to have a relationship with your birth parents or not, you will be a happier person for knowing where you came from."

"And speaking of being a happier person," Quinn said, smiling into Gabe's eyes. "I have something to tell you. I'm pregnant," she said and watched Gabe's eyes light up with joy. It wasn't until that moment that she knew that she was truly happy about her news. She'd taken the pregnancy test while Gabe was with Emma, and the proof now lay at the bottom of the rubbish bin. The test came back positive, just as Quinn knew it would. And she was glad.

Gabe pulled her into his arms and kissed the top of her head. "Oh, that's wonderful news, love. I'm thrilled. Sometimes I don't know who is more psychic, you or my mother."

"What do you mean?"

"I spoke to her this afternoon and she asked me when you were due."

"What?! How could she possibly know?"

"She said that she saw it in your eyes when we came to collect Emma. She said you can always tell, if you know what to look for."

"That's witchery, that is," Quinn laughed. "So, what did you tell her?"

"I told her that I would let her know as soon as you finally decided to tell me."

"You knew?" Quinn demanded, amazed that he hadn't let on.

"I suspected."

"How?"

Gabe arched an eyebrow, making Quinn laugh. "Well, for starters, your period is late. You've blanched the last two times I ate a bacon butty in your presence, and you have declined offers of wine, which is a flashing neon sign in itself to someone who is familiar with your boozy habits." Quinn playfully smacked his arm, acknowledging the truth of everything he said.

"You've also been more tired lately, and often close to tears for no apparent reason." Gabe cupped her cheek and met Quinn's gaze. "You didn't seem pleased with the possibility, so I thought I'd give you a little time to sort your feelings out, if it proved to be true. And it seems that you have."

"You really notice things, don't you?" Quinn asked as she touched Gabe's cheek. "You really care." Luke wouldn't have noticed a thing; he'd been too absorbed in himself, and his reaction to this type of news would have been displeasure and some sort of a rebuke, blaming her for allowing it to happen. Luke wouldn't have cared how she felt, only how the situation would affect him.

"Don't you ever doubt it," Gabe replied, covering her hand with his own. "I love you, and I love our baby."

"I love you too, Gabe. More than you'll ever know. There's no one else I'd rather have a child with."

Quinn leaned into Gabe and he put his arm around her, pulling her close. "We're not making it to the altar, are we?" Quinn giggled. "I'm not waddling down the aisle, looking like a cream puff."

"We have a few months before you begin to show, don't we? I really would prefer to do this right, Quinn. I know it sounds old-fashioned, but I want our child to know that we were married when he was born."

"He?"

Gabe laughed softly, his eyes sparkling with mischief.

"What's so funny?" Quinn demanded.

"My mother asked when 'he' is due. Phoebe Russell hasn't been wrong in forty years, so yes, it's a boy."

Quinn laid her hand gently over her flat stomach. A boy. A son. The idea made her unbearably happy. She would be just as happy with a girl, but the notion of a boy felt right somehow, as if some Earth Mother instinct was alive and well within her.

"So, what are you saying?" Quinn asked, her mind reluctantly returning to their conversation.

"I'm saying that we should set a date. April would be too soon, but maybe in May? Call your parents and tell them to book a flight, and if you don't feel like dealing with the details of planning a wedding, there's nothing my mother would enjoy more. Just tell her what you like, and leave it in her capable hands. All you have to do is buy a dress and show up at the church. What do you say?"

Quinn considered this for a moment. Was it really that simple? She'd always imagined a big, white wedding, but what she wanted at this stage of her life was a small, intimate affair with only friends and family. Suddenly, getting married in Berwick seemed like a lovely idea. They could have a wedding reception at the house or out in the garden if the weather was fine. In May, everything would be in bloom, and with any luck, the sky would actually be blue rather than that particular shade of English slate-gray.

Quinn reached for her mobile and opened the calendar. "May 24th," she proclaimed. "I will be about four months pregnant then. With the right gown, I can pull it off."

"May 24th," Gabe agreed and kissed her tenderly. "Shall we put General Russell in charge?"

"I think your mother has just been promoted to Brigadier. I'll draw up a list of ideas and discuss it with her, and I'll ask Jill to find me a dress. She'll know exactly what I'll need."

Gabe removed the phone from Quinn's hand and pushed her down onto the sofa.

"Oh no, you don't. Emma can walk in at any moment."

"Right," Gabe chuckled. "I keep forgetting we have to act like respectable, law-abiding citizens."

He stood up and scooped Quinn into his arms, easily carrying her to their bedroom and kicking the door shut with his foot. Quinn's last coherent thought was that she quite liked being respectable.

Chapter 55

March 1347

Dunwich, Suffolk

Prior Jacob rose earlier than usual. It would be another three hours before daylight finally chased away the shadows of the night, but he couldn't wait. He was determined to get the unpleasant task over with, even if he had to miss Terce. He never missed a prayer, not even when he was ill; this morning would be the first time since he'd joined the order. The cell was freezing. Prior Jacob's breath came out in vaporous puffs as he slid his feet into his shoes to avoid touching the icy stone floor with his bare feet. He pulled the coarse robe on over the linen shirt he wore to bed and belted it with a rope before genuflecting to the crucifix above his cot and leaving his cell. The leather soles of his shoes made a slapping sound against the floor as he hurried down the dark corridor.

    Father Avery and his lover had sinned, and their son was clearly possessed of the devil, but Christ had healed the sick and forgiven the sinners, so Prior Jacob could not bring himself to condemn them. He would do his duty, but allow someone else to sit in judgment of the accused. Prior Jacob opened the door to his study and was greeted by utter chaos. Scrolls were scattered across the floor, and the chair was overturned, as was the inkwell. The ink pooled like bile on the surface of the desk and dripped onto the floor where it reached the edge. Prior Jacob had to grab on to the door jamb as a strong gust of wind nearly blew him out of the room. The shutter had been torn from the window and a gale seemed to be blowing off the sea.

The prior bent his head into the wind, picked up the shutter, and forced it back into the window, blocking out the wind. Mere seconds later, the shutter exploded out of the frame, nearly knocking him off his feet. Prior Jacob grabbed whatever documents he could carry in his arms and left the study, crossing to an empty cell across the corridor, where he deposited the scrolls. The narrow window faced in the opposite direction, so the scrolls would be safe. The prior stood in the middle of the corridor, suddenly plagued by indecision. He couldn't just leave without warning the others of impending danger, so he headed back toward the friars' cells. Several brothers were already up, calling for the others to wake as they moved down the corridor. They cupped their hands around the flames of their candles to keep them from going out in the strong draft. The meager light illuminated only the bottom portion of their faces, making them look otherworldly.

"A great storm is brewing," Prior Jacob called out to the brothers. "We must secure all the windows and see to the animals."

"The manuscripts must be protected," Friar Gregory called out as he rushed toward the great room where the scribes worked. It had glazed windows, but the wind was so strong that a branch or some other debris could easily shatter the glass. Several friars followed Friar Gregory, while Prior Jacob divided the remaining brothers into groups and assigned them areas to secure. The animals were a priority, but the storage shed, where sacks of flour were kept, was a particular area of concern. If the doors of the shed blew open, the lashing rain would soak into the flour, rendering it unusable. The brothers used the flour not only for themselves, but to bake bread for the poor. They handed the loaves out at the alms gate, which would be mobbed after the storm.

Two hours later, the friars gathered inside the church for Terce. They were wet, tired, and hungry, but would have to wait to attend to their needs until after the service.

"We should offer up a prayer for the townsfolk," Friar William suggested. The friars' heads bobbed in agreement as they took their places. Prior Jacob was in his usual spot at the front of the church. He couldn't desert his brothers during the storm, nor was it safe to travel to see the bishop as he'd intended, particularly since he'd planned on walking the whole way.

**

The wind whipped Petra's cloak, making it billow like a sail behind her. She tried to gather it around herself, but the gusts were too strong and tore away her only protection against the elements. Petra's headpiece was askew, and tendrils of wet hair stuck to her face and blew into her eyes. She could barely see where she was going, so she gave up on the cloak and shielded her face instead, desperate to protect her eyes. Sand and grit blew from the direction of the beach as the storm gathered force, the wind moaning like a wailing woman. A large branch came hurtling past Petra's head and scratched her cheek before smashing against the wall of a nearby house. Several men were in the street, securing the removable shutters by hammering in horizontal planks of wood to keep the shutters from being torn out by the wind. This would protect the interiors of their homes from getting wet.

Petra could see several masts in the distance. They seemed to be thrusting up and down rather violently, their tops disappearing into the glowering sky and then coming down again as waves pounded the shore. Petra took shelter behind a stone building and leaned against the wall, panting with exertion. Lady Blythe would need her today, but she couldn't walk another mile to her house, not in this weather. She would have to turn back and wait out the storm. Petra hoped that Thomas was at home. He would see to the house and his mother. This wouldn't be the first storm he'd weathered.

Petra allowed herself a few moments to catch her breath, then stepped out from behind her shelter and instantly drew back with a cry of alarm. A deluge of water was moving toward her, the wave carrying chunks of wood, household items, and even a cat, who was struggling to keep its head above water and meowing desperately. Petra couldn't see any people, but she heard the screams as the rushing water knocked those townspeople foolish enough to be out in the storm off their feet and carried them along. The men who'd been outside only moments before scurried indoors, slamming the doors shut against the flood. Petra turned on her heel and began to run as fast as she could. The wind was at her back now that she turned for home, so she was able to move more quickly, outrunning the gushing water. She glanced back over her shoulder, relieved to see the water receding and leaving a trail of debris in its wake. The poor cat was still alive, if terrified and soaked to the bone. It ran for its life as soon as its paws found purchase on the muddy ground, instinctively heading away from the sea.

Frightened and out of breath, Petra judged it safe enough to slow her pace. She kept her eyes glued to the opening between the houses, and sure enough, another surge of water came rushing from the beach, this one higher and stronger. Petra watched in horror as a child of about five, who had stepped outside, was swept off her feet and carried along. She was splashing and screaming for her mother, who threw herself into the churning water and tried to catch hold of her daughter's foot. The child was sucked under, and the mother screamed for help, paralyzed with fear as she was nearly knocked off balance and submerged in icy water. A man, who might have been the girl's father, rushed to her aid and managed to fish the thrashing child out of the water before the wave began to recede. The little girl howled with fright and clung to her mother, who was soaked but oblivious to anything besides the child in her arms. The man glanced toward the sea before grabbing the woman by the arm and pulling her along toward higher ground.

Petra didn't wait around for the next wave. She began to run, bursting into her house and throwing her body against the door as she slid the bolt into place.

"Girls, quick, get me a wooden plank," Petra cried.

"Where are we supposed to get a plank?" Ora demanded.

"Get one out from under your mattress," Petra screamed. "Do it now."

The girls scrambled to pull the straw-stuffed mattress off and yanked out one of the planks that formed the bottom of their bed.

"What's happened?" Maude cried. "Why did you come back?"

"Mother, we need to secure the house and leave," Petra screamed. "We must get to higher ground. The sea is coming for us. Children, come. Now!"

"Petra, are you mad? We're more than a mile away from shore. We're perfectly safe here."

"Not this time," Petra threw over her shoulder. "Edwin, put up the shutter, and push it in as hard as you can."

The children looked terrified as Petra carefully opened the door and peered outside. She could see a swell of water in the distance, but judged it safe to run. Petra ushered the children outside and grabbed her mother under the arm. "Let's go, Mother."

She shut the door behind them and wedged the wooden plank between the ground and the door. She had to apply all her strength to push it in. The plank would keep the door from bursting open from the pressure of the rushing water and hopefully keep the water from flooding the house. It wasn't much, but it was the best she could do on such short notice. She prayed that the water wouldn't reach the window.

Maude gasped when she stepped outside and saw the destruction. The water hadn't reached them yet, but in the distance, down the street, a few houses were already in ruins. Several trees had been torn out by the roots and lay on the ground, blocking the street until the next wave would carry them along, their branches and trunks causing further damage. Edwin grabbed his grandmother by the arm and pulled her along, urging her to move faster. Maude lowered her head to keep the rain out of her eyes and allowed Edwin to lead her. Her cloak and barbet were already wet, and her feet slipped on the wet ground, making walking precarious. Ora and Elia were way ahead of them, running like frightened rabbits.

The water had come closer than Petra expected in a very short time, but the storm showed no signs of abating. It must have started during the night, while they were all asleep, believing themselves to be safe behind the walls of their homes. The sea had claimed plenty of houses just like the ones Petra lived in during past storms. She couldn't remember any fearful storms herself, but she'd heard the stories and saw the tops of water-submerged buildings protruding from the sea at very low tide. They looked like the jagged teeth of some sea monster that was about to come up from the watery depths and devour the rest of the town.

Petra lifted her skirts and began to run after her mother and the children. Many others had the same idea, and the streets were congested with families trying to save themselves. Children screamed with fright, and women fought to stay upright as they herded their offspring and clutched whatever small possessions they could carry. Several men tried to help the old and infirm to dry land and then went back for others who were stranded further down the street, but their efforts were hindered. They slipped in the knee-deep silt and, more often than not, needed help themselves.

It was absolute chaos. Everywhere one looked, there was a mass of humanity pursued by gallons of churning water. It was like some Biblical plague come to drown the sinners. Petra swallowed down a sob as she glanced in the direction of Lady Blythe's house. All she could see was destruction and huge, terrifying waves. The masts were no longer there, the ships smashed to pieces by the force of the gale. Every surge brought more silt and debris, but the latest waves also carried corpses, leaving them behind like bits of rubbish once the water receded. A few brave souls tried to retrieve them to keep them from being swept out to sea, but most people just ran for their lives, urging their loved ones to go faster.

Maude was trembling with fatigue by the time they finally reached a safe spot. She sank to the ground next to several other bedraggled elderly people. The earth was wet and cold, but Maude's legs would no longer hold her up, and she was grateful for solid ground beneath her. The rest of the townspeople remained upright, their gazes glued to the normally placid sea. They watched in stunned silence as great waves formed in the distance and crashed into the town with unbridled force. Houses folded as if they were built of paper, their walls falling haphazardly into the foaming seawater and rushing along with the current. The wind was even stronger on higher ground. It tore at hair and cloaks, turning the skin red and raw with cold.

Dozens of people took shelter behind the walls of the Leper Hospital. The stone walls shielded them from the wind, but most folk were too afraid to go near it and preferred to remain out in the open. Petra wrapped her arms about the children as she tried to keep them from getting separated. People were rushing toward them in droves, pushing the stragglers out of their way and knocking them to the ground if they were too slow. The noise was deafening.

Petra froze in terror when she noticed the look in Edwin's eyes. She knew the signs; she'd seen them often enough. Edwin was on a verge of a fit. The fits happened most often in times of stress, and Edwin had been half-dragging his grandmother up the hill for the past half hour. He was physically drained, scared out of his wits, and overwhelmed by the panic all around him.

"Edwin, no!" Petra moaned, but it was too late.

Edwin collapsed onto his side at her feet. The look of fear in his eyes vanished, replaced by the unseeing stare that always accompanied the convulsions. Edwin's limbs began to twitch, and his face contorted into a grotesque grimace as saliva ran from the corner of his mouth. Several people stopped to stare. Their faces twisted with fear and hatred once they understood what they were looking at. Someone pointed a finger and others gathered around to watch Edwin's suffering. Petra tried to shield him from prying eyes, but it was too late. Everyone saw what was happening, and the spectacle momentarily distracted them from the chaos below. The animosity of the townspeople was palpable, and they drew closer, advancing on Edwin, who was still writhing on the ground. Petra's gaze flew from one face to another, searching for a spark of sympathy, but all she saw was hostility. A terrible panic seized her.

"Please," she begged. "Don't touch him. He's unwell."

"Unwell?!" someone snarled. "Look at him. He's possessed."

A few heads nodded in agreement. "He's been taken over by an evil spirit," a woman shrieked as she pointed at Edwin. "He's speaking in tongues."

In fact, Edwin wasn't saying anything at all, but a low hissing came from his lips, which was enough to give credence to the woman's accusation. The woman shrieked in terror, her shaking finger pointing at Edwin as if he were about to attack her. She crossed herself and began muttering a prayer as she backed away, too terrified to turn her back toward the poor boy.

Petra threw herself on top of Edwin. "Leave him alone!" she screamed. "It's nothing to do with you. See to your own children."

Petra cried out as someone tried to pull her off her son. Edwin was just coming around, his eyes regaining focus as the fit began to pass. Petra fought free of her assailant's grasp and crawled back toward Edwin.

"Edwin," she called, terrified. "Edwin."

She suddenly noticed a brown-robed figure rushing toward them and breathed a sigh of relief. The friar would help her. He was sure to know Edwin from the priory and would try to calm the townspeople, who would respect his authority.

"Please, help me, Brother," Petra cried. The mob was upon her, pushing and pulling at her in order to get to Edwin, who was now fully conscious and sobbing with fright.

"You!" the friar screamed. "You are the whore who spawned this bastard. He's the Devil's familiar, and this storm is the manifestation of God's wrath. He sent it to cleanse this evil town from the likes of you!"

The friar was shaking with outrage, his face contorted with religious fervor. Two more friars appeared at his heels. Their damp hair was plastered to their skulls and the skirts of their robes billowed around their legs, exposing milky-white ankles. They were bearing down on her, wooden crosses held in front of them to ward off evil.

"Friar Gregory," Edwin moaned. He tried to sit up, but the friar knocked him back down. People were shouting and cursing, their fear and anger having found a target. They craved violence, and now it was sanctioned by the Church.

Petra screamed like a wounded animal when someone grabbed her by the arms and pulled her aside.

"It's me, Petra." For a brief moment, she thought that Avery had come to their rescue, but it wasn't Avery.

Thomas pushed her out of the way and forced his way through the crowd toward Edwin, leaving Petra at the mercy of the mob. Anonymous hands grabbed at her and tore at her cloak and gown. Someone scratched her face and yanked a fistful of her hair, forcing Petra to her knees. A woman who lived in her street kicked her in the ribs, and several people followed her example, encouraged by Petra's inability to defend herself. People shouted abuse and called her names, but most of the onlookers were more interested in Edwin. It was him they wanted. They'd deal with Petra later. Petra tried to see between the legs of her attackers, searching for the girls. She'd lost sight of them the moment Edwin collapsed. Petra prayed that they were safe and with their grandmother. She rolled onto her side and curled into herself, arms over her head and knees drawn up to protect her head and stomach. She could just make out Edwin and Thomas through the forest of shins.

Thomas lifted Edwin off the ground and held him close. The mob seemed to hold its breath, suddenly unsure of what to do. Lord Devon wasn't one of them; he was a nobleman, a man who commanded respect and obedience, but the indecision was short-lived. The crowd surged forward again, screaming and demanding that Thomas hand Edwin over. The three friars were at the forefront, shaking their fists and calling on God to strike Thomas down for aiding and abetting the Devil.

Thomas roared with fury as he elbowed Edwin's assailants out of the way, desperate to get him out of harm's way, but there was nowhere for him to go. He was surrounded, and there was nothing he could do to appease the mob. The friar's accusation took hold like a flame spreading through dry wood. The mob closed in, their eyes full of fanatic fervor. Petra didn't see who threw the first stone, but it hit Thomas in the shoulder. He barely noticed the blow as he tried to fight his way out, his arms around Edwin, whose face was pressed against Thomas's chest. The second rock struck him in the head. Blood trickled down his temple as his eyes met Petra's. They were full of regret. He was one man, and he was helpless against a mob of dozens.

No one heard Petra's scream of anguish. They were too fixated on man and child. People were closing in. Edwin was torn from Thomas's arms and thrown to the ground. A cudgel was produced. Petra tried to fight her way through the crowd, but someone struck her in the head, and she went down on her knees. The last thing she saw before she hit the ground was Thomas warding off the blows of the cudgel.

"Edwin," she muttered. "Edwin."

Chapter 56

March 2014

London, England

Quinn hurled the cross across the room, desperate to break the connection between her and Petra. Quinn's eyes were streaming, and she was shaking with emotion, shocked and sickened by what she'd just seen. She'd been devastated when Elise and James died in the trunk Lord Asher had locked them in, but at least those two had been guilty of something, had had something to hide. Petra and Edwin were completely innocent, Petra's only sin being her love for Avery. They'd been victims of an enraged and ignorant mob, the people of Dunwich needing someone to blame for what was happening to them. They saw the storm as an act of God, a punishment and a lesson, when in fact it had simply been an act of nature combined with the unfortunate location of the town.

Quinn slid off the sofa, picked up the cross, and reverently stowed it away in its plastic bag. It was the only thing left of a young woman who'd seen nothing but suffering and disappointment in her short life and had been humiliated even in death. And poor Edwin. He'd been a sweet, kind boy who suffered from a condition which could have been brought under control had he been born a few hundred years later.

He that is without sin among you, let him cast the first stone. The words danced in Quinn's mind, making her shake with anger. If people ever looked to their own faults, many lives would have been saved throughout the ages. Someone had cast that first stone, and someone had found a cudgel and attacked Thomas, who tried to shield Edwin with his own body. Quinn now knew what happened to Petra and Edwin, and why. They hadn't found Thomas's grave next to mother and son, but at the moment, Quinn couldn't bear to find out what happened to him.

Quinn grabbed her coat and handbag and fled the flat. She needed Gabe and Emma. She needed to be with those she loved, and to feel that she was safe in her time and her world. Her own baby was probably the size of a pea, but already she felt fiercely protective toward it, which made the murder of Edwin even more heart-wrenching. To watch your baby die was probably the worst thing that could happen to a mother. Quinn hoped that Petra was gone by the time Edwin was killed, and that she had at least been granted that last kindness by an indifferent God.

Quinn headed toward the playground where Gabe had taken Emma an hour ago. They would be ready for lunch by now, and going to a warm, noisy place full of chatter and laughter was exactly what Quinn needed to force the awful images from her mind. Perhaps they'd go get a pizza, or maybe go to a pub. Quinn had a hankering for a steak and ale pie with mash and maybe she could talk Gabe into splitting a sticky toffee pudding with her. She rarely ate a big lunch because it made her sluggish, but she was suddenly hungry.

"It's all your fault," she whispered to the baby in her belly. "Making your presence known already, you little rascal."

The park was a few streets away, but Quinn became aware that something was wrong as soon as she turned the corner. She saw the flashing lights of police vehicles and heard the crackle of radios as she rushed toward the playground. Several mothers were shepherding their children out of the play area, while two police officers interviewed the remaining parents. The mothers held on tightly to their children while they spoke to the coppers and seemed desperate to leave the playground. The children looked frightened and fascinated at the same time, curious as to what the adults were so upset about. A plain-clothes policeman, probably a detective, was sitting on a bench next to Gabe, who had his head in his hands.

"Madam, you can't go in there," a female cop said, but Quinn ignored her and ran toward Gabe.

"Gabe, what's happened?" she cried. "Where is Emma?"

Gabe's head snapped up at the sound of her voice. He looked stricken, his eyes filled with fear and guilt as he met Quinn's gaze. She froze in her tracks, understanding dawning with sickening clarity. The police were here about Emma.

"And you are?" the detective asked gently.

"I'm Quinn Allenby, Dr. Russell's fiancée. Where is Emma?" Quinn pleaded.

"Ms. Allenby, I'm DI Delaney. We don't have a clear picture of what happened as of yet. Emma might have been taken, or she might have wandered off. We have our people scouring the streets, and we are questioning all the witnesses."

"I looked away for a moment," Gabe choked out. "Just a moment. I got an email from work. It's all my fault, Quinn. My fault," he muttered.

Gabe looked as if he were about to cry. His mobile was on the bench next to him, an innocent-looking object that was the cause of so much fear and self-loathing. Quinn pulled Gabe into her arms in a futile effort to hold him together. He was shaking badly. Gabe was always the calm, rational one. He believed that any situation could be resolved if approached with common sense and proper information, and that most mistakes weren't fatal, just foolish. But this was different. Emma wasn't a mistake to fix. She was a child — his child. Emma was a four-year-old girl who was currently out there somewhere, with someone, or alone, but not with her father, and Gabe was coming apart at the seams.

"Gabe, they'll find her," Quinn said, taking his face between her hands. "They *WILL* find her."

"Dr. Russell, is there anything else you can recall? Did you notice anyone watching Emma, or anyone suspicious hanging about the play area? Is Emma prone to wandering off?"

Gabe shook his head. "I didn't notice anything odd. She was right there on the swing. There were plenty of other people about, but they were all still there when I noticed she was gone. She's never wandered off before, but I've only had her for two months."

"Had her?" DI Delaney asked.

"Emma lived with her mother in Scotland until her mother's death. Emma came to live with us in January," Quinn explained.

"How has her mental state been?" the detective asked.

Quinn opened her mouth to reply, then suddenly stopped, recalling a conversation she had with Emma only a few days ago. She'd helped Emma out of the tub and was toweling her dry.

Emma normally loved having a bath, but that evening she had been preoccupied and unusually quiet. She didn't even play with the Little Mermaid toy that she always took into the bath with her. She liked to make Ariel swim, but this time, she tried to drown her, holding her under with her foot and sighing with annoyance when the plastic figurine floated back to the top when released.

"Quinn, will I ever see my Mum and Gran again?" Emma had asked. Quinn balked at the question. She had no idea what Jenna McAllister had told Emma of death, if anything at all. Nor did she have any idea if Jenna had been religious. Perhaps Jenna had mentioned Heaven, but she'd been a scientist, so it was quite possible that she hadn't believed in an afterlife. On the other hand, she'd also been a Scottish Presbyterian, so must have accepted some notion of Heaven.

"Perhaps someday," Quinn replied, knowing that Emma wouldn't let her get away with changing the subject.

Phoebe and Graham had taken Emma to church while she stayed with them in Berwick, but Quinn and Gabe hadn't really discussed Emma's religious education, simply assuming that she would accept whatever they did. They were both Church of England, so Emma would come along to church with them when they went, which wasn't often.

"She's still grieving, Detective," Quinn said. "It will take time for her to accept that both her mother and grandmother are gone." Detective Delaney nodded in understanding and stepped aside to speak to one of his officers.

"How long has she been gone?" Quinn asked Gabe, who sank back down on the bench again as if his legs couldn't hold him up.

"About a half hour, but it feels like much longer," Gabe replied, his tone flat and wooden. "It's all my fault, Quinn. I'm not fit to be a parent."

"Stop talking rubbish," Quinn replied, taking his cold hand in hers. "You are an amazing father, and you will be a great dad to our baby."

"I don't deserve to have a baby," Gabe mumbled. Quinn didn't reply. She supposed that had the situation been reversed she'd be self-flagellating as well. Assigning blame was easier than thinking of what would happen if Emma wasn't found. The longer she was gone, the greater chance of her disappearing forever. The thought made Quinn feel sick. She'd had moments of fear in her life, but she had never felt as terrified as she did at this moment. The thought of losing Emma, or of Emma suffering at the hands of some unknown person was so gut-wrenching that she couldn't even bear to contemplate the idea.

"They will find her," Quinn murmured to herself, needing to hear the words.

Quinn and Gabe sat side by side for what felt like hours, but was probably no more than ten minutes. Neither paid attention to the crackle of the police radios, but the atmosphere in the park suddenly changed. Gabe's head shot up, having instinctively perceived the shift, and his eyes sought Detective Delaney, who was speaking rapidly into the radio.

The detective smiled and gave Quinn and Gabe a thumbs-up. Gabe sprang to his feet as a tall, black officer strode into the park, carrying Emma in his arms. Emma's face was streaked with tears, but she appeared to be unhurt. The officer set Emma down, and she threw herself at Gabe, burying her face in his chest as he lifted her up and held her close.

"Are you all right?" Gabe asked as he stroked her hair and kissed the top of her head. He looked like he would never let her go. "Please say you're all right, Emma."

Emma nodded miserably. "I thought I saw Mum," she whimpered. "I ran after her and called out, but she didn't turn around. It wasn't her," Emma cried. "I just wanted to see my Mum."

"It's OK, darling," Quinn said as she wrapped her arms around Emma and Gabe. "No one is angry with you. We're just glad you're all right." Of course, *all right* was a relative term. Emma hadn't been taken by a stranger, or come to any harm, but it would take years for her to truly be all right. She'd miss Jenna for the rest of her life, and have instances of sudden panic and overwhelming hope when seeing someone who resembled her mother. Emma hadn't seen Jenna's corpse, nor had she attended the funeral. In her mind, her mother was as she had last seen her, alive and well. Somewhere deep inside, she still believed that perhaps she was out there somewhere, and would return one day, suddenly and without a fuss.

"She was standing on the corner, afraid to cross the street," the officer said, smiling at Emma. "Smart girl not to go wading into traffic. She called out to us when she saw us cruising by."
"Emma, please, don't ever do anything like that again," Gabe pleaded with her. "We thought we'd lost you."

"I was scared," Emma cried. "I was calling for you."

The officer smiled. "She just kept saying, "I want my Dad. I just want my Dad." She was terrified."

Quinn didn't need to see Gabe's face to understand what those words meant to him.

"I will never lose you again," Gabe promised. "Ever."

"I don't want to be lost," Emma said. She held out her hand, putting her palm on Quinn's damp cheek. "You're my Mum and Dad now."

"I think it's safe for us to leave," DI Delaney said as he took in the little family. "All's well that ends well."

"I love you, Emma," Gabe whispered into Emma's hair.

"I love you too, Daddy."

"Let's go home," Quinn said. Her legs seemed to have turned to jelly, and she was shaking with relief.

"I'm hungry," Emma protested, making them laugh.

"Of course, you are. Where would you like to go?"

"I want pizza and ice cream."

"Yes, ma'am," Gabe said as he turned to walk out of the playground.

The police cars had sped away, and the onlookers were dispersing, smiling with relief that there had been a happy ending to this family drama. Gabe wrapped his free arm around Quinn. "Are you all right?"

Quinn gave Gabe a wan smile. "I never understood until today how vulnerable becoming a parent makes you."

"Me either. Life will never be the same again, will it?"

"No, but I'm glad of it. I'm ready, Gabe."

"So am I."

Quinn followed Gabe into a pizza restaurant and sat down, glad to be off her wobbling legs. She was ready and excited for the future, but there were still two things she needed to do before the baby was born. She needed to find her biological father and finish out her contract with the BBC. Once that was done, she would never delve into anyone's past again, not in a personal way. She'd been handed this gift/curse, but she didn't have to use it, not unless she really wanted to, and watching Elise's and Petra's tragedies unfold had convinced her that she was more than ready to relinquish the sight.

Epilogue

April 1347

The sea was as calm as a puddle after the rain, its blue-gray surface reflecting the puffy white clouds as they drifted across the aquamarine sky. A chill breeze moved through the newly greening branches, but there was a whiff of spring in the air. Avery stood on a cliff by the priory, gazing out over what remained of Dunwich. The devastation was unspeakable. Hundreds of houses had been washed away by twenty-foot swells, and St. Leonard's was lost to parishioners forever. It was partially submerged in water, its tower rising out of the sea like the arm of a drowning man, begging for help that would never come.

The streets had been blocked by debris and silt for weeks, and many townspeople were still unaccounted for and presumed dead. For days after the storm, people wandered about, unsure of what to do now that they found themselves homeless and completely dispossessed. They searched for victims and anything that could be salvaged, but the sea had been cruel, leaving nothing but destruction behind. The waters had eventually receded, but not all the way. A substantial portion of the town was still underwater, the coast so eroded by the power of the storm that it simply vanished beneath the waves.

Avery pulled on the hood of his robe and began to walk toward what was left of Dunwich. He had two stops to make before he left for good. With Petra and Edwin gone, the bishop had been more than willing to forgive his indiscretions and allow him to return to Oxford after a period of further prayer and contemplation, but Avery refused. He no longer had any desire to be a priest, nor did he have any ambitions for the future. His carelessness and arrogance lead to Petra and Edwin's death, and although he still saw the taking of one's life as a mortal sin, he no longer felt that his life was his to live.

Avery knocked on the door of Petra's house. It had survived the storm, but needed extensive repairs. The water had reached the house and flooded the ground floor, reaching almost to the loft and carrying off household goods and bits of furniture. Chunks of daub were missing from the walls facing the street, while the back walls were still damp even after all this time. Maude was in the house. She tried to restore order to what was left of her home, but her heart wasn't in it, and the place looked a shambles. Elia and Ora were outside, hanging up laundry, their faces solemn and gray and their eyes downcast. They'd lost much the day of the storm, and neither girl would ever forget the sight of their mother and brother murdered by an angry mob. They were lucky to have been spared, and they both knew it.

Avery greeted Maude and stepped inside, but remained by the door. Lord Devon sat at the table, eating a bowl of pottage. His face was still bruised and swollen, and his right arm rested in a makeshift sling and splints, having been broken in two places. He limped when he walked due the damage caused to his knee by a blow from a cudgel, but he was on the mend, physically, if not mentally.

"What do you want?" Lord Devon asked, failing to invite Avery to sit down. He now knew, as did everyone else who survived the storm, that Edwin had been Avery's son and that Petra had been his lover, both before he left Dunwich and after he returned. There was no love lost between the two men.

"I've come to say goodbye," Avery said. "I'm no longer a priest; just a simple Franciscan friar. I leave Dunwich today."

"Where are you bound?" Maude asked.

Unlike the rest of the townspeople, she didn't blame Avery for what happened, at least not completely. Her daughter had loved him, and Avery genuinely tried to help his son. He should have been stronger, and truer, and more honest, but that could be said of many men. Petra and Edwin's deaths had been brought about by fear and superstition, and not only as the result of Avery's mistakes.

"I'm bound for the Holy Land," Avery replied. "Pope Clement VI granted the Franciscan friars *Custodia Terrae Sanctae* nearly five years ago. I will go to the monastery that was built near Mount Zion and spend the rest of my life trying to atone for my sins."

"As you should," Thomas replied. "You don't deserve to be a custodian of the Holy Land, you immoral parasite."

"Lord Thomas, please," Maude pleaded. "He's suffered enough."

Thomas ignored Avery's pallor and the shadows under his eyes. He'd lost more than a stone since the storm, and the robe hung on him as if he were no more than skin and bones.

"No amount of self-flagellation can atone for what he's done. He killed them, as surely as if he'd thrown the stones himself."

Avery backed toward the door. He didn't look at Lord Devon, nor did he respond. He had killed them, and nothing the man accused him of was any worse than what he'd accused himself of already. Lord Devon had every right to despise him, especially when he'd actually tried to help Petra and Edwin and wore the scars to prove it. He'd been beaten nearly half-to-death, and suffered not only broken bones, but the loss of the woman he loved and planned to marry, and the knowledge of her betrayal.

"Go in peace, Avery," Maude said, making the sign of the cross in front of Avery. "Lord Devon will take care of us. He has promised to provide a dowry for the girls when the time comes and will allow me to remain under his roof in my old age."

"And Lady Blythe?" Avery asked carefully. The last he'd heard, Lady Blythe had not been accounted for.

"My mother perished during the storm, as did my daughter and her husband," Thomas spat out.

"What of your brother's family?" Avery asked.

"They are safe, and their home suffered minimal damage," Thomas replied. "Safe journey, Friar Avery," Thomas said, his tone laced with sarcasm. He wouldn't be too upset if Avery's ship went down in a storm. It would be a sort of justice, in his estimation.

"God be with you all," Avery said and took his leave.

He walked slowly toward the Leper Hospital of St. James. His legs felt as if they were weighed down with stones, but this was a pilgrimage he needed to make. Avery broke off two evergreen branches and carried them toward the cemetery, where two fresh graves were visible just beyond hallowed ground. Avery laid the evergreen branches on the graves and fell to his knees, tears running down his face. It wasn't bad enough that the townspeople had executed — for there was no better word for what they'd done — Petra and Edwin, they'd refused them a Christian burial, tossing their remains face down in unmarked graves just beyond the leper cemetery. Avery had pleaded with the bishop, but he refused to relocate Petra and Edwin's remains.

People were frightened and angry, and needed to be appeased, the bishop had intimated. Besides, St. Leonard's cemetery, where Petra and Edwin would have been buried had circumstances been different, was underwater, the graves desecrated by seawater and debris. And the remaining cemeteries were overflowing with the victims of the storm, who were being buried every day. Some were still washing up further down the coast, and grieving family members patrolled the shores, hoping to find their loved ones and give them a dignified send-off.

"Forgive me," Avery whispered to the graves. "Please forgive me." He remained perfectly still, hoping for some sign, but all he heard was a dense silence, unbroken by the sound of the wind or the life-affirming trilling of a bird. He reached into the pocket of his robe and brought out a thin chain with a medal of the Virgin Mary. It was a parting gift from Prior Jacob, given to him only that morning.

"My mother gave this to me the day I left home to join the order," Prior Jacob said as he removed the chain and handed it to Avery. "She said the Blessed Mother would look after me, and she has. I would like you to have the medal, Friar Avery. You've suffered much these past few weeks, and although some would say that you brought the suffering onto yourself, I believe that every man deserves forgiveness if he's truly repentant. I hope you find comfort in our Mother's love."

"Thank you, Prior Jacob," Avery said and meant it. The man had been more generous of spirit than Avery deserved, and gave him a home and a place to pray when all others wanted to banish him from the priory. Avery dug a hole with his hands and buried the medal between the two graves.

"Please, Blessed Mother, watch over those I love," he whispered. "I'm not worthy of your compassion, but they are. I leave them in your care." Avery clasped his hands in front of him, intoned a prayer for the souls of Petra and Edwin, then got to his feet. He was ready to go. There was nothing left for him in England.

The End

Please look for The Unforgiven (Echoes from the Past Book 3)

Coming 2018

Notes

I hope you've enjoyed the second installment of The Echoes from the Past Series. I have something of a fascination with Dunwich, since it's one of those places that's tragic and mysteriously spooky at the same time, being the home to nearly a dozen underwater churches, whose bells still ring, according to some. Of course, coastal erosion and storms were not the result of God's fury or a punishment for the sinners, but for medieval residents of the town they were a directly linked to God's displeasure. Many believed that epilepsy or any other type of mental disability were a sign of demonic possession and blamed the afflicted for anything that befell them, including storms.

In the next book, Quinn will be traveling to New Orleans, which is another place that holds my interest. It's beautiful, mysterious, and slightly sinister all at once. New Orleans' ties to Voodoo and black magic, introduced by slaves brought from Africa and the Caribbean, still draw those who are interested in the occult, like myself. I hope you will continue to follow Quinn's story.

I love hearing your thoughts, so please don't hesitate to reach out to me. You can find me at www.irinashapiro.com or on Facebook at www.facebook.com/IrinaShapiro2/. Please send me your information at irina.shapiro@yahoo.com if you'd like to be added to my mailing list.

And, as always, thank you for your support.

Printed in Great Britain
by Amazon